Echoes of the
Celtic Tiger
and other stories

D1589506

Echoes *of the* Celtic Tiger

and other stories

FRANK O'CARROLL

THE BOGLARK PRESS

First published 2010
Copyright © Frank O'Carroll 2010
All rights reserved.

No part of this publication may be reproduced, stored in a retrieval system, or transmitted in any form or by any means without prior permission in writing of the publisher, nor be otherwise circulated in any form of binding or cover other than that in which it is published and without a similar condition including this condition being imposed on the subsequent purchaser.

All characters in this publication are fictitious, and any resemblance to real persons, living or dead, is purely coincidental.

ISBN 978-1-907593-10-9

Printed in the European Union

The author wishes to gratefully acknowledge the support of the INTO and Comhar Linn, INTO Credit Union.

* * *

By the same author:

ACCORDION MUSIC (short stories)
FOND MEMORIES (short stories)
GRAFTON STREET BLUES (poems)

Frank O'Carroll grew up in North Kerry
before moving to Dublin to teach.
He was educated in St Flannan's College, Ennis,
St Pat's College of Education and UCD.

Some of the stories in this collection
have already appeared in various periodicals.

To my friends in the National Library

CONTENTS

VIGNETTE OF AN ARTIST

For Kevin, it had been a pretty miserable afternoon. He hadn't sold a single painting. In fact, he hadn't sold any for weeks. People, for whatever reason – probably to do with the collapse of the Celtic Tiger – weren't interested. A mere browse was as much as art lovers bestowed on his paintings recently. With the drizzle adding to the gloom of a grey December Sunday littered by a mulch of decaying leaves wherever he trod, it was not exactly the stuff of artistic dreams.

He glanced at his watch. In another hour, he would be packing up and heading for the comforts of his home. Another agonising hour, waiting for a customer to approach him with an offer. Continuing to believe in his star, while wishing and waiting for the day when his pictures would be on display in a reputable, commercial art gallery and he would be spared having to exhibit outdoors in inclement weather like this.

A driving squall reminded him that his fee to the corporation for his slot in the Square and his insurance cover were overdue. Bills! he sighed. For the second time that afternoon, he began having doubts about the wisdom of opting for a redundancy package to devote himself full-time to art.

Glancing at his paintings, he acknowledged he was no Van Gogh. Never would be. But he did have talent, albeit one that worked the socks off him for little financial reward so far. Arty minded friends continued, however, to assure him that there was a niche for his pictures. He mustn't give up. And, in time, who knows?

He could hear the soughing of the wind coming from the park and sensed the early dusk enveloping the city. Any worthwhile prospects that the evening might have held for Kevin were rapidly diminishing. It was a matter of filling in time before calling it a day.

His mobile rang. It was his wife: sceptical, practical Julie, concerned that he had forgotten his cap and gloves and that he must be mad to be standing around in the freezing cold.

'Have you ever known me to be a hot-house flower?' he asked, careful not to let her see any chink in his artistic resolve.

'Any sale?' She measured the worth or worthlessness of his art exclusively in commercial terms.

'None so far, but fingers crossed.' He managed to sound hopeful while steeling himself against the elements.

'It's running rather late, isn't it?' In the Jeremiad league, she was in the premier division. Optimism was his lifeline.

He frowned.

'Better late than never. Cheers!'

He rang off. As a committed artist, he had learned to turn a deaf ear to her negative outpourings. Still, he had to admit, she had been a good wife to him in other ways and a dedicated parent.

If there were days like this, there would be better ones ahead, he consoled himself. Compared to some artists exhibiting in the Square, he hadn't fared overall too badly. It was a question of waiting for things to pick up. Now that he was a full-time artist, he felt confident he could produce the goods.

'It doesn't look as if there's going to be any joy for us this evening either, Kevin,' Paul, a fellow artist, observed gloomily.

A gaunt, bean-pole of a man, his cheeks had rarely looked hollower or more weather-beaten. He kept rubbing his hands to warm them.

'We'll just have to grin and bear it for awhile.' Kevin could see his own despondency magnified in his friend's famished features.

'I've never seen it so slack. In fact, I've decided to pack it in.' Paul looked terminally dispirited.

Kevin was rocked. He couldn't understand his friend not getting the same kick out of painting as he did.

'You can't be serious! Would you not hang on for the tourists?' he pleaded, gutted at having to lose a comrade in arms.

Paul shook his disillusioned head.

'By which time my wife would have divorced me and my family disowned me. Naw. I'm through with it.' He was rubbing his hands again and blowing on his nails. 'To be perfectly honest, I sometimes wonder how I ever wandered into this lark.'

Kevin pressed his arm reassuringly.

'You mustn't talk like that, Paul. You have a gift,' he said.

'I thought, too, that I had a gift for music at one time. But just as well I held on to the day job or I'd 've been busking in Grafton Street for me supper.'

'A Jack-of-all-trades,' a sturdier Kevin acknowledged, trying to persuade him that it was due to the recession and not his fault that people weren't buying art.

Paul blew into his cupped hands and grinned.

'It would have been a lot better had I been a master of one.' He admitted to feeling a misfit in the Square for quite some time.

'I'll miss you, Paul. Are you sure you won't change your mind?'

Paul shook his head then extended a parting hand.

'It's time I faced up to it and called it a day. I'll drop by to see you from time to time.'

If Kevin were to nominate someone who seemed least like an artist at that moment, he'd have picked Paul. He suddenly looked every inch the down-to-earth house painter he once was. His fling with the artistic Muse had not been a happy one. On second thoughts, Kevin agreed it was best that he should return to his true trade that had done him proud down the years.

'Be sure now and stay in touch, Paul. And, no matter what you think of yourself, I'll always admire you for the gamble you took.' Kevin gave him a fraternal hug.

'Cheers, Kev. And keep the flag flying for the turp's brigade.'

First Mandy. Now Paul. He felt bereft. Henceforth he'd have to shoulder the burden of his shaky, artistic future on his own.

As Kevin watched him pack away his few paintings that would never sell, he felt for him as never before. They had soldiered together for years in the Square; swapped yarns and hints about colours and craft; grieved and rejoiced together over bad days and good. Neither had been to Art College. Both had wandered into art via the house painters' route and courtesy of a crash course both attended. Once bitten by the creative bug, they got hooked. They hit it off from the word go and soon became a mutual support system.

An icy blast gusting through the park railings compelled Kevin to zip up his anorak. He could feel his temperature dropping and his ears going red with the cold. If he weren't careful, he could easily catch pneumonia as happened to Mandy, ending her days in the Square.

Free-spirited Mandy, who, for years, hung her erotic paintings in the slot next to his was now prematurely in Mount Jerome Cemetery. Cut down as her talent was peaking. So absurd. So hard to make any sense of it. They were such kindred spirits. How he missed flirting with her, remembering how her banter brightened many an otherwise unrewarding evening! At moments like this, he could still sense her presence close by.

Bereft of his soul-mates, and with a younger, precocious set muscling in, Kevin felt less certain of himself, less comfortable in the Square that had long been his spiritual home on week-ends.

Re-arranging his pictures on the metal railing, he realized that art, for all its lure, was a precarious business. And that life was more often than not an obstacle course for the artist, presenting him recently with a catalogue of headaches he had not bargained for, while leaving him with no choice but to step up to the plate and help out his son – who had been put on short time by his firm – with his mortgage repayments.

Then there was his daughter's expensive wedding. And now Julie was about to hit him with her annual, staggering, Christmas budget. Just as well he had received a decent, redundancy package and enjoyed a reasonable pension. No substitute, of course – as Julie never ceased to remind him – for the big pay-packets he used to bring home during the Celtic Tiger, when she didn't have to watch her spending.

What a day! Even the elements seemed arraigned against him, with a gusting wind buffeting his pictures and the unremitting rain beginning to seep through his anorak.

The fact that he hadn't sold a painting for some time, despite his increased output, convinced Julie that he should seriously consider doing a few nixers during the run-up to Christmas, and then – knowing her – after Christmas too. She still didn't get it that he had retired to paint, and that he was prepared to go for broke for it. Given that the clock wasn't exactly on his side, every minute mattered if he were to fulfil his talent.

A well-clad Yank, savouring a Havana cigar, passed up his pictures for McCann's – an opinionated prat who frowned upon anybody who hadn't been to art college. Graduate though he be, Kevin saw nothing to shout about in his work. For his money, he was just another journeyman landscape painter, forced to sell his work in the Square since the galleries dropped him. It confirmed Kevin's belief that artists are born, not custom-built by art colleges.

Courtesy of the Yank, today would be McCann's lucky break. Kevin had no problem with that, though he recoiled from the prospect of having to suffer the other's conceit for some time to come.

As if that weren't enough, a group of pretentious art students with a slot of their own further down the Square, sniggered as they breezed by. It would have rankled and even resulted in a loss of faith in himself were he not familiar with their unspectacular efforts, which, ironically, were outselling his for all the wrong reasons. Not that he begrudged them, but he took exception to their attitude and to their naive belief in the creative supremacy of youth over age. Nonsense! His best years were still ahead of him.

While stamping his feet and rubbing his hands vigorously to prevent them becoming numb, he was mindful of the famous artists who starved and shivered in freezing attics before being recognised. So far, so good; he didn't have to worry in that regard. And barring a serious financial set-back he would manage.

Another icy blast reduced the over-hanging elm to a skeleton. He realised it was no day to be out-of-doors. One by one, his fellow artists were packing up their kit and making a dash for home. It was some consolation to Kevin to know that it had been a bad day generally in the Square, except for McCann, now strutting about like a peacock and savouring with a supercilious air, a hot toddy from his hip flask.

Kevin defiantly hung on. With Julie's Christmas spending

spree a matter of days away, he couldn't afford to miss out on a deal that would help keep her off his back until his luck returned. She repeatedly disapproved of him being a full-time artist. It was fine with her as a hobby. But the idea of him painting from dawn to dusk didn't make sense. Well and good if it paid accordingly, and she didn't have to constantly budget. The novelty of fraternising with artists in the cafes of Montmartre during a recent holiday in Paris, quickly wore off. It was his scene.

The bohemian life-style was not for her. It was too insecure, too unconventional and remote from her simpler, safer world. She was a home builder. Kevin, with his pony tail, his arty beard and showy, corded jackets, was cut from different cloth – a freer spirit, who shocked her once with a nude portrait of herself as the nubile, young woman he had first met while holidaying in Abbeylaune.

Unlike the uninhibited Mandy, she was a correct woman, who upheld family values. With Julie, it was family first and foremost, which was just as well. With him it was art first thing in the morning and last thing at night. Not that he didn't have his children's welfare at heart or that he ever saw them short.

With the wind whipping up a dirge in the leafless elm, and the Square now all to himself, save for a striking couple approaching from the south side of that illustrious quadrangle of Georgian splendour that once housed the legends of the literary world – Yeats, Wilde and Bram Stoker – he decided to call it a day.

It was time to remove the plastic covering that protected his paintings from the ravages of December and leave the Square to its serenity, to its trees and its ghosts, and the soughing of the wind; time for a warm meal and the comforts of his home – the fruit of his labours from an early age as a painter and decorator.

With respect to Julie, he had paid his dues to the work ethic and deserved to do what he had always wanted: to paint. And even if there were days like this, there would be better ones ahead.

'Can you hold on a minute until I have a peek?' A sleek, snappily dressed gentleman with a stunning lady on his arm stalled him as he was about to put away his paintings.

'Certainly.' The request took him by surprise. Could this be the break he'd been waiting for? Or was he just another, pretentious dilettante trying to impress her ladyship with his little knowledge of art?

'I like that one of the leafless tree with the song-bird clinging to it. It has a bleak beauty about it that would be perfect for our sitting room this Christmas,' the lady suggested in a refined accent that had the ring of money to it.

'And this one of the Roumanian beggar would be suitable for the gallery,' the man said, requesting a price brochure.

Kevin began to doubt for a moment if he were in the real world, and if his hearing weren't suddenly impaired. Snapping out of his trance, he switched on the charm for the benefit of his benefactors.

'Are you not chilled to the bone?' the alluring lady inquired with concern. Probably a model, Kevin figured, from her deportment and her stance, as he made a mental portrait of her exquisite figure.

'Actually, I was on the verge of *rigor mortis* before you came along,' he confessed with a candour that moved her.

Taking a shine to his self portrait, she suggested to her partner that they might as well buy all three. She thought that only someone as dedicated and as crazy as Van Gogh would hang around Merrion Square on a day like this.

'I've suffered worse and for less returns,' Kevin assured her.

She smiled, then suggested that, if he didn't want people

wishing him a happy new *ear*, he had better get in out of the freezing cold.

Jokingly, with Julie in mind, Kevin replied that being a deaf painter might have its advantages.

She laughed.

Suitably impressed, her partner agreed to take all three.

'There now, aren't you lucky I decided we'd take a stroll after lunch.' She beamed, taking some credit for the delighted expression on Kevin's face.

Kevin acknowledged she had made his day. Already the chill had left his bones and, to the west of the park, he could see a clearing in the clouds that triggered fond memories of dappled afternoons when a riot of autumnal shades, blending with those of art, brought a splurge of colour to the Square.

'So, if it's okay with you, I'll ask you to drop the pictures around to my gallery, where I'll take them from you and pay you there and then,' the art dealer suggested.

An overjoyed Kevin nodded, then asked him for the name of the gallery.

'The Omega. You know it?'

'Who doesn't? It's every artist's Promised Land,' Kevin exclaimed.

Chuffed by the compliment, its respected owner declared he would be prepared to consider any new paintings of his.

Kevin thanked him profusely, conveying, in turn, to his gorgeous lady-friend all the gratitude he could summon in a handshake.

'Have a nice Christmas,' she said, as she affectionately linked her man.

'And you, too,' he greeted. Santa Claus had come early to him this year.

Having dropped off the paintings at the Omega and been paid for them, he made a purchase at a nearby supermarket. Then he headed for home with the urgency of a child who couldn't wait to tell his parents that he had won – as he once did – a prize for the best painting in the class.

'A good day at the office,' he announced to Julie, as he placed his soaking anorak on the radiator, thermostatically lowered for economic reasons.

'Don't tell me you've had a sale?' Her expression was a picture of disbelief.

'All three.'

'Well, good for you!' There was a jubilant ring to her voice for a change.

'And that's not all.'

'No?' Her eyes distended with expectancy.

'The owner of the Omega Gallery expressed further interest in any new paintings of mine, so I'm going to be in very select company from here-on-in.'

She chuckled. 'Not bad for a recent house painter.'

'And this for you.' He surprised her with a bunch of flowers and, to keep her sweet, a generous cheque for Christmas.

Overjoyed, she clasped him to her and kissed him in a way she hadn't done since he packed in his job. Then she sat him down to a warm meal and fussed over him for the remainder of the evening.

'Who says art doesn't pay?' he chuckled, savouring a hot toddy, just like McCann, from whose grasp he had snatched bragging rights when all seemed lost.

'You had better keep at it,' she encouraged. Suddenly aware of a silver lining in the artistic cloud, she turned up the radiator.

He appreciated her support. With Julie on his side there would be no stopping him now.

ECHOES OF THE CELTIC TIGER

The house Quirke lived in was the house he would die in. It was the house his parents, too, had lived in and the one that they died in. An old house that was once a new house, though if change be the measure of time, neither new nor old, being essentially the same as the day it was built. In short, a bungalow with no additions or subtractions. Just as his parents kept it. And as he would keep it. For it wouldn't be their house or his house strictly if it were otherwise. And if it were, it would mean he'd have to be otherwise. For, in a sense, the house was his emblem. And for more than fifty years, the capsule of his inner and outer self. Spartan, but homely; a bastion of permanency in a city of flux. His residential memoir.

Such was the house he inherited and that he would leave after him.

'To whom?' I once ventured, seeing he had neither wife nor child.

'To someone who'll keep it exactly as it is,' he declared.

'Do you think you can trust anybody?' I asked, considering it a tall order.

'If not I'll leave it to the Antiquarian Society.' An employee like his father with the Museum, he had turned his home into an ancestral shrine.

I admitted to not having the same attachment to mine. In fact, it wouldn't have cost me a thought to sell up and move down the country to a more spacious residence, like so many who were profiting from the Celtic Tiger boom.

'Unlike yours, mine is a house full of memories I don't want to part with,' he explained reverentially.

'But aren't you missing out on those mod cons that make for comfort?' I was frequently bemused by his reluctance to move with the times.

He frowned.

'Bunkum! If you're asking me to keep up with the Joneses, you're barking up the wrong tree.'

An unswerving attitude, partly inherited, partly his own, and stoutly defended whenever I accused him of turning his back on progress.

'Progress! You've only got to look at Jillian's next door to see what progress has done.'

The storm trooper of the Antiquarian Society wasn't for u-turning. At least not before that eventful New Year's Eve get-together with his next door neighbour.

A rare bird. Foolproof against the state-of-the-art culture Jillian couldn't resist, he remained entrenched and fiercely protective of a legacy many wouldn't think twice about binning. Just to be 'with it' – a catch-phrase that was an anathema to him.

'But you can't go on living in the past.' I disagreed with him as much as I disapproved of Jillian pandering to the in-thing.

He refused to budge.

'The clock stops at my front door,' he'd declare. The buck too, if you ask me. No breakfast for the tradesman. No lunch for the technician. No supper for the painter and decorator. No square meal for the furnisher. The clock stopped, the buck stopped, the future stopped for his bungalow a long time ago while all around him moved on.

'In fairness you've lived up to your principles. But should we dismiss Jillian?'

He grimaced.

'Jillian would bin old Dublin if she had her way. The woman is a Philistine.'

A cultured man, I'll grant you. A lot to be said for him. A lot to be said against him, too. Immune to her attractive looks and her trendy outfits that still turned men's heads, Quirke's withholding of compliments was a sore point with her.

'I suppose women like her keep the Celtic Tiger going,' I said, trying to be fair to her.

He shook his head adamantly.

'Down the chute. That's where it's going. And the sooner the better, if we're not to end up financially and spiritually bankrupt.'

The more she ran with it the more he dug his heels in, fearful, I suspected, of the pressures her unbridled home-building instincts could bring to bear on him were he to follow suit.

'I suppose she could spend her money on worse than her house,' I said sympathetically.

'Given a choice, I'd rather live in a wigwam any day,' he said.

He continued to rail against her doll's house, which grated on his retro sensibility. A tradesman's recreation, renovated, refurbished and redecorated time and time again. Subject of a myriad make-overs, of interior and exterior additions. And lit by a cluster of chandeliers that ressembled a miniature of the Milky Way. Believe me, I've watched this work in progress with a mixture of awe and reservations, wondering, at times, if Quirke weren't right about her sweeping changes that resonated for him with disturbing echoes of the Celtic Tiger.

It began with his dismissal of her double-glazed windows, and it made for a piece of high drama, with more sparks flying than from a welding rod.

'They're not a patch on the previous ones,' he insisted, casting a cold eye on them.

'But they're so easy to maintain. No painting of frames or replacing of glass. You really should install them and reduce your heat loss,' I heard her suggest, much to Quirke's chagrin.

'With global warming on the increase, the ones I have will do me fine,' he snapped, damned if she or anyone would tell him what to do.

She frowned.

'If they're anything like mine, they're fit for the skip.'

'They're not. Not that there was anything wrong with yours. You're just following the trends.'

Fads. How he hated them! Here today and gone tomorrow. Anything to get people spending and working their socks off to pay for them. He had a point.

'They had their day. In any case, I got fed up lookin' at them,' she explained. Money I knew, would burn her pockets while Quirke, she was convinced, would take his communion collection with him to the grave.

'And you'll be fed up looking at the new ones when the next brand comes on the market,' he predicted, suspicious that she could well be touting for business for her husband Darren, a tradesman, who slaved to meet her demands.

'Get out of the Ark,' I heard her retaliate, adding that you'd get pneumonia from the draughts those creaking old windows let in.

He knew better than to give her an inch. Succumb to peer pressure and, in his own words, he'd end up following the herd. His windows, if dated, were fine. Being the original ones, I gathered they were of great sentimental value to him. And a piece of heritage in their own right.

His attitude to the new wave of refurbishments now sweeping the city was no different. The kitchen extension craze left him distinctly unfazed.

'I don't know myself. It's so spacious and so comfortable, unlike the previous pokey one.' We had to endure another spate of Jillian's bragging, hot on the heels of her double-glazed windows.

'It detracts from the original house,' he disagreed, seeing the hand of vandalism rather than enhancement in her renovations.

She shook her head.

'I'd rebuild it from the ground up if I had my way,' I heard her rejoin.

Far from feeling intimidated by her obsessive modernising, a cool Quirke rejoined that he would have a preservation order slapped on all the bungalows on the street and a serious fine for any breaches of it.

'Extensions break the line of light,' he declared.

She stomped off, then volleyed over her shoulder, 'Some woman will break yours some day.'

I doubted it somehow. His romances were short-lived conflicts without resolution. Frequently first night casualties, he once informed me, arising from disparaging references to his house.

'I wouldn't spend a single night in a house without a shower.' Gene was frank with him. Her trail to his heart went dry the next day.

'The carpets are threadbare. You should get rid of them,' Delores suggested. He got rid of her instead.

'No inbuilt wardrobes!' Madeleine was aghast. He handed her coat and scarf.

'Your living room is like a mausoleum. It's spooky,' Irene

shuddered for the first and last time there.

When Tess protested about the lack of central heating, he suggested she warm herself at another man's rads.

Similar short shrifts were, I gathered, meted out to anyone who unwittingly disparaged his home, which was tantamount to disparaging him, as well as his late father, whose motto 'Don't remove a thing,' ensured, in Jillian's words, that the cobwebs were safe.

Unlucky in love, every woman he dated was, by his own admission, a version of Jillian: trend-addicts who put him off tying the knot .

'Clearly you haven't met the right woman,' I'd sympathise with him.

'I don't believe there's one who isn't consumer-driven.'

I concluded that he was looking for his mother in his bridal prospects. Fewer and fewer I noted, as the years sped by, until turned off by women's lib, he eventually bolted the door to any further attachments. His house had won out in the nuptial stakes.

Subsequent affinities were strictly social and mostly with widows, whose material yearnings had given way to spiritual ones. Detached, Platonic and chatty, he was their cup of tea. And many a cup he had with them, though none, I can vouch, with Jillian, who would gladly have put arsenic in it.

'What a Luddite!' she exclaimed to me, making no secret of the fact that she would prefer an historic ruin next door to his drab bungalow that took away from hers.

Quirke remained impervious to her ongoing tirades. We agreed, she had more money than sense. And given her squandermania, she would sooner or later be without either, while the riches he derived from books and from travel were inexhaustible.

I pitied him having to endure her hysterics when he returned from a week in Florence to find his house had been trashed.

'I'm tired telling youse to get a burglar alarm installed like everyone else,' she berated him. Seeing the burglars had to settle for mere handy cash that he left lying around, I couldn't see what all the fuss was about, apart from the damage to his replaceable Yale lock.

Tired of her meddling, I heard him retort, 'I never behave like everyone else. Besides, with a watch-dog like you next door, I see no reason for having an alarm.'

I gathered she didn't want to hear anything about Florence, and Italian cuisine, she let him know, left her cold. Sour grapes, you can take it, because he had one up on her.

I could tell it riled her that she couldn't manipulate him like her hen-pecked Darren.

Having to endure her exaggerated praises of her new Jacuzzi, Quirke was convinced she had finally lost her soul.

I regretted having to inform him that she was already making plans to have a massive new conservatory built.

'Is there no end to her lunacy!' He threw up his hands in despair. He was fated to be the odd one out in a competitive, house-proud neighbourhood. A local voice crying in the wilderness on behalf of values and a way of life to which the Celtic Tiger had put paid.

Critical though she was, I sensed Jillian had a grudging respect for him. Unlike Darren, who never read anything except the tabloids and could talk only about sport, Quirke was widely read and could talk about anything. It might have helped had he managed to suffer her extravagance, as I did, in silence. Incapable of dissimulation, he wore his heart on his sleeve.

'I might as well be talking to the wall as talking to Quirke,' she confessed wearily to me the day he belittled her conservatory as another of her neurotic compulsions to keep up with the Joneses.

I merely shrugged. At least the wall wouldn't give her a smart answer. From what I could see, Quirke's answers were becoming smarter by the day. I tried telling her she wasn't hitting the right note with him. Sadly, where Quirke was concerned, the only one in her repertoire was continually off-key.

'Why did she have to end up next door to me? Why?' I watched him roll his eyes to heaven, then dig his heels in, the day she demanded he have his tree removed – a tree his father had planted, that staged the dawn chorus, and reflected the colourful passage of the seasons! No way!

I merely shrugged, though I could understand her reasons, managing to keep in with both, while thanking my stars that I had Quirke as a buffer between us.

Neighbours! They were no different to the ones I grew up with in my native Abbeylaune, where I was schooled in the fraught art of co-existence.

'Can't you see her life is a spiritual vacuum that all her material acquisitions have failed to fill?' He spotlighted her dilemma after some reflection.

'I suppose she's just a woman of our time,' I replied, trying to see it from her angle.

'She's unreal. Incorrigible. A slave to every new fad on the market. Today it's one thing. Tomorrow it'll be something else.'

I nodded.

'She'll never be satisfied. Never find inner peace or fulfilment. I pity poor Darren. It must be sheer hell for him having to live with her,' he continued.

'So where did it all go wrong?' I asked him, sensitive to the changes that had come over her down the years, and not exactly for the better.

His reply was prompt and straight from the shoulder: 'She

married the wrong man.'

Nothing, in my opinion, could have been further from the truth.

'They could hardly have been more suited,' I disagreed, reminding him that only a tradesman like Darren could have coped with her house-proud mania.

Quirke shook his head firmly. Far from being a proper mentor, Darren, in his opinion, was merely her puppet.

'I suppose with attractive looks and a figure like hers she'd bend any man to her will,' I argued.

He spat.

'Weak men.' Darren, in his opinion, should have stood up to her and pointed her in the right direction.

That winter Darren passed away. From heart failure, it was said, from trying to meet Jillian's endless demands. Merely fifty-five. It was game up, I knew, for her home improvements.

'What was it all for in the end? Jillian should have spared more thought for this.'

A pensive Quirke was quick off the mark as we watched the clay being heaped on her husband's coffin.

'Maybe this will change her,' I ventured.

'If not, the recession will,' he predicted.

After a spell of bereavement, I could see her turning more and more to Quirke for support. It wasn't long before I heard her singing again snatches from the popular musicals of her day, something she hadn't done in years.

I had a sneaking suspicion that Quirke was becoming her surrogate for Darren. Despite their differences, she was suddenly making no secret of it that she could have a worse neighbour.

'As long as you don't try to change him,' I advised her.

She disagreed. 'He'll change alright. We all change sooner or later.'

Was she speaking for herself? Bemused, I sometimes wondered if Quirke was the lost one that women like Jillian try to save. I'd swear, I could sense something happening between them. That he exercised some inexplicable hold over her, I never doubted. How else, I reasoned, could she have been so obsessive about him? I attributed it to the attraction of opposites on her part, though not on his.

When Quirke's house was selected by a television company for a local history documentary, Jillian, I noted, was initially furious that her state-of-the-art bungalow was overlooked. Her highly valued property was now in the halfpenny place while his was elevated to heritage status, vindicating Quirke's defiant stance.

I could tell it didn't help, subsequently, to see passers-by pausing to admire it, instead of hers, as they normally did. That she had been fazed by Quirke's televised input to the documentary was, however, evident. He was no longer the local oddity, presenting instead as a man of exceptional ability. His eloquence and his extensive local knowledge did himself and the community proud.

Even the late Darren paled into insignificance every time she put on a video recording of Quirke's dazzling debut on the silver screen. The more she viewed it, the more spellbound she became. Dapper and attractive in a way she hadn't previously noticed, he was quite a revelation. And to think that all those years she had got him so wrong.

Since Darren's demise, and with Denise, her only child, now living in Australia, her house had an empty ring about it. At night, she felt jumpy and lonely. A spate of local burglaries added to her sense of insecurity.

She knew Quirke to be fearless, having seen him run the gurriers out of the back lane. She relied on him now for her safety. She felt, too, the need for a man in her life, who would satisfy those mental needs that Darren couldn't – needs she had long suppressed, but which were now pressing for attention. What better time than Christmas to kiss and make up! On New Year's Eve, she invited Quirke in for supper and drinks.

I gathered he'd have declined but for the season that was in it. Though he'd sensed a change in her, he'd have preferred to keep his distance. They still walked different roads.

A few stiff drinks helped to bring them closer. The turkey and ham sandwiches were mouth-watering and the plum pudding and the iced cake, I gathered, were like nothing he had ever tasted.

Having fallen prey to good food, he soon fell for the lure of her décor: the plush furniture, the deep carpets, the resplendent chandeliers and the exquisite marble fireplace, radiating warmth and welcome. He was taken, too, by the gorgeous Christmas tree and the polished, upright piano that invited him to play.

And play, I gathered, he did, before the night was over, accompanied by Jillian, by now singing like a nightingale her favourite pieces from her musical society days.

Music, that timeless food of love, would soon dissolve their differences. As the night wore on, both suddenly realised they had more in common than they'd ever imagined.

'We'll have to do this more often,' she said, as he rose to leave.

He agreed. Already, a new-found chemistry between them was kicking in, for having helped him on with his overcoat, I learned she took both his hands in hers.

'You'll forgive me for all the hard things I said about your house. I really meant well,' she apologised, her gaze enveloping him romantically.

'Of course.' He absolved her. 'And may I belatedly compliment you on yours. It's stunning,' he finally conceded, suffused with the season's goodwill and charged with a sudden rush of feelings for her, which he contained with difficulty.

'I'm glad you think so.' I gathered she drew him closer and kissed him with such fervour, that his head went into a tail-spin.

Then she saw him to the gate, where I joined them, along with the neighbours, in a rousing rendering of 'Auld Lang Syne'.

Say what you will about Christmas, it's wonderful the way it brings people as estranged as Quirke and Jillian together.

And estranged, too, from his own house, Quirke admitted to me to feeling that night. After the splendour and comfort of Jillian's, he found it drab and cheerless. She was right. It cried out for a make-over. How else could he invite her in for supper and music and relive again with her those magical moments that they shared on New Year's Eve?

It came as no surprise to me when he commissioned a local tradesman to paint and decorate the living room shortly afterwards, in preparation for Jillian's return visit.

He had finally changed. Just as Jillian, who, too, had changed, predicted.

HOME IS WHERE THE HEART IS

After twenty-five years of marriage to Dara, Kate had come to be regarded in Abbeylaune as a Kerry woman. Even at Munster Finals, those divisive sporting *Táins*, she found herself cheering for her adopted county rather than for her native Cork, partly for the children's sake and partly to keep the peace with her partisan husband whose tribal tendencies peaked on such occasions.

'If you can't lick them, you might as well join them,' she told herself. She soon learned to put up with Dara's conceited airs in the aftermath of Kerry's triumphs over Cork, giving him, in retrospect, more credit than was his due.

Not any more. Part of him, she had come to realise, had never quite grown up. How else could he convince himself that football was the true measure of a man's prowess and that the worth of any county could be gauged by the number of All Irelands it had won. And to think she believed him for so long, and looked up to him as if he were a superman!

'Ye should stick to the small ball and leave football to us,' he would tease her. He considered hurling inferior to football and footballers superior to hurlers.

'Our day will come again,' she would reply discreetly.

After all, she was married to a sporting legend. Admittedly, as a dashing, handsome six-footer, who could pluck a ball from the clouds and loft it over the bar from midfield in his hey-day, she found him so irresistible that she begged him for his autograph after a Munster Final. The rest was history.

Of late, she doubted if he were any different or any better, now that he was slowing down, than any of his Cork counterparts. The glamour and mystique that once surrounded him were past tense. He was becoming noticeably ordinary and vulnerable, like an ageing warrior whose wounds were coming home to roost, while she was experiencing a new elixir.

Now that her family was reared and gone from her, she felt the need to shake off Dara's dominion and be her own woman. Her adopted town of Abbeylaune, to which she was sentimentally attached through her children, was gradually releasing its hold over her. Memories of her beloved Cork city came trooping back to repossess and unsettle her. After all her years in Kerry, she realised she was still, at heart, a Cork woman.

As the current Munster final approached she began to feel a growing restlessness and dissatisfaction with small town fare. The lure of the city that had nurtured her was suddenly becoming irresistible. What wouldn't she give to see a decent film, or for a day browsing in the city's boutiques, which were the rage since the Celtic Tiger took off. Increasingly, too, an evening with her old friends in the Long Valley Bar, the venue for their many, memorable get-togethers, was becoming a must.

'You'll suffocate in this oppressive, little town if you don't get away more often,' her sisters – who looked down their noses on anybody who didn't live in a city – appealed to her on their last visit.

Much as she would have liked to, she couldn't bring herself to leave Dara to look after himself in her absence. He couldn't cook for buttons, and if she didn't call him every morning for work he would sleep through the alarm.

'Could you not persuade him to move, now that your family is reared?' the elder of her sisters suggested.

She shook her head resignedly.

"Twould be easier to move the Magillicuddy Reeks. I've made my bed in Abbeylaune and 'tis there I must lie.'

'I'd make him lie in his own bed if he doesn't allow you visit us more often.' The younger sister deplored the fact that Kate had become a stranger to her own family and city.

The sisters must have got to her, for when the town was hanging out its green and gold flags and bunting for the forthcoming show-down between the two counties, she surprised everyone by flying the Cork colours from her upstairs bedroom window, much to Dara's chagrin.

'What's that flag doing?' He confronted her on his return from work.

'What d'you think? Surely it isn't a crime to fly the colours of my own county?' There was an unfamiliar ring of defiance in Kate's reply.

'It's in your face. What will the neighbours think?'

'Let them think what they like.' She stood up to him with a resoluteness that unhinged him.

Perplexed, he put it down to the onset of the mid-life crisis and to those mutinous, feminist ideas she picked up from women's magazines. Something about her on this occasion told him to let it be.

One evening, while waiting in the porch of the Market pub for a thunder shower to pass, Dara was alarmed at overhearing a group of patrons discussing Kate. It was just what he feared.

'Barbara Frietchie wouldn't be in it with her,' the barber quipped.

'I believe she's threatening to deny him his conjugal rights if Cork lose,' the postman joked.

Long held in high esteem by his community, Dara was annoyed that he had now become the butt of its jokes.

Much to his embarrassment the banter continued.

'I can hear her playing nothin' but Cork rebel songs on the piano for the last week. The Rose of Tralee isn't getting a look-in,' his next-door neighbour put in.

Dara suddenly realised that Kate was becoming the talking point of the town. He felt a rush of blood to his cheeks, then a festering anger in his depths at her betrayal. Were it not for the thunder shower, he would have bolted. Without an umbrella or his shower-proof, he had no option but to endure the drinkers' tribunal.

'Never trust a Corkonian when it comes to a Munster final with Kerry. They'd kill for it.' He could hear the turf accountant who was giving short odds on Kerry to win, admonishing his fellow patrons.

'Would you blame them after all the drubbings we've handed them.' The schoolmaster was more forgiving.

The electrician did not see eye to eye with him.

'Sure, you couldn't stand them otherwise. Football keeps them in their place.'

Much to Dara's relief, the publican insisted, though the sergeant disagreed, that Kate should stand by her man.

'You're not seriously asking her to deny her roots and to bottle her feelings?' The respected member of the local constabulary appealed for tolerance, while making no secret of his enduring fidelity to Limerick, despite his years in Abbeylaune.

By the time the shower ended, Dara's anger had subsided. However much it went against his grain, he was gradually coming around to respect Kate's stance. In any case, he was confident that her little demo would run out of steam after the game.

It was a game Kate was determined to attend. Normally his

brother would have accompanied Dara, but this time, an upbeat Kate, kitted out in her county's colours and emotionally fired up for the fray, would take his place.

She was particularly looking forward to the clash of the Cork Titan, McRour – hailed, because of his flashy boots and dazzling footwork, as the Nureyev of football – and his Kerry counterpart, the spectacular, if feisty, McLean, whom Dara had mentored as a minor and recently had helped with his anger management.

As they made their way to the venue, Kate was determined to make a statement of her intent. From the street hawkers she acquired a huge Cork flag, which she waved defiantly in Dara's face.

In the eyes of the Abbeylaune fans, they looked a pretty bizarre pair, the one bedecked in the green and gold colours of the Kingdom, the other in the blood-red of the Rebel County, as they linked arms with each other from the car park in Killarney to the stadium.

'This is going to be Cork's day. I can feel it in my bones,' she predicted, sensing that her county's football recession was about to end.

'Don't bet your house on it!' Where football was concerned, Dara was incapable of conceding a conciliatory inch to her. She might as well have not been his wife that afternoon, for only Kerry mattered to him on Munster Final days.

Things would soon augur ill for Cork and for Kate as the Kerry forwards got off to a blitzkrieg start, which quickly deflated the guest county. Kate was distraught as, time and again, she watched Kerry's wizardry reduce the Cork defence to tatters.

Her frantic cheering was all the more desperate, being in vain. Kerry were in song and made the opposition look pedestrian.

Far from giving up, Dara had to endure her sustained battle chant at a pitch that would have made Pavarotti marvel at her vocal range whenever Cork registered a score or showed flashes of the form expected of them.

He watched her biting her nails each time McLean outjumped McRour, noted her tugging at the roots of her hair whenever Cork assaults on the Kerry goalmouth were repulsed, and suffered her anguished sighs as she beheld the scoreboard revealing a growing gap between the teams.

Even more annoying for Kate was the triumphal taunting by a nearby group of Kerry supporters as they celebrated the overthrow of the Cork Titan. 'You should exchange your flashy boots for ballet shoes.' And, 'try your hand at Swan Lake instead of football.' Then, 'this is FitzGerald Stadium, boy, not Covent Garden.'

When McRour finally shook the net with a spectacular goal, Kate lost her head, cheering and dancing with such glee that Dara began to see red for the first time in their tranquil union. A further brace of points had her proclaiming yet again: 'This is going to be Cork's day in the sun.'

Much to her annoyance, an unflinching Dara nodded otherwise.

Still grappling with her sudden sea-change, he struggled to keep his cool. All her years of loyalty to Kerry and to him were evaporating before his eyes. She no longer fussed about him and moaned continually about being home-sick for Cork.

At the interval she left him to join an old flame, Weeshie, the diminutive wizard of Cork hurling in his hey-day, whom she spied among a knot of die-hard Rebel supporters. Dara's dander was suddenly up as he watched her conspiring with the enemy. His fists clenched until his knuckles were white and he could be heard muttering angrily between his teeth, 'how dare she!' Grabbing her flag, he furled it and hid it under a seat.

She was so fired up when she rejoined him at the commencement of the second half that she never missed it. Seeing that she was ready to pounce on him any time he got carried away by McLean's feats, he decided to take a cooler stance than usual for the remainder of the game.

Much to Kate's delight, a resurgent Cork team was suddenly living up to its billing and coming in tidal waves at a reeling Kerry defence, while notching up score after spectacular score, until the teams were almost level.

'It's going to be Cork's day,' she repeated, hovering hawk-like over Dara, whose confidence was beginning to wane, as the teams traded score for score in a contest he sensed could go either way.

Then all hell broke loose on the stands and terraces when McRour was red carded for reefing McLean's third jersey of the afternoon, in an effort to contain the rival he'd frequently outclassed.

His marching orders drew howls of protest, reminiscent of the Coliseum, from outraged Cork fans and, notably, from Kate, who, by now, had gone ape.

'Ref! Put on a Kerry jersey,' she yelled.

Dara frowned.

'He did what any right-minded referee in the circumstances would do.' He defended the decision, adding that McRour had it coming to him.

'Go and get your eyes tested,' she screamed. 'A child wouldn't be hanging on to its mother's apron strings the way McLean has been dragging off McRour's jersey every time he solos past him.'

It was futile trying to reason with her. In the meantime, Dara was brimming with admiration for his reformed protégé's refusal to retaliate. Now in control of his feisty tendencies, MacLean had become a shining example of how football should be played, turning the other cheek so often to provocation, that Dara at times feared he was at risk of becoming a wimp.

He needn't have worried. After a cynical tackle by the player newly assigned to mark him, McLean finally lost his cool and – much to a delirious Kate's delight – joined McRour on the sideline.

'He hasn't changed?' She belittled Dara's mentorship.

'We all have our breaking point.' Her husband was more sympathetic.

'Have we now?' she responded, as if smitten by a revelation.

As victory slipped away from a gallant Cork, she turned to blaming the referee, the manager and the sideline assistants – everybody but the team – rather than acknowledge Kerry's supremacy. Such was her annoyance, she even empathised with a rowdy city element who threw bottles and coins on to the pitch whenever a Kerry player was poised to take a free.

In those dying minutes of the game, Kate might well have belaboured an elated Dara with her flagstaff, had he not hidden it and wiped the supercilious snigger off his face as Kerry re-established their supremacy. He still hadn't got the message. She could see that he still looked down his nose on Cork.

As she watched dejected files of Cork fans making for the exits, she could picture the jibes and the condescension she would have to endure from Dara during the week ahead. She would be no better than a second class citizen in her own house. Never again! She would let him see. By God she would!

When the final whistle blew she rounded on him unexpectedly.

'I'm afraid you're going to have to cater for yourself for awhile,' she said.

At his wits' end, he begged to know what the hell was eating her.

She might have replied, 'years of subservience and a denial of her real self.' Instead, she said: 'Darling, you won't mind if I spend a few days in Cork with my sisters? I really need a break.'

He could no longer figure her.

'But you're going to miss the celebrations!' he protested.

'Yours. Not mine,' she said levelly, adding that she would wait until the triumphalism blew over before returning.

'Just a few days, mind! Otherwise I'll be battering down your sister's door for you.' His gaze held hers with an ardour that brought home to her, despite their sporting differences, how much she meant to him.

'Well it's nice to know after all these years that you finally cherish me as a Cork woman.' It was her turn to climb down.

He grinned.

'Don't take it too seriously. It's only a game.'

Was she hearing rightly? The Munster Final only a game! It was more like cold war between them down the years.

'I'm glad you've finally come to your senses,' she said, beaming with satisfaction.

'Enjoy yourself!' he called after her as she headed for the Cork-bound train with a dispirited Weeshie and a crest-fallen group of her old friends, who couldn't get back too soon to their native county. A chastened Dara felt sympathy for them for the first time ever.

Kate chuckled: 'You too. And try and not sleep through the alarm.'

Seeing him still gazing after her as she approached the turn-off for the railway, she gave him a little wave, then fired over her shoulder: 'Up the Rebels!'

A jubilant Dara rejoiced at hearing her confess on her return. while lingering in his embrace, that if home is where the heart is, hers would always be wherever he was.

She was deeply moved to see the Cork flag still fluttering from their bedroom window.

THE DOWRY

It seems only like yesterday. Yet, thirty years on, I can still remember that auspicious evening when an attractive, stylishly dressed woman accompanied by what appeared to be her two daughters, entered this historic hotel bar and sat at the table next to mine.

'I've a feeling I know you,' the senior of the three spoke to me after a discreet interval, during which she must have sensed my interest in the girls.

I responded with a shrug. After years away in Dublin, it came as no surprise to me when people didn't recognise me. I had a similar problem with them.

'Is it possible you're related to the late Con Sullivan who owned the hardware store,' she persisted.

'Why do you ask?' I inquired politely, still cautious of small town intimacies after the anonymity of the metropolis.

'You're the image of him?' Flamboyant, handsome Con! I felt flattered by the resemblance to my late uncle. With looks like his my romantic future was still assured.

'Really?' I kept her in suspense, unsure if she were trying to unearth a family skeleton I hadn't been aware of so far.

Amused by my reticence, she pressed: 'Seriously, you must be a relative?'

'A nephew,' I finally owned up and took her out of her agony.

'I knew it!' she exclaimed with satisfaction at having made the lineal connection.

'Brian Sullivan,' I introduced myself there and then, lest she would think I had something to hide, which I hadn't. Nor had my uncle. With Con Sullivan, what you saw was what you got. At least, that was what I thought.

'Kay O'Brien. And these are my daughters, Joan and Julie.'

Handshakes all round to a chorus of 'pleased to meet you.' I preferred Julie. In my opinion, she was the more attractive of the two, which was no slight on Joan, for if beauty be in the eye of the beholder, she might be considered the prettier by many.

'You won't mind, girls, if I sit for awhile with Brian and take a trip with him down memory lane?' She excused herself to her daughters and picked up her drink.

'Not at all Mum. We trust you,' they teased her. I could hear the birds kicking up a mating racket in the hotel garden.

'Sure, who'd be bothered with me at my age,' she chuckled and sat opposite me.

I ventured she must have turned many a man's head in her day.

'I turned your uncles, for all the good it did me,' she sighed nostalgically, the burden of that memory still weighing on her, I suspected.

'Tell me about it,' I urged, worried that he might have done her some wrong or other.

Addressing her sherry, she confessed they had been madly in love.

'Really! For how long were you seeing each other?' I pressed.

Her expression suddenly hardened.

'Long enough to have made the trip up the aisle, but never did.'

Unsure if she were about to take it out on me for her misadventure with my uncle, I fortified myself with a quick intake of whiskey.

Having recovered, I asked: 'How come? Did he cheat on you? Or did you both just drift apart?'

'It was much more traumatic,' she ruefully recalled.

I could sense one of those long-suppressed confessions gearing up for me, but gestured to her, nonetheless, to continue.

Helping herself to a swig of her sherry, she composed herself on the plush leather chair before hitting me with the next instalment.

'The matter of the dowry drove us apart,' she confessed with a sigh.

'You're not serious!' The painful memory of it still cast a bitter shadow across her features, as she went on to tell me how her parents couldn't possibly meet the demands made by Con's father.

'Utterly senseless!' I could feel something rebelling in me.

She nodded, then reached again for her sherry.

'What was the sum that separated you?' I inquired, having had recourse again to my Jameson.

'Treble what I had to offer.' Her mouth was a thin, hard line.

I frowned, revolted by the idea of marriage with a price tag that spelled the parting of the ways for unfortunate couples like Kay and my uncle.

'If it's any consolation, the loss, I'm certain, was as much, if not more, his than yours,' I tried to assure her.

She smiled.

Remembering something gruesome I'd read about Indian brides being murdered to make way for others with dowries, my heart bled for Kay and for all the victims of this mercenary custom.

I gathered she had set her heart on marrying into the Sullivans, a respectable family, with my uncle running a growing business. Much admired. Much envied. But that was the way it was in those days.

Finance was the monkey on the shoulder of romance. She must have felt utterly hard done.

'And you mean to tell me that my uncle didn't offer to elope with you, and leave his father to hang out to dry until he came to his senses and begged you both to return to help him run the business he couldn't otherwise manage?'

She shook her head, then looked pensive.

Engrossed as I'd been with her story, I couldn't resist sneaking the odd glance at Julie in her stylish outfit, which highlighted an attractive figure, enhanced by an inner beauty I couldn't help noticing.

'I just can't figure him,' I said, deploring Con's subservience to his father.

She shrugged resignedly, then went on to make allowances for him.

'Sons rarely crossed their parents in those days. Besides, his father needed the money to expand the business.'

Pained by the wrong she had suffered, I assured her that were I in my uncle's shoes, I'd have told him to stuff his business and booked my passage to America, rather than lose a woman of her calibre.

'Times have changed. Maybe it wasn't to be. Maybe it was all for the better.'

She suddenly brightened, her exquisite features affirming yet again the prize my uncle forfeited.

'Maybe, but then, maybe not.' Privately, her version of destiny rang a little hollow with me. It seemed much too submissive. I, on the other hand, believed in playing a more controlling role in mine.

As I tossed back my whiskey, I remember wondering why on earth she was telling me all this. Therapeutic reasons? Or the need to settle an old score with my late uncle? I suspected her motives were more complex.

'So where did you go from there?' I inquired, my thoughts turning again to those hapless Indian brides who were sacrificed to Mammon.

Her eyes clouding, she candidly confessed: 'I felt gutted, and for a long time afterwards, I withdrew into myself until the understanding man I married helped me to love again. Thank heavens I've no regrets,' she declared with a triumphal toss of her head.

'I'm so glad for you. And was there any question of a dowry?'

'His family never asked a penny of me.' Her expression softened.

'And rightly so.' Most men, I was sure, would have given their right arm for a woman of her looks and class in her day.

She allowed herself a quick sip of her sherry before hitting me with yet another query.

'Am I right in thinking you used to help out on and off in your uncle's shop before you left for Dublin?'

I nodded. Admitting to being his favourite nephew and to having needed pocket money, I gave her to understand that he usually took me on as an extra hand during the holidays.

'It's such a pity he didn't have any family to whom he could have passed on the business,' she remarked, feeling, I gathered from her expression, the winner in that respect.

Keeping her guessing about the fate of the business, I remarked that given his love of children, he would have been a wonderful father.

She nodded. With a hint of amusement, she recalled how he married rather late in life and remembered him telling her once that it was a match.

'And I'm pretty sure the dowry in question was nothing like

what you were expected to pay?' I ventured, glancing at Julie.

'So I gathered. But by then the business was on a roll,' she said, her tone surprisingly conciliatory.

I had learned more about my uncle over a drink that evening than in all the years I'd known him. It could only happen in a town like Abbeylaune.

'So you made it up with my uncle?' I remarked, liking to think they let bygones be bygones.

'Of course. After all, he wasn't to blame. In fact, I distinctly recall him telling me one evening in this very lounge, after his wife died, that he deeply regretted not having defied his father and married me,' she confided with a touch of vanity.

'He did!' I preferred to think that it was the drink talking on that occasion, for, from what I remember, he got on very well with my aunt. Still, you never know, do you?

Changing the subject, Kay inquired if it were true that the business was to go under the hammer. She too seemed to have fallen for the rumours.

When I informed her that he had left it to me, her eyes widened and she uttered an audible gasp.

'Well good for you!' She extended a congratulatory hand. Then, almost in the same breath, she inquired: 'But aren't you managing a firm in Dublin?'

Was there anything they didn't know about me in this town?

'Not any longer. I've come back to run my own.'

'And your wife and family, how do they feel about your decision?'

I was relieved that not everything about me was known, but that wouldn't last for long. Still, the warmth and friendliness of my home town were preferable any day to the anonymity of Dublin.

'Perhaps I haven't met the right woman so far, for I'm still single,' I confessed, jokingly suggesting that she might keep a look-out for a suitable partner for me.

'It might interest you that I have an eligible daughter.' She gave me a playful but calculated smile.

I gestured cautiously, then discreetly inquired which one. Much though I felt like making some amends for my late uncle's wrong, the prospect of an arranged union repelled me. An incurable romantic, I would decide for myself – unless, of course, some irresistible woman decided for me.

'Well as it so happens, Joan is engaged to be married. But perhaps Julie . . . ?' she suggested tactfully.

My heart leaped with joy. I fancied her at first sight. That she resembled her mother and I, apparently, my uncle, may explain why I was more drawn to her than Joan.

'Perhaps you'd put a word in for me. And you have mine, the question of a dowry won't arise,' I joked, sensitive again to the mating furore in the hotel garden.

Kay smiled, finished her drink, then suggested to the girls they had better be moving if they hoped to beat the evening traffic.

Julie glanced at her watch, then at Joan glancing at hers. In an effort to detain them, I rose from my chair and signalled to the waiter for drinks all around. 'Just one for the road,' I pleaded, wishing to prolong their company.

'We might as well,' the girls agreed.

I wanted to be with Julie. I was thirty and living alone in my uncle's rambling house full of empty rooms, in a town where I was practically a stranger. I could do with a woman's love and support in the trying days ahead. Something told me that Julie might well be that woman.

When Kay announced I was coming back to stay, I could sense

a comforting note of interest in Julie's response: 'Oh, really! We could do with some fresh blood in this town.'

'And he's just inherited his uncle's business.' Kay's announcement really blew them over.

'Congrats! You must be over the moon,' both sisters replied almost in unison.

Aware of the heavy responsibilities that went with a firm that burgeoned during the Celtic Tiger, I had no illusions about the task ahead.

'Hopefully I can run it as efficiently as my uncle did, but he's going to be a hard act to follow.'

'Of course you will,' Julie said. With her by my side, nothing, I felt, would be too difficult.

Getting to her feet, Kay turned to me and said, 'You must call out to see us as soon as you've settled in,' and cancelled her drink. Excusing herself, she went to take a peek at the recently refurbished hotel garden, where dating couples chilled out after the rigours of the ballroom.

'Oh, you must indeed,' the girls chorused and sat beside me.

At that point, I recall, Kevin, Joan's fiancé, joined us. An energetic, clean-cut chap, he worked in a managerial capacity for a firm that had recently gone into receivership. Faced with redundancy, he jumped at my offer of a similar position in my business.

'By the way, there's a dance in the hotel tonight,' he announced, and in a celebratory mood, inquired if we were interested.

I didn't need a second invitation. When Julie confessed she didn't exactly feel like going on her own, I suggested, if it were alright with her, I wouldn't mind tagging along.

'Of course,' she agreed. Already, my heart was throbbing for her.

'Well do you want to stay or meet up later?' Kay inquired when she returned from the garden, which must have held very special memories for her.

The girls had already decided. As she was taking her leave of us, she extended her hand to me.

'I feel so much the better for having met you,' she confessed.

I nodded, relieved that a niggling episode from her past could now be laid to rest.

As I watched her leave I could sense a similar lightness in her step and a song in her heart as was in mine, as I danced the night away with Julie. Even now, that song is there as she crosses the hotel lounge to join me for drinks on yet another happy wedding anniversary.

A BARBER'S TALE

Gary was about to close shop that Saturday evening, when he caught the reflection of a former customer in the mirror, sidling into his barber's salon in Ranelagh. There was always that last minute client whenever he was in a hurry to get home, just like this evening. Being a rigorous business-man, he met such late comers with a smile and a greeting that belied his displeasure.

'Well what do you know! I was beginning to despair of ever meeting you again, Brian.' His greeting on this occasion was genuine.

'Great to see you, Gary!' The big man embraced the smaller one.

'How in God's name are you keeping?' So thrilled was he with the visit from an old and valued client that he forgot his hurry.

Lifting his broad shoulders in a shrug, the big man admitted that, like the Irish economy, he was experiencing a recession.

An astonished Gary couldn't ever imagine the winner of a prestigious Michelin Award to be anything but flourishing and said so, but a deep sigh from the celebrated chef and erstwhile restauranteur suggested otherwise.

'So, what can I do for you?' The diplomatic barber got down to business.

'I've just been given a present of a voucher for a hot shave and a hair-cut,' the other awkwardly confessed to a bewildered Gary who tactfully replied: 'Anything for a gentleman.'

When Brian removed his hacked cromby, Gary noted his sport's suit, too, had seen better days, like those when he cut his hair in Peter Mark.

'I'm glad to see that, unlike yours truly, you haven't lost any of your fine crown of thatch.' Gary set about applying the feel good factor that made him so likeable.

Brian frowned.

'I lost my business instead.' His reflection in the mirror did not belie a man down in his luck.

'I'm sorry to hear that. But you'll bounce back again.' Gary was confident.

The once celebrated chef merely shrugged, then shrewdly observed: 'I can see you're doing nicely yourself.'

The successful barber admitted to making a decent enough living.

'So you left Peter Mark?' Brian noted with interest.

Gary admitted to always wanting a place of his own and to having decided to buy out the lease of his premises when the owners retired.

'A wise decision. And a sound investment. At the end of the day, there's nothing like being your own boss.'

'Indeed. Perhaps some of your entrepreneurial skills brushed off on me.' Gary chuckled, as he applied his scissors to his favourite client's overgrown locks.

'It appears you're putting them to better use than I did,' the other sighed. He was a much leaner version of the previously portly chef whom Gary remembered.

Twenty-five years ago today, Brian, having learned of his engagement to Kay, invited him to dine with her at the Gold

Fish Bowl, the most talked about restaurant in town at the time.

Gary remembered declining the offer at first, unnerved by the prospect of what it would cost him. In any case, he explained that Kay and himself had arranged to dine at the Rainbow, which was more their style and more suited to their pockets.

'You're dining at my place. And that's that,' the restauranteur insisted.

'You realize I only work at Peter Mark. I don't own it.' Gary recalled trying to wriggle out of the invitation.

'You don't have to worry. It will be on the house. So cancel your arrangements for the Rainbow.' The other put his mind at ease.

Suddenly captivated by the prospect of dining up-market, Gary capitulated, only to regret it later.

What he should have said was, 'I'd better consult Kay first.' If there were decisions where she would insist on having her say, this was one. But how could he refuse the chance of a lifetime?

'The usual trim or shall I take a lot off?' Gary enquired of his client.

'A lot, if you wouldn't mind.' His current locks suggested his hair-cuts were few and far between of late.

When Gary broke the news to Kay, she hit the roof, threatened to back out, then went into a sulk. It required all his persuasive powers to get her to change her mind. Even in the taxi, she barely spoke to him and then only to repeat her disapproval.

'We'll be fish out of water,' she moaned.

'Hardly, considering it's famous for its fish menu.' Fearful she would convey any hint of ingratitude to their host, he tried to humour her.

'More suited to big fish than to minnows like us,' she railed.

Gary disagreed. Seeing he could regale them while cutting their hair, he saw no reason why he couldn't cut it with them at table.

She frowned. 'Maybe you can with your gift of the Blarney. I'm going to feel about as comfortable as Jonah in the whale's belly.'

Gary explained that it would have been churlish of him to decline. After all, Brian had tipped him generously down the years and had pointed similar, lucrative clients his way.

'It wouldn't have hurt to say no in the circumstances. You bend too easily.' She was implacable.

Twenty-five years ago – and it seemed only like yesterday – Gary marvelled, reliving every moment of that occasion afresh.

As he listened to the drone of gridlocked traffic, snailing its way to distant homes, he thanked his stars that he lived near his workplace, especially on an evening like this.

'You certainly picked a prime location,' Brian noted. 'And no shortage of customers I'd bet.'

'There are days frankly, when I could do with less,' the barber confessed to the pressures of his business.

'A good complaint,' the other said.

Gary wondered what had befallen the celebrated restauranteur who had greeted himself and Kay so warmly and had the head waiter seat them at a discreet table for two. Enamoured with the breath-taking ambiance and the charming prospect of the sea-front, Kay began to unwind.

A glass of sparkling champagne did wonders for her. Soon, her attractive figure and stylish outfit had more than one head turning. It suddenly occurred to her that the Gold Fish Bowl was not, after all, a bad idea on Gary's part and apologised for over-reacting when the food was being served. And what a meal!

Starters, which were a meal in themselves, were followed by sole on the bone for Kay and a fillet of sirloin steak that would feed a household for him. For desert, the baked Alaska, which for presentation, let alone flavour, still lingered in his memory.

Then the coffee was served in an ornate pot with mouth-watering truffles – all the coffee they wanted. And then there was that unforgettable house wine, that Kay still talked about.

'I see you've retained some features of the traditional barber shop.' Brian cut across his train of thought.

'They help keep me in touch with my roots in the business,' a no-nonsense Gary admitted.

To Kay, Brian had confessed on that historic occasion: 'The reason why I have Brian cut my hair, is not only because he's the best barber in town, but because he's the best story teller.'

'It comes with the package,' Gary chuckled, aware of his indebtedness to the gifted Abbeylaune story tellers of his youth.

'Tell me about him. When he wants to, he can charm the birds off the tree.' Kay too was generous in her praises.

'How else could he have won himself so attractive a fiancée?' replied the restauranteur.

She thanked him for the compliment and for the superb meal she would remember for years to come.

'And speaking about birds, I gather from Gary that you sing like one.' Brian called for a song from her.

After some persuasion, she agreed to entertain her host, the captains of industry, media celebrities and lovers of good food with a compelling rendering of *Love's Old Sweet Song* to a sensitive accompaniment by the resident pianist, which prompted cries for more. Instead, Gary, at Brian's insistence, entertained them with a selection of his yarns which went down a treat.

The crowning moment of their evening, Gary remembered, brought tears of joy to Kay's eyes, as Brian announced their engagement and had the head waiter present her with an enormous bunch of flowers while everybody clapped and wished them well. What an occasion!

'So where have you been exercising your unrivalled culinary talents of late?' Gary inquired, as he snipped away at the restauranteur's greying locks.

'Just catering for the odd function here and there.'

'Whatever became of the Gold Fish Bowl?' Gary was curious as he trimmed the other's neglected, bushy eyebrows.

A forthright Brian confessed: 'It went into receivership, due to bad management on my part, and to stiff competition from a new wave of ethnic restaurants. Then my marriage broke up. I sold the lease of the Gold Fish Bowl and sadly hit the bottle. Since then I've been more or less adrift.'

'I'm sorry to hear it. But you cannot keep a good man down.' Gary consoled him, as he helped him on with his frayed cromby.

'I'm not so sure. Who could have foreseen the twilight of the gourmets?' he sighed, the mirror reflecting his wry expression.

A blushing Brian presented Gary with the voucher, which the barber duly handed back to him.

'Next time.'

Gary let him know it was pay-back time for an unforgettable evening at the Gold Fish Bowl.

'I remember it as if it were only yesterday,' Brian remarked tearfully and thanked Gary for his kindness.

Whereupon, an appreciative barber inquired as his old acquaintance was leaving, if he were doing anything that evening.

Brian turned fully around and paused before responding.

'Why do you ask?'

'Should you happen to be free, you'll be more than welcome at my place. Kay and myself are having a bit of a do for our Silver Jubilee with some friends. We'd love to have you.'

The chef's expression suddenly brightened.

'I'd only be too delighted. What time is it kicking off?'

'Around nine or thereabout,' Gary replied, inscribing his address on the back of his business card, which he handed to Brian.

'Perfect. I'll squeeze in the vigil Mass in Clarendon Street before that.'

A surprised Gary, who had always associated Brian more with epicurean than with spiritual leanings, inquired if he were becoming religious.

Brian smiled.

'Only the Lord's Supper can satisfy our deeper hungers,' he declared as he rushed to grab an oncoming bus for town.

Having closed shop, a more fortunate Gary stepped into his Audi and sped off to celebrate with Kay their twenty-five years of marital happiness in an era of so many broken unions.

Brian surprised everyone when he arrived well ahead of schedule and, with Kay's consent, set about cooking up a treat. Kitted out in his chef's regalia, which he brought along with a carrier bag of ingredients, he looked every bit his former self.

And what a meal he delivered! The roasts were succulent, the baked Alaska mouth-watering, the cappuccinos the real deal. Afterwards, Kay's inimitable rendering of *Goodbye to the White Horse Inn* brought tears to his eyes and Gary's humorous stories had him in stitches.

As he was about to leave, Brian informed them of his second lucky break of the evening. An old friend, whom he ran into in Clarendon Street offered him a job as resident chef at the Rainbow, which he had recently purchased and revamped. Nothing exclusive. Just perfect for hard-pressed, working couples who haven't time to cook. He invited Kay and Gary to the opening night.

Thrilled that things had again turned up trumps for him, they did not hesitate on this occasion to accept his invitation.

It was one of Gary's favourite stories.

FOR WHOM THE BELL TOLLED

McCusker was in an up-beat mood that Sunday morning. It was the 12th of July – the high noon of the Marching Season throughout the North. To-day, the Orangemen were stamping their traditional authority on Ulster, with the exception of the Garvaghy Road, to which they were denied entry. It was a sore point with McCusker, who was bred to believe in the inalienable right of all Protestants to march whenever and wherever they chose, and let no goddamn Fenian or Papist think otherwise.

While checking his watch before belling the Protestant faithful to service, the unswerving sexton of Blackriver Church of Ireland could hear the crunch of the rector's tyres on the gravel. He had little time for the Reverend Grace. Much too liberal for his liking and far too tolerant of Fenians and Papists. He would have peace at any price. An intractable McCusker felt he'd lost the plot since the Good Friday Agreement. That's if he hadn't lost it long beforehand. While most were undergoing the trauma of adjustment in its aftermath, he took to it like the proverbial duck to water.

'Good morning, Reverend. A perfect day for marching.'

'A perfect day for reconciliation, Billy.' Slim-built and with pale, introspective features, he was not what the hard-line sexton would have ordered as a fit successor to the late George Battersby.

'I'm afraid there'll be more confrontation than reconciliation if we're not allowed march down the Garvaghy Road, your reverence.'

The rector grimaced.

'We must seek a less provocative route if we're to live together in peace,' he disagreed.

For McCusker it was the stuff of fantasy, and was asking the wolf to lie down with the lamb.

'If we back down, the Fenians will see it as a weakness on our part and quickly exploit it.'

The rector nodded to the contrary.

'The weak will confound the strong, Billy. Have you forgotten your bible?' The rector had a quote for every occasion.

The sexton suppressed an expletive on his lips. Biblical scholar though he might be, Grace, in his opinion, wasn't a patch on Battersby, his late predecessor. Towering in stature, and with the delivery and bearing of an Old Testament preacher, Battersby was a force to be reckoned with. A product of the die-hard school, he could whip up a storm of Unionist fervour during service on the spur of the moment.

When the mood took him, he'd rail against Papists, Fenians and British Government alike. A fearless, outspoken cleric, he sang from the same hymn sheet as McCusker as well as McCusker's father and his father, too.

'You'll have them walk all over us,' the staunchly traditionalist sexton protested, alarmed by Grace's subversive outlook.

'No Billy. We must walk hand in hand.'

The Sexton frowned, his entrenched mindset recoiling at the prospect. 'To Leinster House rather than Stormont if they get their way.'

The rector grimaced, then reproved him gently.

'You should try to remember that there won't be any Leinster

House or Stormont in the next world.'

Billy shook his head. Grace was so out of step with the spirit of the Twelfth, Battersby would have shown him the door.

As Billy set out the rector's vestments, he could sense sweeping changes on the way. Changes that threatened everything he stood for, with Grace insisting he forgive and forget, as if the Troubles amounted to nothing more than a domestic tiff.

It was a bit rich, especially from someone who came from the South, who had been spared the conflicts and hadn't lost a family member, or been locked away in the Kesh for standing by Ulster. The Good Friday sea-change left McCusker sea-sick. The bitter wounds inflicted on his family and community by the Fenians were still festering. Try as the new rector might, Billy knew that traditional attitudes and loyalties would not be brushed aside overnight.

'The service sheet printed out well.' The Reverend Grace's compliment drew him out of his quarrelsome reverie.

Billy nodded. The content was another matter. Peace-driven and inclusive, it didn't ring with the sexton. A battle-scarred Ulster wasn't ready for it. Not yet. Maybe never. And who should know better than the late Reverend Battersby's right-hand man?

True, there were those Fenians who had sympathised with McCusker over the loss of his son, a prominent UVF activist, shot by one of their kinsmen in front of his family, as he was watching his favourite programme on the tele. A heinous deed, leaving his three traumatised young children without a father.

McCusker had never forgiven them, though there was blood on his son's hands too – Fenians' blood, which the sexton, with his open season attitude to them, justified. Any blow for Ulster was a good one in his book. As he saw it, the best Fenian was a dead one. He had second thoughts since his son's ghastly murder.

'The *Song of Brotherhood* should be suitable for to-day's service,' the Reverend Grace chirped, as if intent on silencing the drums. If he had his way, it would become the new Ulster anthem. In view of the Twelfth, Billy's preference would have been the *Battle Hymn*.

Now that the guns were silent and a new Protestant outlook was emerging, McCusker had begun to feel, especially since the Reverend Battersby's passing, something of a dinosaur. Things were changing much too fast in his opinion. There was too much 'got to move on' and 'forget the past'.

Still rooted in that past, still walking in the shadow of Battersby, he had yet to come to terms with the spirit of the Good Friday Agreement. Unlike the Reverend Grace, it was thus far and no further for him.

'How is our stock of wine, Billy? I seem to remember, it was running low recently'.

'I've placed a new order with McGinleys, our reliable Protestant supplier. It should be here any day,' the dutiful sexton replied.

'Good. But try and remember to give a little business to our Catholic merchants from time to time.'

Imagine Battersby coming out with that! The late rector must have been spinning in his grave recently. His Ulster had been laid to rest with him.

Billy swallowed hard.

As for getting Battersby to row in with the current Ulster, it would have been like pouring old wine into new bottles, Billy knew, as he filled a flagon of port for the Eucharist. He could never understand why Papists only received the consecrated bread, which they believed literally, unlike Protestants, to be the body and blood of Christ.

And dare any Papist receive the Eucharist at an Anglican

service! No give on Rome's part on that score. Okay if it were the other way round. Church unity, how are you, Billy grimaced.

While putting away the port, Billy remembered when Papists weren't allowed to set foot in this very church for a funeral service for a deceased Protestant neighbour. Did you ever hear such bunkum? And to think that they had the neck to accuse Protestants of sectarianism, while insisting that the children of mixed marriages had to be brought up as Catholics. It was a good day that had ended.

As for the controversial question of clerical celibacy and women clerics, Canterbury, Billy was proud, was leading the way for Rome. And if the Vatican had followed suit, he was convinced there would have been a lot less clerical scandals in its church.

'The acoustics haven't been very satisfactory of late,' the Rector noted.

'I regret to report that Mr Gormley tried without success to fix them.' McCusker felt that the entire system needed to be replaced, but the rector had other ideas.

'How about getting the technician who does the repairs for the convent to have a look at them?' he suggested, adding that he'd had a very good report of him.

A shocked sexton felt like exclaiming: 'Over my dead body!' Instead, he admitted discreetly, that the thought never occurred to him.

'Leave it with me and I'll get in touch with him.' The rector's tone was firm. Then, on a more cheerful note, he declared that, if nothing else, it would be a worthwhile cross-community exercise. For a frail man, he dared to tread where even Battersby feared incurring the wrath of his own community.

'I don't think you should.' The sexton shuddered at the prospect of having to eat yet another slice of humble pie.

'Why not?' The rector shot a bemused glance at him.

'His political track record is pretty suspect to say the least.'

'You know what they say about him who is without sin?' The rector eyed him warily.

McCousker frowned. The very thought of asking that renegade O'Donnell to service the acoustics made his blood boil. How could any self-respecting Unionist have any truck with a terrorist thug like him?

It wouldn't surprise the sexton if the rector had O'Donnell and his henchmen around to his house for high tea next, as part of his programme for reconciliation. He must be off his bloomin' rocker. If Battersby had had his way, he'd have had O'Donnell locked up and the key thrown away.

'Did you count the communion breads?' the rector asked, emerging from a silent rehearsal of yet another of his ground-breaking sermons that were in stark contrast with Battersby's thundering denunciations of Papists.

'All in order, your reverence. Sadly, one less than last Sunday.'

'You're referring no doubt to the late George Hamilton?' the rector noted.

The sexton nodded respectfully.

'The very same, distinguished member of the Orange Order. We'll be the poorer for his passing,' he lamented.

Grace again glanced at him suspiciously.

'From what they tell me of his B-Special days, I'm not so sure if the Catholic community would share your views.' There was a note of censure about his remark that Billy resented.

'A man of unshakable, Protestant integrity, he kept the Fenians in their place and law and order in Ulster.' He stood boldly by him, regardless of Grace's opinion.

'It probably cost him his life. It seems his scuffles with the police on the Garvaghy Road may have been responsible for his fatal stroke.'

'He wasn't one to back off. That's for sure,' Billy gave back defensively, though he could see the rector shaking his head.

'Had he done so, he might be moving forward with us to-day.'

The Reverend Grace had clearly come to bury Battersby's legacy rather than vindicate it.

As he peered through the gothic window at the rain-sodden clouds that could spoil the Twelfth, Billy realised he would have to watch his step with Grace. The jibes and jokes he once shared with Battersby at the expense of Papists were no longer politically correct. It rankled that he, who had once been the eye and ear of the late rector, was now effectively sidelined.

'How about this for the theme of my sermon today, Billy?'

A preoccupied sexton gave him his ear.

'Sectarianism has no place in the gospel.'

Billy casually shrugged.

'Sounds okay, your reverence. Just don't rush the fences. There's still a lot of hard feelings out there.'

'That's precisely what I propose to deal with. As I see it, my ministry will be a bridging one,' the determined rector declared, with a spiritual steel that belied his physical frailty.

'Be careful you don't sell us out,' Billy counselled.

The rector smiled, then turned serious.

'We could do with a clearance sale,' he said and reminded his sexton of the ecumenical study group from the local Catholic parish council, whom he had invited to the service.

When Billy told him he had reserved some pews for them at the back of the church, Grace shot him an angry glance.

'I'd suggest you have them sit in the front ones, bearing in mind they're our brothers in Christ,' the crusader for peace demanded.

Billy swallowed hard.

'I suppose you'll be inviting members from the local Muslim community next.' He couldn't resist a poke at the idealistic cleric.

'I don't see why not,' Grace exclaimed.

A frustrated Billy muttered a suppressed swear as he slipped out to ring the bell. Filling his lungs with a mouthful of crisp, morning air, he tried to clear his head of Grace's unsettling views. The distant roll of a kettle drum was suddenly balm to his battered spirits, and his feet drilled to the martial notes of fifes, triggering memories of his own marching days as he proceeded with regimental stride to where the bell chain was fastened. With a fervour that was more divisive than inclusive, he summoned the faithful of Blackriver to service.

As he tugged the chain with heightened zest, he released with each down-pull his pent up frustrations with the Reverend Grace. Ding-dong, ding-dong, clanged the imperious, Protestant bell across town and countryside. Ding-dong. Louder. Dong-ding. 'Drown out,' he could be heard muttering to himself, 'the Priory bell! The convent bell! And every Papist bell within earshot.'

Ding dong. 'Give it everything you have for the sake of the Twelfth. Let it resound with the victory of Craig and Carson over Home Rule. The unflinching stance of Brookeborough towards the South. The tramp, tramp of Ulstermen on their way to the Somme. The up-standing legacy of the late George Battersby.'

Ding-dong, ding-dong.

'Give it a rest, Quasimodo. It's had its day,' O'Donnell yelled on his way to Mass at the Priory, his trade-mark beret affixed to his shaven skull, which McCusker wouldn't half mind cracking, given the slightest pretext.

'Never!' Billy wrung another thunderous clang out of the bell, asserting thereby his supremacy over his arch rival.

'Never' was responsible for the Troubles, Billy. 'Never' should never be on your lips.'

Billy snarled, 'You can hardly afford to talk.' A blow-in, southern Republican from Abbeylaune, O'Donnell had married into a local family of similar political persuasion during the Troubles.

He couldn't bear the sight of O'Donnell, with his leer and his snide remarks. He suspected him, too, of having had a hand in his son's shooting. Now out of the Kesh, where he did time, he was already playing the politically correct card, belying the erstwhile subversive. He had some neck. And to think that the Reverend Grace would have him repair the acoustics, after the mayhem he and his henchmen unleashed on the community.

'I can't hear it, Billy.' O'Donnell cupped his ear in his hand tauntingly.

'The sacred bell of Ulster will never be for your profane, Papist ears.'

'You mean the bell of Unionism. Of Burntollet. And Bloody Sunday. A sectarian bell that ignored the wrongs inflicted by your colonial ancestry on us Catholics down through history.' O'Donnell continued to rile his adversary.

'But not the bell of Enniskillen. Nor Omagh.' The sexton gave as good as he got, then checked himself.

Don't listen to him. He's trying to wind you up. Ding-dong, ding-dong, the rope scoring his scrubbed hands, its back-pull lifting him off his feet of fifty-five years standing by Unionist principles.

'A usurper's, bigoted bell that, despite your Penal Laws, failed to wipe out our one, true, catholic and apostolic Church,' O'Donnell goaded him.

Billy shook his head, then couldn't resist retaliating.

'You mean the bell of the reformed Church, which gave the bible back to the people and the right to their private conscience.'

'Conscience! Just listen to them sectarian drums! And the tramp of those arrogant feet that walked all over us nationalists for centuries. How can you talk about conscience?' O'Donnell switched from taunting to righteous indignation.

Ding-dong. Ding-dong. An embattled Billy tried to keep his cool.

'The truth hurts, eh Billy?' O'Donnell continued to rib him.

'If you don't shove off, it's to an out-patients rather than the Priory you'll be going.' The sturdy sexton shook a clenched fist at his mocker.

'Never again, Billy boy, will you and your sidekicks shove the likes o' me around. And I'm damned if you'll march down the Garvaghy Road this Twelfth.' The leer turned to a scowl; the mocking to confrontation.

Ding-dong. Ding-dong.

'You should try ringing the changes rather than your outmoded prejudices, Billy!'

The sexton did his best to ignore him.

'One o' these days I'll pull the clapper out of that bigoted old bell,' O'Donnell threatened.

'Pity someone wouldn't remove yours!' roared Billy, as his fiery temperament got the better of him. He was confident that if it came to blows, he'd deck O'Donnell, despite his adversary's physical advantages. Billy had beaten bigger men.

Suddenly, the sexton could see the scowl giving away to a look of horror on the Fenian's features. He heard him shout: 'Look out, Billy!' as he advanced towards him.

'You look out! Or I'll put your lights out,' Billy roared back.

'Get out of the way Billy!'

He could see O'Donnell making a dash for him.

'Try and make me. Gwan! Throw the first one! ' Billy adopted a pugilistic pose.

'Move you idiot or you'll be pulverised by the bloody bell! Move!' Billy felt a panic-stricken O'Donnell grabbing him, then pushing him to one side as the bell, preceded by a shower of loosened masonry, came hurtling down on him.

'God forgive me!' Billy prayed, as he was felled under the crushing weight of the bell that he had for so long rung and his father had rung, and his father before him, for the Protestant faithful of Blackriver.

And so it came about, that the bell that put him in a wheel chair had finally tolled for his career as sexton. In reality, it had ended with the arrival of the Reverend Grace. Billy belonged to the old order that was now out of favour.

Expert opinion attributed the bell's collapse to metal fatigue rather than sabotage. A crippled Billy has since made his peace with O'Donnell, fully aware that if it weren't for his intervention, he'd have been an inscription on a headstone like his son – and O'Donnell's son, as well as all the other sons of Ulster who perished at one another's hands during the Troubles.

It was a tragic period in the province's history, which the Reverend Grace and a reformed McCusker, as well as a changed O'Donnell – who fixed the acoustics for free – are determined must never be repeated.

The Good Friday Agreement had finally called the shots.

DISPOSING OF THE ASHES

Even by Manchester United standards, the late Barney Stynes' support for the club had been nothing short of fanatical. Living next door, I ought to know. Picture my disbelief when his daughter, Edel, announced from the altar after her eulogy that it was his dying wish that his ashes be disposed of on Old Trafford's football pitch. Ironically, that's what kick-started our romance. It all came back to me while waiting for the eagerly anticipated Cup Final between United and Chelsea to kick-off.

Like some at the obsequies, I wasn't sure whether to succumb to laughter and embarrass the bereaved or look thoroughly shocked as others looked, which could have been equally embarrassing.

Instead, being a sensitive occasion and very likely a sensitive issue with the family, who seldom saw eye to eye with their father, I greeted the announcement with a respectful nod. After all, it was a dying man's wish. And take it from me, I've seen ashes disposed of in worse places for the oddest of reasons.

'Trust him to make a show of us!' Edel drew me aside afterwards in the pub where we'd been helping ourselves to the customary refreshments. I could see she was left carrying the urn, her brothers wanting nothing to do with it. They had regularly clashed with Stynes prior to leaving home and would never have granted him his dying wish if they had their way.

'He wouldn't be the first not to have his ashes in the family plot,' I said, making light of her worries. I had a crush on her since coming to live next door, though Stynes made it clear he didn't approve of me.

As he saw it, I wasn't, strictly speaking, a United fan. At least not to the extent he expected of a candidate for his daughter's hand. Besides, I was an office boy rather than the stereotype, macho tradesman he had in mind. Big deal! And big though tradesmen's pay-packets were, I figured I was more her type, for she read books and played the piano and was as civil and cool as he was gruff and mental about football.

'Imagine, he was even considering having his coffin draped in the United colours!' she exclaimed.

I nodded diplomatically.

Wrestling with my yearnings for her, year in year out, while watching her enviable dates – the king-pins of the Celtic Tiger – come and go, I vowed I would stretcher Stynes, big-boned and rugged though he be, if he continued to come between us. With youth and a height advantage on my side, as well as those karate skills I'd acquired in my teens, I was confident I'd give him a run for his money any day.

At other times, I dreamed up elaborate strategies for eloping with her, for he had become more and more possessive of her since his wife died, needing someone to lean on and humour him out of those black moods he succumbed to whenever United lost. Like himself, the team were going through a rocky patch since the emergence of Chelsea.

In the meantime, I had to look after my ageing mother who had come to stay with me, putting on hold any thoughts I might have had of settling down until she'd passed away.

'The old Red Devil couldn't let go of United even in death.' An undercurrent of anger punctuated Edel's bereaving.

I told her how he confided to me in the Hospice that he looked forward to meeting his life-long hero George Best.

She grimaced.

'He'd drive him around the bleedin' twist.'

Both Stynes and I kept our distance, but were there for each other in a crisis, like the night he got the fatal stroke after United only managed a draw with Middlesborough, reducing their lead over Chelsea to a single point, and Edel came running in tears to my door for assistance.

'It's such a pity he didn't live to see the Cup Final,' I regretted.

'He saw enough of them for all the good they did him,' she rejoined.

I'd miss Stynes even though I fancied my chances more with Edel now. There were worse neighbours. And he was seldom dull. Though a dyed-in-the-wool Dub, he didn't mind too much that I was a fan of Kerry football. Kerry, like United, were winners. And he had no time for anything else.

Admittedly we had some heated exchanges whenever our counties clashed, though nothing like those between himself and Jones – his other, next-door neighbour – whenever United played Chelsea in what had become a clash of Titans.

All hell broke lose on those tense occasions between the rival neighbours. Shouting matches were followed by prolonged stand-offs.

How Stynes loathed Chelsea and their city-slick supporters. They were the glamorous London pretenders laying claim to the rightful champion's crown. The much-hyped, European outfit versus the home-grown, people's team, which numbered in its time, legendary Irish players like his classmate Anto, one of the stars who helped the club rise from the ashes of the Munich disaster. A crippling blow to United, who would bounce back sooner, I learned, than Stynes, to become once again to football what the All Blacks are to rugby.

I gathered from Edel he would never forget seeing Anto off at Dublin Airport to fame and fortune with his dream team. Though he often gave Anto a run for his money as a juvenile, United would remain a vicarious experience for Stynes. Anto was the one billed for stardom.

'He never grew up,' she regretted.

'I suppose football kept him young at heart.' I tried to make allowances for him.

Throughout the historic year that United won the treble, I scarcely got a nod from Stynes, who walked so tall his head was in the clouds, communing with Eric Cantona, the new deity of the Premier league.

Then came Chelsea. The young Lochinvars set to tear up the form book and blow United out of the water. A rivalry unlike any other in contemporary English football was born. And it boded ill for Stynes.

There were times when I watched him hit rock bottom. When United sank, he sank. When the media gutted them, he felt gutted. Their losses were more poignantly his than theirs. And with Jones gloating over him as Chelsea showed United as clean a pair of heels on the League table as Arkle in his hey-day showed his rivals at Cheltenham, he succumbed to a sustained bout of the blues. All his cheering was in vain. United had had their day, and Jones didn't half rub it in.

'Football for him was a religion,' she sighed. I withheld comment.

My sitting on the fence when he expected me to be supportive, and shouting my lungs out in support of the faltering Reds didn't help.

My friendship with Jones was another, contentious matter. It implied I was neutral, and Stynes had as little time for neutrals as for those who didn't talk football.

Though he was far from bird-brained, I don't think he could talk about anything seriously other than football. It was the be-all and end-all of his simple existence.

'Can I fresh up your drink?' I inquired of his alluring daughter, who was blessed with more sense than her father.

'A gin and tonic, if you insist. I could do with a pick-me-up after that eulogy, which has left me feeling like a hypocrite.'

'Why?' Everything about her fascinated me.

'He didn't deserve it, being married more to United than to my mother, who didn't get a look-in whenever there was football on the tele. I don't know how she put up with him.'

Aware that his heart was in Old Trafford, I nodded tactfully and fetched her the gin and tonic and a Jameson for myself.

In his earlier days, I remember him skiving off to the local with his sons, all of them kitted out in the emblematic red tops of United, shouting down Liverpool or Leeds supporters in the pub and chanting, 'olé! olé! olé!' on their way home. Every room in his house was festooned with football posters proclaiming their loyalty.

Coming from Abbeylaune, with its cooler attitude to football, I couldn't make sense of him then.

'I presume United gave him that buzz we all seek from life,' I explained, more understanding of him now.

'Buzz! In his case it was a high that even drug addicts don't experience,' she rejoined.

I admired the way she stood up to and, in turn, for him down through the years. It's what daughters do.

When I assured her there were worse addictions, she shook her head firmly.

With Stynes, football, I knew, was the measure of everything and everyone. It was your ID. It singled out the wimps from the warriors, the genuine from the shambolic. It was the great class leveller, the common currency of high-brow and low-brow. It made for a bonding of opposites, for tribal loyalties and for enduring friendships founded on the flimsiest of foundations. You could be a serial killer, but if you followed United, you were sound in his book.

'He lived in a football bubble,' she sighed. Tell me about it!

Much as I fancied Edel, I couldn't run with him. His over-reaction to United's wins made as little sense to me as his unreasoning response to their losses. The man was unreal.

In vain, I tried to convince him once that football wasn't all about winning, and that it had a metaphysical side to it, nurturing as it ought, those higher virtues that I considered to be the real purpose of the game.

He glared at me as if I had uttered a heresy.

'If professional football is about anything, it's about winning. About dying in your boots for the club, the fans, the game.' He thumped our boundary fence for emphasis.

I was wasting my breath. He equated Old Trafford with the Coliseum and footballers with gladiators, prepared, if needs be, to face down a pride of lions barehanded.

Refusing to pull my punches, I gave back: 'I would have thought it was about money. Absurd money that gives the edge to a few top clubs that can afford the best players. Any wonder there are so many dismal, one-sided games, unlike the scintillating fare served up by our amateur Gaelic football and hurling teams.'

I might as well have been talking to the wall. That the boundary one between Jones and himself never cracked during their cheering contests whenever United played Chelsea, was a tribute to the craftsmanship of the builder. Oddly, whenever England, whom both regarded as the 'old enemy', were playing, they put aside their differences and roared the place down anytime the opposition scored.

'It's a miracle my hearing isn't permanently impaired from his cheering,' Edel said, as she partook of her drink.

I smiled, sensing that she must have been tuning into my thoughts. Like her, I too was convinced that Stynes' believed that his decibels really carried on the airwaves to Old Trafford, spurring on United against their opponents. Cheering had become a necessity for him And the louder he cheered, the more effective he considered it to be. If the classic performances of Roy Keane made his days, Drogba's, the Chelsea ace, arguably shortened them.

'I wish to God somebody would dispose of these ashes for me. I can't for the life of me see Sir Alec Ferguson allowing me to scatter them on the pitch. Imagine the headlines it'd make if the tabloids were to find out!' Edel shuddered at the thought of the fall-out for the family.

Whereupon, I assured her that Old Trafford had been a graveyard for many a visiting team, and that she needn't have any worries on that score.

A faint shadow of a smile flitted across her features. Then, in a serious mood, she turned to me.

'Quite frankly, I find the whole thing absurd. And if it weren't his dying wish, I'd make a bee-line to Mount Jerome cemetery this very minute and have his ashes placed in the family plot,' she confessed, her eyes moistening with distress.

I nodded sympathetically. Stynes died as he lived, a confirmed head-the-ball who remained trapped somewhere in his teens.

In his favour, he coached youngsters in his early days and took them to Old Trafford, where he arranged for them to meet their sporting icons. The youngsters grew up before he did.

Eventually, he married: a rushed affair, I gathered, after he'd got his wife – a meek little woman who danced to his beck and call – pregnant. It was said she wore shin guards to bed on nights whenever he played in his dreams for United or had nightmares about Chelsea.

'The older he became, the worse he got,' Edel confided. Much though I agreed with her, I was careful not to put him down in her presence.

'I suppose it's not easy to change the habits of a lifetime,' I said and left it at that.

On the plus side, he passed on some marvellous genes to his daughter, resulting in an attractive figure I longed to embrace, a crowning glory of blonde hair I ached to run my fingers through and lips so full of promise I dreamed daily of kissing.

'But having his ashes disposed of on a football pitch beggars belief.' She excused herself as she went to the toilet, where I suspected she must have had a good cry.

Try as I did to help her come to terms with her father's bizarre request, she could only see the senselessness of it, and was amazed that it never seemed to bother him how his family were expected to visit his resting place to pray for him.

'I presume it would have to be when United were playing at home?' I suggested.

'And then there's the cost!' she wailed and dabbed her eyes with her handkerchief.

It seemed to me that Stynes hadn't given that any thought on his deathbed either. As in life, he believed in going for broke for United.

'It's an insult to Ma. I really should have ignored his wish and arranged for his ashes to be placed beside her remains in Mount Jerome. Instead, I'm landed with this mission impossible. All because of an absurd superstition.' His daughter could not make rhyme or reason of it. And could you blame her?

Swept off my feet by her, and eager to impress her, I racked my brains for a solution to Stynes' dying wish. I felt I owed him that much as his neighbour.

'It seems to me he mistook Sir Alec Ferguson for St Peter waiting for him at the Pearly Gates with a complimentary ticket,' she chuckled.

She once ascribed his obsession with United to having never made it like Anto, allowing for a brief, unspectacular stint with 'the Hoops' before being dropped. Due to a knee injury, he told me, though I could never see any evidence of it.

'He certainly had a thing about losers,' I observed, convinced there had to be another reason for it.

'Tell me about it! I blame his father for it. Whenever Dad had an off day with his team as a boy his father would rib him afterwards.'

I nodded ruefully.

'All that matters now is that he's on the winning side in the next life,' she sighed.

After the tea and sandwiches, I had a brainwave.

'Perhaps you'd agree to a compromise,' I suggested, feeling like a knight errant summoned to the aid of the noble lady of his dreams in distress.

Her response suggested we weren't quite on the same wavelength: 'I've been compromised by him all my life. It's no wonder I'm still on the bench and with no offer of a transfer fee at thirty.'

So taken was I by her eulogy, I told her that I'd sign her on any day. Already, her perfumed proximity in the cramped alcove was sending the barometer of my yearnings for her soaring.

Cheered, she inquired if I missed my mother.

'Her death has left a void in my house and in my life,' I confessed.

'I suppose I'm going to miss the weekly football drama in two acts – Home and Away,' she addressed his ashes. 'So why not drop in and keep me company?'

'I'd love to. And in return, you might brighten my gaff with a visit.' I felt an urge to take her hand and give vent to all those pent up feelings I had nursed for her down the years, but realised it was neither the time nor the place.

'So what was the compromise you had in mind?' she inquired, bringing me back to earth.

'I'll tell you what: why don't you sprinkle some of his ashes over your mother's plot and the rest on Old Trafford. That way you can visit his home grave as usual and occasionally his away one.'

Seeing a light at the end of a stressful tunnel, her eyes suddenly shone with relief.

And then I had another inspiration.

'I'll arrange for two tickets for United's next home game which, as it turns out, will be with Chelsea. It should be a cracking game.'

Though the idea appealed to her, she still couldn't figure, in view of the tight security, how she'd dispose of the ashes in United's home ground.

'You leave that to me.' Already, I was working out the details in my head. Crazy about her, I would defy a Praetorian Guard to stop me disposing of them in Old Trafford.

She smiled appreciatively and apologised for putting me to all that trouble.

'Anything for you, honey,' I gave her hand an affectionate squeeze.

A shaft of sunlight lit up the alcove. I could feel the clouds which had weighed upon me since my mother's passing, dispersing. All my fantasising about Edel may not have been in vain.

If the match didn't quite live up to its billing, it didn't lack for that intensity that keeps the fans on a knife edge. Stunning passages of play by both teams, capped with breath-stopping assaults on goalmouths, had me on tenterhooks.

Captivated by the magic of Ronaldo's mandarin skills, Rooney's right-footed pile-drivers and the towering performance of Roy Keane, my sporting instincts were on fire. Was I losing it? Or had Barney Stynes's spirit taken hold of me? Even Edel was bemused to see me leaping out of my seat and shouting my head off for United, for try, as they valiantly did, Chelsea failed to break them. I realised I'd come off the fence and was succumbing to those sporting passions that provide a necessary antidote for so many to the tedium of their working lives.

It was what Stynes would have liked. I could picture him welcoming me aboard as a full-blooded fan of United, once again the undisputed kingpins of English football.

It was a result – unlike this afternoon's Cup Final – that would have made his day. Seeing the prestigious Premiership trophy returning after a painful absence to Old Trafford, Chelsea was welcome to the Cup and Drogba to his day in the sun.

I was so carried away that I would have forgotten all about the ashes if it weren't for Edel keeping me on course. When the fans had vacated the stands and the terraces, I discreetly tossed the remains of the late Barney Stynes on to the sideline, careful to retain some to be placed in his wife's grave.

Caught by a crisp breeze, I watched with satisfaction the ashes being dispersed throughout the legendary pitch, settling on the embattled goalmouths, and even alighting on the anoraks of departing *paparazzi* whose controversial columns were Stynes' bible.

'Who would have thought my father's ashes would be scattered on British soil?' Edel wailed.

I grinned, then turned to her.

'Where football was concerned, he was more English than the English themselves,' I explained.

She nodded, then informed me that his last words were: 'Did United win?'

'At least he died happily,' I consoled her.

Having shed a little tear, she was suddenly cheerful, for I heard her laughing for the first time since his funeral.

'I really don't know how to thank you,' she said. Then taking both my hands in hers, she drew me close to her. With the terrace to ourselves, we melted like the triumphal lovers of legend into each other's eager arms.

I'd finally scored with her. The game that had kept us apart for so long had eventually brought us together.

A CLASH OF CULTURES

I can still hear the battle of wits between Traynor, our PE teacher, and Bernard, at our local college ringing in my ears. Given their contrasting backgrounds, it was hardly surprising: Traynor came from a lineage of army corporals, while Bernard owed his pedigree to generations of booksellers in Abbeylaune.

If the Traynors could point to a proud record of daunting overseas' missions, risky security work and a record of service to the Abbeylaune boxing and sporting clubs for their benchmark, Bernard's family, the Murrays, could claim similar credit for the cultural well-being of the community.

Other than that, the twain walked different roads; the Traynors I gathered, privately regarded the Murrays as high-brow while the Murrays looked down their noses on the Traynors as rough-spoken, feisty soldiers with a turbulent history. Perhaps, theirs was an interface waiting sooner or later to happen.

Don't ask me how, but opposites somehow attract. Quite frankly the Murrays could do with a rub of the common touch and the Traynors would certainly benefit from a smattering of culture. As matters stood, they were like chalk and cheese. Brawn versus brain. The rugged versus the refined. I could sense an inevitable clash on the cards between Bernard and Traynor from day one of our final year in college.

Traynor was a keep slim, trim and fit fanatic, who was convinced, I'd swear, that we were all quarried from the same gene pool, for he made no concessions to the obese or to the frail. In his view, the human body was something to be sculpted, whipped into shape and rendered fit, first and foremost, for sport. Some would say exclusively, for he lived for it. An anathema to Bernard, a bookworm with a literary bent.

I watched him doing Traynor's head in and, in turn, Traynor nearly doing him in. The student who wrote poems felt it his right to be his own man and not Traynor's blueprint for him. His welfare was his own business, not the PE instructor's, however well-intentioned.

For the first time, probably, in his career, Traynor found himself between a rock and a hard place in his efforts to bend his recalcitrant charge to his will; change his attitude to sport; have him shed excessive kilos, and generally kick him into shape in the interests of his health and his appearance, which was suggestive of the Michelin man of the ad in the making, unless he subscribed to the PE instructor's regimen.

Not an easy mission, given Bernard's mindset and his mind – the brightest in our class. Not that Traynor was unduly impressed. Far from it. I soon learned that he subordinated the mental to the physical and the individual to the group. A talented sportsman in his day, with an enviable shelf of trophies to show for it, he epitomised the Spartan ideal. And take it from me, he would have done Sparta proud, for he was a splendid specimen of manhood, standing six foot plus in height, athletic, rugged and handsome. An Achilles of the playing fields, albeit with a blind side, which Bernard was quick to note. Not that Bernard was without his. His fondness for the new deli – a product of the Celtic Tiger – and his obesity would make for a duel I viewed with some trepidation as Traynor took him on.

The instructor, I knew, would not take no for an answer. Kitted out in a trendy track-suit and Nike runners, the gym, the ball courts and the sportsfield were his unchallenged habitat. You could tell our class looked up to him by the way they participated in his sporting routines: vigorous work-outs, competitive sprints and intense but exciting football contests that left Bernard cold.

Unlike the rest of us, he had no desire to acquire a perfectly honed physique like Traynor's, or a collection of athletic trophies on his sideboard. He dreaded the gym with its punitive routines of weight training, to which we willingly submitted for enhanced strength and the bonus of glamorous muscles that accrued from it.

'Why aren't you participating like everyone else?' I overheard the irate instructor take issue with Bernard, who was loafing like a lost sheep on the fringes of the first football game of our final year.

I knew that the very idea of being like everyone else was as repugnant to him as it was appealing to Traynor, for whom conformity was the order of the day.

'I regret sir, sport does nothing for me.' A sympathetic Miss O'Brien had gone easy on him in previous years. He was hoping for similar treatment from Traynor.

'Nothing!' I heard our new instructor bellow. 'Nothing!' I could picture his ears popping as if in receipt of a heresy.

'I prefer a lively walk, sir.' And knowing him, a very short one. And not too lively either.

I could see Traynor's patience beginning to wear thin.

'Sport is about health and fitness. About team-work and character building. Most of all it's about that feel good factor that's in store for you by the time I'm finished with you.'

If sport had a metaphysical dimension for him, it had none for his student, who was now shaking his head gloomily.

'It drains me physically and does my head in, sir.'

'*Mens sana in corpore sano*,' Traynor bellowed, suggesting that he should have spent less time on his play-stations and texting during his years in Miss O'Brien's PE class.

I could tell from the other's cynical shrug that he was on a different wave length.

'Now, get on with it before I lose my rag with you.' The instructor brooked no compromise, treating the aspiring poet no differently to anybody else.

Whereupon, a reluctant Bernard would manage a few energetic bursts for Traynor's benefit, then grind to a halt, getting the other's dander up.

Swift, I recall, was the retribution Traynor exacted. A stickler for discipline, he'd insist in Bernard doing a string of press-ups, followed by punishing laps of the playing field, through pools and puddles, in foul and fair weather, despite Bernard's pleas for leniency, which, more often than not, earned him the derision of his classmates who nicknamed him the *tortoise*. Like their mentor, they had little time for his cultured airs and graces, belittling as decadent his dismissive attitude to sport.

From what I knew of them, they were far from comfortable with the precocious bookworm. He made them feel uneasy, with his sophisticated ideas and his nimble-witted quips, which I found very useful whenever I tried to impress the convent girls whom I flirted with on my way to and from college.

Bernard's romantic exploits, if I were to believe him, were of a seedier order. Salacious ventures, spiced up in their telling with inputs from his dabblings in pornography, which did him no favour with his classmates. If, like Traynor, they viewed romance as secondary to sport, they nonetheless treated their girl-friends with respect.

'He's trying to turn me into a friggin' zombie,' I listened to Bernard rage one day after his laps. 'Can he not accept that I'm a literary, not an effin' physical athlete?'

Not wishing to rock the boat I told him that his dancing skills – a liability to his partners at our local disco – would benefit from it.

'Give me a better reason for not wanting to be a couch potato,' the tortoise begged, and vowed he'd set a record before leaving college, for the slowest lap ever of the sportsfield, long-associated with renowned sprinters.

I merely shrugged. Quite frankly, Traynor made more sense to me than he did. I just don't know how Bernard could look in the mirror and feel comfortable with his reflection, though he was beginning to look better than previously.

'I can tell Gaynor despises cultured types,' he protested as he cleaned himself up on the occasion when he'd done his laps in slow motion – a ploy that misfired, since he had to repeat them, with Achilles breathing down his neck.

'Really! How come?' I had never seen our instructor in that light.

'He has never once set foot in our bookstall to buy a novel or a book of poems.'

I tried to explain that he was not exceptional in that. I could hardly be described as a reader at this point. As for poetry, apart from Bernard's moving sonnets, it was not exactly my cup of tea.

He frowned, then eyed me with suspicion.

'But it's not normal for an academic. It's no wonder he cannot relate to people like me, or imagine that there can be a life beyond sport.'

'Your problem is you can't believe that there can be a life beyond books,' I echoed his classmates' opinion of him.

'Which he's holding against me. What's wrong with being different? Or do we all have to be his athletic clones?'

It riled him, too, to see the magazine racks in the supermarket suddenly groaning under the weight of best-selling, but shallow, sportsmen's memoirs. He viewed it as Sparta grabbing Athenian, cultural territory, still resolutely defended by his family's select bookshop, regardless of the cost to it.

Unlike others, I could see his point. Not that he minded when I didn't, for we went on to become pals, though I made sure to keep in with the others and with Traynor. Admittedly, I was a sporty type and hungry for athletic glory, which Bernard noted with concern, for he felt I was capable of higher things, being no slouch at the books.

'All that physical over-kill is crazy. Thanks to his influence, our college is now more renowned for its sporting than for its academic achievements,' he repeatedly railed, while frowning upon his classmates' preoccupation with body-building and fitness. At least none of them could be accused of obesity or of substance abuse, as, unlike him, they valued their health.

In his biology classes, Traynor never ceased to stress the importance of proper diet. A regular customer at Abbeylaune's, health-food shop, he was a role model for our class, whom he was instrumental in weaning from an addiction to junk food. Many of us, previously, had been a stone heavier than our counterparts of yesteryear. Traynor, in comparison, was as lean as the proverbial greyhound and looked like he'd been quarried from Wicklow granite.

'Fruit fellas! You cannot eat enough of it. Apples, pears and bananas for breakfast, dinner and tea.' He never ceased to remind us in his biology class that we are what we eat.

'Does that mean if I eat curries I'm Indian? And Turkish if I eat kebabs?' Bernard would mutter to me, his breath reeking of pepperoni.

'And fresh vegetables. Not tinned or frozen ones,' Traynor would harangue us.

'Any more laps of that friggin' sportsfield and I'll end up a vegetable,' I could hear Bernard muttering.

'And don't let me catch anyone stuffing his face with chocolate-bars, crisps, ice creams and cream cakes!' the PE instructor warned.

'Yum, yum', from Bernard, his sweet tooth aching for everything on Traynor's hit list. His mouth-watering lunches – baguettes crammed with rich fillings, not to mention those addictive, chocolate brownies and cup cakes from the town's new deli boycotted by Traynor – would tempt a saint.

It was evident to me that the food revolution had by-passed our instructor – a throw-back to the bacon and cabbage era. Tortilla wraps and paninis were foreign to him, as were the current delights of basil and pesto. The Deli's trendy cuisine he dismissed as a fast-track to the cardiac unit, while denouncing the current, fast-food craze as a recipe for a premature plot in the local cemetery.

Instead, he swore by roughage. By the home-grown, home-baked, simple but wholesome, traditional fare. He banned so many things from the dining table it would have qualified for a monastic menu.

'He's out of the Ark,' Bernard sighed, loudly enough to be overheard by the PE instructor, one day.

'I see you don't agree, Murray.'

'You're fighting a losing battle, sir.' Only Bernard had the nerve to say it. The rest of us kept our heads down.

The sports instructor glared at him.

'What matters is I'm fighting. Challenging life-threatening dietary trends. Does that make sense to you? Or would you prefer to suffer from diabetes and a coronary before you're thirty?'

Bernard nodded otherwise.

'Lent begins tomorrow, Murray. So how about turning your back on the deli and the fast-food outlets?' Traynor requested.

'I'll try sir.' Then, taking his cue from Oscar Wilde, decided soon afterwards that the best way to overcome temptation was to give into it, allowing his appetite to rule him.

Proud of our sporting prowess, we sided with Traynor. The idea of waking up in the peak of fitness, rather than as casualties of junk food, binge drinking and substance abuse, appealed to us. It was what Lent, too, was about – the conquest of the appetites and destructive addictions. To the class's credit, everyone, with the exception of Bernard, made some sacrifice on health or spiritual grounds.

You could hardly expect otherwise from Traynor's disciples. Plain spoken and plain mannered, they were hewn from the same, rudimentary block as himself. And the plainer and more rudimentary they were, the more he liked them. The refined, the sensitive and the frail might as well have been evolutionary casualties. In his macho code, it was the supremacy of the fittest. And only the fittest deserved to be supreme. A mindset drummed into him, according to Bernard, by his military ancestry. Regardless of its short-comings, it appealed to most of us, as Traynor well knew.

Hence, the more athletic and sporty you were, the more likely candidate you'd be for the PE instructor's game plan: a coveted place on the football and athletic teams, which enhanced with their triumphs, his sporting reputation and that of the college, while guaranteeing the victors an enduring place in its cherished hall of fame. It's what my classmates and I aspired to, rather than to Bernard's, loftier, cultural aspirations.

You had to hand it to Traynor. The growing list of celebrated footballers who passed through his hands was a glowing testament to his ability, which nobody, with the exception of Bernard, questioned.

'He's trying to make Spartans of us. Well, he can forget it. I'll live and die an Athenian,' he proclaimed to me in between verses of a poem he was trying to compose during the biology class.

I tried in vain to convince him of the positives of football but he wasn't interested.

'It's escapism,' he snapped, deploring the excessive space allotted to it by the media, much of which, he felt, should be devoted to the arts.

Such was his disregard for his physical well being, he confided in me that he had begun to dabble in mind-altering substances. Adventures into the hallucinogenic, he called it. I feared to think what would be his fate if Traynor ever found out, and worried for the consequences to his health if he persisted in doing violence to it.

As our final year drew to a close, Bernard faked a back injury, and, with the aid of a letter from his GP, was exempted from having to run any further painful laps, enabling him to indulge himself with the Deli's latest offerings.

Bernard would be one of Traynor's rare failures. A failure – notwithstanding, his otherwise glowing sporting achievements that year – whose neck, I knew, he would like to wring. But he left him to his fate, knowing that his self abuse would wreak sweeter revenge upon him in its own good time.

I could hardly believe my ears when Bernard confided in me that summer that he had taken up yoga.

'I don't believe it!' I exclaimed, picturing him with disbelief doing headstands and the demanding array of drills that go with it.

'It's cool.'

'Cool?'

'Absolutely. The Lotus posture and particularly the meditation exercises that are part of it, appeal to me.'

I couldn't help regarding him with suspicion.

'And it doesn't do my head in,' he confessed.

I didn't know what to make of him. Had Traynor finally got through to him? Or was it some instinct for self-preservation that prompted him to do a u-turn?

'Don't tell me you're prepared to settle for the Spartan diet that goes with yoga?'

I couldn't imagine him turning his back on the deli.

'I'm adjusting to it. Seriously!' He looked at me as if I didn't believe him.

Could you blame me? An Epicure turning an ascetic new leaf didn't sit comfortably with the Bernard I knew. Oddly, I couldn't help noting a slimmer, spruced-up version of my erstwhile, flabby classmate.

I encouraged him to keep it up, though I didn't think he would, unless, of course, he had a very good reason.

When I learned that one of Traynor's daughters – the one with the film star looks and the figure of a model, to whom Bernard had been writing love poems all summer – was giving the course, I had a little laugh to myself. Romance, I realised, had succeeded where education had failed. It wouldn't surprise me to see him running marathons next and doing those black fasts of bygone Lents.

I was more surprised to learn that Traynor, while resting up after surgery for his cruciate ligament, had begun to frequent the bookshop and was cultivating a taste for literature.

Show me the road that has no turning!

GLOBAL WARMING

The freakishly hot, energy-sapping April of that year was like nothing I have ever known. I should have anticipated it, I suppose, given Greene's dire predictions about global warming. To date, I had turned a deaf ear to him. Who ever listens to the prophet next door?

'You can kiss your April showers good-bye,' he chuckled, seeing me watering the flower-bed. An Emerald Party activist, climate change had become his mission.

As the barometer soared, he was having a field day at my expense. Nothing hitherto prepared me for this. At my age, for God's sake, most men are chilling out. With the sun speeding mercilessly in its chariot of fire across the Tropic of Cancer, there were days when I felt I was approaching melt-down. Reduced to a state of inertia by a heat-triggered respiratory ailment, work was out of the question.

'Are you on a permanent siesta?' Avril, my wife, looked worried as I lay for days spread-eagled on the sofa. Unlike my previous, fleeting bouts of fatigue, my current prolonged paralysis gave her cause for concern.

'I just can't handle the heat.' What wouldn't I have given for the sound of rain drumming again on my umbrella, emblematic, hitherto, of our climate?

She frowned, then opened an extra window.

'If you can't cope with it in April, I can't imagine how're you going to do so in July.' Obviously she was handling it better than I was, which wasn't surprising since she was always complaining of the cold. I usually moaned about the rain.

'I'll decamp to the nearest iceberg until winter sets in.'

'There may be none,' she chirped. As sun –worshippers go, the ancient Celts had nothing on her.

'God forbid! A barbecue on the lawn is hardly my idea of a Christmas dinner.'

When she remarked that Greene may have been right all along about global warming being man-made, I worried she had become another of his converts. And that he would use her against me.

'And it's nothing to do with cars?' Her gaze was suspicious. To her credit, she managed to maintain a fragile peace between us, which wasn't easy.

'Nothing.' I suspected that his doomsday scenarios were not entirely lost on her.

Apparently, the heat-wave was playing hell with his sinus and reducing his lawns to a desert.

As if to prove him wrong, I made a few, tentative efforts to eject myself from the sofa, but failed. I could picture Greene rebuking me, 'I told you so.'

One sweltering morning, an alarmed Avril panicked: 'You'd better get working on your articles for the *Irish Voice*. As for that book you've undertaken to write on the future of the motor car, your publisher will soon put a stop to your advances if you don't get on with it,' she warned, her spryness a rebuke to my inertia.

I tried to explain to her that, in the absence of an air-conditioned system, the library where I normally worked had become a sauna where readers nodded off since the arrival of the heat wave.

Her expression betrayed more than a hint of disbelief, which I set out to dispel.

'If, as Joyce claimed, the summers of Trieste made butter of his brain, you can appreciate why this unnatural weather is making inferior margarine of mine,' I argued.

She preferred to think that it was all in my mind. Give me a break! The heat wave is the problem.

Seeing that my condition wasn't mental, she attributed it to my age. Nothing could be further from the truth. I'm only coming into my prime, for Pete's sake. Overweight and under-exercised, granted. But nonetheless, in reasonable nick. With the barometer continuing to soar, the last thing I needed was a Job's comforter.

When Greene popped his head over our dividing wall one morning, as I was trying to chill out with a bottle of Ballygowan and an ice-pack in the back garden, I sensed I was in for some stick. 'So who was right all along?' he taunted me. A wiry, feisty little man, he maintained that people like me were putting the planet at risk.

'Nonsense! It's just a bloody heat wave So let's not jump to any rash conclusions about climate change.' Beached for days, I was in no mood for another one of his lectures. Give him an inch and he'd take the proverbial mile. Before I knew it, he would have me on my bike and my cars off the road.

To forestall the *dies ire*, he cycled daily to work, installed solar panelling and erected a windmill to economise on the fossil fuels that he held responsible for climate change. So far, I'd resisted his attempts to convert me.

'This freak weather is due to culprits like you,' he continued to remind me.

'Cop yourself on! You're overflagging global warming. Let's face it: there was planet warming, as well as ice ages, in the distant past.'

He scowled.

'Go on! Bury your head in the sand! Never once have I read in any of your motoring columns in the *Irish Voice* about the lethal impact of the car on climate change. Be honest, you've misled the public.'

'Get a life, Greene! The car is indispensable. And, unlike the bicycle, it's big industry.' I adjusted my umbrella, which I was using as a sunshade.

Impaling me with a contemptuous look, he bellowed: 'Indispensable! Do you mean to tell me you have to wait for your house to be burned to the ground before summoning the fire brigade?'

Give me a break! I live for cars. They're my bread and butter. As a life-long motor correspondent with the *Irish Voice*, I've been the car's most passionate advocate. I've recorded all its technical and aesthetic advances, and test driven everything propelled by a combustion engine. As far as I'm concerned, the bike is for the birds. And I've said it loud and clear to him.

'Trust me, it's on the way back,' he insisted.

As the heat wave continued, our exchanges were gearing up for a Kyoto style confrontation .

'With time running out on scientific solutions, I'd suggest you have a dinghy instead of your green-house gas-belching cars on stand-by, given the rate at which sea levels are continuing to rise,' he warned and proceeded to lambaste the multi-car families of the Celtic Tiger.

Preferring to think that nature would right itself, as it did many times in the past, I walked away from him.

'It's not rocket science, so quit your scaremongering,' I said over my shoulder.

He shook his head angrily, then called after me: 'Some morning you'll wake up to find Venice on your doorstep,' adding that it could well take centuries to reverse the process.

Coming from a lineage of cyclists from Abbeylaune, Greene's mindset was understandable. The bike is in his DNA. The car is in mine. My grandfather was a mechanic. My father owned a garage. My uncles were noted rally drivers. My children are set to maintain the technical bloodline and have been driving since their teens. I'd be damned if I'd re-write the script to satisfy Greene.

Frankly speaking, I've always been suspicious of him. Playing up the emerald ticket was politically trendy at the minute. With a general election on the doorstep, he was making capital out of it.

'For too long, the car has been your god. How can you be so complacent with the ice-caps melting and the glaciers shrinking? Can't you see Africa is finally here?'

He continued to proselytise me with the stick rather than the carrot, which I resented, refusing as much out of stubbornness as of self-interest to subscribe to his credo.

Optimistically, I retorted: 'Then the monsoon season will surely follow,' and withdrew indoors, threw open all the windows and put on the electric fan in an effort to chill out. It rankled that the season that I once cherished, I now dreaded, being brought by it to a standstill. And it didn't help that Greene was holding the high moral ground and rubbing me up with relish.

In vain, I looked to the night for relief, but none was forthcoming. A cynical moon shone with indifference upon a city that had become a furnace, emitting unprecedented heat long after sundown. When I wasn't pacing the floor-boards or thrusting my head out the window for air, I tossed and heaved in bed like a skiff astride a tsunami, incapable of sleep and depriving Avril of hers.

After weeks of turbulent nights that saw the duvet on the floor and my pillow where my feet were each morning, we agreed to sleep separately. In any case, and much to Avril's relief, I no longer had the energy for love-making. I could see, the heat was beginning to get to her too, for she was a lot less spry than usual.

With much regret, I cancelled a family holiday that we had booked for the Costa del Sol. I simply wasn't up to it. In any case, we had heard that the heat there was unbearable. Reports, too, of the elderly dropping off like flies, convinced us that there were less mean ways of dying.

'I heard you've changed your mind about holidaying abroad,' Greene observed with glee. Fiercely critical of the effect of air-travel on global warming, he never holidayed anywhere but Ireland. Mostly in Abbeylaune.

When I told him we opted instead for Kerry, he commended our decision.

'Unlike Spain, it should be good for a few cooling showers, for the time being at any rate,' he said, and launched into a lecture on the grim consequences for the Gulf Stream when the ice-caps melted. 'And that's not all.'

'Don't tell me!'

As Jeremiads go, he was in a league of his own. I could sense prophecies grimmer than the Seven Plagues of Egypt assembling on his lips.

'Storms like you've never seen and flash-floods,' he predicted apocalyptically.

I grimaced, then gave back: 'At least we won't run out of tea-water nor, hopefully, Guinness.'

'More than likely you'll be drinking recycled dish-water,' he forecast gloomily.

I'd had enough. As luck would have it my mobile rang. I was glad of any excuse to get away from him.

'You'll be praying before long that rain-drops keep falling on your head,' he trumpeted after me.

I didn't reply. There was no point. Even though I was suffering, I still walked different roads to him.

'You're suffering from hyperthermia. I'd better get you a doctor,' Avril suggested, one torrid morning when she noted my condition deteriorating.

'Forget it. There's nothing any medic can do for me,' I insisted.

She disagreed. 'Your breathing is getting worse. And you've lost your energy.'

I told her I'd be as right as rain as soon as the weather broke.

'I wouldn't hold your breath for it,' she warned, and left me to sleep on till midday.

Some days later Greene roared at me: 'Get rid of it!' as I parked an SUV, which I'd been given to test drive and write about, in my drive-in.

I felt like throttling him. The twilight of the motor car could well be mine. Even if Greene were right, it would clearly not be in my interests to see its fate sealed.

Unknown to myself, I must have been undergoing a sea-change, for, on one scorching afternoon, the message kicked in: global warming could well be here. My belief in the motor was suddenly shaken. Not that I saw the bike as an alternative. It was no longer cool.

Greene's conviction that the fate of the planet was in our hands was beginning to make sense to me. Prostrate on the sofa, I ceased to belittle his Amish life-style, his bike, his rain-barrel, his wind-mill and those solar panels proclaiming his credo from his roof-top. Not to mention the layers of clothing he and his family wore around the house in winter to economise on fossil fuels and minimise the damage resulting from them. A true, blue, eco warrior, I'll grant him.

I should have anticipated his heated reaction when I ventured, subsequently, that bio-fuel could well be the way forward as a renewable alternative to fossil fuels and a lifeline for the car.

He frowned dismissively.

'You can't be serious! It will be competing for space with grain crops and drive the price of food through the roof. And in any case, to meet the spiralling energy demands of tomorrow, there simply wouldn't be enough land to grow it.'

'So it's back to the bike?' I sighed.

'Definitely!'

I frowned.

'If Prometheus had foreseen what you claim, he might never have stolen fire from the gods for us.'

He grimaced.

'James Watt would certainly have thought twice about inventing the combustion engine for today's abusers of the car,' he rejoined.

Despite my ongoing conversion, our exchanges retained a measure of needle, especially with the election campaign heating up.

By now, it was all I could do to write my regular column for the *Irish Voice*. I had put my book on the future of the car on hold. Quite frankly, I was undergoing a radical re-think about it. If the current rate of climate change continued, the car might well become the dinosaur of the future. I decided to hold out for the winter and see how things went. In the meantime, I suspected Avril was privately planning my funeral arrangements, for she finally persuaded me to make my will.

Soon, a fired-up Greene would be hitting the canvass trail, bringing to the people the core message of his party's manifesto: 'Get on your bike!'

After much soul-searching, I gave his party's local candidate my first preference. He was jubilant. To have brought his most recalcitrant critic on board was a feather in his cap. When his party agreed to enter coalition to form the incoming government, I knew the country's reputation as the Emerald Isle was assured.

For the first time ever, I took the Luas to town.

Come June, the weather drastically changed. The temperature dropped. The sun retreated behind a mass of saturated clouds. Then it rained for days. In India and Pakistan, the monsoons, too, were on cue. The climate, I was relieved, hadn't really changed all that much.

In a moment of madness or of irrepressible mirth at Greene's expense, I sang and danced on the patio like Gene Kelly, though without his emblematic brolly, while the rain washed over me in torrents, until Avril, fearful for my health, dragged me indoors.

'I wouldn't read too much into it, if I were you,' Greene advised subsequently.

The summer, strangely, must have been one of the worst in recent memory. In fact, we've had better winters. It was hardly surprising that the jury on global warming continued to be out for many. Could Greene have got it badly wrong?

'The rain, like the poor, we'll always have with us in this country,' I put it to him, unsure whether the atrocious weather hadn't caused him to rethink his position.

He shook his head and informed me that even parts of Britain were being over-run by the very waves it once ruled, as we spoke.

His belief in global warming remained unshaken.

With the rain tap-dancing on my umbrella, it wasn't long before I was firing from all cylinders. Avril was back in my bed and the duvet was no longer on the floor. The library being habitable again, I resumed work.

In the interests of health and climate, I've been seriously

considering giving my old three-speed a run on the recently constructed bicycle lanes. Roll over Stephen Roche!

As for the car, I gather the Emerald Party has extensive plans for a fleet of electric vehicles in the near future. Things couldn't have been brighter for Green and myself, now singing from the same hymn sheet

Fingers crossed, it may not be too late to halt global warming.

AN EXILE'S RETURN

When Oisheen left Oldbridge for New York, he was twenty. He was thirty and newly wed when he returned for his father's funeral. A moving occasion for Oisheen, who, like his wife Hillary, was touched by the genuine show of sympathy from the huge turn-out for the obsequies. So unlike New York, where you could be dead for days without anyone knowing or caring. Father Ryan's moving sermon on death put things in perspective for him; things he had overlooked in his pursuit of the mighty dollar.

Taking stock of the town soon after his arrival, it seemed to him as if it had been trapped in a time warp. Untouched by the progress that was transforming the nearby town of Abbeylaune, it was in deep recession. The creamery had shut down. The mills were mere ghostly effigies of bygone days. Many of the shops looked as if they hadn't sold an item in years. The repeated promises by politicians of this and that scheme had come to nothing. In Oisheen's opinion, it was a town ready for the last rites.

When he drove down its unprepossessing main street in a spanking new Volvo that he had rented from Hertz, he felt superior to and, in turn, concerned for the town. He had done well out of the construction business and could proudly point as a foreman to some of his adopted city's striking new office blocks as his benchmark. Giant feats in a city where everything was gigantic.

So different to Oldbridge, now crying out for the kiss of life. How he wished he could give its community something for which to rise and shine as he had. Regrettably, the entrepreneurial spirit that was such a driving force in America was nowhere visible here. He did well to get out.

After the funeral, he ran the Crossroads' bar a number of times. The sporting hero, who once captained the minor and senior football teams to victory, was putting down his marker. Local boy had done well and he wanted it to be known.

It cheered him to find that whatever the town lacked materially, it made up for in friendliness. Even Hillary was taken by its warmth, recognising a big heart in its emaciated body. With his mother now in need of their support in her bereaving, they decided to see out the week with her.

His father was hardly cold in his grave when Oisheen was asked to play for the local football team in the regional league semi-final. Such was still his repute, though he had hung up his boots, that he was considered worthy of inclusion by the team captain.

'Sure buddy. It's what my old man would have wanted.' Oisheen believed that mourning should be brief.

'We can fix you up with some gear,' the captain suggested.

Oisheen smiled and waved aside the offer.

'I'll take care of that.' The idea of stepping into somebody else's boots was as repugnant to him as it was amusing. Nothing less than state-of-the-art gear would do him.

Though he was short on practice, he played a blinder, finding the goal posts time and again with his expensive Nike sharp-shooters. His sporting skills were as sharp as ever. A devotee of the gym, he outplayed his markers in the air and reduced the opposing defence to tatters with his dazzling solo runs.

Even Hillary was impressed, having seen for herself what his friends told her of his former feats in New York's Gaelic Park, though he had hung up his boots and taken to golf by the time they'd met.

It was just the uplift that Oisheen needed after the funeral. And true to form, the team's many fans paid him a hero's tribute.

'I've managed to keep the best wine till last,' he joked, pleased nonetheless by his performance.

'Is there any hope you'd stay around for the final?' they pleaded with him.

'I doubt it.'

'It's a pity.'

He agreed, but there was nothing he could do. As the days slipped by, he felt Oldbridge growing on him. Drinking sessions with old cronies at the Crossroad's Pub became routine, with selected memories rolled out and relived afresh for his benefit, the trips down memory lane often continuing long after closing time.

A God-send to the publican and a wind-fall for the cronies, who didn't have to reach into their pockets to buy a round. It was nothing less than what was expected of a successful Yank, he convinced Hillary, who had difficulty with his extravagance. In reality, he liked people to know he had money, and that he wasn't afraid to spend it.

Aware that the cronies hadn't a tosser, he knew if the situation were reversed, they'd have been no less generous towards him. He was grateful for their company, their banter and especially their flattery. Their repeated compliments on his youthful looks, his trendy clothes, his Volvo and his attractive new bride, went down a treat with Oisheen, who never ceased to marvel at their cheerful attitude to life.

After a couple of marathon sessions, Hillary settled for the less taxing company of his mother and his sisters, leaving Oisheen to his cronies.

With each day that passed, the prospect of returning to the Big Apple became less and less appealing. The work pressures, the lingering sense of estrangement from a city still foreign to him, and his recurring bouts of homesickness, were not helped by his worries about the draft for Vietnam. He had managed to elude it so far, but the fear that it would eventually catch up with him, and the gruesome fate awaiting him if he were to fall into the hands of the Vietcong, unnerved him. He wished he could postpone his return. He had a lot of catching up to do and he didn't have much time. There were school mates he had yet to meet, places he wanted to see, and events he was determined to be part of, not knowing when he'd be back again.

More importantly, he wanted to help his team-mates win the league final that had last been won under his captaincy. It would break his heart to have to miss it, but there was no escaping that Hillary had to be back at work by Monday or her job would be at risk.

It was the American way. With a pressing mortgage on their newly acquired house, she simply couldn't take a chance. The building boom in New York would ensure he had only to pick up the phone and there would be a job waiting for him. Anytime. Anywhere. But it wasn't all a bed of roses. In New York, you lived to work. In Oldbridge, it was the reverse. That's if you were lucky enough to have work.

For all its shortcomings, he suddenly realised how much he was going to miss it, as well as his family and friends. Listening to a rendering of the 'Londonderry Air' for his benefit at his farewell do at the Crossroad's pub, he was moved to tears by that heart-rending line – "'Tis you ,'tis you must go and I must bide.'

With a heavy heart, he checked in at Shannon Airport, which was reverberating to the din of Vietnam-bound, American jets flying soldiers to fight in a war with which he disagreed, and which wasn't his. Leaving for New York was more gut-wrenching this time than the previous occasion. There was the sense of adventure then, as well as the dream of returning to Oldbridge one day to set up his own business, having made his fortune.

'It's a pity you won't be with us for the final.' His team-mates words kept repeating in his head.

Though Hillary tried to cheer him up, she didn't understand that henceforth, the Big Apple was going to be a life sentence. In marrying her, an Irish American, he had effectively severed his ties with his roots, save only for fleeting visits. She would never consent to live in Oldbridge. And his abandoning her for the cronies didn't help.

There was nothing for it but to make do with his memories. So poignant was the pang of exile, he found himself envying his cronies who belonged in Oldbridge in a way he would never quite belong in New York.

While queuing at the check-in, he thought again about the league final. The prospect of that coveted medal and the adulation of the fans tugged at his heart strings. Having nothing much to cheer about, it would mean so much to Oldbridge. After all, he reasoned, an extra fortnight wouldn't be asking too much of Hillary. The more he thought about it, the more feasible it seemed.

Plan B was already taking shape in his head. He checked his watch, agonised briefly, then made his move. Tactfully, he inquired of Hillary if she would mind him making a last minute phone-call to his mother.

'Of course not.' Her reply was just what he expected.

Unsuspectingly, she went on ahead with a fellow American she'd got talking to in the queue.

Hanging back until she reached the departing lounge, he had her paged, then told her how his mother had taken ill and asked would she mind if he stayed behind, promising to follow her within a week.

An understanding Hillary replied, 'Fine honey. You take care of your Mam. Bye love.'

He thanked her. Then grabbing his travelling bags, he made a bee-line for the car-hire firm where he retrieved the Volvo.

His mother nearly took a fainting fit when he reappeared on her doorstep.

'Don't tell me there's something after happening?' Her face tightened with anxiety.

'Everything is fine, Mom,' he assured her.

She eyed him warily.

'But where's Hillary?' she exclaimed. Her white hair suddenly looked whiter and her physique frailer since his departure that morning.

'She's gone on ahead of me to New York.'

Thunderstruck she exclaimed: 'What! Do you mean to tell me ye've parted?'

'Just for a little while,' he said lightly.

'I don't get you. There is something wrong, isn't there?' Her voice was tense.

He shook his head and smiled.

'Trust me, Mom. Everything is fine. Hillary felt you needed me around until you got back on your feet,' he explained. When it came to producing a plausible excuse, he had few equals.

'Need you!' The room echoed to her exclamation. 'Sure, don't the girls drop by everyday with the grandchildren on their way to the shops?'

She felt his newly-wedded wife needed him much more than she did. And a damn sight more than the cronies who seemed to forget he was married while he was flashing the cash.

'Typical Mom. Not wanting to trouble anyone.' So far so good. His alibi was standing up.

She shrugged.

'Well, now that you're here, I'd better put on the kettle.'

It was nice having her all to himself now that Hillary wasn't vying for his attention. It would come as some surprise to the cronies to see him back again knowing most of them would have gone like greased lightening out of Oldbridge if they had their lives all over again.

'Never mind the kettle! I'm taking you out for lunch,' he said.

Any further reservations she might have had about his return, suddenly evaporated.

He couldn't have chosen a better time to be at home. The fickle Irish weather had suddenly given way to a heat wave, which fitted in nicely with his plans for his extended family whom he felt he had overlooked.

In the ensuing days, he hosted regular get-togethers with no end of partying. On his free afternoons, he chauffeured them to the local seaside resort, swam and picnicked with them, while going out of his way to indulge his nieces and nephews, who, by now, regarded him as their favourite uncle. The life and soul of an ongoing party, he was determined to give them the treat of a lifetime. Wanting them to have those things he craved, but had to wait for America to provide, he took them on shopping sprees to Abbeylaune with no expense spared. Other times he would treat them to a hotel meal and a trip to some scenic spot popular with tourists.

His mother made no secret of it that she couldn't have a better son, though she wished he were more careful with his money. Hillary would see to that when he got back to New York.

'I've worked my socks off for this break,' he would disagree with her whenever she carped about his extravagance.

As he saw it, it was pay-back time for the penny-pinching days of his youth. Now that he had made good, he considered it only right that he spread a little cheer among his less fortunate family members and friends, who had opted to stay and keep the home fires burning.

In his free time, he set about catching up with those things he missed out on before he emigrated, and he was going to do it in style.

The Abbeylaune annual race meeting was top of his agenda. Prior to emigrating, his Saturday flutter at the bookies was as near as he came to a race meeting. Kitted out in an expensive suit and a striking Stetson, he was determined to mix with the racing elite. Courtesy of a contact, he spent more time in the private members' bar than on the stand, regaling the ladies of the turf with tales of New York, while laying on big bets to further impress them. He had a ball, celebrating his one decent win with a bottle of champagne, while taking his losses on the chin, reminding himself, as he tore up his tickets, that it was far from horse-racing he was reared. It was what people liked about him, for all his airs and graces.

Then it was back to the sports field for some rigorous training sessions with his team-mates in preparation for the league final. He even eased up on the drink and tried to get to bed earlier. He felt he owed it to Hillary, who had granted him further leave on the pretext that his mother was still not on her feet, to return to her with a league medal that would be a fitting memento of their homecoming.

In the meantime, he was meeting his social engagements as if he had only days to live. His last port of call was the White Sand's Golf Club, where – surprise! surprise! – he ran into his teen-age fantasy, Marian O'Brien, the headmaster's daughter whom he had adored at one time from a distance, fiercely envious of Billy Burns, the sergeant's son (who hadn't much else going for him, apart from being the sergeant's son) dating her.

What a coincidence! He wondered if she were married. With all the ease and assurance that he had acquired in New York, he approached her.

'Fancy meeting you here!' There was a jubilant ring to his voice.

'And you! I heard you had gone back to America.' She greeted him with a warm handshake. His old heart-throb might as well be his current one, for his feelings for her were unchanged.

'I should have been, but I felt Mom needed me around for a little while longer.'

She nodded approvingly.

'Very considerate of you. How is she anyway?'

'She's coming around gradually.'

'It will take some time,' she said sympathetically, adding that she'd need every support he could give her.

He was moved by her concern and was glad she was still her charming self and no less attractive, despite having put on some weight. If a younger Hillary were slimmer and arguably more attractive, Marian still retained a special niche in his affections.

He signalled to the waiter for drinks, but she settled for coffee. She was queued in for a game in fifteen minutes time and was waiting for her golfing partner to show up. And it wasn't, he was relieved to learn, Billy Burns. The last she'd heard of him, he was in Australia. And from what he gathered, she had lost interest in him.

He watched her sip her coffee daintily while he addressed a Scotch on the rocks.

'So what are you doing with yourself?' he inquired discreetly.

'Nursing. I'm just back from a stint in London.'

'Really! And may I say you look great.'

She beamed.

'You too. So how's America treating you?'

'It's been good to me.' He let her know he'd done well out of the construction business.

'Good for you. And I gather you're married.' Local news, he noted, spread as fast as ever in Oldbridge.

'Only recently,' he said lightly.

'Irish or American?'

'Irish-American.'

In an effort to shift the focus from himself, he inquired about her.

'Still single,' she confessed with a hint of regret.

No way! The woman who turned many a head not married! Hard to please, he presumed. Or perhaps she hadn't met the right man so far. At least she had more sense than to marry that show-off, Billy Burns.

'A dedicated, career woman,' he ventured discreetly.

She shrugged, then took a phone call. Her golfing partner couldn't make it. Whereupon she inquired if he'd like to join her in a game.

He was chuffed to be asked.

'What's your handicap?' she inquired as she got to her feet. Tall and graceful, she fitted nicely into her golfing outfit. One of a new generation of women who preferred to swing a club than wield a tennis racquet, bringing a splash of colour to the course and added lure to the clubhouse.

'Generally twelve.' He had fallen in love with the game after he'd hung up his football boots. Lessons from a pro, then hours on the driving range honing his skills. Good for his image and for business contacts.

'Then you're playing very good golf, which is not surprising, seeing how well you play Gaelic football.'

Must have heard about his feats in the semi-final. One of his classier performances.

'And your own handicap?' he inquired as she led him to the office to sign on .

'I'd be ashamed to mention it.'

'Never mind, we'll play for the pleasure of it.'

She arranged with a friend to lend him his golf clubs.

And a pleasure it would be to play with the unattainable heart-throb of his late teens. A frequent prize-winner with his club, he could have given an exhibition, but he didn't. With a touch of chivalry, he gave her a few discreet tips about her stance (sexy rather than golf-like) and her swing, which he considered too rigid, remembering a time when he'd swing for her. He dumbed down his own game, deliberately missing a few sitters on the putting green so as not to demoralise her.

After all, it wasn't every day one found oneself playing golf with the headmaster's daughter at the reputable White Sand's Golf Course. The pleasure of her company for the evening mattered more to him than winning.

He realised he had America to thank for it. The Land of Opportunity had given him confidence and polish. More importantly, it had given him money. He was a fast learner. And ambitious. He read, attended night classes and mixed with his betters. He liked to think that, were he single, he could score with her. Though he had never set foot on the course in his youth, he was playing as if he had been a life-long club member.

After the game, it was back to the clubhouse for a meal that he insisted was on him. Superb steaks washed down by a cheerful, house wine. His well-rehearsed repertoire of stories about New York, which he spiced up for her benefit, helped bridge those differences that once kept them apart.

She was clearly fazed and even engaged in a little flirting with him. When he offered to drop her off at her place, she cancelled her lift with a club member and accompanied him in his Volvo. Such was the chemistry between them, they might as well have been on a date.

Parked outside the headmaster's home with his daughter at his side, Oisheen felt he had achieved something he'd always wanted even more than that league medal.

'How is your Dad keeping?' he inquired, keen to prolong the pleasure of her company.

She sighed.

'Sadly, he passed away on the eve of his retirement.'

'Good God! I never knew.' He pressed her hand in sympathy, then added his praises to his condolences. 'He was a terrific technical teacher. It's thanks to him I've got to be where I am.'

She smiled appreciatively.

'He'd have liked to have heard that coming from one of his brightest students.'

'May God rest him and comfort your mother,' he responded with all the feeling he could impart to her.

Whereupon, her mother appeared in the doorway. Relieved to see her daughter home safely she withdrew discreetly indoors. It was time to part

Still holding her hand, he thanked her for the pleasure of her company and for the privilege of playing the celebrated White

Sands course with her. 'And God knows I needed that uplift after the father's death,' he sighed dramatically.

She understood how he felt. 'The next time we meet, the treat will be on me,' she promised.

Then drawing him towards her, she kissed him with a fervour that made his day and his extended holiday, while making up for the one romance of his teens he regretted having missed.

'So, when are you returning to New York?'

'Immediately after the league final.'

He suppressed a sigh, as her soft, brown eyes continued to detain him .

She promised that she would make a point of being at the game to cheer him.

Gleefully, he pledged: 'My first one over the bar will be for you.'

'And don't forget one for your wife,' she said, bringing him back to *terra firma* as she made to leave.

He nodded. Then they kissed lightly and parted. Alone in the car, his joy gave way to sadness, now that his stay was drawing to a close. Still, he realised he had a lot to be thankful for as he booted up the Volvo.

His mother met him with an icy reception on his return. 'What delayed you? Hillary has been phoning you all evening. '

'Oh, no! I'll ring her straight away.'

Hillary was understandably cool with him.

'Hey, big spender, when are you going to spend a little of your time with me?' she inquired tartly.

'I give you my word I'll be flying out Monday morning bright and early.'

'And you lied to me about your mother,' she chided him.

Feeling his cheeks crimsoning, he admitted to having exaggerated a bit.

'A hell of a bit from what she tells me. I gather you've been having the time of Riley.'

Apologetically, he replied: 'Let's say I've been doing some catching up with my past. God only knows when I'll be back again.'

'So have you finally caught up with it?'

'More or less.'

'If I were you, I wouldn't get too attached to it,' she advised.

He paused, then assured her that after the league final, he would be on the very next plane to New York. And that he couldn't wait to be with her.

'Just as well.' She sounded like she was giving him an ultimatum.

'What do you mean?' He realised he shouldn't have taken the liberties he did, now that he was married.

'It looks like I'm pregnant.'

'Really!' Winning the sweepstake wouldn't have been better news. Having uttered a celebratory cheer, he declared: 'You've made my holiday. I love you, honey, and I'll see you on Monday.'

And, as if that weren't sufficient grounds for his return, she informed him that America had just declared a truce with the Vietcong and that he need have no further worries about the draft.

He couldn't wait to be with her.

Losing the league final by the narrowest of margins was a bit of a downer for Oisheen, who had been playing a blinder until he was carted off midways through the game, having been on the receiving end of a crunching tackle. It was just as well Marian O'Brien was on hand to treat him, or his return to Hillary might have been further delayed. In a sporting gesture, he left his expensive new boots to a relative who had what it takes to step into them and hopefully win the coveted medal that had eluded him.

The heat-wave had passed. In its rainy aftermath, the town suddenly looked its familiar, drab self. He realised it was time to pack his bags for a sunnier, youthful New York. There was simply no future for him in Oldbridge. Had he never left it, he might have settled for it. Having benefited from the better life the Big Apple made possible for him, there was no going back. Besides, he had something to really live for now.

Seeing the cronies dropping off one by one when he eased up on the free rounds, he realised it was time he stopped playing Santa.

As he boarded the plane at Shannon, he could hear Frank Sinatra recalling him home from someone's transistor.

'Those little town blues
Are melting away
I wanna make a brand new start of it
In old New York.'
C'est la vie, buddy.

THE CELTIC TIGER FICTION

When the Celtic Tiger took off, Peter dug in his heels. I tried to explain that bonanzas like that came with a price, but he wasn't interested. He saw it as a windfall to be blown before it blew over, like all the other booms that burst, leaving the economy to return to its normal equilibrium. History, I should have known, repeats itself. You made the most of the good times and the let the bad ones take care of themselves.

What could I say? With a good number in the computer business, he preferred to spend his nights carousing in Temple Bar rather than worrying about inflation. Whenever I reminded him that house prices were beginning to shoot through the roof, and that it might be a good time to buy while they were still affordable, he'd switch off. Soon enough, he'd be shackled with a mortgage with an 'all work and no play' price-tag.

'What goes up must come down. It's the Law of Gravity, Paul.' He was adamant. Free-spirited, fun-loving, and a big hit with the ladies, he liked to think that he had a lot of partying to do yet. His handsome looks and romantic sensibility ensured he was in great demand for the merry-go-round of parties, which he was determined the Celtic Tiger wouldn't spoil for him.

'By the time gravity kicks in, houses will be about as affordable as a penthouse suite,' I warned him. As a bank official, I had my finger on the pulse.

Girded with a stiff drink in one hand and a Hamlet cigar in the other, he advanced a further reason for his stance. 'If house-prices jump, wages will follow suit. Right?'

I shook my head emphatically. 'Not necessarily. It would be asking the proverbial tortoise to overtake the hare.'

Refusing to take me seriously, he said that he would keep faith with the tortoise.

'You'd better hope that the hare is suffering from Achilles tendon.' I advised him that, with the way the market was going, the same hare would soon be out of sight, and that the developers would see to it that any increases in wages would be quickly overtaken by corresponding hikes in property prices. 'Can't you see it's a vicious circle?'

He preferred not. It would take a dynamite charge to dislodge him from his comfort zone. He had a gambler's belief that eventually everything would turn up trumps for him, and that all he had to do in the meantime was to sit tight and hold his head, while others were losing theirs in a frenzy of house purchasing. In a worst-case scenario, he'd let the last half hour be the hardest.

I refused to give up on him, though I fraternised less and less with him after I'd placed a deposit on a modest semi on the Southside. I simply couldn't afford it. Tony, our golfing partner at one time, was more adventurous, and went one better, purchasing two apartments, with further acquisitions in mind, which he planned to rent out to Polish migrants capitalising on the construction boom.

Peter was unfazed. He rarely saw eye-to-eye with Tony, who dismissed his warnings about the risk of incurring negative equity as balderdash and an excuse for doing nothing.

'I fear him,' he confided. 'He'll upstage Rachman one day.'

I disagreed, pointing out to him that Tony was providing an indispensable service at a time when there was a growing demand for rented accommodation from migrant workers, as well as from those who could no longer afford a home of their own.

He wasn't swayed.

'Bet you he'll be left with empty apartments when the Poles return home,' he forecast, determined to sit it out, to let the market run its reckless course and then cash in on it after it crashed.

I could see Tony had less and less time for him, declaring it was about time he faced up to reality and stopped playing Peter Pan.

I agreed that, for a man about town, he was pretty clueless and suspected, like Tony, that he had lost the plot.

'What d'you expect? He believes, like so many of his peers, that the world should be his oyster.' Tony pictured a rude awakening in store for him.

With the market beginning to spin out of control, Peter took the line that to do nothing was to do something. And that if others followed suit, things would quickly return to normal.

Noting the sea of For Sale signs that, by now, stippled the cityscape as houses changed hands, I felt sure that Peter would pay dearly for his stance. For Sale. Sale Agreed. Sold. Three stages in a selling frenzy that witnessed an unprecedented change of ownership as urban dwellers sold up and moved to cheaper, rural, housing estates to enjoy their new-found prosperity.

To Peter's disbelief, there seemed to be no stopping the trend. The market ruled and purchasers ran with it like lemmings over a cliff. But not Peter, who refused to follow the herd. With a cynical frown, he dismissed it as an auctioneers' rip-off. A developers' El Dorado. A sellers' dream that spared no thought for the buyer. It was panic reaction. And so far, he saw no reason to panic.

'It cannot and it will not go on,' he continued to predict, still refusing to budge.

I agreed it was unreal, but if you needed any proof for the infallibility of the market, you had only to note how the economy was booming. The future was never brighter. So far, the public mood suggested that there was no reason to worry unduly. And if there was one thing Peter didn't like, I knew, it was worrying.

'Don't hold your breath,' I continued to advise him nonetheless.

That he was occasionally unnerved, was becoming progressively evident.

'It defies logic,' he agonised, one evening when I ran into him in Temple Bar.

I shrugged.

'It's simply the old story of supply and demand.'

'Baloney! It's greed,' he was emphatic. 'Greed driving the market crazy.'

Whereupon, he took issue with the Church for its silence, railed against the trade unions for their indifference, and upbraided the opposition political parties for their apathy, declaring that in previous decades the Left would have been at the barricades and the clergy lecturing the culprits from the altar.

'There will be 'weeping and gnashing of teeth' when the Crash comes.' He gazed grimly into his glass like a fortune-teller who had foreseen bad news in store for a client.

I was glad I had purchased when I did. In disbelief, I watched the property index soar like a barometer in a heat wave. It was good news, admittedly, for the bank, and crazy though it seemed, people were prepared to pay tenfold what they would have paid for a similar residence in pre-Tiger times. And still, there were no indications of any easing up or of what Peter hoped would be a general protest. Only a few, lone voices in the media spoke out against it, but soon gave up. The market was sacrosanct, even as it became a runaway train that would soon be unstoppable.

'It can't go on.' Peter continued to ignore my warnings.

'I wouldn't bet on it. The economy is on a roll. And will be for a good while yet,' I predicted, seeing no evidence, so far, of any imminent downturn.

Tossing back his Bacardi he declared defiantly: 'Then let it roll to hell. I'm damned if I'll buy.'

'And you'll be damned if you don't,' I suggested, knowing that things usually get worse before they get better.

He declared he had no intention of committing financial suicide and, in an upbeat mood, signalled for another drink, convinced that he had nothing to worry about that time wouldn't resolve. Tempted though he'd been to follow the trend and purchase in a moment of panic, he decided to hold out until the market slit its own throat and went into free fall.

'You may have a lot grey hairs by the time it does,' I warned him.

I could see he was still living in the previous millennium, when things moved at a slower pace and house prices and incomes weren't poles apart as they were now.

As he waited for his drink, I watched him gearing up for one of his familiar outbursts that were becoming more frequent and more strident of late.

'The confounded unions have their heads in the sand.' Their failure to address the problem of inflation infuriated him.

'What do you expect them to do? Order all their members to stop buying houses?'

He nodded. He was annoyed too with the *Irish Voice* for having refused to publish his letter to that effect.

Despite spiralling prices, the unbridled demand for houses ridiculed his stand-off. Insatiable developers and ruthless auctioneers were creaming it. And the banks, I would later regret, continued to aid and abet them. Not surprisingly, the humblest artisan dwelling was suddenly costing the moon, as the Celtic Tiger went into over-drive.

'I can't explain it. The market has gone pear-shaped.' Peter looked beaten on the occasion when he hooked up with Tony and myself for drinks.

I shrugged.

'Nobody can.'

I noted his first real signs of anxiety.

'It will wreck the very fabric of society. Leave no time for parenting or for cultural and recreational pursuits For anyone with a crushing mortgage, it will be a case of graft till you drop. No thanks.' The playboy of Temple Bar was beginning to sound desperate.

'It's going to be a mobile home for you, pal.' Tony predicted, while pointedly placing a fifty euro note on the counter for drinks.

'Well, you don't have to worry. It'll soon be a landlord's Republic,' an irate Peter, who must have seen his prospects of home ownership dwindling by the day, retaliated.

'Still the old *madra* in the manger,' Tony observed tartly.

'Just your local watch-dog trying to keep the approaching wolf-pack from the door.'

An unflinching, denim-clad Tony reminded his trendily dressed protagonist that he was living in a successful economy that was the envy of Europe.

Peter grimaced.

'Very successful at impoverishing house buyers, while making multi-millionaires of developers. Whatever became of the parable of the rich man trying to get to heaven?' the dapper man about town disagreed.

'Perhaps you'd prefer to live in a Third World economy where the camels are so lean you could drive a herd of them through the eye of a needle?' Tony responded.

I couldn't resist a laugh at Peter's expense, and watched him pull a wry face.

'Who wants a mortgage that would be a millstone about one's neck?'

'None of us. But we took a gamble, rolled up our shirt sleeves and did some belt tightening. So take my advice and quit playing the artless dodger.' A leaner Tony spelled out the price to be paid.

Peter Pan wasn't having any of it and signalled for a drink. I suspected that, deep down, he was worried that he might have got it badly wrong.

'My twist.' Tony ruled him out of order and shoved the fifty euro towards the barman.

Unimpressed by his flatlet and his negative attitude to home owning, Peter's lady friends, I gathered, were giving him short shrift. It must have given him some pause for thought when I moved with my young bride into our newly-built semi, for he phoned me soon afterwards.

'Has the mortgage left you singing for your supper?' he inquired. I wondered if he were having second thoughts about his stance.

Careful not to turn him off acquiring a home, I decided to sweeten the pill.

'On the contrary, it's quite manageable.' Having lived in a congested flatlet since moving from Abbeylaune to Dublin, I assured him it was worth every penny of the price.

'Who knows, one of these days I might win the lottery.' He still held out for a cushioned landing.

I could see him being left behind while his peers moved on, settled down, and acquired homes far a-field, joining the growing commuter generation. And still he waited for the bubble to burst: for houses to be repossessed and resold for a song, as happened in London when the bottom fell out of the property market in the Eighties.

'Wishful thinking.' I tried in vain to convince him.

'Trust me, the Law of Gravity will kick in on of these days,' he forecast. Right now, I knew, the market was kicking his hopes harder than he'd ever anticipated.

Well in his cups, I watched him engage a government minister as we were leaving the Cavern – his favourite Temple Bar pub – on his thirty-third birthday.

'Don't you think it's criminal, minister,' he addressed the politician in a slurred voice, his posture approximating an oblique angle.

The Minister shrugged, then asked him to explain himself.

'The crippling cost of houses.' An unstable Peter drooped over him.

'Nonsense. The property boom is driving the economy,' I heard the minister disagree.

'Into the ground. That's where. And wait till the houses are being repossessed and eviction orders issued, you and your party are going to be out of office for a long, long time.' Peter was now tilting at a perilous angle.

'Trust the market,' the minister advised, more concerned, I suspected, at that moment, that Peter didn't upset his and his partner's drinks than with the housing problem.

'No more than politicians,' Peter replied.

I pushed him towards the exit before he was forcefully ejected and eased him into the passenger seat of my car.

'Keep it for his clinic. ' I managed to restrain him, which wasn't difficult, seeing he was footless.

Determined to give the minister a further piece of his mind for his failure to regulate the market, he tried to force his way back into the pub. Fearful he'd be taken into custody, I pinned him to his seat until he chilled out.

'Why would he want to derail the gravy train?' I asked, clicking his seat belt into position and hitting the accelerator before he changed his mind.

Peter grunted.

'Why would he indeed? Isn't he very likely in the pockets of the developers who are keeping him sweet with stuffed brown envelopes?'

Every time we passed an estate agency he gave it the two fingers for overvaluing houses and for using ghost bidders at auctions.

Earlier that evening he had administered a roundhouse kick to the door of the *Irish Voice* – a paper that played up the property market.

I wasn't spared the rough edge of his tongue either, as we drove past a bank in Rathmines – our former happy hunting ground, when life was uncomplicated and sanity prevailed in both the property and the rental market.

'If you think for one minute I'm letting you off the hook, think again pal,' he said and jabbed me with his index finger.

Annoyed, I demanded to know what I'd done to deserve it.

'Can't you see you and your bank are at the core of the problem,' he drawled, his lip movements like those of a dental patient who just had his gum frozen for an extraction.

Rocked by his reproach, I tried to wriggle out of any responsibility.

'I'm afraid there really isn't much I can do about it,' I said lightly.

He shook his head vehemently, then looked me straight in the eye. 'Don't you realise that in giving one hundred percent loans to house buyers, you're shoring up the market? Reduce your loans and you'll reduce house prices. As it is, you're effectively bankrolling the developers. Get me?' He continued to jab me.

I could see his point, but try saying no to hard-pressed couples desperate for a house, or preaching ethics to your manager when you should be capitalising on the windfall. You'd be out on your ear. I did nothing. And it was beginning to rankle, as tales of hardship from clients who had fallen into arrears with their mortgage repayments were becoming a daily problem for the bank.

'Mark my words pal, there will be a day of reckoning for you when the economy crashes,' he warned, his posture by now more simian than *sapiens*.

As I dropped him off at his place, he positioned himself in front of the car and demanded I roll down the window and hear him out.

'Make it quick.' I told him. He seemed to forget I had a wife and child awaiting me.

'You listen to me. And listen good!' he keeled backwards, swayed, then tilted forwards.

'Go ahead. And then get off the soapbox!' I appealed.

He straightened up, then banged on the bonnet of the car for emphasis as he spoke.

'Not until you reject the myth that the market system that has got us into the mess we're in can resolve itself. And acknowledge, furthermore, that it's up to the likes of you to rein it in.'

'What are you asking of me? That I picket my own work-place?'

'Just say *no* to the next house buyer who comes looking for a hundred percent loan for a mortgage.'

I merely shrugged. As I pulled away, he gave me the clenched fist salute, then staggered up the steps to his flatlet, which, however congested, spared him, so far, from the fate of his commuter-weary, mortgage-burdened contemporaries, who depended on crèches to rear their children and whose lives would henceforth be from work to bed. Whether he stood to lose or to gain ultimately was anybody's guess. For now, at any rate, he could indulge his addiction to the *dolce vita* and sleep with a relatively easy mind.

I could picture him dancing with glee when the Tiger Economy crashed, literally, overnight. For the disgraced banks, and especially for yours truly, it was a grim scenario, now that my job was on the line and most of my savings wiped out.

Even Tony, as Peter predicted, had taken a drastic hit. With the construction industry ground to a halt, his Polish tenants had returned home, smiling all the way to their native banks, while leaving him in the red and his empty apartments now negative equity. A companion in distress.

When I answered the door one troubled evening, I was greeted by an elated Peter who announced he'd just bought a house.

'Congrats! Whereabouts?' I inquired. I was never more relieved to see him and invited him in for drinks.

'Within a stone's throw of you. A cool, little terraced job. And at the right price. Apparently it had been repossessed.'

'Lucky you!' I admitted to being in a state of shock all week, having learned that one of my clients, whose pension schemes had suffered a similar fate to my savings, had committed suicide. A foiled bank robbery that afternoon at the branch where I worked left me further traumatised.

Peter reached for his glass and having taken a swig of its contents, grinned.

'And there'll be a lot more of that as the recession worsens,' he predicted ominously, and suggested that I wear a bullet-proof vest to work.

I grimaced, then looked into space, wondering, like countless others, where it all went so disastrously wrong.

'I see you picked up a shiner,' he observed during a lull in our exchanges.

'Aye, for saying *no* to a client.'

'A bit late in the day, don't you think?' he remarked acidly.

On a brighter note, he confessed to having found the woman with whom he wanted to spend the rest of his days – hence, I gathered, the pressures on him to acquire a house.

I commended him on his sense of timing.

'I told you the tortoise would catch up with the hare,' he trumpeted triumphantly.

I nodded, knowing that it was now my turn to eat some humble pie.

'You should have listened to me. Instead, you threw business ethics, along with your conscience, to the winds.' He smiled a thin, mocking smile as he consulted his glass.

Ruefully, I replied: 'Who could have foreseen the outcome?'

With a dismissive gesture he declared that the dogs in the street were barking it.

'At least you've come out of it alright,' I said, a little envious of him.

He nodded, but couldn't resist a dig at me.

'It looks like I'll be spared the debtors' prison, now awaiting many of your unwitting clients.'

'Just hope your firm doesn't relocate to India,' I warned, having seen many recently taking that profit-driven route and many more going to the wall.

Shaken by the spectre of insecurity, he threw back his drink and got to his feet.

As we were parting, he remarked with a wry smile, that I had a lot to answer for, and that I should be wearing sack cloth and ashes for my sins.

I've been told worse. As the recession deepens, giving rise to wage cuts and to unprecedented unemployment, I've repeatedly been given to understand that, along with my colleagues, I should be lined up against a wall and shot.

With my hand on my heart, I'll readily admit that, when we could have done something to avert the catastrophe, we did nothing, preferring to make a killing in the market.

A jubilant Peter on the other hand, continues to believe that by having done nothing, he did something genuinely cool. And if others had followed suit, the economy wouldn't be in the mess it is in now.

We are finally agreed that the Celtic Tiger was a fiction that kept us all in suspense, and guessing, in the way all fiction does, right up to the end.

A CHANGE OF HEART

There was no way, Jane was sure, though her friends disagreed, that the new Jack Byrne resembled – apart from his appearance – the previous Jack Byrne, since his heart transplant. She wondered if they were being discreet, or if they had enough problems of their own to be bothered about hers.

Their response: 'We all change sooner or later. Be grateful he's alive and well!' smacked for her of Job's comforters.

None of them had the foggiest what she was going through. For goodness sake, she might as well be living with another man. A man as different as chalk is to cheese from the man she had lived with for thirty years. And they couldn't see it!

Not that the current Jack wasn't what she secretly wished for at times. She agreed there were plusses. In the place of the rugged, controlling man who previously ran the show was a gentle person who treated her as an equal and entrusted her with decisions, from which he'd previously excluded her. It was too good to be true. And it kept her awake at night. In her entire, nursing experience, she had never come across anything like it.

Riffling through an old album for a clue, there was no mistaking the dashing fellow in the faded photo, with whom she fell in love in her mid-twenties. Captivated by his looks, his personality and his drive, she preferred him to worthy rivals who came with flowers and presents to her door. Her opposite in many ways; her refined, sensitive temperament was in marked contrast to his swashbuckling manner. Even then, she could sense a winner in him. Despite a certain, raw edge to him, there was a glamour about him that she found irresistible.

She looked at her watch. Better make him some tea. Strictly herbal, don't forget! One Earl Grey tea-bag rather than Barry's rich blend, which he preferred before his operation.

While it's drawing, I'll have a peek at another photo. Perhaps her favourite: holding one of his many trophies. He was the toast of the golf club and a big hit with the lady members, who frequently enjoyed his generosity. He played, she recalled, like he lived: to win. Not any longer. Now he was taking the scenic route in his study, reading and reflecting when he should be up and doing. It didn't make sense. There had to be something seriously the matter with him.

'Your tea, Jack! Can you hear me, Jack? Jack, your tea! Uhoo, Jack!' she trumpeted towards the study, his sanctuary from the business routines that he had left in the hands of his staff.

'Mind if I have it later?' His request was as predictable as it was irksome..

'It'll go cold.'

'Hot or cold, it will still be tea.'

She sighed, bemused by the ascetic man with whom she now lived.

He was still engrossed in those philosophy books he turned to for consolation. Still seriously at odds with his previous self. She remembered when he wouldn't have to be called a second time to his elevenses. He'd be ripping into the cakes before his tea was poured. Now his appetite was for higher pursuits, he told her. She couldn't figure him. Prior to his operation, she rarely ever saw him with a book in his hand. While academically bright apparently, he preferred sport to reading, and the active to the reflective life.

Placing a cosy on the teapot to keep it warm for him, she perused a snap of him on a building site wearing a metal hat. Whatever he lacked upstairs he made up for with his hands. A tradesman's hands she remembered, strong yet gentle, his nails always meticulously manicured. And those enviable muscles that were a by-product of the building sites rather than the gym.

Having no desire to follow in his father's footsteps as a woodwork instructor, he apprenticed himself to the building trade as soon as he left college. It was where the money was. And Jack made no secret of it to her that he liked money. Lots of it, which appealed to her, having had her fill of the tight household budgets of her Abbeylaune upbringing. Far from being impressed by his current, frugal life-style, she worried he was losing it.

As she placed some tea cakes on a plate, she remembered how the previous Jack capitalised on the periodic construction booms. Out-stripping his white-collared peers who had outshone him at school, he drove flashy cars they would never afford, while surrounding himself with upmarket, attractive women who massaged his ego in return for good times. Still, it was she, the girl in the nurse's uniform, peering at her from the album, who would capture him soon after they'd met at the Outpatients', where she had been on duty the day he fell from a scaffolding and effectively into her arms.

Jack was a good catch, admittedly. He was a fast learner. Experience quickly taught him what his teachers didn't: that good connections make for good business, and that the way to the top was by having a Minister in one pocket, a bank manager in the other and, at all times, a Merc to boost his image.

What on earth had come over him? She agonised as she continued to flick through the album. He was the least likely candidate for his current life-style.

'Your tea, for heaven's sake, Jack!' Her patience was wearing thin.

Another photo of him in his yachting gear brought a smile to her lips. It wasn't, she knew, for the novelty of sailing before the mast, like his seafaring boyhood heroes, that prompted him to embrace the brine. Nor, for that matter, was it for the privilege of an entry card to an exclusive club. With Jack it was business first and foremost, and the yacht club, he told her, presented him with the right contacts that would further his career as a developer. So different to the recluse now confined to his study, and whose wallet was at the service of the every street beggar, rather than his coterie at the club, which he'd ceased to frequent, preferring to browse occasionally around the city's bookstores.

'Can't you see I'm imbibing the wisdom of the great thinkers? Just bear with me until I finish this chapter,' he requested his tea to be put on hold.

The previous Jack, she remembered, also viewed life as an on-going, learning curve. No year passed that he didn't add to his repertoire of skills. Soon he would be a Jack-of-all-trades, his services competed for by friends and neighbours, as soon as he set up his own business.

'Jack I need a new bathroom installed.'

'I'd like you to put in a new kitchen unit for me, Jack.'

'Can you do a patio for me Jack?'

'Can you queue me in for a drive-in, Jack?'

The list was endless. With his growing reputation came self-belief in his ability to handle bigger projects. A stand of semis, she remembered, established him as a fully fledged developer. If soaring house prices spared little thought for the victims of the property boom, he excused himself by saying that the market was not of his making. There was no room in his line of business for the thin-skinned. She would have preferred if it were otherwise, but ran with it.

Browsing over an enlarged snapshot of him standing beside a billboard bearing his name, she remembered how proud she had been of him. They would move to a posher estate and to a larger residence for his increasing family, for whom he had big plans – wanting, she knew, to be reflected in their success.

A driven man, he bristled with energy and ambitions, literally stampeding through life.

If she were seeing too much of him recently, she saw less and less of him as his business grew, his time taken up with planning hearings and appeals, and fraternising with politicians he bankrolled in return for their favours. She didn't mind. He was providing well for her and their family.

'Your tea will be stewed, Jack!' she appealed, concerned that the man who once lived to eat was now fasting to live.

'Be with you in a sec.' He told her he was gradually finding what he was looking for.

'Good. But what have you suddenly got against food?'

'A little abstinence is good for the spirit,' he replied.

'You'll love the fresh Danish pastries.' She was trying every trick in the book to lure him from his lair.

'Not good for my cholesterol count. Remember what they did to my previous heart? Eat, drink and be sorry!' he reminded her.

She felt like screaming. The new Jack was a complete enigma, his sudden indifference to his business causing her sleepless nights.

How he could dismiss his achievements, proudly catalogued in the family album, was beyond her? Those impressive, suburban semis and those towering office blocks, which were his benchmark, had to mean something to him – not to mention the esteem and the wealth that accrued from them.

Now he was under her feet day after day, until she felt at times like shooing him out if it weren't so soon after his transplant.

Like most men who have made it, he had begun to ease up long before his operation, delegating more and more responsibilities to his eldest son, who was beginning to make his way in the firm. Instead of bestriding the building site, issuing directions and pressing for deadlines, he was hanging out more often at the yacht club. Not that she had any serious crib with that, as long as he kept his hand on the tiller.

She needn't have worried. Gratis of the Celtic Tiger, property prices continued to shoot, like his cholesterol, through the roof, as if money grew on trees and rainy days were about as likely as a wet season in the Sahara.

Then came the set-back, with Revenue discovering a gaping shortfall in his tax returns, along with an undeclared, offshore account and secret donations to a politician, who pocketed them for his own rather than his party's use. She felt like binning that embarrassing photo of him in one of the tabloids, taken as he emerged from the Tribunal.

Days of cross examination by lawyers and relentless exposure by the media were traumatic for himself and his family. Named and shamed, his reputation was seriously tarnished, resulting in many of his former friends shunning him.

Replacing the embarrassing snap in the album, she dumped the cold tea and put on a fresh pot while trying to shut out that regrettable episode from her mind.

He was spared the embarrassment of imprisonment, but not a massive heart attack. Shock waves of disbelief sent shudders through his system when told he needed a transplant. For the first time ever, the possibility of death, she knew, gave him serious pause for thought and put his aspirations and his achievements in perspective. After months of anxious waiting, a donor was found. To her amazement, he was back on his feet, though not in his head, in next to no time.

'Ready, Jack! I've just made you a fresh pot.' She put aside the album.

'Coming! And no sugar or milk, honey!'

She presented him with a beverage that would have repelled, rather than cheered, his previous self. Then she watched him sip it gingerly. At least he was shedding his excess kilos and looking none the worse for it.

'Excellent tea,' he declared. Asserting his dominance over his former appetites, he continued, to her amazement, to refuse the Danish pastries.

'Care for some more tea?' she inquired, as he pushed aside his empty cup.

'One cup will be fine.'

When she inquired if he were doing penance for something or other, he grinned. In truth, his lack of interest in food worried her a lot less than his disinterest in his business. Even his gait, she noted, was different: relaxed rather than rushed, and he carried himself with an absent air, his feet, she feared, no longer on *terra firma*.

The brand new man sitting across from her at the coffee table would soon pose serious issues for his staff, who began to suspect that his problem wasn't confined to just a coronary one. As the weeks went by, the familiar, ebullient developer presented more like a member of a monastic order, than someone hell-bent on making a killing in the market.

'You won't mind, honey, if I return to my study. I want to finish that book I'm reading,' he'd excuse himself.

She would nod half-heartedly, then release a sigh of despair when he was out of earshot.

Various were the explanations for his withdrawal from society. The damning effects of the tribunal were cited, as well as the possibility that he had made his money and wanted out. Happily, his elder son managed to deputise for him for the time being.

'He's reading philosophy,' Jane unburdened herself one morning to the firm's accountant.

'He's what!' The number cruncher raised both eyebrows. Philosophy had never been his cup of tea. Metaphysical issues were above his head.

'Day in, day out, he's holed up in his study, immersed in books I've never heard of,' she explained.

'They may not be what the doctor ordered. On the other hand, they shouldn't do him any harm.' The accountant saw no reason for panic at this point.

She shook her head, then ruefully remarked: 'They already have. He has completely lost interest in the firm.'

The accountant looked up from his figures and observed a brief, bemused silence.

'Give him time. After all, he's been through a life-changing trauma,' he suggested after a prolonged pause, then cheered her up with a healthy statement of the firm's finances.

When Jack informed Jane one morning during his scant elevenses, that he planned going back to college and doing a philosophy degree, she freaked.

'It's a degree in business and marketing you should be thinking of doing,' she snapped.

He shook his head gloomily, then confessed that he had had his fill of business.

'Seriously, Jack, you need counselling,' she appealed, having observed him for weeks now, padding about his study like an over-petted poodle rather than the former, focussed jungle cat.

'Nonsense! I've moved on,' he declared emphatically.

'So I see; sadly to cloud-cuckoo land.'

He shook his head and, with a show of contriteness that was out of character, claimed that for all his success, he had been spiritually bankrupt up to now. Money had failed to bring him contentment or an easy conscience. Somewhere on the business ladder he believed he had lost his way and, he feared, his soul.

At breaking point, she sought the advice of a psychologist.

'He hasn't set foot in the firm since his operation.' She opened her heart to Mr Digby, a paternal figure of advanced years.

'And you're sure he has lost all interest in his business?' an attentive psychologist twiddled his biro thoughtfully.

'Completely.'

After some reflection, he concluded that Jack seemed to be running away from something or other.

'But that's not all.' A tense Jane readied herself for further disclosures.

'No?'

'I must inform you that he's no longer the person he once was.'

Mr Digby suddenly raised a bemused, bushy eyebrow.

'He spends his days reading philosophy,' she sighed, sensing that she wasn't the only one who was perplexed.

His curiosity further roused, Digby urged her to continue, whereupon she admitted that the current Jack, in fairness, was much more attentive towards her, and a lot more patient and understanding with the family, than the previous Jack.

He nodded approvingly.

She didn't mention that he was less demanding in bed and more tender in love-making, too. Love words she'd never heard him use were readily on his lips during their recent couplings. At times it seemed to her that their intimate moments released a latent bard of the bed in him, in place of the highly sexed man of few words whom she had lived and slept with for 30 years. Such was his restraint at other times, it wouldn't surprise her if he were contemplating celibacy.

'I still want the Jack I used to know.' Her sigh was a plea for help.

'As I see it, it's imperative he gets back to work as soon as possible.' The psychologist's response was prompt.

She frowned, making it clear to him that any attempts on her part on that score had been firmly resisted, and that he wouldn't hear of a counsellor.

After some reflection, Mr Digby had an inspiration.

'D'you think he'd listen to a philosopher?' he inquired softly.

She hesitated, then rowed in with the suggestion.

'Who knows? It would certainly be worth a try. Can you suggest someone?'

He paused for a moment, then recommended his friend Barkley from Trinity, who practiced briefly as a psychologist before taking up philosophy.

'Why philosophy?' she inquired, all the more wary of it since Jack took it up.

'I gather he is looking for answers that psychology doesn't have.'

It seemed a good ploy. Nevertheless, she'd better get Jack's agreement before arranging a meeting. Discretion had always been her trump card in her dealings with him.

Mr Digby handed her his card and suggested she get in touch with him as soon as Jack consented to a meeting.

In the meantime, the new Jack was becoming increasingly philanthropic and had his accountant write cheques for this cause and that. No Romanian reached out a supplicating hand who wasn't rewarded generously. Few were the AIDS-, tsunami- or famine-hit parts of the globe that didn't benefit from his benevolence. In contrast, he was spending next to nothing on himself, spurning luxuries and dressing down, having donated most of his clothes to Oxfam.

Jane worried. There was a recklessness about his generosity. His sudden preference for Abbeylaune over Italy for holidaying, hardly made sense to her, much though she shared his approval of it for not having lost the run of itself during the Celtic Tiger.

A lapsed Catholic, he surprised everyone by resuming his religious practices, making no secret of it to his mockers that he had found his spiritual road map again.

When he terminated his membership of the golf and the yacht clubs, and downsized from his Merc to a Ford Focus, she felt it was time for her to seek the help of the philosopher. A delighted Jack readily agreed to have Mr Barkley to tea one evening, on the understanding that the professor wished to set up a fund for a migrant student, who had come to Ireland to study philosophy.

He took an instant liking to the bearded, silver-haired professor, who seemed to take a reciprocal liking to him. Jane's superb cooking, along with a quality Chateauneuf, made for the kind of evening that ended all too soon for Jack, who was so charmed with Barkley that he paced about the house excitedly long after his guest had gone. His contribution to the bursary was put on hold until Barkley had completed the necessary arrangements.

'Well, what did you make of him?' Jane inquired of the professor as she saw him to his car.

After some reflection, he informed her that cases like Jack's were rare, but well-documented.

'Are we talking about a psychotic sea-change?'

Barklay nodded otherwise.

'More about one arising from a heart transplant, whereby the recipient manifests characteristics of the donor,' he said gently.

'So what should I do? Run with his new self?'

'I'd suggest you first try and find out more about his donor. And then we'll discuss procedures.' He got in his car, leaving her more hopeful than she'd been in months.

The following day, she contacted the cardiac unit in the hospital, where she had briefly worked as a nurse before retiring to parent a big family.

It didn't take her long to discover that Jack's Polish benefactor had been doing his doctorate in philosophy in Dublin while working his way through college. Like so many of his fellow countryman, he had been attracted to Ireland by the Celtic Tiger boom. His untimely death, due to a fall on the building site where he worked part-time, put paid to a promising, academic future.

So Barkley was right. Pleased with the professor's diagnosis, she had him to tea again.

After a hearty meal, of which even Jack partook with more relish than usual, Barkley got down to business.

'Before we get around to the subject of philosophy, there's a little matter that could present a problem unless we first get it out of the way,' he said.

She watched Jack nod, then give his undivided attention to the professor, while he revealed to him the sad saga of his donor.

'A philosophy student!' Jack was more excited than saddened for his benefactor.

'So that accounts for your sudden pre-occupation with the subject.' Barkley's diagnosis was more clinical than philosophical.

Jack looked bewildered.

'You're not confusing a heart with a brain transplant?' he protested.

The professor shook his head, then proceeded to put his mind at ease.

'On the contrary, research has shown that the heart, in some cases, would appear to be a storehouse of memories.'

'Lucky me,' Jack chuckled.

'Why lucky?' The professor eyed him curiously.

'After all, it could well have been the heart of a serial killer, or a paedophile, or God only knows whom.'

Barkley grimaced, whereupon Jane intervened.

'Personally, my preference for you would have been for one more down to earth than your present one.' Realising what she had said, she promptly apologised to the professor for her inadvertent remark.

He made light of it, then proceeded to work out Jack's solution.

'Are you happy with your new self?' she heard Barkley inquire.

'Absolutely. It's a higher self.' He added that he felt much more comfortable with it and more in harmony with himself and with others.

'Good. But, I gather you've been neglecting your business recently.' Barkley glanced discreetly at Jane, then critically at Jack.

'It no longer interests me. Maybe I'll get back to it; maybe not.' The developer shrugged indifferently.

'Why not?' Barkley held his gaze, his great beard investing him with an air of profundity.

Jack made a dismissive gesture that had Jane worried.

'It means nothing to me. Just a bad conscience,' he confessed, then added that, for too long, he had sacrificed his cultural and spiritual development to the pursuit of Mammon.

'Is that what your new self tells you?'

'Yes.'

Barkley drained his glass, then pushed it aside.

'You mustn't be it's puppet, Jack. From what I can see it's calling the shots. Are you with me?' the professor appealed for his co-operation.

A disillusioned developer shook his head

'Have I not taken a more virtuous route?' he protested.

Barclay placed his cards on the table.

'Suffice, you were delivering a very valuable service prior to your transplant. Building the new city. Providing homes and offices, as well as jobs, for impoverished workers from all over Europe. It must count for something. So think about it, Jack and give your old self a look in. Perhaps you might even consider building more affordable homes in future, and paying your migrant workers standard wages. Then you'll be at peace with your old self. But remember, you're in the driving seat.'

Jack nodded, and Jane could tell by his expression that everything would be fine again.

'Good. Just keep in mind, Jack, philosophy does not have all the answers. And if the legendary Descartes were alive and present in this room right now, he'd be at sixes and sevens.' The professor prepared to leave, himself not a little bemused.

A grateful Jane held his coat for him.

'About that fund?' Jack reminded him.

'In your own good time. Something to compensate the Polish family for the loss of their son.' The professor finally explained the reason for the fund.

A grateful Jack reached for his pen and wrote him a generous cheque there and then, while Jane breathed a sigh of relief that her ploy hadn't backfired on her.

'And now I want you to promise me that you'll be in your office bright and early on Monday morning.' Barkley sought his assurance.

'You have my word.' The other placed his hand on his heart.

Jane could hardly contain her joy. The familiar Jack, whom she loved with all his faults, was about to make a comeback. She was further relieved to hear the professor sensibly suggest to him that, when he got his act together, he would start him off on a course of extra-mural philosophy lectures. 'No exams. Study at your own pace. Lectures at night, leaving you free for your daily tasks. And when your son is ready to step into your shoes, we can discuss further options.'

'Brilliant.'

An overjoyed developer saw the professor to his car.

When Jack stepped into his Ford Focus and headed for his office the following day, Jane knew it was business as usual.

SCIENCE ON THE CURRICULUM

If you're looking for a reason why Abbeylaune remained something of a backwater for so long, you could point a finger, as its Three Wise Men once did, at the local college's former curriculum. A modest town then, it mostly owed its survival to shop-keeping and to its monthly cattle fairs and markets. Factories might as well not have existed. The Industrial Revolution, which had long ago overtaken Europe, had by-passed Abbeylaune –your original green town, long before that eco-concept became currency.

It may have been green, but for many, believe me, regrettably in the red, and with few employment prospects, unless you owned a business or had a profession.

For most working-class families, it was a case of the one-way ticket to England or America, or alternatively, a life of subsistence on the dole. It was a grim scenario – you can take it from one who'd lived through that era when the home fires, more often than not, were kept alight by registered letters from the Bronx and from Britain, which was benefiting from a post-war building boom.

It took the Three Wise Men, as they came to be known, to see through the failures of the old ways and to realise that what the town needed was a factory.

Regrettably, the business sector showed no great enthusiasm to date for one, which they considered, in any case, incompatible with a town where cattle were still bought and sold in its Square. In retrospect, I suspect that the shopkeepers' apathy was rooted in their fears that a factory would steal their staff, with offers of higher wages and shorter working hours.

The Three Wise Men, though, had other ideas. Putting their heads together, they came to the conclusion that the local college's curriculum, which no longer addressed the needs of the current generation, was a contributory factor in the town's retrograde mindset. Having pinpointed the problem, it remained for them to devise a strategy for change – a fraught undertaking in those reactionary days when the old ways were sacrosanct, and new ideas were regarded, even in academic circles, with a suspicion that stymied progress.

I gathered that in their time, as in my time, the college's curriculum was essentially classics-driven, with English literature a close second. Science, in any shape or form, had no place in it. The beauty and wonders of nature, as expressed by the romantic poets, summarised most of what our respective generations knew about it. Educationally speaking, we were mired in the previous century, with the gaping blanks in our information filled by what, in retrospect, were old wives' tales, which, in the opinion of the Three Wise Men, were for the birds.

On the plus side, I'll credit the system with nurturing a literary clime unfettered by the empirical perspectives of science, which rarely come to grips with the soul, while ring-fencing the imagination – the launching pad of poetry. Few will deny that the bards and balladeers of Abbeylaune helped raise the spirits of the jobless with their songs and lyrics, even if they couldn't provide a single job. Hence the brain drain and the irreparable loss to the town of its youth.

Determined to change all that, the Three Wise Men – an

engineer, a shopkeeper and a journalist – finally arranged, I've been told, a meeting with the president of the college, a formal man of the cloth whose views commanded a respect that owed as much to his position as to their worth.

He hosted the meeting, of which I was given a blow by blow account in later years, in his plush study, which was lined with burnished bookshelves stocked with rare Greek and Latin texts and precious, leather-bound works of the romantic poets.

'Well, gentlemen, what can I do for you?' he commenced with a brisk, business-like air, his tone however, hinting of impatience.

'A little matter to do with the curriculum,' the engineer, a sturdy, forthright man, was the first to speak.

'Ah, the curriculum! I wasn't quite sure what precisely you meant when I read your letter,' the tall, imposing head of the college responded condescendingly.

The engineer got straight to the point.

'We've come to discuss the possibility of having it brought up to date with the inclusion of science.'

'And why science, might I ask.' The president, I was told, eyed him suspiciously.

'Well to begin with, many students going on to third level colleges are at a decided disadvantage in not having done physics and chemistry,' the engineer explained.

'I wouldn't have thought so.' The president, I learned, began to drum on the polished surface of the conference table. Not exactly a good omen, as most of his former students would have known.

A surprised, but resolute engineer was not put off by the academic's apathy.

'We'd also like to think that, should the curriculum cater for it, it would encourage more students to pursue a career in the sciences,' he persisted.

The president stopped drumming and sat bolt upright.

'And what's so special about the sciences?' The classicist looked critically at their proponent who, by now, must have felt a little overwhelmed by the heady scent of waxed floors and the stately decor, proclaiming the exclusiveness of the surroundings and of their esteemed incumbent.

It was Nolan, the plump proprietor of the leading hardware store in Abbeylaune, who responded to the question.

'If we're ever to promote an entrepreneurial spirit in this town, it will have to start with the educational system.' The words bolted from his lips after years of imprisonment.

The president cast a chilling gaze at him, then asked him to explain himself.

'I'm talking, Father, about the town's crying need for industrial development.'

'You're talking, I gather, about a factory.' The drumming started again.

The hardware merchant nodded and went on to affirm that in view of the shift from agricultural to manufacturing industry, a factory was a must if emigration were to be curbed.

The president, I gathered, frowned, then held himself erect as he pronounced, with an air of infallibility, that the addition of science to the curriculum wouldn't make one iota of difference to that objective.

Nolan, as I would expect, stuck to his guns.

'With respect, Father, shop-keeping has failed to provide sufficient jobs for our youth.'

'Mind you, it has served us well.' The clerical son of a retailer continued to have faith in it, even as the trio shook their heads in unison.

A rebuffed Nolan refused to back down.

'As we see it, the chances are that a scientifically educated community could well give rise to an entrepreneur who'll save Abbeylaune from the misery of unemployment and emigration.'

'And if not? And there's no guarantee it will.' The president met optimism with scepticism.

'At least we'll have an educated workforce in the event of an outsider setting up a factory here.' The merchant's confidence was not shared so far by a stalling president, hopelessly entrenched, I was given to believe, in his ivory, academic tower.

'And what do you think, Mr Doran?' He directed an imperious glance at the third member of the delegation, a life-long champion of causes in his newspaper articles.

'I'd be singing more or less from the same hymn sheet. Except…'

'Except?' The president adopted a more commanding posture.

'As I see it, science is also a language and a way of seeing things denied to your students by the current curriculum,' the bespectacled journalist replied.

The president, I was told, pulled a contemptuous face.

'I'm surprised at you, a man of words, lauding the technical jargon of science. What scientist ever spoke about nature like Wordsworth? Or expressed the horrors of the Industrial Revolution like Dickens?'

'That maybe so, but attributing thunder storms to the wrath of God and bad luck to superstition, rather than to natural causes, is the mindset of the Dark Ages.'

In retrospect, the journalist must have sounded agnostic to the cleric's ears.

At this point, I learned, a maid intruded discreetly with an offer of tea and withdrew as promptly when there were no takers.

The meeting back on track, the president assured Mr Doran

there was more to heaven and earth than science conceives, and that the Greek myths have served us well as our cultural road maps for centuries.

The journalist nodded respectfully while clinging to his convictions.

'I'm sure there is, and I'm not for one minute suggesting that science has all the answers. But it's the way forward. And right now it's pioneering new discoveries that I feel students should know about.'

The president grimaced with disapproval, then proceeded to bombard him with objections, which have been repeated over drinks right down to my time.

'Like the Big Bang theory that rejects the Book of Genesis! Not to mention the destructive secrets of nuclear power. I don't imagine, Mr Doran, that you'd fancy another Hiroshima?' He glowered at the science enthusiast, who realised his adversary was more formidable than he anticipated.

'Heaven forbid, Father.' The journalist would confess to me years later how, for once, he felt pinned down by the presidential firepower.

'Or perhaps you're prepared to accept a materialistic biology that takes no account of the soul, or the scientific doctrine that denies that the universe has a purpose, contaminating our curriculum?' The president continued to pound him.

The journalist was about to give up when the outspoken engineer cut in: 'If we continue to turn our backs on science, we'll end up resorting to Biddy Early's bottle.'

'And without manufacturing industries we'll continue to depend on imports,' the shopkeeper rowed in.

The president brushed aside their submissions with a dismissive wave of his beringed finger.

'As it stands, we have a clean, healthy environment. And long may it continue.' He expressed no wish to live in a local version of the Black Country or the Ruhr Valley – the heavily polluted heartlands of heavy industry – and left his seat to bang a window shut on the intrusive din from a nearby forge.

It was the hardware merchant, I gathered, who returned fire.

'You can't live on fresh air, Father. Without a factory this town is finished. After all, this is the Lemass, not the De Valera era. So why not sow the seeds of a prosperous, new future for the community by introducing science to the curriculum?'

Much to everyone's annoyance, the academic shook his head.

'Science, gentlemen, has made the world a more dangerous and more irreligious place than ever.'

A recovered journalist looked the smug figure on the plush, leather chair in the eye.

'That may well be, Father. But the idea of Socrates contemplating the stars from a suspended chair as the ideal of education is all very fine, but it's hardly going to put bread on the table.'

The president responded with a nod of disapproval.

'Was he not the wisest man on earth?' he said.

From what I heard in later years, he appeared to have heard enough .

Glancing at the Queen Anne clock on the marble mantelpiece, he explained that he had a meeting to attend, whereupon he rose abruptly from his chair and discreetly, but firmly, led the Three Wise Men to the door, thanking them for their interest while insisting that only the classics and literature could deliver a proper education.

Such was their respect for the cloth, I gathered, that they left it at that. Abbeylaune, unlike its more enterprising, industrialised counterparts, went into a rapid decline. It was heart-breaking to see the unemployment figures soar and the town being depleted of its youth, its beauty and its talent year-in, year-out. Not surprising, it remained untouched for another generation by that entrepreneurial spirit that gives communities the kiss of life.

When my classmate, Andrew, the genius of our final year in the college, got his hand on Darwin's *Origin of Species*, I could see at first hand the disturbing effects that science can have on one. I listened to him repudiate the Book of Genesis, then dismiss the Garden of Eden and subsequently, though briefly, drop out of church attendance. Having sampled that book, he was in open revolt during religious classes, challenging an uninformed teacher who should have known better than to dismiss his views out of hand.

Eventually summoned to the president's office, Andrew was lucky, I believe, not to have been expelled. Like Galileo, when confronted by the Inquisition, he retracted publicly what he continued to hold fast to privately. Having come to hear about Andrew's revolt, even the Three Wise Men began to wonder if the wily, old president hadn't been right after all. For them, too, God made the world in six calendar days. And the human race descended, unquestionably, not from primates, but from Adam and Eve. It was the dogma of their day and they ran with it. And anyone who, like Andrew, didn't, was considered a heretic.

If the three wise men privately harboured any doubts to the contrary, they refused to say so. Conformity in matters of this kind was not up for negotiation then – a regrettable state of affairs, that resulted for generations in a clampdown on essential new ideas.

Regrettably, we would have to wait for Teilhard de Chardin's appealing new perspective on Evolution before the president finally did a u-turn. Such was his regard for the celebrated French Jesuit, that he became, overnight, a convert to science.

Confident that it was in safe hands, he promptly sought funding for a college laboratory from the Department of Education. With the advent of a new curriculum, the foundation stones of a future, progressive Abbeylaune were laid.

Like so many local prophets, the Three Wise Men would have one foot in the grave before receiving the recognition they richly deserved for their foresight. Gladly, they'd live to see their dream come through when a brilliant young entrepreneur, who was a former science student of the college, set up a major food processing factory, which would bring employment and prosperity to a dying town that suddenly rose like the proverbial phoenix from its medieval ashes.

The industrial revolution, having finally caught up with Abbeylaune, would prepare the way for the digital one and, subsequently, the Celtic Tiger.

Would it have happened, I've often wondered, without science figuring in the college's curriculum? Suffice, that future generations were saved by that factory – the trail-blazer for others – from the heart-break of emigration and from that sense of hopelessness that for too long had dogged our community.

To that historic factory I, too, have been indebted for having met there my beloved, who rescued me from the fate of those hapless bachelors who had missed the bridal boat in the destitute days of the town.

Having cut its industrial teeth, Abbeylaune, despite the grumblings of the eco watch-dogs, and the sentimental hankerings of the elders for the old days, has never looked back.

Remaining stand-still, you'll agree, is simply not an option.

RICH IN THE GRAVE

It wasn't until he had left his relaxed post at Dwyer's that Joe realised what he had missed. By then there was no going back – not with Imelda holding the gun to his head.

Ten years he had worked at Dwyer's. Ten laid-back years, during which he seldom raised a sweat and could never recall being even remotely stressed, anymore than his father, who had worked there in a similar manner, and his grandfather too, making for an easy-going family dynasty. It came as no surprise when Joe decided, though he was capable of better, to follow in their footsteps soon after he'd left school.

Dwyer's, he soon realised and came to accept, was not for the aspiring. Fine, if you made it to managerial level. But only those with long service and extra drive landed the few plum posts that, in return, carried extra responsibilities, visible at times on the tense features of the incumbents. Dedicated men, whose tireless efforts kept the firm on course, and the boss – a pushy, cigar-toting businessman – happy. And happy he must be, Joe figured, watching his business grow from its modest beginnings into a creditable enterprise.

Joe opted for the scenic route until Imelda changed all that after she'd got him up the aisle. A mutation unlike anything previously in his lineage was about to take him by storm.

Fresh from their honeymoon, a previously undemanding Imelda revealed her true nature. If ever a marriage was suddenly chalk and cheese, it was theirs. The ambitious, spendthrift wife and the laid-back husband would prove an explosive cocktail, which would soon catapult the easy-going Joe out of his comfort zone.

'What did I do to deserve this?' he'd exclaim, as the bills for this and that began to queue for his attention, sending his adrenalin shooting through the roof.

If his romancing of the alluring Imelda had been blind, their marriage would prove a stark eye-opener. Her carefully cultivated charm–cum-sex appeal disguised, up to now, a Jekyll and Hyde. The suddenness of her sea-change convinced him that she had kept her true colours under wraps until she had hooked him – a reliable enough bloke, but needing the skids to be put under him, which she set about in no uncertain manner from day one of their union. Confirmation of their first child on the way gave added impetus to her mission.

'Dwyer's is a dead end.' She was brutally blunt with him one frustrating week-end when the figures didn't tally with her designer aspirations.

He shrugged helplessly, then rallied to his job's defence.

'At least it's secure,' he said. Not programmed for hardship, it was as much as he had ever wanted.

'So is the dole,' she snapped. 'And with all the perks that go with it, you wouldn't be faring much worse than you are now.'

He looked aghast at her.

'You're not suggesting I give up work and go on the labour?'

Her expression was a snapshot of disapproval.

'Of course not. I couldn't bear having you under my feet day after day.'

'So what are you on about?' He had an uncomfortable feeling

recently that she was hatching a punishing game plan for him .

'That you apply for a position as a van driver. We simply cannot manage on your present income.'

He nodded half-heartedly.

'I can try. But I wouldn't give much for my chances.'

'Ask!' she commanded him, as if Dwyer catered on demand for everyone according to their needs and not their seniority. 'There are perks going with it, like overtime and tips, which would help us to furnish the house. And you're well able to drive.'

Ask, Joe did, for the sake of peace with Imelda. One bleak, February morning he mustered the temerity to set foot in the boss's office, where he could hear the rain pounding on the window pane, which overlooked the recently extended delivery yard. It was the first time he had ever been in that office with its ledgers and computers, and it was unsettling. It didn't help that Dwyer looked more aloof than usual. Or so Joe thought, unnerved at having crossed a forbidden line in a firm where the boss called the shots.

'So what can I do for you, young man?' An unusually brusque Dwyer must have sensed something untoward on the cards.

Joe could feel a tightening in his throat.

'I want to apply for a job as a van driver.'

'Van driver!' Dwyer roared in a declamatory tone.

A low-sized Joe felt himself shrinking in metres. He hoped his colleagues downstairs hadn't overheard the boss's put-down.

'You know how it is, sir: a big mortgage, a child on the way and the house only partly furnished.'

Dwyer relit his cigar and posted a plume of acrid smoke towards the stained ceiling.

'May I ask if your wife works?' he inquired.

'Part-time.' But spending as if she had won the lottery, he might have added.

'Then you shouldn't have any problems.' The boss believed that only men in his shoes had problems. Real problems. Which Joe didn't have until he married. And which his father and his father before him didn't have, because their wives cut their cloth to measure and were prepared to settle for much less than Imelda.

He realised that their problems were more of her making than Dwyer's. Nothing would do for her but state-of-the-art this and designer-labelled that, just to keep up with her peers at the Women's Club, while he performed unprecedented feats of juggling with his weekly pay to keep a costly roof over their heads.

'I can no longer manage on my wages,' Joe pleaded, the congested office feeling by now like a compression chamber.

The boss replaced his cigar on the ash-tray, gazed blankly at his employee, then shook his head .

'I'm sorry Joe, but there aren't any openings at the moment in the delivery section. And I don't see any sign of our senior drivers opting for early retirement. Besides, if that new chain store earmarked for the town materialises, I may even be forced to shed some staff. You get me?'

Joe nodded. He should have known better than to bother asking. It would be easier to rob a bank than to force Dwyer's hand in the circumstances. He was a stickler for protocol but, in fairness, a decent enough employer. At least Imelda couldn't accuse him of not trying.

'Pack it in! Dwyer's is no place for a young married man with ambitions,' she ordered him subsequently.

After a relaxed decade at Dwyer's, Joe's dormant energies were more suited to recreational ventures like pitch-and-putt, fishing and viewing the latest releases from his local video outlet on nights when he wasn't exercising his elbow at the Market bar. Living with his parents until recently ensured that the line of least resistance had sufficed to keep him comfortably afloat.

Like most of his colleagues, he carried his day and enjoyed the seasonal changes reflected by the big chestnut, with its choir of song birds, at the corner of the delivery yard, which he viewed from his counter in the hardware department. The various, national wage agreements took care of his modest needs. He slept comfortably. But suddenly he was sleeping less and less.

'It's easier said than done,' he protested, his attachment to Dwyer's still outweighing his marital obligations to support the glamorous Imelda in the manner of her friends, whom Joe regarded as rivals competing to upstage one another in the state-of-the-art stakes.

Annoyed, she reminded him how he had given her to believe he was an achiever while dating her.

'I mustn't have been sober,' he chuckled. Married, he reverted to type.

'Your problem is you're too damn sober. I want to see more fire in your veins. More get up and doing like the other young, married men in Abbeylaune.'

He pleaded for time. At least the bird-in-the-hand ensured he didn't have to sing for his supper so far, though his evening meal was fast approaching anorexic proportions, the small change from his pay packet befitting a vow of poverty, and his conjugal rights more often than not tantalisingly suspended, as Imelda grew more shrewish by the day.

'You've had plenty of time. Ten years at Dwyer's and what have you to show for it? It's high time you looked around for something better,' she screamed at him.

He knew, if he were to stay put, there would be no rest for him. An ad in the *Evening Herald* for a rep's job with Munster Products, a spanking new car going with it, threw him a lifeline.

Imelda suddenly made sense to him. It was get out now or remain mired at Dwyer's.

'You're right,' he admitted to her. 'It's time I stopped being an under-achiever.'

If variety was the spice of life, then his routine up to now, he agreed, was a recipe for a slow, if easeful, death. The lure of the open road and the novelty of different towns and people were suddenly irresistible.

Having landed the job, he broke with a long-standing family tradition when, much to his colleagues' disbelief, he handed in his notice to Dwyer and was given a rousing send-off and an invitation to return, should he ever change his mind.

He got off to an agreeable start. He had a way with people. His mercantile experience at Dwyer's stood to him, and he was enjoying the challenge and the adventure that were part and parcel of the job. If he missed the camaraderie of his colleagues, he preferred being his own boss. The BMW gave him added status and was a joy to drive. With a meal ticket, bonuses for extra sales, and a smart outfit at the firm's expense, the world was his oyster.

Initially, he came out with marginally more than he had at Dwyer's – something that Imelda was prepared to overlook until he got to know the ropes. In the meantime, she enjoyed the use of the BMW on week-ends and the occasional perk from the firm, like tickets for a show, which she loved to trumpet about at the Women's Club.

By the third month, she changed her tune.

'We cannot go on living on status, now that we have another mouth to feed,' she protested as she presented him with a worrying statement of her expenditure.

When he tried to explain that he was still on a learning curve, and competing with seasoned reps who had cornered the market, she didn't want to know.

'With youth and energy on your side, you can hold your own with the best of them.'

She gave him a reassuring hug, her kisses promising as yet uncharted bliss as soon as he delivered.

When his best was not good enough, he decided there was nothing for it but to ask for a rise. Having faced down his previous boss, he felt less uptight about approaching his current one – a polite, accessible gentleman whom he had been advised, however, not to underrate. Well briefed by Imelda, he was confident of a better showing this time than with Dwyer.

His *tête-à-tête*, with Mr Jackson began agreeably. His new employer was disarmingly tactful. Instead of hitting you with a blank refusal like, 'out of the question', or a thunderous, declamatory 'what!' which effectively had you jumping out of your seat and looking for the nearest exit, he engaged in more subtle diplomacy.

It soon became clear to Joe that Mr Jackson was a past master of negotiations of this kind and that he himself was merely a novice. Lacking the skills and the persistence that wring bargains from reluctant employers, he was effectively a push-over. When a wily Jackson politely inquired what time he started work, an unwitting Joe replied nine o'clock.

'And if you don't mind me asking, how much time do you set aside for breaks?' the boss gazed benignly at him, his expensive suit and his Rolex watch, confirming for Joe, the legend with whom he was dealing.

'Generally half an hour for elevenses and an hour for lunch.'

'And you finish at what time?' The gaze a little less benign, but still agreeable.

An unsuspecting Joe replied, 'generally around five o'clock'.

'Fair enough.'

Joe believed that all was going according to plan as he watched the boss remove the lid of his expensive Parker pen and do a quick calculation on his notepad. At least his office was so much more cheerful than Dwyer's dingy lair, which resonated of parsimony. And he was listened to, instead of being shouted down.

'As I see it, your time-table is your problem.' The boss quickly grasped his problem.

'Really? But…'

Before he could advance his viewpoint, Mr Jackson intruded firmly.

'You're working as if you were in a nine-to-five job. That's basically your problem.'

Joe managed to squeeze in his reason.

'I assumed when I got the job that I could work out my own schedules.'

The boss smiled, then continued to edify his new recruit.

'As a former rep, I'm merely offering you my prescription for success and for enhanced, financial dividends.'

Joe had no objection to being his understudy. Respectfully, he listened to Mr Jackson – a successful, self-made man – speaking from hard-earned experience, then observed him do another quick calculation on his notepad before spelling out his winning formula.

'All the successful reps of my acquaintance were early birds,' he recalled, adding that he was regularly on the road by six a.m.

Joe wasn't sure if he were hearing rightly. 'But places are closed at that hour,' he protested lightly.

'I said on the road. By the time you reach your outlying clients you can bet they'll be open for business. Big firms in particular. And don't you ever forget you're in competition with other early birds in the business. Do I make sense?'

Joe glanced at his Rolex, then nodded.

'Then perhaps you'll give it a try,' he said.

A convinced Joe got to his feet and thanked the boss for his advice and his time. It wasn't quite what he had in mind, but coming from an incredibly successful rep in his day, Joe was prepared to put his blueprint to the test. Perhaps Imelda's claim that he was still suffering from Dwyer's syndrome had more than a whiff of truth about it. Well, he was going to show her.

Strictly an afternoon man, he initially found the early start on inclement wintry mornings pure penance that, far from whetting his appetite for success, brought home to him how much he missed his relaxed constitutional to and from Dwyer's, which, even on the gloomiest of days, was brightened by the banter of the townsfolk.

He accepted there was no going back. With two children now to fend for and Imelda's demands unabated, there was simply no room for nostalgia of that kind.

While his new time-table made for improved returns, it fell well short, so far, of the crock of gold the boss had predicted. Spurred by the need to make ends meet more than the dream of hitting it rich, he soldiered on, coping with fatigue and fickle clients, not to mention fierce competition from a new breed of university whiz kids, armed to the teeth with marketing techniques. Still, he reasoned, if Jackson succeeded, there was no reason why he shouldn't.

Keeping faith with well-tried techniques and his growing ability, he charmed deals from female clients where others would have failed, while wringing purchases from their male counterparts by tapping into their sporting and political preferences gleaned from fellow reps over drinks. Besides, he had what many of the whiz-kids didn't: the common touch, as well as hands-on experience from his time at Dwyer's.

Gradually he mastered the art of being all things to all men, changing his political loyalties more often than his clothes to suit certain customers, and his sporting ones to suit others. Knowing the power of humour, he had more jokes to hand than a stand-up comedian. So convincing were his well-honed, commercial gems that he wrestled deals from skin-flints, while his repertoire of compliments, reserved for business women, would have earned him ladies' man of the year. They were survival techniques he had not needed at Dwyer's, where his job was predictable and safe.

Suddenly, things were looking up as the Celtic Tiger began to spread its tentacles down the country, resulting in an unprecedented construction boom that boded well for him.

Never more hopeful, he continued to hit the road at six a.m. in all moods and weathers, achieving ever greater sales and increased commissions and, eventually, salesman of the month.

To keep Imelda sweet, he surprised her with a handsome sum, which he had received from a colleague in exchange for his coveted prize – a week-end for two in a five-star hotel in London.

Thrilled, she sang: 'I always knew you had what it takes,' and showered him with kisses.

His worries would soon be over now that the El Dorado he dreamed of was suddenly materialising for him, as the property boom went into over-drive. With towns and villages expanding into housing estates, Joe's order book was full beyond his wildest expectations.

An elated Imelda rejoiced that he was living up to her belief in him, as they enjoyed foreign holidays, designer-this-and-that, as well as meals in expensive restaurants, while no expense was spared on the house and the children.

It would be her turn to hold bragging rights at the Women's

Club, in return for which, she rewarded him liberally with what men most desire.

Impressed by his spectacular success, his former colleagues at Dwyer's regretted not having followed in his footsteps. Not that it was all the bed of roses they imagined. Far from it.

If they had to settle for a fraction of his income they were, however, spared the mounting pressures to which he was increasingly subjected. Dashing from one town to the next in pursuit of orders, and chasing up debtors faltering in their payments, it was frequently a case of snatched meals and forty winks on a lay-by to save himself from nodding off behind the wheel.

His children, more often than not, were in bed when he got home and his cherished sporting pastimes had to be put on hold. It was a question of capitalising on the boom which everyone knew wouldn't last, and making the proverbial killing in the market while the going was good. It was the way of business and he ran with it, regardless of the human cost.

On New Year's Eve, while speeding past the Regional Hospital, he suffered a massive heart attack. Thankfully, it happened where it did. Minutes meant the difference between life and death. With three little mouths to feed and Imelda's soaring demands to be met, it was imperative he should get back on his feet quickly.

While his firm stood by him during his convalescence, it soon became clear that his days on the road were over. Wracked with anxiety about his family's welfare, he felt gutted and embittered over the cruel hand he had been dealt just when everything was going his way. Then, remembering the fate of two of his fellow reps who had been killed instantly in car crashes, he realised the story could have been worse.

Recovering slowly from a triple by-pass that put paid to his dreams and brought Imelda to her senses, they both realised that there had to be more to life than the pursuit of Mammon. It was the wake-up call that would turn them spiritually around.

'Sitting around feeling sad for ourselves, will get us nowhere,' Imelda declared one morning. She decided it was her turn to bring home the bacon. Updating her computer skills, she acquired a secretarial job with the local credit union where she had previously been one of the leading customers.

When Joe sufficiently recovered, he applied for a job with his old firm and was given the prodigal's welcome by a supportive Dwyer.

'There will always be an open door here for you. I haven't forgotten how your father, and his father before him, worked here. And if your sons should ever want to, they'll be welcome as well. But you appreciate that you'll have to settle for considerably less than you've been earning with Munster Products, now that the Celtic Tiger is winding down,' Dwyer reminded him before taking him on.

Joe jumped at the offer, and, with a song in his heart, went to join his colleagues, with whom he fitted in seamlessly in the hardware department, where nothing seemed to have changed. He thanked his stars that the chain store had not materialised; otherwise, he might well have been singing for his supper.

Through an open window, he could hear the familiar choir in the big chestnut and the cheerful rustle of summer in its leaves again – a summer he would enjoy with Imelda and their children, with whom he would have more time to play, now that he was freed from his punishing schedules to meet crippling targets.

Grateful to be alive, he realises that there isn't much point in being rich in the grave.

THE NEW FOOTBALL BOOTS

While placing a present of football boots for my grandson beneath the Christmas tree, I remembered Seán Mulvey's late uncle returning from England with a pair of spanking, new Supremos for him. News of their arrival spread like wild-fire throughout our neighbourhood. In those penny-pinching days, only professional soccer players across the water could afford football boots of that calibre. Most Gaelic footballers, who could afford boots – and not everyone could – settled for Blackthorns – reliable kickers, if suggestive of Clydesdales rather than the thoroughbreds that the Supremos brought to mind.

In retrospect – the forerunners of the sterling Nike and Adidas brands, which are the standard boots of today's Celtic Tiger generation. Low-cut, light-weight, and with a toe-cap that would kick a dead ball into space, they were every sportsman's dream then, rather than reality, due to their prohibitive price. Now, enviably, Seán's – a belated Christmas box resulting from post-war shortages – but as luck, or ill-luck, would have it, they were on cue for our 'friendly' that Easter with Kilown, who regarded us as rustics and themselves as townies, living as they did on the outskirts of Abbeylaune.

To refer to those encounters with Kilown as ' friendlies', would, in retrospect, be an inaccuracy. From my recollection they were more like wars of attrition. Frequently, on our way home from school, we squared off with our adversaries and boxed for the pride of our respective communities. Currently, Kilown had the edge at football. But that was all about to change, courtesy of the Supremos.

As we gathered around, feeling their texture, testing them for flexibility and marvelling at the breath-taking craftsmanship that went into their making, we sensed victory in the air.

'I can picture Kilown's goalie clutching air as your raspers fly past him,' Malone exclaimed as he scrutinised the cogs. His comment might have been taken from *Champion*, our favourite sport's comic.

'With these boots, we'll beat the socks off them,' Seán declared, with a resolute look that suggested his game was about to move up a gear or two.

'I can't believe you wear two sizes bigger than me!' I heard Kinsella exclaim, as he measured them against his own hobnails.

Seán shot him a derogatory look.

'Why not? Aren't you smaller than me, you gawm.'

'Then how come Sheehan takes a smaller size than you?' Kinsella couldn't figure either, seeing he was taller than Seán, who was too busy lacing his boots to answer him.

'He'll be a lot smaller by the time we've finished with him. And don't spare his ankles with those boots,' O'Connor prompted Seán while testing their toe-caps.

I didn't like what O'Connor had in mind. He was a rough diamond, bristling with aggression that drew him into frequent scraps with his Kilown counterparts, who needed no encouragement to fight.

'I don't think we should let them know about the boots until Seán sets foot on the pitch,' O'Keefe suggested, as he assessed the ankle-pads.

Everyone, with the exception of yours truly, agreed that the element of surprise could work in our favour. And that an unsuspecting Sheehan would feel intimidated by the boots. I knew him better, but I kept my counsel, careful not to dispel the optimism that was driving our team.

'We're going to put Kilown in their box,' Seán declared, as he fitted on the boots.

Though they looked the real deal, I was less convinced than the others about their worth. I figured it would require some time for Seán to get used to them. And that this 'friendly' was at too short notice for comfort. Besides, I believed it was the wearer, not the boots, no matter how acclaimed, who really mattered. Otherwise, I reasoned, any gobdaw in possession of a pair would be a top-flight footballer.

My doubts were not shared by my team-mates, who accepted at face value the mythic powers imputed to them by the *Champion*. I'd have to wait and see if they made any difference to Seán's game. And if anyone would put the Supremos to the test it would be Kilown and their ace, Sheehan.

Kitted out in togs that were too long or too short for us, with faded, patched jerseys belonging mostly to older brothers, and boots the worse for wear, we must have looked a motley squad as we set off on foot that unforgettable Sunday afternoon for the appointed venue.

As far as we were concerned, the only item of gear that really mattered to us was the Supremos, concealed in a knapsack until the last possible minute, in the hope of springing a surprise on the opposition.

As teams go, Kilown had a pretty fearsome reputation. Hard hitting, they made liberal use of the elbow and engaged in a lot of nasty stuff behind the ref's back.

Not that our team were all saints either. We had our hard chaws like O'Connor, but we generally played clean football, aware that, if we resorted to the rough tactics of the opposition, we'd come off second best.

And it paid off, for I never remember any member of our team receiving a ticking from the ref or being sidelined for dirty play. The same could not be said of Kilown. In Griffin's words, they were a bunch of hackers, who tried to win by foul or fair means.

Our captain's last minute appeal that we keep a close watch on Sheehan – that he was 'dynamite' – met with a chorus of approval that suggested he was speaking to the converted.

'He can score with both feet, which makes him very hard to mark,' I heard Kinsella warn.

'And he's deadly in the air,' Griffin added.

'A county minor for sure before long,' O'Neill predicted.

I watched Seán frown defiantly.

'So what? As yet he's only a juvenile,' he rejoined, vowing he'd run him ragged and give him a lesson in Gaelic football.

'Hear! Hear!' we cheered him. By now, I too was beginning to believe in the efficacy of boots.

O'Connor's final reminder to Seán not to spare Sheehan's shins caused me to shudder. It would be inviting retaliation. And I feared what that would be.

Besides, I wouldn't like to see Sheehan hurt, for I had a secret crush on his sister Marian, whom I sat beside at school and fantasised about after school. Even though she relied on me for her maths, she had a figure and looks that blew me over.

By the time we got to the pitch Kilown were already kitted out in their stylish regalia and working out their moves. I noticed some slick passing, well-drilled positional play and the use of the high delivery to the lanky, lightning-fast Sheehan – a joy to watch if you didn't have to mark him and, unless the Supremos worked miracles, a headache in store for Seán – a useful player in his own right, but not in the other's league.

Much to our dismay, Kilown didn't seem to mind Seán's new boots. I concluded they were either too over-awed and didn't want to show it, or too under-awed to be concerned. Initially, at any rate, they pretended to ignore them, which annoyed Seán, who wanted them to be admired and feared and to work miracles for him against a superior Kilown, captained by a future, county minor prospect.

Instead, they jeered our tatty gear and vowed they'd kick us all the way back to Doire while the captains faced off for the toss, which we won, our side opting to play with the wind – a light, April breeze – and with the slope favoured, coincidentally, by it.

As for the latter preference, some perceived it to be towards the moor, while others thought it was the opposite, and others still were convinced it was non-existent, the field, in their opinion, being as flat as the proverbial pancake. I held my tongue for fear of adding to pre-match confusion, not to mention post-match recriminations.

With the wind and gradient, real or imaginary, on our side, we got off to a flying start. What we hadn't calculated on was the sun, a glaring disc shining with the blinding clarity of a search-light that effectively rendered our target – two bundles of clothes so many strides apart – practically invisible. It was a serious oversight on our part and one that would cost us dearly as the game progressed.

'We shoulda brought sun-glasses,' Kinsella said over his shoulder to me.

'Or picked a dull day, more suited to yer drab football,' Bruiser Brady, who was marking me, taunted, hoping I would retaliate physically.

Instead, I snatched the ball from his brittle grasp and laid it off to Seán, who recorded his first score – a beaut of a long-range point. Another spectacular point gave him an aura of invincibility. And if it weren't for the sun blinding him, he'd have put the game beyond Kilown's reach early on, despite Sheehan's growing mastery at midfield.

Such were the Kilown ace's aerial talents, his sure hands and his elusive range of dummies, that he left his markers flat-footed and frustrated. I watched anxiously as his deft, long-range passes and scintillating solo runs had our backs reeling and in disarray.

Soon Kilown were level. And a jubilant Marian Sheehan was cheering for my opponent, despite all the help I'd given her with her long division. Yet, it was for her as much as for Doire I played out of my skin that afternoon, giving the Bruiser the run-around, and laying off pint-point passes to Seán who seemed suddenly to be having trouble with his boots, shooting inexplicably and to our dismay, wide of Kilown's goalpost time and again.

When Sheehan put the ball between our two clothes' stacks from midfield, the Kilown supporters, now swollen to a crowd, went wild. That score, in my book, had all the trademarks of a future county star.

Even O'Connor began to flounder as Sheehan rode his heavy tackles like an ice breaker, and led him a merry dance, posting a further brace of spectacular points, to his marker's chagrin.

It was left to Seán to carry the can at centre-field. Whatever plusses the Supremos had on the ground, they were of little benefit in the air where Sheehan ruled the roost.

It saddened me to see an out-classed Seán becoming increasingly deflated as the game went on. The much-hyped boots had ceased to contribute anything further to the score-sheet. To add to his misery, the Kilown supporters were jeering him and calling him

Puss-in-Boots while Sheehan, in his frayed, canvas sandals, was kicking rings around him.

Reading the game from the relative comfort of the wing, where I'd been giving Bruiser a torrid time, it became clear to me that unless Seán could pull something off quickly, Doire would be disgraced and his vaunted boots become a joke.

The taunting must have got to him, for I've never seen such resolve in his expression. When Sheehan grabbed a kick-out way above his head, Seán drove at him with such venom that the ball went flying from his adversary's grasp and sped off ahead of them. Tensely, I watched them as they raced for it, the fleet-footed Sheehan getting to it first. As he stooped to pick it up, Seán administered a slide tackle, connecting – accidentally, he swears, though the opposition believed it was deliberate – with the other's ankle, rather than the ball. The agonised screams from the up-ended, prospective county minor brought the outraged Kilown supporters charging onto the pitch .

It would have been curtains for Seán, and probably for the rest of us, if we hadn't made a run for it to the safety of the moor – that no man's land that separated our two communities. Breathless, we raced through its terrifying expanse pursued by what now had become a mob, screaming vengeance and raining missiles upon us. Even O'Connor, for all his bravado, was scared stiff and Seán's Supremos, now cutting into his heels, were more of a liability than an asset in his frantic flight.

It was a classic rout, with every man for himself, as we tore in disarray through thickets of heather and soft, peaty soil, where some got their shoes stuck and had to run barefoot, as the mob closed in on us like a wolf-pack.

Lambs to the slaughter we'd have been, but for a swamp that Griffin knew a way around, leaving our pursuers knee-deep in it, and waist-deep as they proceeded further, and beyond which, even the most reckless among them ceased to venture out of concern for their safety. Mercifully they withdrew – winners and, in turn, losers, for though we lost the match, we won the race.

It was only when we got back to Doire that I realised I'd left my football after me. A quality, hand-sewn gem for which I'd saved for over a year, now in the possession of our opponents from whom I'd never retrieve it, after what Seán did.

I recall feeling more sorry for him than for myself as I watched the tears welling up in his eyes, while he ruefully assessed the damage to his boots, now soaking and fouled, and to his feet that were chafed and hurting.

'The Supremos are a write off,' he sobbed bitterly.

In vain, we tried to console him, for nothing would convince him they'd ever be the same again. As far as he was concerned, they were as tarnished as his reputation.

'You hadn't broken them properly in,' I heard Griffin apologising for their failure to live up to their billing.

We agreed they'd take getting used to, while his mother scrubbed them and placed them over the range to dry.

'The next time we play them you'll dance rings around Sheehan.' Kinsella's confidence in the Supremos was undiminished.

'And don't forget to dance on his ankles,' O'Connor chortled, though he got no hearing, for we all knew how badly Seán felt about his tackle.

I distinctly remember my heart river-dancing in my ribcage when Marian strode into the school yard the following day with my treasured, leather football, which she handed to me apologetically. Much to the dismay of my team-mates, I gave her what, in retrospect, was an impulsive kiss. It would the first of many, having fallen more in love with her than with football, which I continued to play to keep the respect of the Kilown players, who initially resented me, but eventually came to accept me, now that I was a boyfriend of their hero's sister.

We didn't have long to wait for the phenomenal Sheehan to regale us with a stunning display for our county before a packed Croke Park, kicking points from impossible angles and hitting the roof of the net with a rocket-like penalty that won him his first All Ireland medal.

A prodigious talent, he would unite Doire and Kilown in his support, his neat feet fitting perfectly into Seán's classy Supremos, while their proud owner, glued to the radio, basked in a vicarious glory, which is still etched in my memories: the nest egg I rely on to see me through the rainy days of uneventful old age.

THE ELOPEMENT

When Grace Lovett and Dermot Lawless eloped on the early Dublin-bound train from Abbeylaune, they felt they were doing the right thing.

Holding hands, they nestled like love-birds in the sun-drenched carriage, rejoicing as the procession of villages, the last vestiges of their captivity, receded like episodes from their anxious past. Then their lips met tenderly, sealing a love-pact for which they had taken a considerable risk.

They were approaching the Midlands when Grace succumbed to doubts, which she thought she had put to rest.

'I trust we're not taking leave of our senses.' Strange towns and unfamiliar landscapes sowed seeds of uncertainty in her mind.

'No way. We had no other option,' Dermot insisted, as decisive as he was handsome.

'I hope Mum won't be too upset.' It was something she hadn't given much thought to up to now.

'She'll understand,' he assured her.

'And your Mum?'

He smiled. 'What she doesn't know won't trouble her.'

Grace laughed. They were so different, yet so attracted. She remembered the first time she set eyes on him: he was installing some electrical sockets in her bedroom. It was love at first sight.

They had been dating secretly when Finian, her father, came to know about it. He reacted swiftly, ordered Dermot to stop seeing her and ensured that Grace, just gone sixteen, stayed indoors at night-time and kept to her studies. Two fraught years would pass before they were finally driven to this.

Thurles, Portarlington, Portlaoise. Pick-up points for people leaving for the metropolis of promise that she and Dermot had long set their sights on, like so many of their generation. But first she had to complete her Leaving Cert – the indispensable safety net for the precarious years ahead – and he, his apprenticeship.

In the meantime, their courtship became clandestine, confined to brief but rapturous dates in the pine-wood that bordered on her father's property on the outskirts of the town. She would steal out to be with Dermot when the family was asleep, trip across the dew-laden meadow and glide like a faun into his waiting arms. In the fastness of the wood, their love grew, became defiant, demanded public assent.

'Tickets please!' A brisk conductor checked theirs and wished them a pleasant journey. They thanked him, keeping their exchanges to a minimum and discouraging any familiarity that might lead to their discovery. Knowing the kind of man Finian was, both were aware they would have to watch their backs for awhile.

The sooner they got to Dublin the better. They had had their fill of evasion and could take no more. Grace would never forget the scene her father had made on hearing that she and Dermot had been to a dance. She had defied him, been disloyal. He read her the riot act. Determined not to be outwitted again, he became more vigilant, watching her every move.

From then on, they had to settle for the odd date in the pine-wood, where they watched the seasons come and go, the fox creep out at night for prey, the pine needles form a carpet of rust beneath their feet, which were itching to get away from an unrelenting Finian.

Grace sat her Leaving Certificate exams and, having completed his apprenticeship, Dermot made a successful application for a post with an electrical firm in Dublin. They decided without further ado to up and leave.

'Let's get some breakfast,' he suggested, and escorted her to the dining car.

'Just in case we'll have to eat our hearts out when Dad finds us,' she joked, looking very attractive in her bright summer-wear.

'No way.' Dermot was confidant. Resourceful and free-spirited, he coped with crises in his stride – hence his appeal for the less adventurous Grace.

Their first brush with Dublin during the mid-day rush, was intimidating. Such hustle and bustle! The pavements were thronged, the traffic crazy, the anonymous crowds spewing in and out of shops and offices. It was all so different to easy-going, friendly Abbeylaune.

'Can you ever see us adjusting to this?' Grace again succumbed to doubt.

'Of course I can,' Dermot said, his chin firmly set, his eyes ablaze with the spirit of adventure.

They spent their first night in a B&B. The following day, they procured, with the assistance of the owner, a suitably furnished flat in Rathmines. Dermot made his debut with the electrical firm and Grace did a cursory tour of the big firms that took her breath away. Dublin, she was thrilled, lived up to everything she had imagined in this regard.

As yet she could only afford to fantasize about the stunning range of fashions that greeted her everywhere, begging to be purchased. The pleasure she derived during those early days, riffling through racks of clothes and fitting on dazzling footwear in search of a bargain, was unspeakable. She couldn't wait to get a job and go on a buying binge.

In response to an ad, she managed to land holiday work with the accounts department at Dodders.

Soon, she and Dermot were sampling the popular bars and cafés, enjoying a rock concert at the stadium, and a much-hyped film that might never make it to Abbeylaune.

'I'm glad to see you've no longer any regrets about burning your boats,' he observed with satisfaction.

She nodded positively.

Dublin, she realized, bristled with possibilities. Dermot's colleagues were supportive and friendly. Caught up in a roller coaster of entertainment, any lingering concerns she might otherwise have had about leaving home soon evaporated. She was finally her own woman, having the time of her life and more in love with Dermot than ever.

When Finian Lovett heard that Grace had flown the coop that evening he went berserk, stormed about the kitchen thundering vengeance, and brought his fist down with a smash on the dining table as if Dermot were the recipient of the blow. A towering hulk of a man, few ever dared to cross him when he was roused. Apart from the odd, domestic flare-up, which usually spent itself in a transient torrent of emotion, he was an even-tempered and genuine family man.

'Take it easy, or you'll do harm to yourself,' his wife appealed.

A meek little woman, she had learned to cope with such outbursts.

'I'll tear his limbs apart,' he roared, manifesting with manic gestures his homicidal intentions.

She sighed, her helplessness serving to further infuriate him.

'I just can't figure what's got into Grace,' she exclaimed.

'You might, if you hadn't spoiled her.' His enraged bellow made her cower into her fireside chair.

'It was a sad day when that fellow crossed our door-step,' she whimpered.

'It'll be a sadder day when I get my hands on him. Over my dead body will he mix his seed and breed with my daughter's.'

Whereupon, he clapped his frayed hat on his head and stormed out of the house.

She could hear him revving the car frantically, then watched him speeding out of the farmyard like a lunatic.

When Finian rapped on Pat Lawless's door, it was his wife Nora who answered it, greeting him with a disarming welcome. She still retained some of those looks that turned many a man's head in her hey-day, and Finian recalled often dancing with her at the local hops in his youth and having a crush on her, which had not been reciprocated.

In later years, it often baffled him what a woman of her qualities could have seen in that dandified leprechaun of a tailor, Pat Lawless, for whom she bore the redoubtable Dermot – a dapper whipper–snapper whom Finian was determined to bring to book.

'Sit down, Finian, and make yourself at home while I make you a cup of tea. It must be years since we had a chat.'

She proffered him a chair, but he remained on his feet.

Determined not to allow his former feelings for her to temper his resolution, he refused her offer of tea, then bluntly asked:

'Where's himself?'

'Gone for a round of pitch and putt. 'Tis the only bit of exercise he gets these days.'

'He'd need to exercise some control over his son,' Finian barked.

Jolted, she inquired: 'What do you mean, Finian? Is there something the matter I should know about?

He glared at her in disbelief.

'Well you know there is. Well you know, Nora.'

'If there's something I should, but don't know, tell me for God's sake and maybe I can help.'

She reached out to him with convincing concern.

With a lump in his throat, he told her that Dermot had eloped with Grace. His voice had a ring of father's grief about it that registered with Nora.

'Don't tell me! Oh, dear God!' She covered her mouth with her hand.

Sensing he had a companion in distress, his gaze softened and his demeanour became less threatening. A supportive Nora drew closer and placed a compassionate hand on his shoulder.

'I want to put a halt to their gallop, Nora,' he resorted again to firmness. 'Nothing good can come of it. Grace is only a slip of a girl and still green in the ways of the world.'

She nodded sympathetically.

'I know how you feel, Finian. It's a sad day for me that a son of mine should do a thing like that. After all my rearing. So that's why he applied for a job in Dublin,' she let out.

'Did you say Dublin?' His ears snatched at the information.

While still nodding, she gave way to doubt.

'Now that you tell me they've eloped, sure 'tis to London or to Amsterdam they could have gone for all I know.'

'Oh, my God!' Finian exclaimed, suddenly racked with fears of Grace wrecking his plans for her by becoming pregnant before he could catch up with her.

'Have a cup of tea with me, Finian. I don't know what's come over the young people of to-day. The rock groups have driven them crazy.'

She placed the kettle on the hot plate of the range but at that moment tea was about the furthest thought from Finian's mind.

'I'm afraid I've no alternative but to contact the police,' he said and made for the door.

Throwing herself across his path, she appealed to him not to.

'It's up to you, Nora. So, what do you propose to do?' Moved to pity for the aggrieved woman standing before him, he stopped in his tracks.

She pleaded for time. Then promised that, as soon as she heard from Dermot, she would let him have his address.

'I'll wait, but not for long.' Finian knew there was little the police could do in the circumstance but played on Nora's fear of finding herself on the wrong side of the law.

Instead of returning home, he went straight to the presbytery, where he was received by Father Devine, the parish priest, who invited him in for a drink. As a leading contributor to the parish dues, and with a brother in the Jesuits, there was always a welcome at the presbytery for Finian. Before he left, he had the priest's assurance that in no circumstance would he provide Dermot and Grace with a Letter of Freedom.

A resourceful man, Finian was spurred to action where others would have bowed to adversity. He was at his most inventive when under duress.

When the postman called with the mail the following day, Finian sat him down to lunch. Their friendship went back a long way. They had played together with distinction on the Abbeylaune football team, and Finian liked nothing better than to reminisce over a snack in his spacious, farmhouse kitchen about the games they'd won.

He had been generous to the postman, too, at Christmas, and occasionally stood him a drink at their local. On this occasion, Finian decided to call in his debts.

During the meal he confided his grievance to a sympathetic Cunningham, who agreed to set aside postal ethics and duly report to his benefactor any correspondence from Dermot to his family.

'No better man!' Finian thanked him.

'Don't mention it,' Cunningham said.

Finian felt relieved, but come night, a procession of black feelings seeped like poison into his soul. The house, deprived of Grace's lively presence and the lilt of her laughter, had the empty ring of a tomb. Rankled by her betrayal, he seethed privately. His wife's pathetic response, coupled with his son's seeming indifference to his plight, served, if anything, to cast doubts upon their loyalty when he most needed their support.

Only with the help of a well fortified night-cap could he manage some sleep.

Meanwhile, in Rathmines, things began to come a cropper for the elopers.

'Is there something needling you, Grace?' Dermot inquired, seeing her brooding one evening.

'I feel as if I'm being followed,' she confessed.

'By whom?' he exclaimed in disbelief, as if the idea of being tailed in Dublin was the stuff of fantasy.

'It looks as if everyone who left Abbeylaune for this city in recent times, has ended up in Rathmines.'

He shook his head, then motioned to her to continue.

'For starters, I ran into the Beagle sisters in the supermarket.'

'So?' He shrugged.

'Then whom do you think I bumped into next, on my way back to the flat, but Michael Hunt, now operating with the Special Branch and curious to know what I was doing. So much for the anonymity of Dublin. I thought we'd be safe here from the prying eyes of Abbeylaune. Instead it looks as if Rathmines is going to be from home to home.'

Taking her hand in his, Dermot declared: 'What we do is nobody's business but ours.'

Knowing how news travels, she felt, however, they should consider moving out of Rathmines.

'I'm not moving anywhere.' Dermot dug his heels in defiantly.

Given that it might not be easy to get a flat as reasonable or as suitably located as their current one, she finally agreed to stay put. Besides, for their age group, there was no place like Rathmines for the *craic*. And oddly, the prospect of having a few of their former school-mates close by, appealed to Dermot, who was not hiding from anyone.

Then he put on her favourite Beatles' record, while they tucked into mouth-watering curries from the nearby Chinese takeaway. Later they made love on the divan – passionate young love, without having to look over their shoulder for her vigilant father.

True to his word, the postman duly reported to Finian Lovett that he had delivered a letter bearing a Dublin postmark and addressed in Dermot's hand, to the Lawlesses. It was music to his ears.

But it was a music that swiftly faded when Nora flatly claimed she hadn't heard high up or low down from her son, adding a little tear for good effect. Not wishing to implicate Cunningham, Finian bridled his anger and appealed to her instead to keep him posted about any sightings of them. As he was leaving, Nora let slip where her loyalty lay.

'They'll come to their senses in their own good time,' she said, just a little too cool for his liking.

Finian disagreed.

'Can't you see they've lost the run of themselves?' he rejoined, just about managing to contain his distemper.

'Have you no heart, Finian? Have you forgotten what it's like to be in love?' she appealed to the romantic man she had once known.

Unmoved by her sentiments, he barked: 'There's love and there's infatuation. I don't want Grace to rue the difference for the rest of her days.'

Nora looked him in the eye for an answer she had been seeking in recent days.

'But who are you to decide? Or do you propose to choose Grace's husband for her? Or is it that Dermot isn't good enough for her?'

Finian looked through her.

'Don't pit yourself against me, woman. Your son has done me a grievous wrong.'

Nora's gaze drifted affectionately to a picture of Dermot on the sideboard.

'Having looked into my heart in recent days, I can't but help feeling for them,' she confessed.

'You should be looking into your conscience,' he volleyed, then bolted for his car. When out of earshot, he exploded, 'you conniving bitch!'

Diplomacy was futile. Nora was simply playing cat and mouse with him. A new strategy was required. He was damned if she'd get the better of him. He would go to the ends of the earth to retrieve his daughter. A republican activist in his youth, before switching politics, Finian was no stranger to strong arm tactics.

It would be a last resort and one he would not undertake lightly, but the Lawlesses had left him with no other option. He spent the afternoon refining his strategy with the precision of a military campaign.

Confirmation by Cunningham of another letter from Dublin, catapulted Finian into overdrive. Early next morning, he ordered his reluctant son, Michael, to accompany him on a bit of a journey. It was only when they knocked on Pat Lawless's door that Michael noticed the shot-gun he used on foxes, protruding from inside his father's overcoat.

The tailor's door shot open before he could register a protest.

A frail, timid man; Pat Lawless looked down the barrel of a gun for the first time in his docile existence. He uttered a little gasp, raised his hands in an impromptu gesture of surrender and back-pedalled into the safety of his kitchen.

'In God's name what's come over you, Finian? 'the tailor asked, his knees on the point of buckling under him.

'Your son's address,' Finian demanded, advancing on his adversary.

'Wha..wha..what address?' the tailor stammered.

'Dermot's Dublin one. And make it quick.' Finian cocked the hammer of the gun and thrust its muzzle against the tailor's right temple, swearing that he wouldn't think twice about blowing his brains out if he didn't comply.

Never a man to dice with death, Pat Lawless sensibly retreated towards the dresser, fished out Dermot's letter and deposited it in Lovett's outstretched hand. Having made note of the address, Finian returned him the letter and preceded his apologetic son to the car in haste.

'Where are you heading for?' Michael inquired as they sped out of the village in the Hillman Avenger.

'Dublin,' his father barked.

'But we're not properly dressed!' The thought of showing up in Dublin unshaven and in his stained, working gear, scenting of the farmyard, ran counter to Michael's sense of decorum.

'You'll only be seeing your sister,' Finian muttered.

'I don't think she'll be too pleased,' Michael protested, but knew it was too late to back out.

His father grinned.

'Someone else will be less so before I'm through with him.'

Michael shuddered at that prospect.

'What do you propose to do Dad?' He worried that his father would do something he'd live to regret.

Finian winked at him. 'You leave that to me son.'

When Dermot Lawless answered the door of his flat that evening, he became rigid with shock. Before he had time to rally, Finian Lovett up-ended him with an upper-cut that unpacked all the vengeance he had nursed for weeks. Stepping over the prostrate figure, he barged into the flat like a commando on a clearance mission. An alarmed Grace sprang to her feet at seeing him, screamed, then broke into tears. He took her in his arms, stroked her hair gently and spoke words of endearment to her. Then he told her to pack her bags.

'I don't want to go Dad. Can't you understand? I'm in love with Dermot,' she pleaded tearfully.

'You mean infatuated,' he said, and reminded her of her plans to study for a university degree.

'I want to be with Dermot, Dad.' She told him of their intentions to get married as soon as he got his career up and running.

Finian frowned. Faced with stubborn resistance, he resorted to guile.

'If that's what you want, then go ahead, and put your mother in an early grave.'

He placed the travelling bag he'd brought for her things on the table before proceeding.

'Have you any idea what you've put her through since you left?'

'Tell me!' Her resistance began to crumble.

Exploiting her concern for her mother, he gave it to her straight.

'Dosing herself with sedatives, pacing the floorboards night after night, worrying about you and crying in her sleep. Is that all you care about her?'

Grace was moved to remorse.

'Oh, no! I'll go then. Not that anything is going to come between me and Dermot,' she told him.

'That goes for me too.' Dermot staggered into the room, still groggy from the *coup de grace* that had found him physically wanting and clearly no match for his assailant.

Michael Lovett ushered his sister past him and got her into the car before she could change her mind. His father stayed behind to complete the packing, literally bundling Grace's belongings into the battered travelling bag. As he made a bustling exit, he grabbed Dermot by the lapels and lifted him off his feet.

'The next time you elope with my daughter, buy yourself an obituary card,' Finian advised him before putting him down.

'I'm not good enough for her, isn't that it? Well I'll show you,' Dermot declared, though suddenly not half the man he thought he was.

'Your problem is you're too big for your boots.' Finian brushed him aside as he breezed out of the flat.

The car was stuffy with the heater on. The pendulum motion of the wipers mirrored the tumult in her soul, while a drizzle that thickened to a downpour cast a pall of gloom upon the landscape, in keeping with her mood. Even Michael's best efforts to reach her failed. She remained glum throughout the journey, tuned in, she would later recall, to snatches of a Beatles' song that kept recurring in her head.

Yesterday. All my troubles seemed so far away
Now it looks as though they're here to stay,
Oh, I believe in yesterday.

Much to everyone's relief, her spirits suddenly lifted and tears of joy streamed down her cheeks at seeing her mother awaiting her on the doorstep.

Ejecting herself from the car, Grace ran to her and embraced her with all the warmth and misgivings of a repentant daughter for an aggrieved mother.

Finian rejoiced that his resoluteness had paid off. The postman did the rest, handing over Dermot's pleading missives to Grace to her father, who promptly lit his pipe with them.

When Grace opted for a job with the local bank, rather than for a degree course in Dublin, Finian was satisfied that she had outgrown Dermot.

That Dermot would in time outgrow Grace seemed to him no less inevitable. Now that they were apart, there were better things for them to do.

In time, Grace would become a career woman and would cease to have any interest in men. As the years drifted by and she was still single, Finian began to worry that she was married to the job.

'She still hasn't outgrown Dermot,' his wife remarked one night.

'Nonsense!' he barked.

'I know her better,' she said.

He didn't want to know.

When a successful Dermot, now rumoured to have set up his own electrical firm in Dublin, arrived in Abbeylaune in a spanking new Volvo and dressed to kill, it was hardly surprising, when he dropped into the bank to make a withdrawal from his impressive deposit account – which would eventually surpass Finian's when the Celtic Tiger took off – Grace felt her heart skip a beat. When he invited her out for a meal, she did not think twice. The man of her dreams had come back for her – still the woman of his dreams.

A bemused, if relieved, Finian did not stand in their way.

OPTICAL ILLUSIONS

When Aengus showed up for his appointment at the optician's, he expected Mr Solomon to do his eye test. Instead, he was escorted by a female addition to the staff to the testing laboratory upstairs – a high tech chamber that housed the latest optical advances. Having sat him down on a comfortable, adjustable chair, she checked his records while he made a furtive appraisal of her. She was probably in her late twenties, and possessed of those well-defined, expressive features that he had favoured in his previous attachments, which, for one reason or another, came to nothing – ships passing in the night. His preference for his freedom, though he was approaching thirty, had so far won out over the urge to settle, which was further impeded admittedly, by the prohibitive cost of houses due to the Celtic Tiger and his refusal to sacrifice his intellectual pursuits to a crippling mortgage.

'I see it's been two years since your last eye-test.' She had a soft, provincial accent, not unlike his own, still resonant, despite his years in Dublin, of his Abbeylaune roots.

'That long? It seems only like yesterday.' Eager to impress her, he assured her that he only used glasses for night reading.

'Time steals a march on all of us,' she sighed to the accompanying chimes of a clock in the next room. While not unkind to him, it was distinctly generous to her.

'And sadly our sight,' he lamented.

'I suppose, otherwise, I'd be out of a job,' she chuckled and introduced herself as Iris.

'Pleased to meet you.' He beamed, very pleased indeed, as he sensed an immediate chemistry between them – modality of the visible enhanced by her striking looks.

Having consulted his previous records, she proceeded tactfully with some medical inquiries. The flaws in his genetic inheritance. His Achilles heel, so to speak.

'Any history of glaucoma in your family?'

'None that I'm aware of.' He noted her deep-set eyes and her long eye-lashes.

What a fetching figure too! Tall, but not too slim and with great legs – pity she wore trousers, denying him a closer glimpse of them. Black trousers, black top. The in-colour, and very suited to her. Could she be a dark horse?

'Are you on any medication?'

'None.'

In truth, his rude health was due to sound genes rather than correct dieting or rigorous exercise. He hoped, however, that Iris would overlook his excessive kilos.

'Any injuries worth mentioning?' she inquired lightly.

He shook his head with a measure of satisfaction.

'Some minor sporting ones at one stage, but they seem to have cleared up.' He wondered what she did with her spare time. Line dancing or power walking? A figure like hers usually came with an exercise tag.

'Good. Then we can proceed with the testing.'

Whereupon, she moved nimbly towards the windows and drew the drapes, reducing the laboratory to semi-darkness, confirming for him that there was no seeing without an object of perception, however blessed were those who have not seen and yet believe.

A business-like Iris, had him sit at the auto-refractor to have his distance vision assessed for prescription and for any indications of astigmatism. As he gazed into a microscopic device, first with his left eye and then with his right, he was aware of a hot air balloon set against an emerald background. As to what it signified, he hadn't the foggiest. On a more personal level, it might well signify the vehicle of his fantasies *en route* for Iris, by now more a sexy silhouette at the controls than a luminous presence. Just as well she couldn't read his amorous thoughts at that moment. Transparency in that regard was just not on.

He wondered how Mr Solomon, her Jewish boss, saw her with his gold-rimmed spectacles, and she him, knowing how racial and religious labels often prejudiced people's seeing. The way others see us can be at such odds, he knew, with the way we see ourselves, which must be tough on those labelled for the rest of their days for some crime they committed, despite having reformed.

Still gazing into the auto-refractor, he pictured what it must be like to see through the eyes of the sexually abused, having once witnessed an abuser being brutally beaten up in a laneway by his victim.

The second phase of the test, conducted on the tonometer, he would find discomfiting, having to suffer air puffs being fired point blank at each pupil. Painful little executions, which made his eyes pop and his lids blink, but essential to diagnosing glaucoma, an eye disease that was rampant in Africa.

Imagine, he pondered, not being able to see the changes of the seasons and the beauty of the female figure!

'Terrible what those African children have to suffer from want of eye-care,' he exclaimed suddenly, though lip service was the extent of his concern so far.

'Indeed. And to think that it's curable if caught in time.'

He was astonished to learn that she had done voluntary service there, treating its victims. Challenged, he realised that seeing was about seeing problems and, in turn, solutions – as the Government now realises, faced with a mammoth recession of its own making, having shut its eyes to the abuses of the Celtic Tiger.

'You're a shining example to us all.' He was blown over by her altruism.

She shrugged modestly.

'Just something for my sins.'

For the letter-reading test, she fitted him with specially designed frames that must have resembled those night vision ones worn by special forces during night-raids on enemy positions. To his relief, he read the first two lines effortlessly, amused by the inversion of the words SIGHT and TRYST. He even picked out the number 2 on the third line but failed, unlike the previous test, to decipher the blurred letters that accompanied it.

Clearly there had been some deterioration in his eyesight, which was offset, he was confident, by some gains in insight. Nothing to be alarmed about, he hoped, for the thought of having to wear distance glasses was off-putting, knowing how they would impede his sporting activities and leave their imprint under his eyes. A nuisance, too, on a date when kissing. Iris, he was pleased to note, wasn't wearing any. Very kissable, too, were her neatly sculpted lips.

As she experimented with a range of lenses, the plight of the sightless set him wondering if there could be something to the charge that evolution was a blind watchmaker, considering the register of flawed humans to its discredit. He preferred to think otherwise: to see the glass half-full; to stay metaphysically positive.

'How are we doing?' she inquired.

'Fine.' In truth, he was so spellbound by his optician that he was no longer capable of seeing the wood from the tree. Love's blindfold. Sadly, he sighed, the besotted eye was all too short-lived. No lens, he regretted, to offset that so far.

Still, if he were to choose between seeing and hearing, he would opt for seeing. The ancients, he recalled, would seem to agree, perversely, in many cases, choosing to blind their captives. King Lear. Samson, too, love-blinded in advance by Delilah.

'And how about this one?' Iris proceeded with a rigour befitting the windows of his soul.

'Much better.'

He wondered if blindness restricted the soul, or if visual privation made for the inner enrichment that mystics experience? He would find it hard to live with, given that to see was to possess, in a manner of speaking, those beauties he glimpsed daily that were physically off-limits for him.

His gaze again caressed her, then lost her as he slipped back into visualising Jesus giving sight to the blind. Admittedly, one cannot wait around for miracles, as Iris, who must have restored sight to hundreds, testified. Still, it was some comfort to know that, presumably, there will be no visual defects in the next world.

As Iris continued to try out further lenses, he was reminded of Nostradamus looking into the future. No lens for that. Not that you'd need to be a prophet to predict most lives – so routine they might as well be programmed.

As the test progressed, he sensed his feelings for her moving into overdrive. Her heady scent and the resonance of her honeyed voice triggered a turbulence in his soul that was reflected outdoors by the frenzied behaviour of the birds in their mating fever.

'It shouldn't take much longer,' she assured him, as she meticulously assessed lens after lens for their subtle differences.

Starry-eyed, he told her to take all the time she needed, that he wanted to be able to see a mile by the time she was through with him. Granted, with respect to Aristotle, that hearing be more informative, seeing Iris, he wouldn't deny, was immensely more pleasurable.

'I'll have you reading between lines,' she chuckled.

He smiled, then wondered how people ever managed without specs. Imagine trying to read with poor eyesight in the dim light of the past! While acknowledging his indebtedness to science for providing him effectively with an extra sense organ, he agreed, however, with the philosophers that what we see are mere appearances, rather than the thing in itself.

Not that he hadn't some reservations, even as a philosophy student, about Plato's views that the things we see are but imperfect copies of their higher, transcendent forms. He wondered what Iris's looked like? A *spéirbhean* [a beautiful woman]?

'Try this lens.'

The eye as the avenue of learning – a big shift from the previous, mental route. Polyphemus had only one eye, the other dislodged by Odysseus. If thy right eye scandalise thee, pluck it out. The lusting eye. The adulterous eye. The paedophile's eye. The evil eye. He wondered how much of our seeing was due to nurture, and if it could be weaned from the lure of consumerism to which Buddhism attributes our unhappiness .

'And this?' She pressed ahead with her quest for the appropriate lens, which could never match his ardent perception of her at that moment.

'Better still.' Her well-formed hips, suited to child-bearing, aroused his paternal instincts from their bachelor torpor.

He tried to picture Iris's expression if he were to ask her out. The eye was so expressive. It could invite or repel. One glance at

Medusa and you'd be turned into stone. Lot's wife, too, suffered a similar fate for having looked back. Iris can only refuse. Then something prompted him to wait.

He marvelled at how the blind cope, picturing Raftery groping through the rutted boreens of Mayo, regaling people with his poetry and his music. He wondered if nature somehow compensated him for his defect, or if he resolved, against all the odds, not to be the person he was, in order to become the indomitable one he was not.

'Now this,' Iris cut across his thoughts, presently assessing the worth of his own view of things against a more objective viewpoint.

'Perfect,' he exclaimed, convinced he'd seen the inversions of the words *SIGHT* and *TRYST* at peak definition.

Iris seemed pleased.

'We're almost there,' she said, unaware of how much he wanted to prolong the pleasure of her company, even in the dim chamber. He remembered, at the point of laughter, how Berkeley held that there were only perceived objects. Try it in a dark room and you'll get a rude eye-opener. Ouch! Wouldn't mind bumping into Iris.

'No rush,' he told her, conscious of a growing bond between them.

As the testing drew to a close he inquired if he would need distance glasses.

'Not for some time yet,' she assured him and proceeded to set up the next stage of the test.

He emitted an audible sigh of relief.

'Great!' Not that he would deny that seeing had often been his problem. Seeing faults in his girl-friends had discouraged him from venturing up the aisle. Better in retrospect, if he were to see less. He wondered, if in that regard, the blind fared better, and if they were any less blind to their own faults than he was.

Gazing discreetly at her, he liked to think that beneath her attractive features were those qualities he admired in women; qualities that women, too, set more store by than looks in men – prepared, if needs be, to overlook shortfalls in the attractiveness ratings. Or so he hoped, in view of his.

Her reflection in a wall mirror, illuminated by a chink of light from a parting in the drapes, confirmed her the fairest of all his exes – a joy to the eye and a treat to the ear, and exciting, too, he'd wager, to touch and to hold. Touch me, honey!

Her mobile bleeped. A text message. Could it be her boy-friend? Relieved that she ignored it, he remembered with satisfaction that the heart in her Claddagh ring was facing out. And she wasn't wearing a friendship ring either, he noted with satifaction, before she drew the drapes. Could it be they were fated to meet?

A snatch of a song his mother used to play on the piano intruded on his thoughts.

'When Irish eyes are smiling,

Sure 'tis like a morn in Spring.'

'Next stage!' Iris cut across his infatuated ramblings.

She had him sit again on the adjustable chair, which she raised prior to proceeding with the final scrutiny. Producing a torch, she probed each eye in turn for any indications of cataracts, while issuing a list of instructions: 'Look up ! Look down ! Now to your left! And now to your right!'

Vision, he knew, was so drawn to beautiful women, which, come to think of it, is a bit unfair to the plain ones, considering the beauty often residing beneath the plainness. More often than not, in reality, he settled for the happy medium, content to make do with his fantasies of the stunning.

As she drew back his eyelashes and bought the light closer, he found the subtle scent of her perfume intoxicating. The titillating brush with her hair as she bent over him, accompanied by the rapturous sensation of her fingers as she drew back his eye-lids, fired him to arousal .

He felt an wild impulse to press a strand of her wavy hair to his lips, then an urge to ventilate his feelings for her in a cascade of words. His fantasies running amok, he pictured her in his arms, their lips pressed together, his entire body aching with desire. Catching himself, he realised he was succumbing, yet again, to love at first sight.

As if sensing his unruly vibes, Iris skipped out of reach, drew back the drapes and escorted him promptly downstairs, where she had him try on a range of specs. He was surprised at how similar their tastes were, and their sense of humour, too, as she had him try some exotic samples popular with celebrities. He finally settled for sensible reading glasses.

'You look terrific in them,' she complimented him, with an approving gaze.

'Really! And may I say you, too, look stunning.'

How he appeared to others mattered to him. No Narcissus, he would have to admit though, that the self he glimpsed in his shaving mirror, was, he suspected, more handsome than the one Iris saw. It's the way we are. How else, he mused, could we look at ourselves day-in-day-out and feel comfortable with our reflections?

'It must be the glasses,' she chuckled.

What a lovely laugh she had! There was no denying the chemistry he sensed between them.

Thanks to Iris, he was suddenly seeing everything through rose-tinted ones.

Dredging up courage, he inquired when he could see her again. The more he saw of her, the more he wanted to see.

'I presume you'll be collecting your new glasses this Friday.'

She didn't appear to get his drift. Or was she giving him the brush-off? Admittedly, he was rushing his fences. On the other hand, he couldn't let slip an opportunity that might not come his way again.

'I mean for drinks and a chat some evening after work.' The words came pleadingly if impulsively from his lips, causing him to blush.

She hesitated, her distended blue eyes appraising him seriously.

'I'll have to see,' she finally said, and gave him an agreeable smile, which raised his hopes as Mr Solomon intruded and announced that another client awaited her – an unwitting, young man, he gathered, who sadly had lost an eye in a violent dispute at a disco, over a girl on whom it would have been better had he never set his eyes, considering the short shrift she gave him soon afterwards. Given his feelings for Iris, a gallant Aengus was certain he would risk his sight for her, if it ever came to that.

As she saw him out, he felt reasonably confident that she wanted to see him again, unless, of course, he was suffering from optical illusions.

In a worst-case scenario, he wouldn't be any the worse for having seen her.

THE EMPRESS WITHOUT CLOTHES

Sheryl's rise to fame as a model was nothing short of meteoric. Endowed with a figure women dream of and men fantasise about, she took the fashion world by storm. Soon, her stunning looks and her remarkable flair would have the fashion columnists, who referred to her as the empress of the catwalk, vying to extol her. Anything she wore she enhanced and was, in turn, enhanced. The leading fashion houses head-hunted her throughout the Celtic Tiger, while the media pursued her relentlessly, capturing her every nuance for public consumption. In a sense, they created her, endowing her with an image more mythical than real, while waiting in the wings to dismantle it, given half a chance.

I followed her ascent to stardom from the vantage point of the accounts department at the House of Livia, a celebrated clothing establishment that capitalised on her reputation – a lucrative commodity, my figures will testify. She had only to be associated with an item for its value to soar and its sales to rocket. Whenever she did a catwalk in town, tickets sold out in a matter of hours, due to the hype that accompanied her.

What it is that cult figures like Sheryl have, I'll never know. Call it x-factor or what you will. It's indefinable. Unlike her less successful contemporaries, she clearly had the charisma and the class that make for a household name, which is tough when you consider the sacrifices they make to keep themselves in shape.

How often did I hear Sheryl's fans aspiring to emulate her!

'I'd live on fresh air for a figure like hers.'

'I'm really going to start dieting and exercising again, and bin everything sweet in my shopping basket'

'I'm definitely going to shed a stone before hitting the beach this summer.'

If we're supposed to be what we eat, then figures like Sheryl's, I knew, were a pipe-dream for most. It is so difficult, I agree, to say no to the appetites. Some can, others fail, lacking, unlike their role model, the willpower to persist. Hence, their on-going battle with obesity, in an effort to meet the criteria of the fashion gurus obsessed with slimness, regardless of the damage to health and to many women's self esteem.

Being the high noon of the Celtic Tiger was certainly in Sheryl's favour. Boutiques and fashion designers flourished as never before. For the fashion-conscious, she had brought an exciting new dimension to their lives. Wearing her designer clothes was considered trendy and the hallmark of good taste.

I failed to see the logic in it, but trust me, I've heard women rave about her shows as if they'd been through a life-changing experience. The premiere of a stunning new film or play wouldn't have moved them in the way that she did. I suspected that it had more to do with the aura of stardom than with the fashions she modelled, that somehow had her followers believing that we are what we wear.

Sheryl's catwalks were, indisputably, theatre in their own right. You had only to observe her fans turning up for them in droves, with an infectious sense of expectancy, to realise her appeal. I sometimes wondered, if what they really saw, wasn't Sheryl but her media image, which misled them into mistaking the wood for the tree.

To watch their heightened reactions, and listen to their glowing tributes, you would think a goddess had come among them, for most behaved as if they had seen an apparition, rather than a creature of flesh and blood. She was stunning, I'll grant you, though I refused to be taken in by all the hype.

Having seen celebrities like Sheryl come and go like the seasons, I've come to cast a cold eye on them. As for the fashions they popularise, they all too often conceal, rather than disclose, women's inner beauty. Give me the soul beneath the finery any day, rather than the body-serving breath-stoppers Sheryl brought to the catwalk. But try telling that to a bevy of fashion-besotted women. I'd be lynched – or told to get a job with Oxfam, with respect to that noteworthy charity.

'She's the hottest property since Kate Moss,' I kept hearing her fans confirm.

A tiny minority of sceptics felt her clothes were much too daring.

'You don't expect her to wear a burqa and clothes down to her ankles in this day and age,' I frequently heard her fans disagree with the sceptics.

Then the first chinks in her armour appeared. Whether Sheryl was responsible for them or not is questionable. Reports would suggest that she was tacking too close to the precipice for her own good, and that fame was going to her head. Like many celebrities, she took everyone by surprise when she hooked up with a rising rock star.

Jeff had the charisma that lures women like Sheryl, as well as, admittedly, some talent – insofar as rock musicians require any, which I sometimes doubt, having been mugged all too often by their ear-shattering emissions in city pubs. Suffice, each benefited from the other's image. Together they were Posh and Beck.

You didn't have to be a seer to predict that Jeff would soon be overshadowed by Sheryl. It is generally the case, isn't it, when you hook up with a legend. Give me a lower profile partner any day for comfort.

And I think Jeff would have preferred one, too, for it wasn't long before I heard rumours that their relationship was in trouble. It came as no surprise when he was charged with possession of cocaine – the statutory fall from grace by rock stars.

The tabloids, for some reason, went relatively easy on him. Their real interest I suspected, was in Sheryl – the big fish they hoped to fry some day. Jeff, I knew, amounted for them to no more than a minnow. If it weren't for his ties with Sheryl, whose shows furnished them with exciting copy, he'd scarcely merit a mention.

Despite carefully packaged evidence to the contrary, the downward trend for the celebrity partnership continued. Rumours had it. The lyrics said it. Acquaintances remarked on it. The sceptics were congratulating themselves, while the tabloids were moving in for the kill. If anybody can sense a celebrity rift, it's the media. It thrives on break-ups.

Sheryl, they noted, looked thinner. Then ghastly thin. Was she suffering from anorexia? Or just succumbing to the dieting trend? Slim sightings of her, skimpily clad, on the beaches of St. Tropez, with shadowy figures, led to a raft of tabloid speculations, which were, more often than not, unfounded.

When the bubble finally burst, it came as no surprise. Jeff did her a huge favour when he packed his bags and rode off into the sunset. Few of her fans would have her stand by her man a day longer.

Meanwhile, I noted the House of Livia was busily reinventing her. It was a clever ploy. Otherwise, I knew, people would tire of her. Celebrity scandals these days are just seven day wonders, while reputations built on firm foundations are more enduring. It was time she presented as something more than the model of yesteryear.

When it comes to investing their stars with a winning new image, few, I knew, could match the House of Livia. Years of experience had taught them that the way to overcome a private crisis was to embrace a public cause. The brand-new Sheryl was about to be relaunched. In place of the iconic, sexy model was a model of compassion and concern seen campaigning against global warming.

Pictures of her in Africa bearing a pail of water on her head went down well. Soon she would be photographed with influential politicians, campaigning on behalf of the Kyoto Agreement, while making weighty pronouncements about the imminent risk to the planet of rising sea levels, unless drastic steps were taken to prevent it. The empress was back in business and more esteemed than ever by her adoring fans.

'It's just an act. A publicity stunt to further her career,' I heard her sceptics complain.

'But consider the good she's doing.' Her fans stood staunchly by her.

Genuinely concerned or otherwise, you could hardly pick a better representative for the cause in question. Take it from me, beautiful women get a hearing plain ones rarely get. I don't think they should, but that's how it is. Add in celebrity status and you have a captive audience.

At the peak of her popularity, she threw caution to the winds. In a fit of whimsy, or in a logical response to a record-long heat wave that turned Ireland into a tropical zone, Sheryl, for some reason, pushed the bounds of decorum in dress to unprecedented limits.

In fairness to her, our attire is seriously unsuited to heat waves like the current one. Consequently, we douse ourselves with a range of anti-perspirants harmful to the ozone layer.

Sheryl cleverly read the situation. Clothes were intended to be functional as well as fashionable. As the heat wave continued, the demand by youth for mini-skirts and skimpy tops soared. Provocative mid-riffs and alluring legs that would tempt Providence, not to mention susceptible young men, became the order of the day. The city, reeking of sun-tan lotions, had gone Mediterranean .

For a free-spirited Sheryl, there was nothing too daring or skimpy that she wouldn't model it. Global warming became her signature tune. She believed in dressing for it. The House of Livia didn't stand in her way.

Inspired by the unprecedented heat wave, she continued to revolutionise fashion, as if she hadn't gone far enough already in that respect. Good God, I shuddered, what next? Any skimpier and there would be a public out-cry that would bring the house of Livia crashing down around my ears.

Sheryl obviously didn't think so. Such was her standing with her public, she believed she could bring off anything. She had a mission. If global warming had to be met head on, traditional attire would be as absurd as sleeping with an electric blanket turned fully up during the heat wave.

Driven by her larger than life ego or by genuine concern, her catwalks began to border on the outlandish. At first it was the flimsiness of the material that caught the attention of her fans. Then the skimpiness of her attire, progressively approaching zero while managing to steer clear of damning controversy.

Her catwalk featuring a broad-brimmed sun hat and a topless G-string, with her nipples cleverly concealed by two deftly arranged strands of her hair, drew some fire from the media.

'Sheryl's gone African,' radio observed.

'Leaves less and less to the imagination.' The tabloids were surprisingly discreet.

'Titillating, but hardly functional.' The fashion magazines were less fazed.

An economist humorously predicted that the clothing industry would soon be facing melt-down if Sheryl had her way.

Overall, a muted dissent – arguably understandable in the context of the unrelenting heat wave, which was setting record temperatures. Besides, what do you expect from a liberal clime where bikinis were the in-thing at the beach? Sheryl was ringing the changes that signified, however, for yours truly and her increasingly vocal critics, the Last Post for Irish modesty.

But who was I to complain, as her fans never ceased to remind me. I never once refused those generous bonuses I owed to Sheryl, who was on a roll, and raking it in for the House of Livia with her startling new outfits. Lacking that moral fibre that compels men to stand up and be counted when it's unsafe to do so, I left it to others to speak for me.

Apart from an audible gasp from her more senior fans on the occasion when she appeared wearing a fig-leaf, I could detect no evidence that a storm was about to break. It was enough to spare her, though with nothing to spare, of the charge of indecency. Far-fetched though her audience rated it, they considered her outfit more suited to the frolics of the bedroom than to the beach and could never see it, anymore than I could, catching fire in Ballybunion or Bray.

But who can put a halt to the march of fashion? However daring and exotic the fig-leaf be, it was novel. And fashion these days, for better or for worse, has to be novel if it's to survive.

I was more than surprised, and not a little relieved, that the episode was received in the spirit of humour. A little frivolity on the catwalk was seemingly acceptable.

After all, I gathered she was modelling in a crisis context for women rather than men, who, in any case, were not supposed to over-react nowadays to a mere fig leaf – turned on, yes, in the way that a nude painting by a Renaissance artist moves you to aesthetic rapture. Quite frankly, I couldn't imagine many women being tempted to take a leaf from her book. It was one thing for models to take liberties on the catwalk; another thing for their fans to disport their wares in public. So far, the protests of her critics fell on deaf ears for, as yet, Sheryl could do no wrong by her fans.

With the heat wave showing no signs of abating, and confirmation of melting icecaps and shrinking glaciers sending shudders through the scientific community, Sheryl crossed her Rubicon. Given the persistent absence of rain, she predicted she would soon be able to catwalk across the Red Sea.

To her credit, she promised to donate the proceeds from her forthcoming and, what was billed to be, her most ground-breaking show yet, to fund a programme for sinking wells in Africa – a worthy humanitarian cause, I agreed, like most who turned up to see and be seen at her show.

And what an expectant turnout! And what a reaction, as a jam-packed, stunned house watched her fanning herself as she strode casually down a dimly lit catwalk in what seemed, if you discount her broad-brimmed sun hat, her birthday suit. It beggared belief. The day of the full Monty on the catwalk had finally dawned.

Unhinged by the spectacle of her shapely breasts, her exquisite figure and stunning legs, I struggled to maintain my composure and strove for that detachment exercised by artists and fashion designers towards their models, however tempted.

I was less sure of the audience because, quite frankly, I was convinced that Sheryl had gone too far. Her topless catwalk and her appearance with the fig-leaf were shocking enough, but this! Ah, come on! Alarming though the mini-skirt and the bikini were at first, they didn't hold candlelight to it for sheer bravado.

My first impulse was to leave, albeit discreetly. Instead, I sat glued to my seat, numb with disbelief and asking myself what on earth could Sheryl be up to. Was she losing it, or treating us to a risqué, Berlin-style cabaret, or what?

From what I could gauge, the initial response of her audience was one of similar bemusement. A solitary titter was followed by an uneasy cough. For a moment, you could hear a pin drop, then a mounting chorus of muttering.

As Sheryl made a coquettish exit in the full glare of the lights – which did justice, admittedly, to her vital stats, though not to her image, I heard the little boy in front of me exclaim with disbelief: 'Mummy! The empress has no clothes!'

Whereupon, a red-faced porter cried 'shush', then glared at the offender, while pressing his index finger to his lips.

'He's right. The cheek of her!' an indignant woman trumpeted from the back of the hall.

'Shame on her! She must think we're all blind,' another dissenting voice railed from the more mature wing of the assembly. I could sense the tide turning against Sheryl as the tirade continued.

'I'd like to think we paid to see a fashion show, not a striptease,' I heard a younger disciple reproach the organisers.

Whereupon, a shout of 'hear, hear!' rose unanimously from the audience, now united in protest, irrespective of age and outlook.

I could see they'd had enough and were determined to speak their mind.

There was no containing the barrage of outcries, as her outraged fans competed to denounce her.

'What does she take us to be? A bunch of cave women?' I heard the woman at the back again complain.

It was time to cry halt to Sheryl's excess, which the furious columnist from a respected Catholic newspaper – and one of Sheryl's persistent critics – promptly did with a vengeance.

'What's the world coming to! Is it any wonder that rape and sexual assaults are on the increase?' he cried, as he cast his eyes heavenwards.

I nodded, then watched an outspoken group from my native Abbeylaune leave their seats in disgust, declaring they'd had their fill of Sheryl's brazen antics.

Others would have followed suit, but for a desperate plea by the organisers for calm.

'Please remain seated, ladies and gentlemen. I'm afraid you've missed the point.'

'Just as well, or we'd all perish from skin cancer or from pneumonia,' a respectably–clad woman in the front row rejoined, supported by her friend, who declared she had no desire to join a nudist colony.

It was the voice of moderation finally reasserting itself, and about time.

'I regret if the message has been lost on you.' The master-of-ceremonies appealed again to everyone to be seated.

Judging by the mood of the audience he would have some explaining to do.

'Really?' the incensed gentleman from the Catholic press exclaimed. 'I would have thought it was in your face.'

The master-of-ceremonies shook his head and looked the protestor in the eye.

'That may be, but for a very good reason. So please bear with me while I explain that what Sheryl is saying to you this evening is that, given the current pace of global warming, clothes, every woman's delight, will soon be superfluous, unless we do something to halt this impending disaster. You'll all agree that, for too long, we have been much too complacent about it, and need a sharp wake-up call – which is precisely what Sheryl, at considerable risk to her reputation, undertook to administer this evening.'

Everybody was now seated and attentive again, as he went on to further justify the show in such beguiling terms that few could resist.

'And finally, I appeal to you to spare a thought for our African sisters, who have to travel ever greater distances for their food and water due to climate change. So do, please, forgive Sheryl, who has generously donated her share of the proceeds from this show for the provision of drinking wells for them. And we deeply regret if she has in any way offended or shocked your sensibilities, for that was never her intention.'

Whereupon, the becalmed gentleman from the Catholic newspaper nodded a qualified approval. Then the audience started clapping, at first singly, then in unison, until the room reverberated to their applause.

Sheryl was saved. It would be her last catwalk in the nip. The downpour that night, and the rainy summer that followed, put paid to her skimpy outfits and allayed fears, for the present, that global warming, with its terrifying consequences, had arrived on our doorstep.

A wiser Sheryl has come to accept that *the less the more*, will never quite sit with Irish fashions. The dress-code of Eden is simply not on.

CONCESSIONS TO LEISURE

St Valentine's Day, like any other day, saw Aisling Khan labouring on her thesis. She was almost there – just some minor tweaking and some spit and polish and she would be rid of it. For the second time that afternoon, she pictured herself being conferred with her university degree and having a framed photo of herself in her graduation gown gracing her upright piano in Trim. Aisling Khan, MA – the first of her siblings to graduate. Then the eagerly awaited graduation celebration with her family and relatives and a male friend whom she had yet to consider as her escort.

She wondered if Pauric would oblige. His appearances in the library were regrettably fewer since he had taken up a post with the Institute of Advanced Studies. He was a brilliant young man, with whom she had much in common, and she enjoyed their stimulating chats over coffee in the library café. He liked what she was doing and he gave her some valuable hints, which she found helpful. She would have liked to have had his overall opinion on her thesis, but decided to keep him guessing about its worth and her ability, knowing that she was not in his academic league.

Scrolling through her mobile, she paused to browse over a photo a friend had taken of them in the café, where she remembered having taken an instant shine to him. In addition to his striking build and reasonable looks, he had a sense of humour and was a good listener. The fact that he rarely wore his learning on his sleeve appealed to her. Yet, behind his modest front, she knew, was a formidable talent.

Unlike Jason, the library Lothario, who considered himself to be God's gift to women and to whom she had given short shrift, Pauric was sensitive and reticent to a degree that suggested it might be for her to make the first move, if their relationship were to progress to the next stage. She wondered what he did for his week-ends – if he played football or tennis, or if he fraternised with his friends in pubs and cafés. She wouldn't mind doing some hill-walking with him and immersing herself again in nature, the heady scent of heather and pine suffusing them with the eros of Spring.

She glanced anxiously at her watch. The week-ends were becoming a bit of a drag, and Saturday evenings, in particular, posed a problem for her. Having little free time for leisure, she wished the library would remain open as on week days. She found it hard to focus in her flatlet. There were so many distractions, and that niggling feeling that she should be partying in Temple Bar, instead of having her head in her books, didn't help.

Nor did it help that the weather was unusually mild and charged with that unsettling presence of an early Spring. Even the birds outside her window were in a frenzy since early morning. And the laughter of little children at play outdoors, rekindled her dormant, maternal instincts.

She gazed again at the photo of herself and Pauric. She liked to think that the attraction she felt for him was mutual. Whenever he strode into the library, she felt a warm glow suffusing her and a heightened sense of expectancy at the prospect of their joyous meeting of minds. They hit it off from the word go. She knew that coming from Abbeylaune, a town that had something in common with Trim, helped.

She had yet to establish if he had a girlfriend. A rival to her fantasies and a shareholder in the man for whom she increasingly yearned. She tried to picture such a woman, ascribing to her attributes that might appeal to Pauric and, in turn, assessing them against her own. So far she had only an inkling of what he sought in women, wondering at times if he really knew, or if he were leaving his fate in that regard to chance, or in the lap of the gods.

Meanwhile, his mere company sufficed to make her happy. And if it meant playing second string, she'd gladly settle for a platonic relationship that would compromise neither.

On days like this, she wondered if she had done the right thing in going back to college, rather than getting on with her life. Many of her former classmates were already married and parenting. In the meantime, the years were passing her by and repeatedly asking questions of her in this regard.

A stretch limousine bearing a cheerful bride and groom, followed by a spirited cortege of wedding guests, sped past her window, but didn't arouse any longings in her for the trip up the aisle. In truth, she felt no desire to settle down yet. Romances, yes, as soon as she was through with her thesis – that ball and chain that had pinned her down for the second year running. Like a child, it monopolised her attention even on Valentine's Day, when young men should be trooping to her door with cards and roses.

It was no reflection on her looks, her mirror confirming an attractive figure, which she owed more to her Arabic than to her Irish genes, the former manifesting themselves in characteristic raven hair, much admired brown eyes and enviable slimness; the latter more evident in her personality.

Tweet-tweet, tweet-tweet. Those birds seemed to be saying something to her all afternoon. So spontaneous, so uncomplicated in their mating rites, unlike humans. Her own romantic ventures hitherto, she would have to admit, were as fleeting as they were unsatisfactory.

In the meantime, her quest for Prince Charming had to be put on hold. It was the price she willingly paid for academic success and a future, fulfilling career, rather than a soul-destroying job in a dead-pan office like the one she had left. On days like this, she wondered if it were worth it. And whether she should have run with her amorous impulses, like the fun-loving girls downstairs.

Her father, with his strict, Muslim rules of courtship, was not exactly helpful. Suspicious of Western, liberal attitudes, his protectiveness deprived her of those essential, romantic experiences in her teens, which had been enjoyed by most of her classmates. Hers, regrettably, was the proverbial, nuclear family, culturally ring-fenced for much of her youth, from racist jibes of ignoramuses who could not accept her being different.

All of a sudden, as she paced restlessly about the room, Spring or St Valentine was urging her to break out and let it rip. She might as well down tools, for her mind was adrift and her emotions were running riot and overflowing, like a river in flood, those embankments her father had rigorously erected for her safe-keeping. Even the strict routines she adhered to for her studies were being seriously derailed by inner, rampaging forces she had suppressed up to now.

As the house vibrated with a partying mood and the streets resonated with revelry, she was suddenly her fun-loving mother's daughter. The steely character she had inherited from her father had all too often repressed her maternal inheritance, which he considered much too indulgent, and responsible for the mess society was in today: single parents with multiple live-ins, separated and divorced couples, feral children out of control, not to mention the appalling legacy of drugs. Instead of the island of saints and scholars he anticipated when he fled war-torn Iraq with his family, he arrived to find a more secular society that was increasingly turning its back on religion.

She closed the windows, pulled the Holland blinds and switched on her desk light, in an effort to create a working atmosphere. Running her eye over the final chapter of her project, she was finally seeing light at the end of a tortuous tunnel.

The thesis, she was relieved, would soon be as near to perfection as she, a perfectionist, could achieve. She was happy, too, with her choice of subject. Having grown up in Meath, its historic legends had become the stuff of her fantasies. It was no surprise when she chose the Pursuit of Diarmaid and Gráinne as the theme of her thesis.

From the moment she first became acquainted with the story of the ill-fated lovers being hunted down by the vengeful, jilted Fionn Mac Cumhaill and his sleuth-like Fianna, she relived it in her imagination as if it were her own story.

In time, her discovery of the Celtic myths would supplant her addiction to the *Arabian Nights*, with which her father had regaled his children at bedtime – magical tales that had set her infant imagination on fire and prepared her for the Celtic conversion ahead.

Browsing over a framed photo of herself in Iraq at the age of six, she wondered what might have been her fate had her family opted to stay. Natives of Baghdad, they fled, like so many others, the brutality of Saddam Hussein's regime during his war with Iran.

The bombs of a fanatical Khomeini's air force, she remembered, had made that city even more dangerous than in peace time, when people who dared to question the tyrannical Hussein disappeared in their thousands, making for an unnerving scenario that led to their decision.

Her father and her mother, who met during her secondment to the Irish embassy in Baghdad and subsequently married, decided that Ireland was a safer place to raise a family. Aisling would have no regrets on that score. As she switched off her mobile, she muttered: 'Stay away from me, Ali!'

In retrospect, Trim, her mother's home town and henceforth Aisling's, until she moved to Dublin to do her degree, proved to be a very attractive alternative. It was as if fate had had a hand in her relocating, for whenever she fished the nearby Boyne with her brothers, it was for the Salmon of Knowledge rather than for sprats. Every swan that went by might have been one of the Children of Lir. And at Easter she imagined the nearby hill of Tara ablaze with the Paschal Fire of St Patrick, who converted the High King to the faith that was her mothers and her siblings. Her father, understandably, remained faithful to the Koran, which, for all its virtues, never appealed to her in the way the New Testament did.

Why she should be thinking about all this, this evening of all evenings, baffled her – as if she hadn't enough on her mind, given that the deadline for her thesis was upon her.

She rose from her desk and put on the kettle. A cup of hot chocolate might help to settle her and get her back on track. Funny, she mused, how unruly one's feelings can be on days like this. No matter how focussed her mind had been hitherto, it could not quell those instincts that were troubling her all afternoon. Perhaps they deserved a break, and she, a new direction.

When she was through with her thesis, she would hang up her academic head and immerse herself again in the day-to-day, like the girls downstairs who, at that moment, popped in to inquire if she were doing anything for Valentine's Night.

'Nothing planned. I've got to get this thesis finished,' she sighed wearily

'Pity you can't join us.'

'I'd love to if I weren't faced with a pressing deadline.'

'Any cards?' they inquired. Shop assistants, they set great store by things like that, yet they envied her, in the nicest way, her university education and being able to discuss matters that were beyond their grasp.

She shook her head, then sighed.

'I'm afraid I haven't time for romances.'

'It's all ahead of you,' they chirped and left her to her project. Even by Celtic Tiger standards, their tireless pursuit of entertainment never ceased to amaze her.

She realised, as she sipped her hot chocolate, she would have to re-jig her life-style. Five years had passed her by while she had been immersed in her studies – five irretrievable years of missed romances and fun-filled nights on the town.

The girls downstairs brought home to her this evening what she was missing, triggering a wave of misgivings and compelling her to question the demands of the academic life. Admittedly, her thesis gave her something to strive for, and, as it neared conclusion, a sense of achievement, but at a price.

Casting a baleful look at her electronic calendar, she realised she was living in a world as vaporous as a dream; more mired in a mythological past than alive to the present. She wouldn't deny that there were week-ends, when her housemates were living it up, that she felt like abandoning her project and teaming up with them.

As to whom was winning out in the living stakes, she was pretty certain this evening that it wasn't Aisling Khan. As soon as she dotted the last *i* and crossed the final *t* in her thesis, she was resolved to let her hair down and to smell the roses again.

She rose from her desk, finished her chocolate drink, then, finding herself incapable of bending her mind to the rigours of revision, she lay on her divan to clear her head. Unknown to her, she nodded off and started to dream.

She felt herself being spirited away through an ancient land of deep forests and vast moors by a young man of striking stature and warrior mien. His voice, which was vaguely familiar, was comforting and his protective embrace reassuring as they continued to elude their pursuers, whom she dimly identified as her father and Ali, his wealthy, ex-pat friend to whom he had tried to marry off Aisling, despite their differences in age and interests and the absence for her of anything remotely resembling chemistry.

Arranged unions of that kind were out of the question. She would enter an enclosed order rather than agree to a loveless marriage for financial advantage.

In her dreaming state, she had never felt so captivated by any man or so suffused with love – an emotion with which she had effectively lost touch.

As the dream ended in the cloudy way that dreams often do, she was suddenly startled by the strident ringing of her door-bell. Who on earth could it be? Picking herself up, she glimpsed at herself in the mirror, glad she had her hair done the previous evening. She could hardly believe her eyes when she beheld Pauric on her doorstep, holding a card in one hand and a bunch of roses in the other.

'I suspected you'd be working on your thesis and that I'd catch you in,' he said, presenting her with the traditional gifts.

Still midway between dream and reality, she exclaimed: 'Oh, my God! What a surprise! It's so thoughtful of you,' and invited him in.

He suggested, instead, that she join him, with some friends, for a meal.

Concerned about the deadline for her thesis, she hesitated for a moment, then, remembering the girls downstairs putting aside their cares to celebrate St Valentine's Day, she decided she owed it to herself to make concessions to leisure.

'Just give me a minute to gear up,' she appealed, so overjoyed that she all but lost the run of herself.

A considerate Pauric assured her that there was no rush and said he would wait for her in the car.

'By the way, how did you come by my address?' she called after him, as she sniffed the roses.

'A little bird told me,' he chuckled. She left it at that.

As she sat beside him in the car, his bearing, and something about his voice, reminded her of the handsome young man in her dream. Pauric was everything she would have wished for on St Valentine's Day. Elated, she felt as if life were spreading the red carpet for her and inviting her aboard after a prolonged spell of abstinence.

As they turned the corner, she caught a glimpse of fundamentalist Ali – who would have her wearing a burqa and insufferably subservient – heading, she knew, for her flatlet in his ostentatious new BMW. She hoped he'd get the message when he found that she wasn't there to receive him. Ali and she walked different roads, and the sooner he realised it the better.

She felt closer than ever to Pauric, and surprisingly comfortable with his friends, who helped to make it a memorable St Valentine's night for her. The Westbank's ethnic menu lived up to its billing, and the resident pianist's dazzling repertoire would prove as the evening progressed, to be the food of love .

Having put the final touches to her thesis later, with Pauric's assistance, and wrapped it in readiness for delivery, she felt she had paid her dues to the mythic lovers who inspired it.

Jubilant and, in turn, relieved, she let herself go and sat around drinking wine and listening to music, while being wooed by the man of her dreams, who was only too delighted to be her escort for her graduation.

NO ROOM AT THE INN

Christmas Day can be the loneliest day of the year if you're on your own, like Noel, and nobody has invited you to dinner. In recent years, Christmas had presented him with a predicament. He realised he was partly to blame, being one of its shrillest critics. He refused to pull his punches with the consumerism, the prohibitive gifts and excessive drinking that had become a part of it. It was not the Christmas of his youth: the modest but wondrous Christmas, so eagerly awaited after a year of basic fare; a Christmas, which the Curries accused him of confusing with Lent, and that had gone out with the Ark.

While adjusting his tilted Catholic calendar, Noel felt the novelty had gone out of the current festival. Even the ceremonial turkey and smoked ham were no longer a luxury. Unlike the mouth-watering plum pudding and the delectable, Christmas cake that were his mother's forte, they could be had any day in the supermarkets. As for toys, children had a surfeit of them. He could see a day very soon when Santa would be redundant. Admittedly, though, the Christmas dinner retained much of its traditional appeal.

He moved away from the calendar. How time flew! Already seven Christmases into the new millennium – the decade of the Celtic Tiger.

It was at moments like this that he took stock of the season and wondered where it had gone wrong. Never more than in recent Christmases, was time the measure of change, and not for the better, he lamented, as the mantelpiece clock chimed once.

Time, somehow, saw him still mired in his parental mindset. Okay in its day, but out of synch with the present. Sentimental lip service was as much as it commanded, putting him on a collision course with the current generation, for whom Christmas was a season of unbridled indulgence, typified by the neighbour from hell across the way, who kept him awake last night with his loud, barbaric music and his boozy revelry. Not a single Christmas carol did he hear sung by the Caliban.

He remembered how his late mother, now gazing at him from a fading, framed photograph, had repeatedly remarked that the traditional Christmas was giving way to a festival of squandermania.

'This city is losing the run of itself this Christmas. Mark my words, people will be queuing up at the pawnshops in the new year.'

How often he had listened to her grim forebodings. A thrifty woman, she instilled in him the sensible values of her Abbeylaune upbringing – values he adhered to even to this day.

His broadsides, which began in early December, with the city's lights being switched on, continued unrelentingly all through the festival. Spiritually on fire, he duelled at every hands' turn with the consumer trends that blindfolded the faithful to the real significance of Christmas.

Defiant, he refused to succumb to the orgy of buying that proceeded it, while abstaining from the manic celebrations during it. A Franciscan novice briefly, before deciding that the religious life wasn't for him, he was determined to uphold many of those principles he acquired from his mentors.

Drawn to the humble crib on the sideboard, he worried that the miracle of Bethlehem was turning into a twelve-day spree.

'Your Christmas would bar the Three Wise Men from bringing gifts. Seriously, you should join the Jehovah Witnesses,' the younger Curries jeered him.

'It was the true Christmas and, in time, it will come around again,' he would reply, sensing a growing disillusionment with the current, materialistic one.

'It's the festive season, for heaven's sake. So be kind to yourself for a change,' they'd appeal, dismissive of his frugal version and less welcoming as they grew older and dropped out of the Church.

He refused to follow the trend. Impelled by his example, he liked to think they would take a leaf from his book some day and turn back again to their Faith.

As he sat listening to the intrusive ticking of the clock on the mantelpiece, he considered whether he should postpone putting on his casserole – a portion of chicken, three diced carrots, an onion and two medium-sized potatoes.

It was not at all the meal that he had in mind, nor the solitary afternoon that cast an unseasonable gloom upon him. Admittedly, it was a pretty poor showing on the part of the Curries not to have invited him this year, considering the many Christmas dinners Noel's mother had treated Alan Currie to before he married.

Listening to the patter of raindrops on his sitting room window, he realised that he should have booked himself into a hotel, like most single men in his shoes. Instead, he waited, as he always did, for that last minute summons he rarely failed to get.

Not this Christmas, he sighed, gazing at the solitary tree in his rear lawn. No room, seemingly, for him at the proverbial inn like other years. Or rather, he suspected, no room in the Curries' hearts for a contentious, middle-aged bachelor, who, more often than not, brought conflict rather than harmony to the Christmas dinner. He'd have been better thanked if he had kept his views to himself and amused his hosts instead.

The whining of the wind in the eves was a further reminder that he should have joined the growing exodus to Lanzarote and spent Christmas in the sun.

Admittedly, it wouldn't be the same – missing out on the Vigil Mass in Clarendon Street, and the choir's stunning performance of the *Halleluiah Chorus* – the highlight of his Christmas – would have put a damper on it.

He would miss, too, the customary get-togethers with old friends from Stephen's Day onwards – a drop in here for a cup of tea and iced cake; a stop off there for a glass of Port and a slice of plum pudding. It was a time, too, for renewing old friendships and for sharing reminiscences, which he would be reluctant to exchange for Lanzarote.

Feeling a chill about the house, he turned up the thermostat, aware that he would be missing the warmth and cheer of the huge coal fires at Curries' to-day.

Instead he would have to settle for the fickle output of a dated radiator that was no match for the seasonal draughts, as he sat out the evening tuned in to his own, bleak thoughts.

He should have seen it coming. Their invitation to the one dinner he valued above all others had become increasingly tentative – an eleventh hour phone-call that left him with the feeling he was being done a very special favour. Arguably, he'd never invited the Curries to dinner. He knew they would decline, suspicious of his catering skills and, in any case, preferring their own lavish menu to his simpler fare.

Pacing about the room, he paused to peruse their Christmas cards: impersonal, clichéd, brief, mere token acknowledgements of his existence. Surely they could do better. In contrast, his effusive greetings were reinforced throughout the year with concerned phone calls about Damian, his godson, who had gone off the rails.

It was a sensitive issue and a tough call that had Noel frequently skating on thin ice. His adopted role as Damian's *in loco parentis* was not always welcomed and resulted, more often than not, in run-ins with him and his older siblings over their liberated lifestyles, which he attributed to Alan, a free thinker and a lapsed church-goer.

Year in, year out, Noel stuck to his guns under increasing fire from a stubborn opposition, who had come to regard him as something of an old fossil.

'Your religion is your road map,' he'd insist, seeing how wayward they had become of late.

It was the tender to the powder keg, an unlidding of a Pandora's box of conflicts that would set the table at loggerheads: he taking an uncompromisingly orthodox stance on the burning religious issues of the day, while they countered with liberal, secular arguments; no give by either party.

'Your theology went out with the Indians, Noel,' they'd protest, using the rash of clerical scandals to justify their dropping out of Church, and the AIDS crisis in Africa as a stick to beat him for his stance on contraceptives.

The fact that they were grown up and capable of thinking for themselves didn't count with him. In their case, sense had yet to come with age. Already, they were reaping the fruits of their unwitting sowing and needed some frank advice to help them mend their ways.

For Noel, the family was as morally strong as its weakest link. In the Curries' case, Eleanor, the lenient mother was as culpable in his book as the lax father. Never one to flinch, he seized on the

Christmas dinner when they were all together, to counsel them.

'Give us a break from the religion and a tune on the piano instead,' his godson would soon appeal, uncomfortable with his sermonising.

He would oblige, though not before he had spoken his mind, while extended family members kept a tight lip, too discreet or apprehensive to stand by him.

The clock on the mantelpiece chimed two. In another hour, they would be sitting down to their meal: generous helpings of turkey and smoked ham, served with scrumptious stuffing and creamed and roast potatoes; the rich gravy and cranberry sauce adding their mouth-watering flavours. Then the plum pudding, with optional sauce or whipped cream, washed down with a full-bodied red wine, followed by servings of invigorating coffee and Christmas cake – a meal fit for a king and a tribute to his hostess's culinary talents.

He thought again about the casserole – best leave it until he had worked up a real appetite. No point in eating for the sake of eating, or to kill time.

He ran a check through the herb shelf before selecting a suitable one. He wouldn't deny being finicky and hard to please where food was concerned. Adhering to moderation, even on Christmas Day, his hosts weren't exactly complimented by the portions he left untouched on his plate.

'Were the ham and the stuffing not to your liking?' Eleanor would inquire.

'On the contrary. I'm just limiting my calorie intake for health reasons.'

Privately, and in keeping with his monastic training, he was denying himself, proud that he had done Lough Derg again this year.

'For heaven's sake, Noel, go and eat, drink and be merry, and stop behaving like an anorexic,' Alan would appeal.

Whereupon, he'd reply that he didn't have to overeat to be merry.

Then there was his much-derided hit list, adhered to *de rigueur,* regardless of the occasion. He avoided whipped cream and insisted on boiled, rather than creamed potatoes. If anyone forgot and put sugar in his coffee, he would promptly hand it back. He limited his intake of wine to a single glass and was similarly sparing with spirits. He was surprisingly partial to the cappuccinos, the current rage with coffee drinkers.

On a day excused for indulgence, he could be something of a trial to his hosts, ample folk with robust appetites and serious weight problems, unlike him – slim, trim and as fit as the proverbial fiddle.

The mantelpiece clock having chimed thrice, he switched on the tele. A celebrity chef doing a demo of an exotic Christmas dinner reminded him of the Mansion House, where excellent meals were served free that afternoon to the homeless and the hard-up. He was neither. To-day it was the poverty of loneliness that was eating him.

'Dammit!' he snapped, while switching off the tele, 'it wouldn't have been asking too much of the Curries to have him for a single meal each year.'

Even though they walked different roads, he had their best interests at heart. He suspected it was the older siblings who were responsible for his omission.

Glancing at a group-photo taken at the Curries' last Christmas, he acknowledged it would have made his day just to be able to say to his neighbours that he was invited out to dinner – not that it was the food that mattered so much as the conviviality and the festive atmosphere.

He rose from his chair and switched on the lights on the

Christmas tree. It brought back memories of childhood Yuletides: the Christmas tree from the pine forest, the candles in the jars, the sprigs of holly and the mottoes by Kevin O'Higgins.

Then the excitement of his siblings, now living abroad, as they ripped open their presents on Christmas morning. Modest toys, that were all the more magical for being rare, they'd be cherished and played with for months after, rather than discarded within days, like the current ones by spoilt children.

For dinner it would be roast goose instead of turkey, and the traditional plum pudding, which had been suspended from the ceiling for weeks in its gauze wrapping, to be resisted until Christmas Day.

He couldn't wait for the relatives to arrive on Stephen's Day, to be part of their banter and the sing-song around the piano. Party political disputes would follow as the drink took its toll, though none was as heated as the one he provoked at Curries' about Iraq, and prior to that the Divorce Referendum, when all hell broke loose at the dinner table. Controversy followed him.

Ting-a–ling-a-ling! Better check if that's the phone ringing in the hallway? No such luck. Must be the widow Gillespie's next door – one of those women whose extravagant Christmases never compensated her enough for the frugal ones of her youth.

Glimpsing his own few presents under his mini Christmas tree, he could picture her unwrapping hers, surrounded by her adoring grand-children, whom she showered with gifts. In fairness to her, she never failed to invite him in for food and drinks on St Stephen's Day. Regrettably, not this Christmas, which she was spending with her youngest daughter.

Slipping into a reverie, the framed brunette – his romantic, last chance saloon – on the sideboard, triggered in him a raft of recriminations.

'You should have married me,' Irene spoke to him.

He sighed.

'Perhaps, I should never have left the novitiate.'

'Nonsense. We could have made a perfect couple.'

He shook his head.

'It looks like I was meant to be a bachelor.'

'No way! How you would enjoy watching our children breaking open their toys on Christmas morning. Then, in later life, being invited to their place for Christmas dinner.'

He swallowed hard, then said: 'Too late for that now!'

'And you'd have me in your bed at night,' Irene persisted.

He could picture it: her tongue probing his mouth while he thrust himself deliriously into her again and again, as love words cascaded from his ecstatic lips, harmonising with little screams of pleasure from hers. Christmas would be every night in each others arms.

'Enough. I've made my bed. Too bad, honey, I let you slip through my fingers. Then you went away. Entirely my fault.'

Perhaps not entirely, having had to look after my widowered father. Couldn't bring myself to put him in an old folk's home. In the meantime, the years stole by, at first slowly, then at a sprint, until before I knew it, I was seeing my ageing reflection in the mirror. For some reason or other, I didn't respond.

Be honest, you preferred to be fancy-free and footloose and to be able to take off at a moment's notice. Last year to Lourdes. The previous one to Medjugorje. Next year to Rome. The perks of singlehood.

'Bye honey.'

He thought again about the casserole — mustn't forget the seasoning. Didn't bother to get a plum pudding or an iced cake. What'd be the point? He'd never get through them. A candle on the other hand, would brighten up the meal. And a little music to go with it would help cheer him up.

Irene's favourite, 'I'm dreaming of a white Christmas,' sung by Bing Crosby, would be perfect and would help conjure up for him the white Christmases of his youth, which had recently become the casualties of global warming.

He unwrapped a bottle of Chardonnay, which he had intended giving to the Curries, and set it on the table. It wouldn't be quite the same drinking it on his own. Still, nothing like a helping of the grape to lift the sagging spirits, especially on a day like this.

'Go and make your own Christmas and don't be dependent on others,' his comforting inner voice urged. 'It's just another day that will pass,' a second voice consoled. 'Strictly speaking,' a third quipped, 'it's not at all about turkey and ham, but about the birth of the Lamb.'

As if to prove that no man is an island, the door-bell rang. Who on earth could it be? Not even the travellers beg on Christmas day. Should he answer it? How could he explain, if it were a neighbour, that he was on his own on Christmas day?

Ting-a-ling. More strident this time. Could it be one of the Curries with a last minute invitation for him. Ting-a ling-a-ling. The bell resonated with an urgency he could no longer ignore.

Partly hopeful, partly uneasy, he responded to it. The pleasure he felt at seeing Linda from down the street left him at a loss for words.

'Thank God you're at home!' Her face lit up.

He asked her to step in out of the rain. He always had a welcome in his heart for Linda.

'Sorry to have to disturb you, but I'm in a spot of trouble.'

Like a knight in shining armour, he was at her service and asked her if there were anything he could do to help.

He fancied Linda. On more than one occasion, he had stopped short of asking her out, fearful that a refusal would compromise their friendship.

'Do you think you could fix a running tap in my kitchen sink? I don't suppose there's a hope in hell a plumber would do a call out to-day?'

'I doubt it. But don't worry. I picked up a few hints about plumbing from my father, so I should be able to solve your problem.'

How well she looked! And so chic! He would do anything for her at that moment.

'You're an angel.'

He smiled.

'Just your average DIY man,' he chuckled, and went to fetch his tool-kit.

Linda's visit would brighten a dismal afternoon for him. She was brightly dressed, too – in cerise, her favourite colour, matching her lustrous, auburn hair – the crowning glory of a cute little figure, which set his heart river-dancing whenever their paths crossed.

'Amn't I steeped you were in!' she exclaimed, a flash of relief lighting up her neatly arranged features.

'Unlike previous Christmas Days, I happen to be on me own.'

He gave her to understand that the Curries, for whatever reason, hadn't invited him this year.

She too, he gathered, was on her own, her relatives having gone away to Lanzarote. They wanted her to join them, but she had agreed to stand in for some ministers of the Eucharist who were spending Christmas with their children.

'I don't know what the local clergy would do without you,' he praised her.

She smiled, then admitted modestly: 'Sure I have to do

something for my sins.'

Surprising she never married. Probably hard to please. Or simply never met the right man.

As he popped his tool-kit into a bag, it occurred to him that she might well be the right woman for him. Then he accompanied her to her place.

'At least I won't have to listen to that tap running during Christmas, or wake up some morning to find the kitchen flooded.' Her face was etched with relief.

'If you ever have any problem in that regard, don't hesitate to contact me. After all what are neighbours for?' he said, always glad of her company.

After he had fixed her tap, Linda invited him into the lounge, where she served him a Jameson on ice. Soon they were immersed in their favourite topic – religion.

They had so much in common. He could sense a chemistry that was mutual, drawing them closer. Her vibrant personality, enhanced by her subtle sex appeal, never failed to turn him on. Soon, the gloom that hung upon him all day, evaporated. Linda was just what the doctor might have ordered for him.

'It's worrying to see such a decline in church attendances,' she lamented. Caring and committed, he recognised in her a kindred spirit.

'And no less distressing is the fall-off in vocations,' he added.

'It looks like celibacy is too big an ask,' she concluded.

He nodded, every cell in his system radiating with affection for her. She was such pleasant company. Time seemed to evaporate when they were together. When he next glanced at his watch, he realised the evening had flown.

As he rose to leave, Linda insisted he stay for dinner. The roast would be done shortly, and would otherwise go to waste.

'Are you sure I'll not be putting you out?' he inquired.

'Not at all. I'm only too delighted to have you. It's one of those days that can be a bit of a drag if you're on your own.'

'Tell me about it.' He was relieved she felt as he did.

Linda was an accomplished cook. The roast lamb was succulent and tender. In a bout of self-indulgence he put away portions of it that he would normally have passed up, doing justice afterwards to a generous helping of dessert and iced cake.

'I find turkey a bit dry,' she apologised for breaking with tradition.

'The lamb was just perfect,' he assured her.

As he savoured his cappuccino, he realised the Curries had done him a favour in not having him for dinner. He couldn't have wished for a better or more charming host than Linda. He felt completely at ease with her, and, if his instincts were right, the feelings were mutual.

When he offered to help her with the wash up, she wouldn't hear of it. He had done his bit for her.

Later, they would sing together like love-birds at mating time, to the accompaniment of a DVD of Christmas songs, her sweet soprano blending nicely with his robust tenor, honed from his years with his local church choir.

They would finish Christmas Day in each other's arms. And who knows, future Christmases too.

A HALLOWE'EN ENCOUNTER

If there's one thing I've learned to avoid, it's a dust up with your local gang. You might get more than you bargained for, like my friend Oscar got on Hallowe'en. The culprits in question were well known to the police, who have had them charged, down the years, with a shopping list of petty crimes – nothing terribly serious so far, though some would have already done time for one thing or another. Few tears, you can take it from me, would be shed were they to be locked up and the key thrown away.

A Draconian solution, I'll grant you, but that's the way the community feels. And I can understand, even though I disagree. Unlike the liberal do-gooders who live in the posh, trouble-free side of the city and who drool with sympathy for them until one of them gets mugged, or has his or her car stolen and torched – whereupon you'll hear them screaming over the airwaves for more police and stiffer, prison sentences – I'm prepared to engage with them, though it's still at the good intention stage.

'They should be hounded out of the community.'

Oscar, like most, believed in passing on the problem rather than solving it. I'll say this much for him, he's gutsy. Too gutsy, as it turned out, for his own good. You can bet though, he'd never look away while someone was being mugged, which is probably why, in the first instance, he took a job with Liffey Security .

'Let the police deal with them,' I continued to advise him.

I could tell from his comments and the grinding of his teeth whenever we ran into them at the banklink – where they lurked like predators looking for odds – that he was itching to have a go at them.

'They're laughing at the police. Unless they're caught red-handed they get off scot-free in court.' Taking the law into his own hands seemed a more effective way of dealing with them.

'Perhaps there's a better way,' I ventured, preferring to take a cooler route.

Clenching his fist, he declared: 'The only solution for them scumbags is a visit from the Dissidents.'

'Knee capping, base-ball bat beatings, and broken limbs! Is that what you want?'

He spat.

'Hell would be too good for them.'

I knew it was his sinister side that was talking, and that he was only echoing the vengeful aspect of the community. And I can understand. Law and order is breaking down. Crime is soaring, drive-by shootings a daily occurrence as rival drug gangs engage in relentless feuds with one another.

'Society must have something to answer for them,' I said.

'Nonsense,' he ground, flexing his bulging, tattooed biceps. 'I had a tough upbringing, but I didn't turn to crime.'

I reminded him that he didn't grow up in the flats that have been a fertile breeding ground down the years for criminal activity. While neither sentimental nor naïve about the gang in question, I knew only too well from where they came and the sinister influences that have moulded them into the marginalised, foul-mouthed, screwed-up ass-holes they've become.

'No excuse. There's lots of decent people living in those flats.

As for those scumbags, they'd mug their own grandmothers.' He declared he'd gladly swing for them.

I feared for him. Useful though he be with the mitts and the karate, he'd be no match for a gang like them.

'Hopefully they'll grow out of it when they go to work,' I tried to talk sense to him. With the country in recession and few job prospects, I could understand why they hung around the banklink looking for odds.

'Work!' he exclaimed. 'They wouldn't turn in the bed for you. Naw. They'll settle for the dole queue rather than raise a sweat. And for the five star menu of the Joy for spells.'

'Let's be honest, putting them away is a costly solution."I tried to reason with him.

Hence the need, I felt, for pre-emptive action. If only I could muster up enough courage to cross the divide that still separated us and rescue them from a life of crime before it was too late.

'I'd put them in a chain gang, if I had my way,' he ground, becoming more combative by the day.

I disagreed, and tried not to see them in terms of their wrongdoing.

'It'll take somebody from outside the gang to turn them around,' I remarked to him subsequently, toying more and more with the possibility of being that one.

He frowned dismissively.

'Go ahead Colm. Just count me out when you try converting them.'

'It might be more prudent than playing rough-house with them.'

The cool, Christian alternative to aggression had served me well in the past, with no shiners or broken bones to show for it.

He shook his head vehemently.

'You'd be wasting your time. They have the instincts of animals and the mindset of cavemen.'

He was convinced that if you were on fire they'd light their cigarettes off you and watch you burn.

Which is why I've kept a discreet distance from them while maintaining a nodding acquaintance, suspecting that they or I weren't ready yet for my venture. Otherwise, it would have been as daft as entering a lion's lair bare-handed and hoping to emerge unscathed.

Even though they nearly did Oscar in on Hallowe'en night, I refused to give up on them. I don't know why. Perhaps it's some inner impulse, however crazy, in Oscar's opinion, that's driving me.

'How did it come about?' I asked him while he was recuperating in St James' Hospital, where he was being cared for by an attractive young nurse whom he introduced as Niamh.

Having propped himself up on his pillow and taken a swig from his bottle of Ballygowan, he proceeded to give me a blow-by-blow account of his misadventure.

'I was passing the banklink when I noticed Florence Nightingale here getting hassle from the gang.'

'What were they up to? Trick or treat?'

'More like 'your money or your life' as they tried to rob her purse,' Oscar explained through swollen lips.

I could picture Niamh's dilemma. Terrified screams, giving way to sighs of relief, as Oscar rushed like a knight in shining armour to her assistance.

'So what did you do or say to them to merit your battle scars?' I inquired.

'I basically tore into them and managed to grab the purse from them.'

Not bad for starters.

'And then?' I inquired about the main course.

'There was a manic struggle as they tried to wrest it back, leaving me with no choice but to weigh in with a flurry of punches and karate kicks.'

'Hmm!' So John Wayne throws back his whiskey, and squares out to his assailants, knocking the first one over a bar-room table and the second over the counter.

At this point Niamh chipped in. Kitted out in her smart nursing attire, she looked a picture: the kind of woman for whom most men would do battle.

'They swooped on him and knocked him to the ground, though not before he had decked three of them. Helplessly, I watched him battling with them like a tiger, even though he was outnumbered. Having overpowered him, they punched and kicked him. I was sure they'd kill him. I could see blood gushing from his nose and mouth as they laid into him like frenzied wolves tearing their quarry to pieces. I tried to drag them off him but they pushed me aside.'

'And did nobody come to his assistance?' I inquired, noting again her attractive figure and her exquisite features that must have helped arouse Oscar's, chivalrous instincts.

Angrily, she went on to relate how a crowd, who had just emerged from the nearby pub, just stood around like frightened lambs while Oscar was being clobbered.

'And you mean to tell me nobody even rang for the police?' I exclaimed, sharing her outrage.

She shook her head, her expression changing from one of annoyance to sadness.

'You know how it is. Too scared to get involved, or to have to give evidence in court.'

I couldn't but help feeling overcome with disgust.

'Appalling ! So how did it end?' I was beginning to have second thoughts about my mission to them.

'You won't believe it,' Oscar said, a sight to behold in his bandages and with a crutch at his bedside.

'What?'

'Out of the blue, the cavalry arrived.' I might have guessed – just as the fort was being over-run by the Apaches.

'Somebody was praying for us,' Niamh said.

'You'd better believe it,' Oscar, whom I had never known to be overly religious before now, agreed.

'So who was it?'

'Tell him Niamh,' Oscar said. 'You saw more of him than I did.'

Dramatically, she responded: 'As true as God, this tall, robust man wearing a dark, leather jacket and carrying a shoulder bag, appeared from nowhere and made a bee-line for us.'

'Really! And what then?' I couldn't wait to hear.

'Next I saw him taking a club from his bag and wading into the gang whom he scattered in all directions. Then he pulled Oscar to his feet, flagged down a passing taxi and popped him into the back seat, while I held the door open. Concerned for Oscar, I accompanied him to the out-patients in St James Hospital.'

'Superman to the rescue,' I ventured, suspended between belief and scepticism.

'Supernatural man if you ask me, for he vanished as readily as he appeared.' Oscar sounded like a man who'd been through an extra-terrestrial experience.

'Presumably one of you must have spoken to him?' I pressed for more conclusive evidence.

Whereupon Niamh volunteered: 'When I thanked him, he just nodded.'

'Very strange.'

'But stranger still . . .' she went on.

'Tell me!' Steeped, in my youth, in the folklore of Abbeylaune, before moving to Dublin, I was suddenly a captive audience.

'The following day I recognised the stranger in an old family album I happened to be riffling through.'

Bemused and in turn intrigued, I pressed her to name him.

'If not my Godfather, who had emigrated to the Isle of Man and was drowned in a mysterious, boating accident on Hallowe'en, it must have been his double.'

'I get you,' I exclaimed, after a prolonged pause.

'Get what?' Oscar looked at me curiously.

Unsure if he'd believe me, I evasively referred to an old pagan belief about the dead being allowed back to earth on Hallowe'en, and left it at that.

His quest for satisfaction was not exactly appeased on hearing from me, in the course of my subsequent visit, that the gang's prison sentence had been commuted to community service. 'So you won't find them lurking around the banklink again,' I assured him.

'Good enough for them,' Niamh said and readjusted his pillows.

'Not half good enough.' Oscar was less satisfied.

I could understand his feelings and proceeded to outline the positives of their sentence.

'At least we won't have to support them in prison where they'd be treated to bacon and eggs for breakfast and steak for dinner, which you and I can't afford. Not to mention the additional, criminal education they'd receive from fellow prisoners.'

He nodded. Then swore: 'May what goes round come round to the scumbags.'

Whereupon, Niamh, who had seen worse outcomes from similar dust-ups, put in: 'Be thankful you got away with relatively minor injuries. You could have been permanently brain damaged.'

I watched his features break into a sudden smile.

'Admittedly, if it weren't for that brawl, I might never have met you, honey.'

He took Niamh's hand and raised it to his bruised lips.

Was I imagining things? Oscar tumbling for an attractive nurse to whose rescue he went! Or the attractive nurse fallen for the felled Oscar? I was beginning to believe in destiny.

'Don't keep me in suspense Oscar,' I pleaded.

Niamh couldn't refrain from laughing as she spoke on his behalf.

'Having met accidentally, it was only inevitable that our first date should be in the Accident and Emergency ward,' she chuckled.

'As you can see, I first of all had to prove myself to her,' he said, pointing to his injuries.

'Which you did with colours flying, darling,' Niamh praised him, then kissed him tenderly.

I commended him for his chivalry.

'Sir Galahad will never die while you're around. That's for sure.'

'I still have a score to settle with them buckos,' he snarled as I was leaving.

'You mustn't!' I heard Niamh again appeal, concerned for his safety.

When I visited him prior to his discharge, and reported that I'd finally succeeded in involving the gang in a community scheme, he shook his head in disbelief.

'They'll walk all over you.'

'They're a handful I'll grant you, but with the help of a female member, who put me in touch with them in return for a small favour, I'm gradually getting around them.'

Oscar grunted.

'Knowing you, you'll be dating her next. That's if you aren't already.'

Knowing how he still felt about his attackers, I merely smiled.

When they apologised to him one evening, I was sure they had turned a corner. A corner he, too, has now turned, grateful to be alive and to him who never failed the Gael in their hour of need.

A VISIT TO THE BREWERY

It was Damian's idea that we visit the Brewery for its 125th anniversary celebration. For the former cooper, it would be a well overdue trip down memory lane. For Jude, our local ex-barman, it offered the prospects of a few drinks on the house. My interest was purely academic.

'Fair play to ould Arthur, he really looked after me,' Damian bragged loud enough for everyone on the top deck of the bus to hear.

A jaunty, dapper seventy year old, he radiated success.

'I regret I can't say the same.'

A shabbily-dressed Jude stank of failure.

'I'm proud to report, I wrung a lot more outa him than he'll ever get outa me,' the sleek ex-cooper crowed, scenting of an expensive after-shave.

Jude scowled.

'Quite frankly, I don't know how you can live with yourself.' Even at that hour, he was smelling of drink. I've never known him to smell of anything else. It's his deodorant.

I could sense an all too familiar quarrel in the making.

'You should ask yourself that. With a pension on a par with the average industrial wage, a house practically for nothing, and a retirement lump sum that will see me out in comfort, I don't have any problem,' the retired cooper declared unapologetically.

'You did alright, Damian,' Jude reluctantly agreed.

I watched him gazing sadly at the work-bound traffic – an indictment of his purposeless existence.

'I did more than alright,' the smug cooper proclaimed.

'Out of fools like me,' Jude ceased to agree.

I could see Damian getting defensive, then heard him retort: 'Don't blame the Brewery.'

'Then whose to blame?' Jude barked.

'Yourself. Who else?' Damian pulled a derisive face.

I watched Jude adopt a penitent pose. 'Trust me, I've tried every trick in the book to kick the drink.'

'You didn't try hard enough. And if I know you, Jude, you'd kick yourself before you'd kick it.'

Jude cursed. He cursed a lot of late.

'You haven't the foggiest what it's like to wake up in the morning with that craving eating you and having to retire to bed at night still achin' for a jar,' he ground.

His love-hate relation with the bottle never ceased to bemuse me. I figured, if his hatred ever won out, he might manage to kick it.

'Say what you like, the pint's the workin' man's nourishment,' I heard Damian insist.

'And curse,' Jude drawled.

A dishevelled, scarecrow of a man, he epitomised the evils of addiction. Having lost his home, his wife and his family, he didn't have much to live for these days. Giving him a reason to get up, we invited him along on the tour.

As we bussed past the firm's sports club, Damian's attention was fixated on ladies in immaculate white outfits playing tennis, and on men in formal regalia competing at bowls – games at which he claimed to have excelled.

We heard again how he met his future wife during a mixed, tennis tournament. Fast on her feet and with a powerful return of serve, she was the pride of the tennis court. He recalled being so taken by her that he lost all concentration, conceding the concluding games of the final set at love–40, to the disbelief of his colleagues.

Mabel was the prize that interested him. He lost, or so he claimed, to win her and scored with her soon afterwards, netting himself I was given to believe, an Amazon, who reputedly had him under the cosh and effectively teetotal after his bibulous, bachelor days.

A disenchanted Jude admitted to having met his wife in a pub. So fazed were they with each other, she had a bun in the oven and he up the aisle ahead of her within months of their acquaintance – her father and a troop of her brothers, I gathered, hot on his heels, just in case he changed his mind.

'She really fell for you,' I heard Damian chuckle.

''Twas a sorry day for her she did. I was no good to her, or to me family.'

The former barman was having one of his contrite moments.

I gathered that Damian's sons, who followed him into the Brewery, were currently among its top-paid reps – chips off the old block and the reverse of Jude's: drop-outs and drug-casualties.

'It'll be the Iveagh Hostel for me.' Jude was again looking out the window anytime we passed a pub. His landmarks.

I disagreed and tried to cheer him up, having noticed him deteriorating in recent months.

'You picked the wrong end of the business, Jude. The brewery with its daily quota of free pints would have been your baby. You don't know what you missed,' Damian had him know.

'Just as well, or I'd probably be dead by now,' the ex-barman admitted.

That he hadn't drunk himself to death already was a tribute to his survival kit. Addictions! So few manage to lick them.

We dismounted from the bus in Dean Street and made a bee-line for the Brewery, with Jude setting a cracking pace for us. That walk through the Liberties, with its network of little streets with names like Pimlico and Marrowbone Lane, resonated for me with memories of the clippity-clop of Clydesdales' hooves and the rumble of drays, pub-bound with their freights of Guinness.

Then, greeting us magisterially above the huddle of artisan dwellings, the historic brewery we were about to tour. My first visit, I'm ashamed to admit. But then, what do you expect from a holly and ivy drinker?

Jude maintained I must have been a Muslim in a previous life, with an alcohol-free address somewhere like Saudi Arabia. He could have done with a stint there, for nearly every pub in Dublin had been his Mecca at some time.

With a spring in his step, Damian piloted us to the Hopstore, where a simulated version of the original Brewery had been recreated for the benefit of tourists now flocking to it like pilgrims.

That the lure of his old work-scene hadn't waned for him was soon obvious. He was clearly in his element as he gave us a rundown on the technical details, before taking us step by step through the elaborate, processing system that produced the legendary brew.

'I had great times here. And great mates,' he confessed.

I figured it must have been an exciting place to have worked. Given the perks and the unrivalled wages available to its employees, I could understand the nostalgia and the loyalty it still inspired in him.

When we came upon some wooden casks in the cooper's yard, I could see the years sliding from his shoulders and his eyes light up, as he gave us a blow-by-blow account of their making. If he could have taken one away with him, I'm certain he would erect a shrine to it.

'Take my word for it, the best pint came out of those wooden casks. The Iron Lung wasn't a patch on them,' he assured us, running his hand over the polished surface of one, as memories came flooding back.

'You can say that again. Many the wan I tapped,' Jude agreed with him for once. Rivers of Guinness, I figured, passing through his hands year-in, year-out. A tonic for some, the downfall of others.

'Picture a quarter of a million of them stacked in a pyramid awaiting delivery. And then, picture three hundred coopers at full spate. God be with the gifted craftsmen of those days,' I heard Damian sigh.

We nodded, then agreed it must've been some sight. I regretted not having seen it for myself before it all went high-tech and the coopers were made redundant. The unforgiving price of progress.

A video which brought tears to Damian's eyes didn't do much for Jude. I could see he was becoming increasingly uneasy as he twitched and fidgeted, long before it was over.

'Let's grab that bleedin' drink on the house!'

He bolted for the pub as the video ended. It was about the only interest he had in the tour.

As we followed him at some distance, while taking in the historic surrounds, I listened to Damian giving vent to his annoyance. Jude, he insisted, should have been fazed instead of bored to tears by that documentary. A unique record of a unique firm as Damian remembered it.

It was obvious to me the ex-barman had only one thing in mind. Already, Damian, I gathered, was having second thoughts about having brought him on the tour. Strictly speaking, it was wasted on him. If anyone should have been fascinated by the brewery, it should have been Jude in Damian's opinion.

In the rooftop bar, reverberating by now to a chorus of toasts to the legendary founder of the firm, we were treated to as good a pint, Jude swore, as he'd ever drunk, as well as to a stunning view of the city, so changed to the Dublin of Damian's youth that it brought tears to his eyes.

Even the Hopstore was now a museum-piece. Nothing seemed permanent.

'It's a changed city alright. And not altogether for the better,' Jude lamented.

Seeing he had already guzzled his pint, I gave him mine which was still untouched and settled for a Harp Shandy. I just don't have the head for Guinness. And anyway, after a few pints, it would be a case of 'show me the road to go home. And what day is today?'

'Dublin may be a changed city, but Dubliners' love of Guinness will never change.' Damian was emphatic.

I could see Jude shaking his head sceptically.

'It wouldn't surprise me if we're about to witness the twilight of the pint drinkers.'

'Nonsense Jude! The pint is part and parcel of our culture and will remain so.' I could picture him worrying about his sons' future.

Whereupon, the ex-barman presented an even bleaker scenario.

'With the strict, new drink-drive regulations, the smoking ban in pubs and the ridiculous cost of the pint, not to mention the collapse of the Celtic Tiger, it wouldn't surprise me if the Brewery has had its day. There's even a rumour that it could be moving to some Third World country where labour is dirt cheap.'

I watched Damian grimace, then reach for his drink.

'No way, Jude. The Brewery is here to stay.'

'Seeing we're rapidly becoming a nation of wine-drinkers, it might survive as a museum,' he disagreed.

A rattled cooper rejoined: 'I still think you're seeing the glass half empty.'

'Was it every otherwise for me?' Jude moaned, seeing the one I gave him wasn't exactly half full by now.

Whereupon Damian asked him what he thought of the video.

'It was a whitewash job,' I heard Jude object.

'You were obviously not listening?' Damian accused him, above the din of tourists partaking with relish of the global beverage that had made Arthur Guinness, its original brewer, a household name.

'I'm tellin' you it's a con job,' Jude insisted.

'Nonsense?' I heard the ex-cooper reply, whereupon Jude exclaimed:

'It was a blatant denial of all the broken homes, the battered wives and neglected children for which, incidentally, your legendary firm has been responsible.'

I couldn't believe my ears. Jude knocking the Brewery! Could he be winding Damian up? Or too sickened by the victims of drink he'd known as a barman, to celebrate the Brewery?

'It's an authentic record of it,' Damian insisted, reciting the benefits enjoyed by its staff.

I watched Jude locking eyes with him.

'Then how come I didn't hear any mention of the hangovers, the missed days from work, and the trips to the pawnshop associated with drink? Surely that's part of the picture?'

Refusing to allow his venerated firm to be disparaged, the indignant cooper stood his ground.

'I'm sure, as a barman, you must have seen for yourself the conviviality and the festive mood to which a few jars give rise. Not to mention that feel-good factor that helps us all to make a bonfire of our troubles.'

I watched Jude nod to the contrary. Normally argumentative, he could be really disagreeable after a couple of drinks.

'Cripples and bereaving families caused by drunken drivers. That's what it's giving rise to these reckless days. None of which gets a mention in that video,' Jude continued to lambaste it.

'C'mon, Jude. There's a lot more to drink than that,' I listened to Damian trying to reason with him, to a background chorus of toasts to Arthur.

A remorseful Jude exclaimed: 'You're damn right there is. Why did I ever believe in that ad that claimed Guinness was good for you?'

The ex-cooper's insistence that to drink or not to drink was one's own free choice didn't wash either with the former barman.

'Free to begin with. And then, sadly for many, addictive, resulting in alcohol-fuelled rapes and unwanted pregnancies, not to mention the mayhem that makes out-patients look more like field hospitals in a war zone after closing time on week-ends.'

I could sense Jude's scathing indictments were beginning to get under Damian's skin.

'You're referring, surely, to a minority who give drink a bad name,' he protested.

I felt sorry for him having to take so much stick today of all days.

'The truth, Damian. That's all I'm asking for. The truth that might save potential addicts among teen-age binge drinkers from a fate even worse than mine.'

In a last-ditch defence of the product, an embattled Damian drew our attention to a picture of a trinity of Irish writers as celebrated for their drinking as for their literary achievements.

'Make no mistake, Guinness brought the best out in them.

It was the rocket fuel that launched their imaginations and inspired them with wit and eloquence that made them the toast of society.' The cultured ex-cooper would have us believe.

An unconvinced Jude frowned: 'At that rate, I shoulda been bleedin' Shakespeare.'

'I'm tellin' you. I've seen them for myself at the Palace Bar. The more they drank, the more brilliant they became.' Damian's eyes were alight with conviction.

Whereupon, Jude made a dash for the bar to order another drink, which could only have the reverse effect on him. I knew there'd be no stopping him now.

I purchased a plate of sandwiches and watched him wolfing them, confirming my suspicion that he hadn't been eating properly of late.

'Three free meals a day we had at the Brewery. And the best o' grub at that,' Damian engaged in a face-saving exercise as he partook of his ham salad portion.

'While the families of dipsos, as often as not, went to bed hungry,' Jude rejoined, as he tore into the last one – a ham and cheese.

'Give it a rest, Jude!' Damian was becoming fed-up with his sniping. And I could see why. Today was meant to be special and Jude was spoiling it for him.

Quite frankly, I, too, was becoming tired of the ex-barman's, negative outpourings. Like most, I could see the plus side to drink taken in moderation, and the indispensable role of the pub, especially in rural villages and towns like my native Abbeylaune.

I could see Damian glancing at his watch. Then getting to his feet, he suggested we'd better be making tracks if we hoped to beat the rush-hour traffic, as Jude started to sing:

'I've been a wild rover, this many a year,

And I spent all my money on whiskey and beer.'

'What's your hurry? Why don't we make a day of it, given the occasion that's in it?' Jude appealed. Ever since he was turfed out of his home, the pub had become his refuge.

Why, I don't know, but I agreed. After some hesitation, Damian, too, opted to stay and stopped glancing at his watch.

We'd soon regret it. Jude was on song and belabouring us with those *come-all-yes* that drunks try to sing when they've had a skinful. Not having a note in his head, it was painful to have to listen to him. And if that weren't enough, he had forgotten some of the words, while getting others all mixed up.

It wasn't long before he was crying into his glass over the mess he'd made of his life, and blaming everyone and anyone who had any input into it. So pathetic was his plight as the evening wore on, he'd justify prohibition.

'*Mná na hÉireann* cost me my home,' he grieved as he gazed at his dwindling drink.

However much I felt for him, I was very definitely on the side of those long-suffering women.

Damian had less sympathy for him

'If Matt Talbot could give up the drink, so can you,' I heard him challenge an unsteady Jude.

'It'll give me up first. Still, I'd hate to perish for want of a drink like that what-you-call-it, unfortunate bird in the poem we learned at school,' he chuckled.

'You mean the Yellow Bittern?' I said.

He nodded, then looked forlornly again at his glass, which after years of abuse was more toxic than tonic for him.

Whereupon Damian signalled to the Polish waitress for one for the road.

'A true blue cooper.' A revived Jude raised a cheerful glass to his benefactor. Then changing his tune: 'Present company excluded and between you and me, martyrs for the gargle. Am I or am I not right, Damian?' I could see Jude trying to wind him up.

'Wrong Jude. We were limited strictly to two pints at work.' I could see Jude's eyes popping, as Damian secreted a fifty euro note from his wallet for the drinks.

'Two pints at work and twenty-two after work. Right Damian?' the ex-barman sniggered, his eyes twinkling with mischief as he gulped his drink.

'Wrong again, Jude.' I could see Damian was beginning to purple.

'You remind me of that video, Damian,' the other continued to taunt him.

'Go to hell, Jude.'

'I don't have to. I'm already there. And although I destroyed one family, God only knows how many you've destroyed. But I forgive you, Damian, for I honestly don't think you knew what you were doing.' I watched Jude absolve him in the manner of the confessional.

'Shut the fuck up, Jude!' Damian threw back his drink and made for the exit.

We finally managed to get Jude home to his grotty bed-sitter, which reeked of discarded empties and unwashed delph. Reduced to the bare necessities, and so unfit for human habitation, it would have driven even me to drink.

'We must do this more often,' he said, wringing Damian's hand as he thanked him for the outing.

I could tell it was about the last thing in Damian's mind.

'And be sure an' give my regards to your good missus, but for whom you might have ended up in my shoes.' The unstable ex-barman clung to him as he swayed like a skiff in a storm.

Damian frowned.

'I don't think she'd approve of all the nasty things you said about the Brewery,' he reproved him.

Whereupon, Jude apologised to him.

'Nothin' personal mind, but you know what they say about one man's meat ... You know what I mean?'

Damian nodded, then disengaging himself from his detractor, made a discreet exit.

True to form, Jude tapped me for a tenner as I was leaving, not for booze, he crossed his heart, but for a little present for his grandson's confirmation.

I pretended to believe him.

I'm glad I did, for he was discovered dead soon afterwards, clutching, oddly, an empty coke can.

GENETICALLY MODIFIED MANNA

When big Bill Looney, reputedly from some Mid-West American Institute of Advanced Sciences, beat local bidders to acquire Maguire's farmstead next door to me, we were taken aback. Being outflanked by an outsider was a sore point with them. It was inevitable that the Yank would incur their initial resentment, then, grudging acceptance when the dust settled – an acceptance not helped by an off-putting eye-patch, suggestive of a buccaneer, rather than the benign blow-in, he would pose as subsequently. When we learned that the loss of his eye was due to a genetic defect, we were less suspicious.

I must have been one of the first to extend the hand of welcome to him. The days when men killed and boycotted for land in Ireland were long over. I knew only too well, that the knell for modest holdings like Maguire's, had begun to toll. Its addition would admittedly help make a similar, small farm viable. I figured, nonetheless, that due to its prime location and its modest asking price, it would invite a lively but measured, local interest. Admittedly, there is still an odd one who is prepared to go for broke for land, as anyone familiar with auctions in nearby Abbeylaune will tell you.

Hence, the sizeable turn out and, initially, the discreet bidding, until Looney put his hat in the ring. With a big cheque book at his disposal, it soon became evident that he was resolved to acquire, at any cost, a farmstead like the one from which he claimed his ancestors had been unceremoniously evicted during the famine. Not that his ancestral ties would count for much in the circumstance, with local pride and prejudice banded against him .

A mere observer, it didn't seem right to me that my neighbours should be bidding up the farm well beyond its value. Their attitude: if they couldn't have it, then the Yank wouldn't either, short of paying through the nose for it. And even if Looney proved to be the winning lottery ticket for the work-shy Maguire, for whom the farm was more a liability than an asset, I still didn't approve of the Yank being ripped off.

Not that it seemed to worry him. Whenever the auctioneer appealed for any advance on the previous bid, he was nodding, convincing everyone that he had nothing to fear from local punters, who eventually conceded defeat, satisfied that they had made the Yank pay.

As to what might be his motive, apart from sentimentality, in acquiring a run-down place like Maguire's in our obscure neck of the woods, it was too early to say.

Acknowledgement of his Irish ancestry helped win him a provisional welcome after the cut and thrust of the auction. The possibility that he might even start up a much needed industry in the area by-passed by the Celtic Tiger, further helped bridge the divide that initially separates strangers from a cautious community like ours.

His generous contribution to the party thrown by a jubilant Maguire, made, however, for a good start. From my experience, there's nothing like a few drinks on the house to win over the opposition. The reconciling powers of Guinness are unrivalled where a quick-fix for conflict is required. With the rivalries inspired by the auction giving way to camaraderie, I watched him play the native card with resounding success.

'My ancestors just about made it in a coffin ship to the States. Being the smart cookie he was, my great-grandfather headed out west to become a rancher,' he confirmed his farming background.

When he removed his stylish Stetson, which had been exciting some attention, he revealed a well-groomed head of silvery hair peculiar to a man in his mid-fifties.

'He made a wise move,' Bracken, an active member of the Farmers' Union, ventured.

The Yank nodded.

'So you've come here to reclaim your roots?' an upbeat Maguire, who could now retire in comfort to Abbeylaune, observed.

'You bet.'

I looked forward to having him as a neighbour. In a parish like Oldbridge, where only the weather seems to change, any novelty was welcome.

Speculation about the Yank's possible plans for his farm would soon be rampant. Most believed we were about to witness an exciting, new agri-venture in the near future. The Americans, after all, were the pioneers of progress, trail blazers for the sciences, who put men on the moon and mobiles on Mars. While little was expected of transient migrant workers from an expanded EU, much was expected of the Yank. And that air of expectancy was already palpable, as we dreamed of cashing in on the fruits of his project that could well be our Celtic Tiger.

The sense of anticipation I, too, felt at seeing him move into Maguire's bungalow next door was nothing to what I experienced that spring, as I watched a contractor he'd hired, dress the river meadow for tilling. The traditional cattle-grazing practised by Maguire and his predecessors did not make sense to Looney, who had a different agenda in mind. But would it work?

I listened to the local Jeremiads arguing to the contrary, their cynicism suggesting they were still hurting from the outcome of the auction.

'If the Yank knew anything about farming, he'd know that Maguire's was totally unsuited to tillage,' Bracken remarked.

Kelly nodded and declared it wasn't fit for scrub never mind tillage, while a sceptical Dillon said the Yank was welcome to his roots, which, he maintained, shouldn't be hard to find given the shallowness of the soil. Only O'Brien believed he'd make a go of it, given his scientific credentials.

If there's one feature of our community I deplore, it's its attachment to the past. I'm all for change and for ventures that generate employment. If the Yank had a game plan up his sleeve, then more power to him!

Come April, he informed us, during one of his rare appearances at our local, that he was about to kick-start a new enterprise. It was more or less what I'd come to expect and couldn't wait to hear about it.

'Anything to do with those spuds you're planting in the river field?' I heard Bracken inquire.

The learned professor nodded, then went on to correct him.

'What you refer to as spuds, I prefer to call Genetically Modified Manna.'

'Manna!' Coughlan disapproved of Looney's irreverent use of a biblical term, and he felt like protesting, but couldn't find the courage or the words to do so.

Looney smiled, then took him out of his misery.

'In layman's terms, a super potato that will rid the world of famines,' he explained.

I could see Bracken shaking his head.

'What's wrong with the reliable, ould spuds we've always

enjoyed?' he asked, and looked to me for support, which I withheld, unsure at this point of what the Yank had in mind.

'They've had their day. Their prolific, disease-resistant successor, suited to all climes, will prove to be one of the marvels of science.' The Yank could hardly contain his excitement.

Only a deformed Dillon, a thalidomide victim, ventured to voice his suspicions.

'It's pie in the sky,' he snapped.

The Yank glared at him, then declared it would be a winner on all fronts: in flavour, vitamins and yield. In short, a complete food.'

Whereupon he lit up his Havana – a majestic cigar that added to his status.

'Then it looks like we'll be having spuds for breakfast, dinner and supper,' Kelly observed with a snigger.

I watched the Yank nod, then address his Scotch and soda with an air of satisfaction.

Ground-breaking though his enterprise might be, it seemed rather surreal to most of us and initially invited banter.

'You're going to miss your mother's apple tarts,' I heard Kelly tease Murphy, who found the Yank's slimmed-down, revolutionary diet off-putting.

'So it seems,' Murphy sighed theatrically.

An amused Yank humorously remarked that, had Eve not been such an apple tart, Adam might never have fallen for her forbidden fruit.

Murphy prefaced his response with a wry smile.

'On the other hand, if she hadn't boxed the fox, we might never have had apple pies,' he rejoined.

Kelly laughed, then suggested to Murphy that he'd have to settle for potato cakes.

'And hope the new spuds don't turn out to be forbidden fruit,' Dillon cut in.

When the banter subsided, I heard a doubting Bracken query the food value of the controversial spuds – a relevant concern in the circumstances.

The professor allayed our fears.

'This newly cultured, super potato will be a totally sufficient food. As near to manna as you can get.'

'Roasted or boiled?' Kelly continued to clown.

'Either way.'

'Good for the figure?' the barmaid inquired.

'Perfect for slimmers.'

'It sounds really sexy,' she chuckled. Tall and slim, most of us would agree she didn't need genetically modified manna to look sexy .

'And it's performance-enhancing,' he confirmed, giving rise to laughter from the men.

When Bracken complained that he'd miss the few slices of turkey at Christmas, the professor assured him to the contrary. And that very soon 'turkey' would strictly refer to a country and not a bird.

If fazed, I was still unsure whether the plusses of this controversial product outweighed its minuses. Though a rep for a seed company specialising in cereal crops, I hadn't the foggiest about cutting-edge science of this kind.

'What assurances have we that this what-d'ya-may-call-it won't be responsible for another potato famine?' Bracken too had his doubts.

'Genetically Modified Manna will be blight-proof,' I heard the professor insist as he called for drinks for everyone.

When the barmaid remarked that any food had to be better

than the junk food that youngsters were hooked on nowadays, the Yank assured her that its days were numbered.

'And the sooner the better,' he declared with a ring of finality that left us in no doubt that he meant business. And with everyone now on board, his project was greeted with raised glasses and a chorus of best wishes for his thing-o-me-bob.

'Genetically Modified Manna,' he repeated for the umpteenth time, his patience with their linguistic fumbling beginning to wear thin.

'Genetically modified balderdash,' I heard Dillon mutter under his breath, then ask if the something modified spuds would be compatible with a pint of Guinness.

Appreciative of the popularity of the brew, the professor smiled.

'Definitely, until such a time as science incorporates it in the new potato.'

'At that rate, we'll have atin' and drinkin' in it.' Kelly continued to find it amusing.

I could see a worried look casting its shadow over the publican who must have seen the writing on the wall for his licensed premises, already hard-hit by the recent spate of drink-drive regulations.

'By the way, have you tried it yourself?' someone was heard inquiring, as the Yank rose to leave.

Beamingly, he replied: 'This summer, all going to plan,' and invited us all to a gala dinner.

Murphy assured me he would be giving it a miss. A spuds only menu would never be his idea of a meal.

It would take some time before the neighbours got their tongues around the new term. Some confused the word manna with banana and wondered if the professor had gone bananas. Others mockingly predicted a 'manna republic' in the making.

Few, however, risked using the unfamiliar scientific title, lest they get it wrong and be jeered. In any case, it sounded a bit high-brow for our community who would never use a big word where a small one sufficed.

Not that they minded the learned professor using such lingo, as long as he didn't mind them using theirs. They were certainly having lots of laughs at his expense. I'm sure he had some at theirs – or, at any rate, until my old flame, Jane Conroy, a science lecturer at the Regional College of Technology, intervened while home on holidays for Easter.

Up to speed with the latest, scientific advances she was in no laughing mood when appraised of the Yank's project. Springing into action, she insisted on seeing him at once.

Knowing the Yank better than most by now, I was press-ganged into escorting her. I knew her to be a keen environmentalist and recently, an advocate of organic farming. I knew a different side to her, too, having dated her in my teens, before losing her to the higher education that I had turned my back on in favour of my current job.

Though my feelings for her still ran high whenever we met, I'd have preferred not to have been her escort on this occasion. Something about her suggested trouble ahead. The last thing I wanted was to be partner to a show-down with my new neighbour, whom Jane suspected was far from the real deal I imagined.

We bearded him in his hastily constructed conservatory, where he grew samples of his super product in huge pots while monitoring their growth .

Introductions over, Jane confronted him with a temerity that rocked me. No longer the willowy, coy brunette I once had courted, she was now a commanding woman of striking looks and forthright views.

'I gather you propose to introduce genetically modified potatoes to our community,' I heard her discharge her opening salvo across the Yank's boughs.

'Yes. The seed in fact is already in the ground. So the project is ready to roll. '

'Not if I can help it,' she rejoined, moving into assault mode. 'I'm sure you're well aware of the lethal side-effects still associated with this product.' She gestured reproachfully at a pot hosting a massive stalk, now ringing alarm bells in my head.

An unruffled Yank didn't envisage any. And in any case, he claimed it was scientifically done and dusted.

'Far from it,' she declared, circling him like a prize-fighter.

I watched him light up a cigar and post a plume of smoke in her direction. 'You've been reading the wrong literature. Protest, reactionary stuff.' His expression was suddenly a portrait of hostility.

She shook her head, then eye-balled him.

'On the contrary. The latest scientific findings convince me you're being totally irresponsible.' Her voice resonated with outrage.

Retaining his composure, the Yank declared that, if feeding the hungry of the Third World were irresponsible, then she'd need to have her head examined.

I could see Jane losing her patience, while he managed to keep his.

'The deformities arising from Chernobyl may be nothing compared to those that could, in time, result from this unproven product. You must call it off,' she insisted, sending shock waves through me, as I thought of Dillon with his spinal defects.

In disbelief, I listened to the reputed member of the Institute of Sciences, dismiss her warnings rudely: 'I find it depressing, that a person of your academic standing can be such a Luddite.'

I noticed his shifty right eye avoiding hers.

The rebuff served, if anything, to inflame her, as she pranced about the conservatory.

'You know what they say about the one-eyed man in the country of the blind?' I heard her remind him. If the Yank was planning to put one over on us, he'd better think again. He had not bargained on Jane.

'I assure you I haven't met any blind folk since arriving here.' The Yank adjusted his eye-patch, looking every inch the buccaneer we first took him to be.

Outraged at having been duped by my new neighbour, who had been pulling a fast one all along on our unsuspecting community, I readied myself for action.

I felt an overwhelming urge to destroy the potted plants as I listened to him casually explain, while adding a shake of fertiliser to them, that science had always managed nature in humanity's best interests. Otherwise, we would not be enjoying the range and quality of food we consume today.

I could see June firmly shaking her head.

'This is one serious case of mismanagement. Heaven help the consumers!' she volleyed, as she looked apprehensively again at the river field

I admired the way she stood her ground. She knew her stuff and didn't hesitate to point out that rats test-fed on G.M potatoes developed cancerous tumours – and that there was no telling the risk to humans of allergies and irreversible ailments from the same product.

Rocked by each fresh revelation, I would have bolted from the conservatory there and then if it weren't for Jane, who refused to walk away from her mission and abandon the community to its fate.

'Ground-breaking, perfectly safe potatoes – you can take my word for it.' I watched the Yank fondle a stalk, then add with a dismissive frown, that Jane's version of nature was for the Serengeti.

Whereupon she accused him of treating a gullible community like unwitting guinea pigs for a venture that would wipe out all existing varieties of potatoes, with their unique histories and flavours, in favour of a single, unproven specimen.

The more I listened to her, the more sense she made to me, though obviously not to the Yank who rose from his wicker chair, thrust open a window and directed an approving gaze at the river field.

'I just can't understand what all this fuss is about,' he sighed. To me he sounded as evasive as he was unconvincing.

I could tell by the way she glared at him, that she had not finished with him yet.

'I fear to think what will be the outcome, should your herbicide-resistant organisms migrate into our local weeds. So don't lecture me about the benefits of such advances!' I listened to her admonish him in the shrillest of tones.

Drawing himself up to his diminished six-foot-plus stature, the embattled professor thundered in his booming bass: 'You cannot put a halt to science. Otherwise, we'll regress to the dark ages.'

A resolute June was not persuaded.

'Nature is not for exploitation. So stop patenting it! How dare you alter the genetic structures of things that have taken millions of years to evolve to their current state! And you won't rest until you've reduced the eco-system to a few, genetically modified plants that will seal the fate of insect life,' she continued to harangue him.

I could see him becoming increasingly exasperated, then looking irately at me for not standing by him. No way. I was through with him.

'You've got it all wrong,' he drawled in a voice that was showing signs of weariness.

She shook her head defiantly.

'I believe in safe science,' she cried, seriously concerned for the casualties of a genetically modified food, resistant to antibiotic medicine.

I watched the Yank sink into his wicker chair and relight his shrinking Havana before replying: 'So, in the meantime, millions must go to bed hungry while you and your camp followers protest on full stomachs.' I could tell, by the way he kept glancing at his watch, that he wanted us to leave – a hint which Jane refused to take until she had spoken her mind.

'Hardly worse than waking up terminally damaged by your toxic mono-menu.' She flounced angrily around him.

If Jane had him on the ropes, I could see that he was still not conceding defeat.

Unmoved, he predicted that time would prove him right, whereupon, nothing would give him more pleasure than to see her eat a very large slice of genetically modified humble pie. I thought for a moment she would smite him on the good eye.

'I'd starve first,' she snapped, then gave him a final warning: 'Take my advice and confine your unproven product to your conservatory. I wouldn't like to think what might be your fate at the hands of the community were anything to go wrong. You just might lose your other eye.' Whereupon she drew a swipe at a plant as she stormed out of the lab, with yours truly in tow, relieved at having daylight between myself and the deceitful Yank who, by now, had forfeited my respect.

What a woman! Filled with admiration for her, I gave her a heart-felt hug.

'You were magnificent,' I exclaimed.

'Do you think I've managed to stall him?' She looked to me for reassurance.

'You've certainly rattled his cage.'

I was in love with her again and ready to do battle on her behalf.

Back in the car she said: 'You've got to call a meeting. I want to wise up the community to this con-man.'

With the health and well-being of the community at stake, and my job as a rep for the seed company at risk, I simply couldn't refuse her.

The huge turn-up for the meeting at the Abbeylaune Arms Hotel reflected the esteem in which she was held. You could hear a pin drop as she showed up genetically modified manna for what it was. Spellbound by her charisma, I watched her win over the gathering with her remarkable, persuasive powers.

As expected, the Yank didn't show up. Given the mood of the meeting, it was just as well. When Jane called for a total boycott of his product, she had our support to a man.

In the pub afterwards, it amused me to hear the locals putting their own dismissive spin on the product they had previously, unwittingly enthused about.

'It could have left us impotent.' Dillon shuddered.

'And infertile,' the barmaid exclaimed, horrified by the prospect.

'Not to mention cancer-ridden.' O'Brien's faith in science was suddenly shaken.

'Potatoes for breakfast, dinner and supper, did you ever hear the likes?' I heard Kelly guffaw.

'Just as well we'll be giving his gala dinner a miss. It might have been our last,' Murphy said.

At that moment, Bracken thumped the counter. I knew it was a signal for action.

'We must put a halt to the Yank's gallop,' he thundered, and advocated that we take a leaf out of the Land Leaguers' book.

His proposal was greeted with shouts of 'hear! hear!' Judging by the mood of his supporters, I knew it wouldn't take much to turn them into a rampaging mob.

'So what's your plan of campaign?' A less amused Kelly readied himself for action.

'That we dig up his spuds and destroy them, while he's away on one of his week-ends in Dublin,' the intrepid union man suggested, and pledged he would take full responsibility for whatever the outcome, even if it meant going behind bars for it.

'Nobly spoken, but it won't be necessary,' Jane announced as she joined us. A torch to my feelings that were more on fire for her than ever.

I watched the intrepid union man shaking his head.

'There's no other way,' he declared, determined not to be cheated of his moment of glory.

Jane shook her head.

'Happily there is.' Whereupon she went on to inform us that, not only was Mr Looney not a professor, but, as she discovered, a front man for a suspect American organization, determined to get its genetically modified foods into the European market. 'And given our historic association with the potato, what better base from which to launch its new product than Ireland?' she exclaimed.

I could hear a murmur of suppressed anger that might have been a prologue to a lynching party, had Jane not managed to cool matters.

'Right now, the gárdai are bringing him in for questioning. As for his genetically modified spuds, it will be the job of the Department of Agriculture to dispose of them. So sit back everyone, and have a drink on me,' she invited as she sat down beside me.

'And another on the house.' The relieved publican rejoiced, safe in the knowledge that his business was secure.

It would be a memorable night, with Jane's praises repeatedly sung, while everyone present, be they sober or sozzled, pledged their undying loyalty to the Kerr's Pink, the Rooster and the Arran Banner – our unrivalled, native potatoes.

'I'll have to trouble you for a lift home,' Jane requested at closing time.

I was only too glad to oblige. Besotted by her since her arrival, but fearful of a rebuff, I recoiled from taking the next step. She was no longer the uncomplicated girl I'd once known. All evening, however, I'd been receiving some very encouraging vibes from her.

As we walked towards the car park, she slipped her hand into mine, igniting again the romantic ties of our teens. Later, sitting together in the car outside her parents' place, we slid, as we once had done, into each other's eager embrace. This time I was determined not to lose her.

For big Bill Looney, it was a case of history repeating itself. Having disposed of his farm at a thumping loss, he returned to the States as empty-handed as his ancestors – that's if he ever had any who could even remotely claim to be Irish.

'At least Maguire had his Celtic Tiger,' Jane chuckled.

Still, were it not for Looney, I might never, as in the song, have met my future wife 'in the garden where the praties grow.'

LIFE MUST GO ON

Paul delayed discussing with his mother the vexatious question of Michael's current liaison until the last possible minute. He knew he would be treading on a minefield and running the risk of reopening old wounds. It was a duty he'd prefer to pass up, were it not for an urgent letter from a relative, appealing for his intervention. After some deliberation, he took the early train from Dublin to Abbeylaune, with a view to looking into the matter.

Fortified by a hearty meal prior to his departure, he finally popped the contentious question, as he sat across the table from his mother.

'By the way, is there any sign of Michael getting married?' he asked lightly, careful not to provoke her at this point.

'None whatsoever. Sure, hasn't he plenty of time?'

Paul shook his read.

'Time is not exactly on his side, Mum. And the older he gets, the harder it will be for him to find a suitable partner.'

She frowned, then looked suspiciously at him.

'Isn't he better off than being in a broken marriage? And now that divorce is available, there'll be an avalanche of them, according to the latest reports.'

She hadn't changed. Commanding and statuesque, she was still in the driving seat. He regretted that time had not mellowed her or taught her to take a back seat in the family's affairs.

He knew he'd have been better thanked if, like Michael, he didn't speak his mind. He was different. Frank and forthright, he was not averse to putting his cards on the table when the occasion demanded.

Rising to the challenge, he said: 'Seriously, don't you think that, at thirty-five, it's time he had a wife?'

She shook her head, then responded frostily: 'He hasn't time for a date, never mind the responsibilities of marriage.'

'How come?' He refused to accept her lame excuses.

'He's run off his feet with the shop.' She wrenched herself away from the table and, in a typically evasive ploy, busied herself at the kitchen sink.

Though he could sense a growing distance between them, he was not prepared to back off.

'I don't think the business would suffer were he to set aside some time to romance a suitable partner,' he protested.

She ran the hot tap noisily, her expression an overstatement of annoyance, as she declared that romance went out with cross-roads dancing. And that, now, it was more about living together and costly separations.

'Not quite.' He stood his ground, fully aware that he had a fight on his hands.

She pulled a wry face.

'Not half. Since the Celtic Tiger, young couples have lost the run of themselves.'

A resourceful Paul decided to try her with a different approach.

'Don't you think that at your age you could do with some help around the house?'

'Help, my foot! Most modern wives wouldn't soil their hands with housework. Michael and I are doing fine. And in case you don't think so, I'm well able to cope.' She put on an energetic display at the sink for his benefit.

Control freak! Michael felt he would have to meet her head-on, just like he did when he decided, against her wishes, to leave the Christian Brothers for Helen, whom she resented for having lured him – as she liked to think – from his vocation. She couldn't have been more wrong. If there were any luring, it was on his part. Celibacy was not for him. The sex abuse by members of his Order, served to fast-track his leave-taking.

Having met her while holidaying abroad, Helen would become the love of his life. In time, his mother came to respect his decision and Helen as her daughter-in-law, even though she didn't quite measure up to her expectations. No woman could, he knew.

'I'm sure you can. But you mustn't tar all young wives with the same brush. Besides, traditional roles are changing.'

'Tell me about it!' she snorted scornfully.

Michael, he knew, was no better than her puppet. For the sake of peace, he kept his private life secret from her. His attitude: what she doesn't know won't trouble her. In the best interests of both parties, Paul felt he had no choice but to appraise her of his brother's liaison. As yet, he preferred to approach the issue gingerly until it was time to present her with the unpalatable truth.

'This house is but a ghostly shadow of itself.' There was a nostalgia in his voice for the vibrant, familial atmosphere that had once been its hallmark. Today it was noticeably cheerless and its décor looked dated and dull. Filigrees of cobwebs suspended from a smoke-stained ceiling, testified to his mother's increasing ineptitude.

'Well, you can afford to be sentimental. Here today and gone tomorrow. Look to your own house. There's nothing the matter with this one,' she snapped and ran the cold tap.

He fed her more line until she was ready to reel her in.

'It's dying a slow death.'

She glared at him.

'It's anything but.'

'Seriously, what future can there be for it and for the shop if Michael doesn't marry?' His gaze was again fixated on the cobwebs and the smoke-stained ceiling, begging for a fresh coat of paint.

She swung around and brandished a warning finger at him.

'The last thing I want is to live out my few remaining years with a disagreeable daughter-in-law, having seen the way my own mother was ill-treated by hers. As it is, it gave me all I could do to keep the peace with your other brother's wife during their recent stay. Just as well I don't have to put up with her whims on a regular basis.'

Determined not to capitulate, he suggested that Michael could surely get a place of his own.

She shook her head resolutely.

'He has ploughed every penny he had into upgrading the shop,' she informed him. Then added reproachfully: 'Do you think, for one minute, he'd leave me on my own?'

'Then I regret you're in for a bit of a shock.' Paul felt there was no longer any point in beating about the bush.

'I am! Am I? Is there something I ought to know? Sure Michael tells me nothing.' She reclined heavily on the sink while holding a cup in suspense.

'It's obvious why.'

'What d'you mean?' she demanded abruptly.

'Seeing you disapproved of all his other girl friends up to now, I seriously doubt if you'll approve of his current one.'

'Who?' Her face tightened with apprehension.

'Mrs Fitzroy.'

Her eyes widened with shock.

'Are you referring to that high-flying, loose-living, protestant divorcée?'

He nodded ruefully.

'God be between us and that woman!' The cup slipped from her grasp and fell with a splash into the sink. 'And to think he's carrying on like that behind my back!' Tears sprung to her eyes as she withdrew from the sink and slumped into her fireside chair, looking every day of seventy.

Paul allowed her some time for the matter to sink in. Then he upped the ante.

'And if they should tie the knot, there will be serious problems,' he warned.

'As if marriage isn't problematical enough,' she wailed.

Marshalling his arguments, he directed them like a cannonade at her defenses.

'In addition, you can look forward to a registry office, instead of a church wedding, inheritance disputes between her first and her second family, and a division of the property in the event of a divorce, if you persist in putting obstacles in his way with other women.' Paul presented her with a scenario he hoped would induce a u-turn on her part.

'Over my dead body!' His mother was on her feet and ready to go to war.

'I don't really know if there's much you can do to stop it. Unless . . .' He was about to pop his solution when she cut him short.

'Damn right there is. I'll sell the business and send him packing before I'll let a protestant divorcée darken my door.'

Paul played his final ace, hopeful that it would bring her to the conference table: 'You mightn't have to.' He took her place at the sink and began to dry the dishes.

He watched her wringing her hands, then heard her exclaim: 'What kind of a *meawe* is he? Of all the eligible girls in Abbeylaune, he has to fall for that Fitzroy wan.' She rolled her eyes to heaven for an answer, then gazed abjectly at the unswept floor.

'Love isn't particularly clear-sighted at the best of times. And I'm sure Mrs Fitzroy had good grounds for her divorce,' Paul disagreed with her.

'Her husband certainly had,' she ground, adding that she'd break the Central Bank.

Whereupon she catapulted herself out of her chair and made a bee-line for the cabinet, whence she plucked a copy of her last will and testament. Reaching for a scissors, she would have shredded it, had he not managed to wrest it from her.

'Are you crazy Mum? Chill out, for heaven's sake! I may even have a solution,' he appealed for sanity while keeping custody of the document until she calmed down.

'You have?' She regained her composure and resumed her seat again.

'It might interest you to know that I met up with an old flame of Michael's on the train from Dublin.'

'Tell me about her!' Her shoulders straightened and her eyes glistened with interest.

'I gather she's still keen on him, even though you discouraged him from seeing her,' Michael rebuked her.

'I must have had my reasons,' she replied archly.

He shot her a critical glance.

'Isn't that why things are the way they are? Your perverse reasons. Your road-blocks. Your refusal to let go of him.'

Defensively she responded that, where women were concerned, Michael didn't see beyond his nose.

He grimaced, then made a dismissive gesture.

'Maybe he sees beyond yours. And try and bear in mind that chemistry is an essential ingredient for any genuinely romantic relationship. And that your idea of the perfect partner isn't necessarily his. So butt out and let him choose for himself!' he told her.

She heaved a heavy sigh.

'Where was the chemistry in my match-made union? And wasn't it happy?' she protested.

Friendly, practical and procreative, Paul would have to admit, but hardly romantic.

'I'm sure it was happy, and I'm equally sure there were many such unions that weren't, but were suffered in silence out of religious subservience.'

A tense silence dropped between them as she reconsidered her circumstances.

'So who's this old flame of his you met?' She put aside her stalling tactics and gave him her attention.

'Does the name Carmel Mullins mean anything to you?'

'Of course it does. At the time, I didn't think she was cut out to be a shopkeeper's wife. Still, anybody but a promiscuous divorcée, and being barred from the sacraments for life. At least Carmel comes from a good, Catholic family,' she admitted with hindsight.

'And she's charming and attractive. And I'd bet she doesn't mind soiling her hands with housework,' Paul added, confident that he had neutralized her objections to a prospective daughter-in-law.

She emitted a deep sigh of relief.

'Can you arrange to bring them together?' She was on her feet again and, grabbing the tea towel from him, resumed drying the dishes.

'I can try. But it's not like turning on and off a tap. You

understand, I'll have to see firstly how Michael feels, though I gather he recently sent her a gift token for her birthday.'

'I know how he'll feel after I've finished with him,' she chortled.

Whereupon, Paul slipped out to the shop to talk things over with him.

After all, what are brothers for? And daughters-in-law, if not for mothers-in-law to become grandmothers?

Life must go on.

FORTUNE IN A TEACUP

Aidan was one of those rare birds that a town like ours throws up once in a while. Unconventional, often labelled eccentric, he was indisputably his own man. That he was still a bachelor at thirty didn't surprise us. Wedded to his antiques, some so old they'd qualify for carbon dating, there was simply no space in his life for a partner. In any case, not many women would care to live amid the trappings of previous centuries. And who could blame them? Stepping into his cluttered bungalow was like entering a time capsule. where the past proffered you its geriatric hand and divested you of your youth for the duration of your visit. A shrine to the past, where only a faithful minority came to pay their respects so far, keeping alive his faith in his mission when others would have long given up.

Considering I was living next door, I should have understood much sooner the lure that the antiques' business held for Aidan. It just didn't make sense to me, initially, how he could spurn the rewards of a well-paid, nine-to-five job like the rest of us, to pursue a precarious career. Conventional to the finger tips, I differed in most respects to my flamboyant neighbour, remarkable for his trendy, corded jackets, his arty ties and bohemian hats, matched by a carefully cultivated Van Dyke beard and a ponytail. which made him stand out from the rest of the townsfolk.

On winter evenings, for want of something better to do, I'd help him catalogue his stock, which owed its modest beginnings to his father, who had dabbled in antiques as a hobby, which would one day become his son's passion.

For my sins, I'd have to suffer the din of myriad clocks chiming in strident tones peculiar to their era – the hours and the half hours – while we re-located items, many of which I would have binned, if I had my way.

Quite frankly, I despaired of him ever getting rid of his mounting stock, by now cluttering every room in his bungalow. He was more optimistic. Dated paintings gathering dust and obsolete machinery rusting in an old barn could be used some day for an historical film. Period items of furniture were beginning to be sought after again and restored. There was nothing, contrary to what I might think, in his bizarre collection, that didn't have a commercial future.

'They are my orphans. It's my duty to provide a home for them,' he'd insist, foregoing a decent living due to his reluctance to part with them.

His modest returns somehow ensured that, even if he never hit it rich, he would never go hungry. Intuitively, he predicted an inevitable reaction to the mass-produced kitsch of the day, and a renewed demand for the rigorously crafted products of yesteryear. With the Celtic Tiger taking off, he saw clear indications of an uptake in the antiques' market in Dublin, though not to date in Abbeylaune, where few showed any interest in, and less foresaw any prospects for his business.

Little faith though I had in it, Butler, his other neighbour. had less.

'That stuff has had its day,' he declared dismissively.

When I told him there was a growing demand for it in Dublin, he simply spat.

'There's growing demand, too, for scrap. How he manages to live in that cluttered bungalow of his beats me. Creepy though it be by day, even Dracula wouldn't sleep there at night.'

As far as Butler was concerned, antiques were a waste of space, and Aidan a joke. Anything that didn't register a decent profit was pointless in his view.

To date, Aidan's clients consisted mostly of tourists and a sprinkling of local businessmen's wives who stopped by occasionally, in search of the odd item to enhance their trendily furnished sitting rooms. Something old, something new, if you know what I mean. Enough to keep the receiver from his door, though I gathered his father didn't leave him short.

'What do you see in it?' I put it to him once, intrigued by his dedication.

'The culture and the craftsmanship of the past.' His expression radiated enthusiasm.

He could talk for hours about a vase or a particular piece of plate if we, his neighbours, were prepared to listen. We weren't – at least, not yet. Sceptics to a man, we'd only be convinced if he hit the jackpot. After all, what use had we for those period pieces he raved about? State-of-the-art this and designer-labelled that were more our line and in keeping with a town in a modernising frenzy.

'Have you ever considered doing modern stuff?' I heard O'Leary inquire one evening when we were gathered at Aidan's place.

I watched Aidan shake his head emphatically.

'This is my mission.' He gestured devoutly towards his hoard, in which he had invested, I suspected, most of his inheritance.

'But have they any use?' Murphy, too, needed convincing.

'Of course they have. Antiques are an indispensable legacy of our past. They're part of our story, as well as a shaping influence on the craftsmanship of the future,' the connoisseur replied, adding that to understand the present one had to look to the past.

Butler frowned.

'Do you seriously believe that tea drunk from antique bone china tastes any better than tea drunk from an ordinary mug?' I heard him ask while wetting the tea.

'A mug for a mug in your case. Stay away from china,' Murphy advised the tea-maker, whom he likened to a bull in a china shop.

Aidan smiled, then proceeded with his defence, though I don't think anyone was really interested.

'It's more to do with one's sense of history, as well as one's aesthetic enjoyment of a rare item, than with the flavour.'

A confused Butler shook his head. Whereupon, Murphy volunteered to edify him.

'When you drink out of quality china, you're drinking with the gentry you clearly didn't come from. *Comprenez* bonehead?'

'Knowing as I do about your ancestry, it was buttermilk and not tea they drank. And that out of earthen-ware jars rather than rare china,' Butler retaliated.

'I'll wait till you're in your cups to mug you,' Murphy declared.

Fearful for his tea-set, Aidan discreetly suggested that, if they were contemplating a Boston Tea Party, they might consider having it in the chipper downtown.

At that point, we retired amicably to his cluttered kitchen to partake of his favourite Darjeeling tea from a set of cups so exquisitely wrought that they might have been purchased in the fabled markets of Araby.

A converted Butler spoke for all of us when he confessed that his second cup was as good as his first. And that a third would very likely be better still, but that he never drank more than two.

'You should try drinking more often outa china, it might help civilize your primitive taste-buds.' Murphy couldn't resist a dig at

Butler as we were leaving.

'You're not fit to drink out of a horse-trough, let alone china,' the other rejoined.

After that, we gave Aidan more respect. You couldn't but. And even if his precious possessions failed, so far, to yield him the jackpot and the esteem he deserved, we stood by him, seeing him as a feather in our community's cap, rather than the oddity who had, hitherto, made little sense to us.

It was left, however, to those discerning tourists who came knocking on his door each summer, to flag up the worth of his collection and convince me that it would only be a matter of time before his business took off.

In the meantime, I could see Aidan was content to settle for the long haul and for the odd fleeting attachment. Enduring ties were not yet practical. Besides, his career so far lacked that whiff of success that is a priority with most women nowadays.

In any case, I gathered, they were soon repelled by his domestic chaos and the cacophony of his clocks, which only the deaf could endure at night-time.

They wisely, we both agreed, parted company. Resignedly, he would admit afterwards that a partner who had no use for his cherished antiques would be as insufferable as a step-mother who couldn't abide her adopted children.

Watching him unwrap and, in turn, rhapsodise about an acquisition, convinced me his collection was the love of his life. The fascinating history an item of delft would evoke for him never ceased to amaze me. An old vase, about which I could see nothing special, would provoke him to flights of ecstasy, while having to part with a book of poems bearing the signature of some long-deceased bard, was as painful for him as parting with a limb. Money still didn't matter to him as long as he could get by.

In his fitful moments, he was known to dine from a Wedgwood plate, drink a rare wine from a Murano glass and round off his meal with a silver pot of exotic tea, which he'd drink from a Dresden china cup, causing the townsfolk to shake their heads and declare he was for the birds.

Nothing, of course, could be further than the truth. Aidan's talent for organization was remarkable. If I forgot where I'd stored something, he would locate it in a matter of minutes, give me its history, the auction where it was purchased, its aesthetic virtues and its market value. A professional to his finger-tips.

Whenever I disagreed with him about holding on to marketable items, he'd dig in his heels, fearful they might end up abroad or in the wrong hands. Knowing how frugally he lived, and fearful he'd be left with them, I pressed him time and again to part with them and give somebody else the pleasure of them.

'They're part of our national heritage that must be safeguarded,' he'd insist, irritatingly scrupulous.

He seemed to me to derive more enjoyment from acquiring than from disposing of them – and much more pleasure from browsing through them than from any money they'd make. Where business was concerned we clearly walked different roads.

'If you're going to turn this business around, you'll have to get rid of your scruples.' I stopped short of yelling at him on more than one occasion.

He simply shrugged, letting success come to him, rather than chasing it.

On Valentine's Day, while we were doing some stock-taking, it knocked on his door in the guise of a stunning young rep from Jaspers, one of Dublin's leading antique dealers. Being on short time from my firm – presently in the process of slimming down its work force – I was spending more and more time helping Aidan.

'I presume I've come to the right place.' She seemed a little unsure, flicking back a lock of her auburn treasure, as she spoke.

'It depends on what you're looking for,' Aidan replied, taking in her exquisite figure with a captivated glance.

'Aidan O'Brien's antique shop,' I heard her chirp in a cultured accent.

'This is it.' He was promptly all over her, inquiring if there were anything he could do for her.

'A pretty big ask, I'm afraid.' She heaved a little sigh that was more like a cry for help.

He smiled, then looked hopefully at her.

'There's no ask too big or too costly if I have it.'

I could tell by the way he fussed over her, that if she asked for the moon, he'd go all out to fetch it for her.

'You won't believe it, but I'm looking for a missing cup from a very rare, *Mandarin* tea-set,' I heard her ask.

He racked his brain – a veritable database now in over-drive on her behalf.

'"The cup that cheers but never inebriates." Belongs with the golden age of Dutch delft,' he recalled with satisfaction.

'Let's say it will be a cause for inebriation if you should find one.' She beamed at him and in turn at me, by now as spellbound as Aidan by her summery presence that brightened the drab surrounds, as well as the prospects for their contents, after decades of repose.

'Fingers crossed. I'm nearly sure I have one. And possibly a saucer to go with it.

Yes. I distinctly recall picking them up at a local auction some years back. And if my memory serves me, they were originally rescued from a local manor house torched during the War of Independence.'

'Really? What a shame! If you can locate it, it would be the find of the decade.'

Her doe-like eyes sparkled with expectancy.

He nodded positively.

'Just bear with me a moment,' he appealed.

I watched him skip on winged feet into the store room, his feelings for her I could tell, running amuck. When he returned with the elusive cup, his hair was quiffed, his tie straightened and he smelt of Old Spice – his favourite aftershave.

'O my God! I can't believe it,' she exclaimed as she held it to the light for inspection. Then setting it down carefully, she gave him a delirious hug.

'Amazing what you can find in a neck of the woods like this,' he remarked, delighted to have been able to oblige her. Could this, I wondered, be his lucky break? His reward for years of diligent service to antiquity?

'Amazing is no word for it. I've searched high and low for it to no avail until now.'

If ever a woman were his for the asking, it must have been Olive at that moment.

Presenting him with her card, I heard her ask if he wouldn't mind her not making him an offer until she first conferred with her boss.

He nodded deferentially.

'No problem.' Such was the chemistry between them, and knowing how little money mattered to him, it wouldn't surprise me if he made her a gift of it.

Remembering her boss was on a golf outing and was not to be disturbed while playing, she'd text him later. He'd ring her back from the clubhouse. She could picture his joy. The elusive missing piece of his prized set of delft was his at last.

As she was leaving she said: 'I'll ring you as soon as I get word.

Then you might be good enough to pop around with the cup to the Abbeylaune Arms where I'm staying. The least I can do is to treat you to a meal.'

'Provided it's on me,' I heard Aidan protest but was over-ruled.

'Nonsense. It will be on the company. The early bird menu is well within my expense account. So how about eight o'clock?'

'Perfect.' I could tell by the way he kept glancing at his watch, that he couldn't wait to be with her.

'What a woman! What a night, Joe!' Aidan exclaimed to me the next day, rejoicing like an adolescent over his first date.

'I seriously hope you wrung a good deal from her.' I tried to steer him back to reality, which wasn't easy in his present mood.

Recklessly, he proclaimed: 'Never mind the deal! I'd gladly let her have the cup for another intoxicating evening of her company.'

I grimaced anxiously.

'Get a grip, Aidan!' I'd never seen him so giddy. I'd long suspected he was a soft touch for women.

He refused to listen.

'You don't understand, Joe. I've just found the woman of my dreams.'

'Did you name your price?' I asked, worried he'd lost the run of himself.

He shook his head, then told me her boss insisted on seeing the cup before making him an offer.

'Just keep your head on your shoulders until you've sealed the deal,' I warned him.

He nodded, though I don't believe he heeded a word I'd said.

A week later, the longest ever in Aidan's experience, Olive phoned. She had wonderful news for him. The really wonderful part of it, I could tell, was hearing her voice again after an agonising week of waiting .

'Care to guess how much your cup is valued at?' I over-heard her ask Aidan, who had the phone on loud. He was so engrossed, he was oblivious to me standing vigilantly by, just in case he said something rash.

'Not as valued as its buyer.'

'You old charmer. Come on! Give a guess!'

'A dinner for two at the Trocadero.'

'You'll have to do much better.'

'A week-end together in London?'

'Try again.' The lilt of her laughter was resonating through every fibre of his being.

'Make me a three figure offer.'

'What are you running? A charitable organization?' I heard her echoing my own convictions.

'I'll survive.'

I felt like grabbing the phone from him and taking over.

'Well how about this for your survival fund?' The offer in question left us both speechless.

'You can't be serious, Olive!' he responded as if he'd won the Lottery. The thought of haggling for more, as most dealers would, never once crossed his mind.

'I'm very serious. Congratulations.'

His persistence had finally paid off. Still shaken, but curious, he learned that her client was a wealthy oil sheik who owned a renowned stud farm in the Midlands.

'It'll take me a lifetime to recover.' I watched his hand tremble as he held the receiver.

'I'd suggest you do so before you come to Dublin to collect your cheque. Or would you prefer to have it posted to you?'

He opted to collect it, the money, I knew, paling into insignificance at the prospect of another evening with her, this time in the capital.

'And when you're there, I want you to have a browse around our magnificent show rooms. It might encourage you to consider applying for a post with our celebrated firm.' I wasn't sure if she were romancing him or head-hunting him.

'Certainly.' If he should ever decide to up and leave, I felt it would be for Olive. And judging by his absent air in the ensuing days, it wouldn't surprise me if he were seriously considering it.

'So how come you sat on that fortune for so long?' I inquired more confused than ever.

He winked at me, then admitted he'd been waiting all along for the right customer.

'I had a feeling you'd hit it rich,' I finally confessed.

'You did! You must have been reading my tea cups,' he chuckled.

Though everything appeared to be going his way, I could sense a hint of unease about Aidan. It annoyed him that it took Olive so long to get back to him. He noticed, too, a certain brusqueness about her exchange. A business-like edge, rather than a romantic resonance to her voice, which left him guessing.

'What d'you expect?' I tried to reason with him. 'That she'd trumpet her feelings for you in the presence of her colleagues, having met you only once?'.

'Hmm! And you don't think it was all an act on her part at the Abbeylaune Arms, just to wring the best possible deal from me?'

Seeing him about to whip up one of his characteristic storms in a tea-cup, I couldn't but help laughing at him.

'If anyone got a good deal it's you. Thanks to her, the Celtic Tiger has arrived on your door-step.'

He shrugged, then proceeded to pace tensely about the room.

'If only I could trust her. Have it from me, Joe, career women in this line of business can switch on and off the charm like an electric bulb. It's a ruthless business.'

I finally managed to convince him that he had achieved the kind of success that women find irresistible, and left him to draw his own conclusions.

'Then it's the first train to Dublin for me.' He regrouped, packed his travelling bag and left me to keep an eye on things for him in his absence.

I gathered, on his return, that all the red carpet treatment he received at Jaspers, and the cheque that had his eyes popping, counted for next to nothing on learning that Olive was away in London for the week-end.

'I've been duped,' he ranted repeatedly, as he paced about the dining room the same evening. Nothing would convince him but that she had given him the slip.

'How can you be so sure?' I asked, and suggested a wait and see approach.

Wringing his hands, he fumed that she didn't think it worth her while to leave even a note of apology.

How often had I seen him lose the run of himself at the early stage of his romances, only to be brought abruptly to his senses subsequently.

When I saw him pluck the cheque from his pocket and reach for the scissors, I grappled with him, managing after a manic struggle to wrest it from him.

'You mustn't look your gift horse in the mouth!' I appealed to him.

He shook his head distraughtly.

'Without her the money means nothing to me,' he assured me and continued to torture himself with imaginary betrayals.

I told him to chill out, while keeping the cheque out of his reach.

Ignoring my plea, he pounded the table.

'The woman of my dreams has done a runner on me. And you're asking me to chill out!'

When he finally simmered down, I returned him the cheque.

Olive's re-appearance a week later during stock-taking, had more the ring of the bad penny turning up than a repeat of the previous apparition that blew him over.

'Surprised to see me?' It wouldn't surprise me if she were the one surprised by his icy reception.

'Oh, not at all. Most of our customers return time and again.' I could see it was all an act with him and that he was still as mad about her as he was with her.

'By the way, I owe you an apology for failing to meet you at Jaspers,' she said. Though I'd removed myself to the next room to allow them privacy, I couldn't but help overhearing them.

'I'm sure you didn't travel all the way from Dublin to tell me that,' he responded curtly.

'In case you mightn't think so, I do have a heart.' Her voice was as pleading as it was plaintive.

'So does a deck of cards,' he said tartly.

She sighed audibly.

'Speaking of cards, it may not occur to you, but I do have to play mine with the boss.'

'You didn't seem to mind dealing me a pretty miserable hand. You could at least have left a note,' he rebuked her.

She cut him short.

'You don't seem to understand that with big money like that changing hands, I had to be extra careful not to show my hand.'

He began to see reason. And in a reasonable manner he inquired: 'So what took you to London?'

She explained that she had to step in at literally five minute's notice for a colleague who had taken ill, to represent the firm at a very important auction. 'Really, Aidan, you should treat yourself to a mobile phone for emergencies.'

I could see him smiling.

'I'll wait till they've become antiques' he chuckled. 'So, what brings you here again?' There was a cheerful ring to his query.

'The saucer.' I could picture him swearing under his breath. A saucer! It sounded so business-like. So unromantic. He'd tell me later his first impulse was to scream. Happily, his business instincts prevailed.

'Anything but a flying saucer,' he quipped. 'Whatever happened to the original one?' he asked, as he withdrew to the storeroom.

'Don't ask me how it happened, but we suddenly discovered a hairline crack in it,' she called after him.

'I can't imagine the original owners hurling plate of that quality at one another during their family tiffs, but you're welcome to the companion piece. And don't bother about the cheque,' I heard him telegraph from the storeroom, then watched him emerge minutes later and present her with the indispensable saucer, though not scenting of Old Spice on this occasion.

I was on the point of protesting when Olive intervened.

'Don't be silly.' She reminded him again for whom the delft was intended. I admired her for her honesty. Wind him, though she could, around her little finger, she refused to take advantage of him.

'Then make me a modest offer.' Typical Aidan. He should have been running a pound shop.

She waved aside his request.

'The same as the cup. And a meal together in the Abbeylaune Arms.'

He said he'd gladly settle for the latter.

What wouldn't I have given to be in his shoes. I could sense his spirits lifting and noted a lilt in his voice that had been missing for days.

'Now, now! Business is business. Otherwise, what would the boss think of me?' she took issue with him.

'I imagine he'd be pleased.'

She stared at him in disbelief.

'I'm pretty certain he'd want to know what I did with the money.'

'Women!' I heard Aidan sigh.

'Have their reputation to maintain. So if it's not too much to ask, you might pop around with the saucer to the hotel around eight.' Her voice was suddenly dulcet and her smile beaming with invitation.

He nodded eagerly.

I joined him in the porch as he saw her off.

'Tonight the world will be your oyster,' I predicted and wished him well.

'For me, she's the only pearl that matters,' he professed with a candour that was moving.

The ensuing week-end in Dublin – the first of many – would be a turning point for Aidan. The city, with its teeming prospects, was as irresistible as Olive. Very soon, there would be much coming and going: she to Abbeylaune one week, mixing business with pleasure, he to Dublin the next, mixing pleasure with business, and Jaspers providing him with a lucrative outlet for his antiques – the fruit of his tireless pickings from auctions throughout the country.

When Jaspers advertised a vacancy for a post, his application was successful. I could tell he was through with Abbeylaune. From the moment Olive first set foot on his premises, I sensed the dice was cast for him. I'd miss him. Now that he's made it and shaken its dust from his shoes, Abbeylaune laments the loss of one of its more enterprising sons.

With the proceeds from his windfall and his subsequent business deals with Jaspers, he shrewdly placed a deposit on an attractive semi on the city's south-side, where he and Olive propose to live when they marry, which I gather will be shortly, with yours truly press-ganged into doing best man.

In the meantime, I've agreed to act in a caretaker capacity for his business. It will give me something to do and help to tide me over until I find something better, having recently been made redundant by my profit-driven firm, nowadays outsourcing much of its work to cheap, foreign firms.

All going well, I might even continue to stand in for Aidan now that I've got a handle on the antiques. And who knows, a stunning woman like Olive, in search of a missing piece of delft, might walk into my life some day and spirit me away to the metropolis of opportunity.

It's every bachelor's fantasy in Abbeylaune these days.

POETIC JUSTICE

It was Grandad who confirmed, with a story about Donlon, his neighbour, what our teacher once told us about Gaelic poets of the past possessing magical powers.

A strong farmer with a dodgy reputation for women, Donlon, I understood, lived alone in a rambling residence of gloomy rooms and an eerie attic after he'd fired Lisa, his maid – a mere slip of a girl in her early teens – having got her pregnant. A felony he'd have done time for to-day but which went unreported then, scared as most people were, in those days, of the law courts. Previous, more street-wise maids left his service before suffering a similar fate.

From what I gathered, Grandad felt sore about her ill-treatment, and regretted in later life not speaking up for her at the time, seeing her as an unwitting victim of grievous abuse. So sweet–natured and winsome a colleen, much praised for her housekeeping and her appetizing little suppers greatly appreciated by the card players who frequented Donlons, deserved better in his opinion. The hitherto cheerful house would soon be the poorer for her absence, the neat kitchen becoming noticeably unkempt, and the suppers rough-and-ready.

With Lisa gone, Donlon's household consisted, after his neighbours had dispersed, of his collie and his three black cats, which he sometimes felt like strangling for keeping him awake with their mating rites – a stark reminder of his misadventure with Lisa.

When I suggested that he needed them to keep the mice in check, Grandad pulled a wry face.

'Mice were about their size, for on the fateful May Eve night when the rats descended on his farmhouse, they effectively spread the red carpet for them.'

'You mean to tell me they turned tail?'

He nodded, and drew his chair closer to the fire.

'Would you blame them? Even a pride of lions would have taken to their heels in the circumstance.'

'And Donlon?' I could feel a knot gathering in my stomach.

Grandad went on to relate how he was rudely aroused from his sleep by the deafening din of the invaders. The house, which was normally as silent as a tomb at night-time since his brothers and sisters dispersed, was suddenly pulsating with the patter of paws on the ceiling, which was nothing compared to the frantic clawing beneath the floorboards, and the bedlam in the cupboard. All hell seemed to have broken loose.

'They picked their time well,' I observed with a shiver.

Grandad nodded and reached into his pocket for his pipe.

From what I could gather, Donlon thought, at first, that he was dreaming and tried in vain to go back to sleep, as wave after unnerving wave of din shook the house. Each time the delph rattled in the cupboard, his ears popped. When things began to topple and smash, his heart was in his mouth.

He was definitely not dreaming. A menacing presence, like that of a burglar in one's room, soon routed him from his bed.

Feeling frantically for his matches, he sent them hurtling onto the floor in his panic. While groping for them, his hand brushed against a furry object, which scurried at his touch. Shocked to his toenails, he realized there were rats in his bedroom.

'Ouch! It must have been pretty scary,' I interrupted, reliving the sensation.

'Scary is no word for it.'

Grandad's tone grew more dramatic as he gave me to understand that Donlon was in a cold sweat. 'Never, in his experience, were the small hours so dark or so terrifying. Never did he feel so alone,' he assured me.

'I'd bet he missed Lisa,' I said, picturing myself in his shoes.

He frowned and went on to tell me how Donlon spent the rest of the night banging on the floorboards and sealing crevices, in an effort to secure his sleeping quarters from further incursions. Suddenly religious, he was said to have dipped frantic fingers in the holy water font that must have been dry for years.

'Wouldn't you if you were in his shoes?' I asked Grandad.

'You'd better believe it, son. And hope that it was Knock or Lourdes water that was in it.'

'So how did he deal with the rats?' I inquired, liking to think he had the upper hand.

'There was nothing much he could do. Unopposed by the household guardians, they just took over the house and soon the outhouses.'

'Are you serious?' I couldn't wait for him to light his pipe and settle into his fireside chair. A born story teller, he liked to keep his listeners in suspense.

'Very soon, son,' he resumed, 'I witnessed with my own two eyes, the dictatorship of the rodents.'

He then went on to relate how they grew more fearless and terrifying by the day.

I grimaced, picturing Donlon's dilemma.

He recalled how, within a week of their residency, they subdued the cats and the collie. Whether these household minders had a surfeit of their prey after the initial killings or had made their peace with them, nobody could tell. One thing is certain, the rats were ruling the roost.

Even the card players, my grandfather among them, were bewildered by the rodents' antics.

'You mean to say they weren't normal?' I wasn't sure what he meant.

Reluctant to confirm or deny it, he merely shrugged, while admitting there were local rumours to that effect.

'Did he not turn his gun on them when the cats gave up?' I inquired, picturing myself picking them off like a Texas Ranger.

He nodded, then went on to relate how Donlon opened fire one night on two rats mating near his bedroom door. When he missed, the gun fell from his trembling hands, leading him to believe that there was something unnatural about them.

Unreal or otherwise, Grandad conceded that there was an air of invincibility about their defiance of conventional remedies.

When he suggested to Donlon that he should set more traps for them, his shattered neighbour had him know that they were wising up to those he had already set for them. More effective methods were required if his home weren't to become uninhabitable.

Determined to find a solution, the resolute card players continued to put their heads together, eventually settling for poison.

'I don't know if it'll work.' Donlon, who no longer had faith in any remedy, again doubted.

'I see no reason why it shouldn't. Unless of course they're *pisheógs*.' A superstitious member, I gathered, cast further doubts on it.

'Balderdash! The strychnine will wipe them out.' The others were convinced.

With the card players dispersing earlier than usual, Donlon was left to endure his relentless nightmares without a woman to comfort him, the smell of the rodents a constant reminder of their presence.

'Did the poison work?' I enquired.

A perplexed-looking Grandad shook his head.

'For every rat that perished, there seemed no end to others taking their places. Not that there weren't considerable casualties. Every morning the scene of carnage by the little stream at the rear of the house resembled a battle scene, strewn with the bloated bodies of the victims.'

'Donlon must have felt like giving up,' I said.

Grandad remembered him becoming more and more desperate, as he watched the rats wreaking havoc on his thatched roof and springing leaks in his attic.

'Could they have been *piseógs*?' I asked, intrigued by the possibility.

Assuming a mystified air, he toyed with the idea.

'They were pretty weird I can tell you. And there was simply no end to their destructiveness,' the *seanchai* added, pausing to relight his pipe, which was forever going out.

I waited with baited breath for the gory details while he tended to his pipe – a ritual I had grown used to by now.

When he resumed, I learned that the rats had a field day in the corn loft, where they ripped open the sacks and gorged themselves on the contents. Even the cattle were terrorised in their byre at night and frequently broke their chains, as the rats descended ravenously on their food troughs. Nor, I gathered, was Donlon's own larder spared. Eventually, he was too scared to eat for fear of being poisoned.

Bemused, I was curious to know why they had picked on Donlon's place?'

Grandad paused, then, after some deliberation, said: 'It was generally believed that they were sent.'

'Were they?'

He merely shrugged and went on to relate how he watched his neighbour cracking up. If matters continued, he feared Donlon would have to surrender his home to the squatters – a home from which, in Grandad's words, rack-renting landlords had failed to evict his ancestors. A home, too, that had been a popular rambling house in the past and kept an open door for travellers, now in the throes of destruction.

Many, he gave me to understand, were the failed ploys hatched by the card players but still they refused to give up. Believing in their supremacy over the animal kingdom, they continued to pit their wits against the vermin.

Eventually, I gathered, a ferret was suggested and procured from a local fowler.

'Did it succeed?'

Yet again, I watched Grandad nod otherwise.

'The rats played fox and geese with him. Like the cats and the dog he too tired of the conflict and was found dead one morning beside the stream. Poisoned.'

The knot in my stomach grew tighter as he told me how, one night, a rat crept up the leg of Donlon's trousers as he dozed off by the fireside. Luckily, I gathered, he awoke, and managed to crush the intruder in his groin, though not before it left the marks of its teeth on his private parts – the excruciating pain he must have endured conveyed by Grandad's agonized expression.

'Donlon must have been at his wits end,' I ventured, feeling sympathy for him despite what he did to Lisa. So gripping was Grandad's account, I relived every step of the nightmare he'd been through.

'You can take my word for it, he was a broken man.'

I gathered he slept with the light on in his bedroom that winter, and with an ash plant by his side to ward off the rats and to bang on the floor boards whenever the noise became unbearable. Sometimes he woke up in the morning to find his shirt and his socks chewed to bits.

'How on earth was he able to get up for work?' I mused.

Grandad remembered that, more often than not, the wretched man went about his chores sleep-walking and muttering to himself.

Things, seemingly, got so bad that Donlon eventually had to sleep at Grandad's. By then, the once fearless, powerfully built man had become a mere shadow of his former self. Emaciated and drooped, his prolonged silences and his blank stare had the card players seriously worried about his health.

'So how did it finally end?' I was getting impatient for the outcome.

In no hurry, the story-teller refuelled his pipe before going on to relate how the Redemptorists were giving a mission in Abbeylaune. As it drew to a close, a despairing Donlon invited a missioner to his house to bless it and pray that it be rid of the rats.

'Did the prayers work?'

After some deliberation, he responded with a characteristic shrug.

'If you're asking me did the rats move out there and then, my answer is no. But, for what ever reason, help was soon on the way.'

'In what form?'

Impatiently I waited for him to add some fuel to the fire before resuming his seat.

It came about, he told me, that an elderly travelling woman knocked on Donlon's door one day, seeking alms. In a penitent or a charitable mood, Grandad saw him place a florin in her palm, which, in those days, was a princely sum. And it worked.

'Really? He'd want to do better in today's money,' I ventured.

He nodded, then proceeded to give me a blow-by-blow account of what passed between his neighbour and the travelling woman.

'I believe you've rats,' she said.

'Who told you? '

'I heard it in my travels.'

'I can't get rid of them,' a beaten Donlon sighed.

'You can,' she said, feeling sorry for him.

'I've tried everything.' He wrung his hands in despair.

The travelling woman disagreed.

'Then what in the name of blazes am I to do?' he exclaimed.

'I presume you've heard of the bard McPhelim?'

He nodded, but thought he was dead.

'He may have one foot in the grave, but there's still a step in the other one. So take my advice and get in touch with him, or 'tis two feet you'll soon have in the grave.'

'You mean to tell me that McPhelim can succeed where a Redemptorist failed?' Donlon, I gathered, began to doubt her.

She nodded emphatically.

'Sure who knows but 'twas the holy missioner's prayers sent me to you with an answer. Trust me, McPhelim can rid you of them rats,' she assured him, adding that somebody had obviously sent them.

A bewildered Donlon shrugged wearily.

'Get in touch with the bard at once. He may not have long to live,' she warned as she was leaving.

'Did he?' I inquired, my mouth by now dry with anticipation.

'You're damned well right he did. Straightaway, he collected the bard in his horse and buggy and sat him down to a hearty meal, which was graced before and after with liberal helpings of whiskey, while he informed McPhelim of his plight.

The bard, having drained his glass, reached out a bony hand across the table and held his host's in its firm grasp.

'Tonight you'll sleep in your own bed,' he assured him. 'Somebody has put a curse on you for a wrong you've done, but it's in my power to lift it. I haven't forgotten the hard times when your father kept the bailiff from my door. And for that I'll repay you.'

'God bless you and spare you your health.' Grandad, while fixing a hot punch in the scullery for the bard, overheard a grateful Donlon pray.

I gathered however, that McPhelim demanded poetic justice for Lisa. What the exact figure was, Grandad wasn't sure. It was generally deemed to have been substantial.

Whereupon, Donlon and himself witnessed the bard – a gaunt, hieratic figure – rise to his shaky feet and recite a frightening chant that was peppered with imprecations. It was as if he had suddenly turned himself into one of the shamans of old and was communing with all his strength with mysterious, spiritual forces.

Grandad distinctly remembered how McPhelim's body had vibrated, and his voice, issuing like thunder from his depths, had the commanding resonance of a priest's conducting an exorcism. Not exactly, I'd venture, a scene for the faint-hearted.

No sooner had he finished his unnerving rite, than a thunderous patter of paws could be heard, heralding an exodus, that sounded for all the world like an army of occupation moving out after the signing of peace terms.

The Bard, having regained his composure, was seen by Grandad to raise his refilled glass to Donlon and wish him luck.

'Come now and see for yourselves what I've done,' he proudly said and proceeded both men into a crystal-clear night, floodlit by a new moon, as far as the eye could see.

They could hardly believe their eyes as they watched the huge phalange of rats, their leader borne on the backs of four of his lieutenants, heading towards the river, where McPhelim consigned them to a watery grave.

I gave a little gasp of disbelief, then inquired about Lisa.

'Donlon was as good as his word. You can take it from me, neither she nor her baby lacked for anything.

'And what became of Donlon?'

Grandad told me that he eventually married a woman who failed to give him a family. In his declining years, he surprised everyone by leaving his farm to the son Lisa bore for him.

'Fair play to him. And McPhelim?'

'He died shortly afterwards, just as the travelling woman had predicted.'

'Poets are really cool,' I marvelled, convinced more than ever of what the teacher said about them.

Grandad nodded, his mind drifting away into the mists of his past – that storehouse of memories he'd draw on to regale me another day during my holidays in Abbeylaune many years ago before he, too, passed away.

QUICK TO JUDGE

When David Cashman entered Abbeylaune's leading bank that ill-fated, Friday afternoon, with his redundancy cheque from the electronics firm, you can take my word for it, he couldn't have foreseen the unwitting outcome arising from his investment, recently the talk of the town. Unlike his colleagues, who couldn't wait to splash theirs out in the Market pub and the bookies, he intended his as a nest egg for the rainy days ahead.

A thrifty but simple man, who always put his family's interests first, he was an easy prey to the promptings of the assistant bank manageress that he might consider investing his lump sum in the lucrative, overseas' Midas Account, which guaranteed much richer dividends than the local credit union, where he normally lodged his few savings.

David, whose wealth, I suspected, was his health hitherto, saw no reason why he shouldn't make a bit of a killing in the market. A lifetime of modest deposit accounts had not put money in his pocket, and his regular expenditure on draws and quick-picks proved even less fruitful. Money, he maintained, walked the other side of the street to him. Yet he lived in hope for one of those windfalls that come peoples' way when they win the lotto, or are left money by a deceased relative – one of the reasons, I'd venture, why he tumbled unwittingly for the lure of the Midas Account.

Placing himself in the hands of his attractive mentor, the future of his investment was assured with a wink and a nod and 'mum's the word'. Or so the word in the street goes. And in Abbeylaune, it's usually on the button.

When news of the scam broke and an amnesty was granted to those who made a disclosure of their investments, David, like so many others, refused, for some reason, to avail of it. Why, I may never know. And it's anybody's guess whether it was deliberate default or a naïve belief on his part that he could beat the system, as some had done in the past. Admittedly, the penalties were pretty stiff. Yet, I would have thought it was a golden opportunity for him to come clean, pay up, and be forgiven for his misdemeanour. David, obviously, thought otherwise.

Byrne, who claimed to know him better than most, gave him his full support.

'He did what any man in his shoes would do, given half a chance.'

David's failure to respond to the second amnesty, I found even more baffling. The reduced penalty for evasion was still within his reach, unlike its costly alternative.

Instead, he spurned the offer, hoping, or so the rumour goes, to give the tax sleuths the slip, like his ancestors, who, for various reasons, hid their savings under their mattresses and slept very comfortably and securely on them, immune to the whims of the financial system that cost others sleepless nights, and drove others still to jump to their doom from skyscraper windows, as happened in America in the wake of the Wall Street Crash. Who knows, if such events may have influenced his decision?

'I'm sure he had his reasons.' Reynolds, too, was forgiving.

I watched Cribbins shaking his head, then proceed to knock him.

'It beggars belief that he could have walked himself into such a trap.'

Admittedly, for much of David's life, tax evasion had a whiff of Spartan ethics about it. The crime was in being caught. And far from being a corrective, the biblical perspective of the unpopular tax gatherer served, if anything, to make light of the offence.

'There's got to be more to it than we think,' Byrne continued to make allowances for him.

Unfortunately for David, tolerance had given way recently to transparency and accountability. I felt, however, that the bank that initially misled him had a responsibility to him, even if he weren't entirely innocent of the cock-up he'd made of the amnesties.

Like most of my fellow patrons in the Market Pub, I agreed that the idea of setting up an overseas' account in the first instance, would have been foreign to David, for whom the local credit union was as close as he ever came to investment banking.

Cribbins disagreed, claiming to have suspected him all along, and that all his sanctimonious posturing in recent times was nothing more than a carefully rehearsed cover up. I gathered he saw himself as above all that kind of underhand dealing.

'We'll just have to wait to hear David's side of the story.' I was relieved to hear the publican plead for his popular patron, as the inevitable tribunal got off the ground.

Quite frankly, I suspected Cribbins's reaction had more to do with begrudgery of his neighbour's generous redundancy package, and the considerable profit he stood to make from his overseas' investment, than with principles.

The self-employed among us were more understanding of David. I suspected from their response that their tax returns, too, left something to be desired.

'For cryin' out loud, he was only beefing up his pension book.' Lenehan glared at Cribbins.

'He'll have something else to beef about now,' the righteous

Cribbins snapped.

Night after night, I listened to him making a meal of his next-door neighbour's downfall since the news broke. Admittedly, controversies of this kind were nothing new to the Market Pub. And the closer to home, the more controversial they generally were. It comes from living in a small town where everyone knows everyone else's business.

'I'm sure the thought would never have crossed his mind had he not been made redundant. So who could blame him for trying to shore up against his losses?' Byrne, too, rallied to his defence.

Cribbins looked at him with disdain. 'He thought to get rich quick by pulling a fast one on the taxman,' he sermonised, for the benefit of David's redundant colleagues, who provided him with a captive audience. Though they had drunk their way, by now, through most of their redundancy money, they would have no undue regrets, having enjoyed every penny of it.

It was an attitude I deplored, seeing how little thought they spared for their families. It hurt me, too, to see David being put down in his absence. Out of circulation since his name appeared among the hit list of offenders named and shamed by the newspapers, he was rumoured to be lying low with his daughter in Dublin, until the storm blew over.

Like most, I couldn't wait, regardless of his offence, for his return. I missed his lively contribution to the company and his ability to put the bumptious Cribbins in his box.

'He must have been blown over by the sexy assistant manageress,' I heard one of the factory hands trying to belittle his disgraced colleague during the on-going pub assize.

I watched Lenehan shaking his head.

'She didn't have to be sexy to pull the wool over his eyes. The man hadn't a clue what he was letting himself in for,' he insisted.

It annoyed me that the small guy should be the fall guy in scams of this kind.

Cribbins frowned dismissively.

'Whatever else David is, he's not stupid. He must have known that sooner or later Revenue would catch up with him.' He was relishing his tenancy of the high moral ground, and had even appropriated David's stool in his absence.

'Whatever he knew was less than the bank that misled him, knew,' Reynolds disagreed, and signalled to the publican for another pint.

A politically correct Cribbins refused to listen. For all his outspokenness, I sometimes wondered if what you saw was what you got, or whether he hadn't some skeletons in his own cupboard. He was certainly known to have his finger in a number of pies, though nobody seemed to mind so far.

I watched him, another night, raise a patronising glass to the factory hands, as he commended them for their good sense.

'Sensible lads were ye to have put yer money in the Credit Union instead of being sweet-talked into a dodgy deal by the bank.'

Seeing that the real beneficiary of their redundancy lump sums was the Market Pub, I would hardly rate them sensible.

'You can sing that again,' I heard the revellers reply. Their heaven was a high stool and a skinful of Guinness. Then: 'What day is today? Show me the road to go home! And let tomorrow look after itself.'

David, on the other hand, would have nothing to show for his investment but embarrassment and the prospect of a crippling penalty he could ill afford, having been reduced to odd-jobbing since his firm shut down. With the clock hardly on his side, his job prospects looked slimmer now that Abbeylaune's Celtic Tiger was winding down. Not exactly, I knew, the happiest scenario for a man married to a demanding woman and with a dependent son and daughter – the last of a large family – still at college.

As the pub tribunal continued, it riled me to see David's credentials taking a hammering from Cribbins, now revelling in his new-found role as judge and jury of his neighbour, with whom he had so often crossed swords only to come off second best.

David's apologists, I was relieved to note, did not come up short in their exchanges with an antagonist who refused to let up. Having no stomach for arguing, I tried to keep aloof, as the rights and wrongs of tax evasion were hotly debated, some taking the absent David's side, while others supported Cribbins, who was becoming more judgemental by the day.

'Try and remember, David doesn't have a secure, pensionable job with the Council like you,' I heard Reynolds reprove him at the height of the fall-out.

'So what? Are we to throw the rule book out the window and give the tax dodgers a free ride?' Cribbins considered David's underhand arrangement with the bank unprincipled and unpatriotic.

Much to my relief, one of the factory hands unexpectedly rounded on him.

'As it stands, there seems to be one set of rules for the bank and another for the poor suckers it misled.'

Whereupon, some one inquired how much David had been caught for, giving everyone, bar Cribbins, pause for concern.

'By the time the taxman has finished with him, he won't have the price of a pint,' he ventured with satisfaction, drawing further fire from his erstwhile supporters.

'It's friggin' outrageous, diddling a redundant workin' man out of his nest egg.'

Another factory hand changed his stance much to Cribbin's chagrin.

'Not to mention all the untaxed wealth in this country.' A third cried shame.

I nodded, certain that he spoke for most in the Market Pub.

After a heated controversy about the likely penalty, some presumed David could plead inability to pay and hope for leniency, while others saw no reason why he should have to cough up a single penny, having been more wronged than wrong-doing. A sympathetic publican felt as I did that, if the bank had any decency, it should bail him out. Only Cribbins dared to suggest that David should be given a prison sentence.

The rousing reception given to him by his friends and work-mates the night he made a discreet rear entrance to the pub, went a long way towards atoning for all the harsh things that were said about him in recent days. It was as if he'd been granted a general absolution and the blame for his plight placed fairly and squarely elsewhere.

Bloodied but unbowed, I could tell that David was bouncing back. Like most I saw no reason why he should be shunned. It wasn't as if he were the first man to try and beat the taxman. Nor the last for that matter, if the tribunals currently investigating political corruption, were anything to go by.

And after all, what are accountants for? I felt it was only right that we should make liberal allowances for him, considering that in the pecking order of tax offenders, he would be at the bottom of the league table.

I watched as, having been stood a large Jameson on the house by the publican, he moved towards his familiar stool, only to find his critic firmly enthroned on it, without so much as a hint of recognition or welcome.

'I see you've taken my stool,' I heard David observe good humouredly.

Declaring that it was public property, his neighbour refused to budge.

'With respect, it's private property. Mine, if you wouldn't mind,' The publican corrected Cribbins, whose custom he'd gladly do without if the truth be told.

'It's a bar stool for Chrissake. First come first served,' its occupier insisted.

David told him he was welcome to it and sportingly stood at the counter.

Whereupon his adversary began to play to the gallery.

'Just as well. I wouldn't like to see you make a footstool of yourself again.'

David stared at him, then told him that he, of all people, couldn't afford to talk. I could sense one of those confrontations that frequently make for theatre in our local, warming up.

Cribbins sniggered.

'Oh, really? Well, so far I haven't tried to pull a fast one on the taxman.'

I've seen punches thrown for less below-the-belt digs.

'There are many who would disagree. And rightly so.' I watched a cool David trade him a withering look.

'Not me!' a holier-than-thou Cribbins denied anything of the kind.

'Not half! What about those nixers you do around town from time to time? I bet you never declare them for tax.' David proceeded to grill him.

'Why should I?' I could see Cribbins shifting uneasily on his stool.

David scowled.

'Can you give me any reason why you shouldn't?

'Just a few quid for feck sake.' I watched as Cribbins's face dropped, then recovered awkwardly. A Pharisee unmasked.

David continued to dismantle him.

'Few or otherwise, it's tax liable. And by the way, that profit you make from those deliveries you do on week-ends? I'd bet you don't declare it for tax.' Bull's eye. I could see David gradually pulling the stool from under him.

'Small beer.' Cribbins was on the back foot and looking to his mates for reassurance, but it was no longer forthcoming.

'Big or small, it doesn't alter the principle,' David insisted.

A crimson Cribbins began to back down, admitting that, like everyone else, he had his tight moments.

David guffawed. 'You ... tight! I'm damned if I've ever seen the Vincent de Paul helpers making tracks to your doorstep.' I could tell it was going to be a fight to the finish. The low-sized, light-weight David versus his stockier, bull-necked adversary – I'd bet on David having the last word.

'Relatively speaking,' Cribbins mumbled. He appeared to be running out of steam

'Relative my foot! Two foreign holidays last year? Not to mention that state-of- the-art conservatory you had installed in your home recently. If that's being tight, then the rest of us are millionaires.' David suddenly looked leaner and meaner. A prize-fighter in disputation. And we were relishing every minute of it.

'Don't say I didn't graft for it. Or that it was unearned income,' his knocker protested.

Their eyes locked.

'Paid for, no doubt, by those Christmas trees you sell around the town every December. And I'll be damned if that isn't another undeclared source of income on your part,' David accused him, slicing through his adversary's self-righteous facade.

I could see Cribbins beginning to crumble. To reach for his

Guinness for support. To twist uncomfortably on the high stool that was neither his nor David's, but strictly anyone's with or without a cleaner sheet than either while drinking in the Market Pub, which was never known to refuse anybody, whether saint or sinner.

'What's so wrong with a few quid under the table for those luxuries that make life worth living?' Cribbins appealed for tolerance now that his bluff was being well and truly called.

A conciliatory David responded: 'Isn't that the point? So just keep in mind, chum, the advice given to the stone throwers in the bible.'

'Hear! Hear!' we cheered, relieved to see his critic finally vanquished.

Whereupon, a crestfallen Cribbins relinquished the high stool to his neighbour. Unlike David, who'd have to pay dearly for his offence, he could thank his stars that so far he had managed to get away with just being named and shamed in his own local.

I didn't feel sorry for him. Seeing that it would only require a phone call from a whistle-blower to the taxman to have him nabbed for a backlog of unpaid taxes, he'd be less quick to judge in future.

From now on, he knew he would have to watch his mouth. And his back. The tax net was gradually closing in on everyone. And nearly everyone, you can take it, was guilty of some bit of evasion or other.

When a resolute David vowed, at closing time, that he wouldn't rest until he had cleared his name and brought the institution that misled and embarrassed him to book, he had our undivided support.

There are times, you'll agree, when it takes a David to bring down a Goliath.

THE WEDDING

It was touch and go that Shane's wedding didn't go down in history. Is there no escaping it? It only takes a diehard dissident like Cormac to stir it up.

Otherwise, the wedding was a multi-cultural triumph, bringing together Shane's and Lissa's diverse guests for a memorable evening at his stunning, new home in picturesque Ashgrove, on the outskirts of London. Unlike Cormac, Shane's best man, I usually get on well with the Brits. Maybe it's because I speak their language and have been a lifelong fan of their football.

'Welcome to Gatwick!' A chic air hostess greeted, as our Ryanair jet taxied to a halt.

The sense of expectancy I experience when touching down in a foreign country was not shared by Cormac.

'There was a time when English factories carried signs: 'Irish workers need not apply.' That was the welcome they had for us,' he ground.

His response wouldn't have been more hostile had he been parachuted behind enemy lines.

'I'd suggest you put aside your historical grudges until after the wedding?' I appealed. As cousins, we're chalk and cheese.

I can see where he and people like him come from. I appreciate the Brits treated us Irish pretty badly, though probably nothing like he'd have you believe.

Admittedly, there is some damning evidence, like the Famine and the Penal Laws, which he never ceases to exploit whenever I try to persuade him to let bygones be bygones. So far he has refused.

'No way. Not until England gives us back what is rightfully ours,' he snapped. History brings out the worst in him at times, though, in fairness, he always buys Irish and is a keen supporter of Gaelic culture.

Shane, I'm glad, has not taken a leaf from his book. He works in the *City*. A financial whiz kid I gather, unlike yours truly – a fan of the arts, which is why I have to settle for a modest terrace house in Dublin, rather than a stately home like his, with its swimming pool, its tennis court, its extensive front and rear lawns graced with stands of mature trees and geometrical flower-beds, which left the best man speechless. The arts don't give you that, but they help you to see outside of the box. Burdened with historical grievances, Cormac has become their unwitting puppet.

I suspect it was due as much to Lissa as to Shane, that he volunteered to act as best man. He loved the Scots and never forgot our historical indebtedness to them. It wouldn't surprise me if he had other reasons too, like that visit he had in mind to Hever Castle. With Cormac what you see isn't always what you get.

'Shane has done us proud,' he remarked haughtily, as we continued to explore the impeccably kept grounds, the fruit-laden conservatory, the well-stocked tool shed and a charming out-building housing an impressive wine rack, which brought to mind an older England with its passion for gardening and high living.

"Something smaller would be more my cup of tea." I admitted to feeling a bit overwhelmed by it.

'But can't you see he's showcasing us Irish abroad?' Cormac saw nothing incompatible about his nephew assuming the mantle of the English country squire as long as he didn't forget his roots.

I couldn't help sniggering. I knew Shane, a product of the Celtic Tiger prior to moving to London, had better reasons for acquiring the property. History for him, with respect, is usually more about playing the market and about shrewd investments than about patriotism. If it were in his financial interests, I'm certain he'd down-size tomorrow without second thoughts.

'Though they kept us down for centuries, we're catching up.' Cormac bragged and adjusted his tam before launching into one of his dissident tirades.

I switched off. I wished he weren't wearing that tam. Not that I've ever seen him without it. In the circumstances, I felt, it was as provocative as it was inappropriate.

Sensitive to the English presence arriving for the wedding, I joined the guests, leaving him to continue his tour of the grounds and to grind his political axe in private. As we set out for the church, my heart unfolded to my host country and to all manner of races and religious persuasions.

Younger clerics being in short supply, the wedding ceremony was performed by Father Osborne, a retired priest and a late convert from Anglicanism. A moving rite as weddings go, if you allow for the sermon – a fundamentalist statement on marriage and its responsibilities, followed by a swinging attack on the evils of divorce, which he held accountable for countless broken homes and lives throughout Britain.

The very walls of Hever Castle must have shook, as he thundered in his cracked voice, against the polygamous Henry VIII, in a manner reminiscent of medieval, mendicant preachers. Judging by his mien, he'd have gladly suffered martyrdom rather than submit to the reprehensible Tudor, whom he held responsible for English Protestantism, which, inspired by his hero, Cardinal Newman, he had come to reject.

At any moment, I expected a resounding 'hear! hear!' from a rapt Cormac, sitting bolt upright within the altar pale. The sermon, I knew, was right up his alley. I was relieved he had removed his tam, which he knelt on as a protection from the unpadded kneeler.

Watching him present the wedding ring to the celebrant, I wondered if he'd ever marry. Several times during the ceremony, I couldn't help matching him in my thoughts with Emily, the attractive, English bridesmaid. Wishful thinking! I should have known by now that the only wedding he'd ever consider would be a political one.

In a joyous tone, the former Anglican welcomed Shane and Lissa into the local Catholic community, and went on to praise the Irish contingency for their fidelity to the Faith handed down to them by their ancestors, who stood by it in the face of persecution and death, ashamedly at the hands of his fellow countrymen. Even Cormac must have been moved by the way he apologised for, and in turn, denounced their barbarity.

As we taxied back to Shane's place after the photographs, a fired up Cormac applauded the sermon, for having been, as he put it, 'straight from the shoulder and right on the button.'

It was just as well the chauffeur was a Rastafarian and that he was plugged into Bob Marley rather than Cormac's outpourings about the Protestant legacy of sectarianism in Northern Ireland. You'd think, by him, that, as a religion, it didn't have a single redeeming feature. As to how he managed to reconcile terrorism with his own religion, I could never quite understand.

I couldn't wait to get away from him and wished Siobhán were with me. Refusing to entrust the children to a baby sitter, she gave the wedding a miss, leaving me stuck with Cormac – though kin, no kindred spirit.

The wedding reception was getting underway when we got back, the air scenting of a heady blend of odours as hired caterers served up a treat in a huge tent rented for the occasion. The idea of having it in Shane's place, rather than a hotel, appealed to everyone. It had the ring and charm of by-gone days about it. Even the recently unpredictable weather came up trumps.

Having wined and dined royally on a menu inclusive of multicultural tastes, Cormac's humourous speech, which went down a treat, prompted the ladies to tease him.

'It's going to be your turn next,' they predicted .

I watched him shake his head, then offer his usual laughable excuse.

'My mother is the problem. I cannot serve two mistresses.'

'I'm sure she wouldn't object to you having an heir to carry on your name and your business,' a relative disagreed, seeing he was now approaching his mid-thirties.

'I might end up like Henry VIII,' he quipped.

Given his handsome looks, his personality and his thriving little business, which benefited from the Celtic Tiger in Abbeylaune, I knew he was much sought after, though married to the *Cause* – a united Ireland by physical force, rather than by constitutional means – to which I subscribed.

As the wines and the spirits took effect, I watched him moving into a partying mood and bantering with the bridesmaid, with whom he seemed to be hitting it off. When it came to doing his party piece, however, his rendering of his favourite dissident ballad fell, to his dismay, on unresponsive ears.

Bemused by its low key reception, he drew me aside afterwards.

'What was wrong with it?' he queried.

'Put it this way: would you approve of 'God Save the Queen' being sung at a dissident's wedding?'

Not that such ballads haven't their place. And, like it or not, they are part of our culture that continues to survive.

He frowned irately.

'Isn't it time we reclaimed those ballads? How long more are we going to have to deny them?'

Deploring their political misuse, I gave him a deaf ear. Then, in response to popular demand, I unpacked my violin and obliged with a selection of waltzes, to which the guests danced the night away on the huge patio, presided over by a breath-taking new moon.

After the party ended and the guests had departed, I noted Cormac ambling with Emily around the grounds, flicking on and off his Ronson lighter as they picked their steps between the dusk-mantled trees. Respectful of their privacy, I kept a polite distance.

'So how come a charming attractive lady like you is still single,' I heard him inquire of Emily, her silhouette confirming, yet again, a fetching figure, enhanced by shoulder-length, auburn hair, which must have turned many a head.

She shrugged, then frankly admitted that, so far, the right man hadn't come her way.

When I overheard him declare that he hadn't given up on meeting the right woman, I suspected it was the drink talking.

'I'm sure there must be some woman who would make you a good wife,' she said encouragingly. Could she be speaking of herself?

'Hopefully.'

After a lull in their exchanges, he observed, 'I believe your parents were Irish.'

They seemed to me to be linking arms, as they drifted out of sight into the stand of trees.

'Believe it or not, they were both from your county,' I heard her reply.

'I might have known,' he exclaimed, as they emerged again into the moonlight, his long shadow merging with hers.

'Really! How come?' She was curious.

'I've been picking up certain expressions of yours all evening that give you away,' I heard him remark. As they sought again the seclusion of the trees, I left them to it and went indoors, relieved that Emily had taken him off my hands.

I could swear there were lipstick stains on his collar when they finally rejoined the extended family for a night-cap.

As I was making for bed, he reminded me again of our intended visit to Hever Castle the next day. Emily, he gave me to understand, had made him a present of two complimentary tickets for it, which she'd recently won in a local draw. Knowing something of its controversial history, I couldn't wait to see it.

That sense of awe I felt as we entered the stunningly refurbished castle, was in stark contrast to Cormac's, dismissive response.

'Built, no doubt, on the backs of the wretched peasants,' he ground, indifferent to its splendour and its spectacular story.

'Then why did you come here if you find it so upsetting?'

He chuckled. 'A long overdue audience with his royal highness, Henry VIII.'

'He'll expect you to take the Oath of Supremacy,' I teased, surprised that he'd removed his tam.

'Over my dead body,' snarled the rebel, who claimed his phone was tapped and who'd had more than his share of run-ins with the Special Branch.

I could see he had already undergone a sea-change and was no longer the cheerful person who charmed Emily the previous evening.

As we wound our way through a mind-blowing succession of beautifully restored chambers, I could sense his dissident adrenalin ticking like a time-bomb primed to detonate any minute. He had so many historical bones to pick, I lost track of them.

The concealed alcove where an outlawed priest said Mass riled him. Then it was the wax figures of the tragic wives of Henry that got his dander up. The spectacle of the fearsome instruments of torture and death that accounted for Saint Thomas Moore and numerous others were the final straw.

'May he roast in hell!' he bellowed.

I refused to go down his unforgiving road, and tried to see the castle and its chequered history from a cooler perspective. Historical places like Hever never cease to fascinate me. And what a fascinating history it had!

'To think that English Protestantism had its seeds in that failed bed of Anne Boleyn,' I remarked, as we entered the boudoir she had shared with Henry. 'One thousand nights they slept there, questing for a male heir to the throne. Tragically for her, it wasn't to be.'

Cormac pulled a scornful face.

'How could that lecherous, murderous Tudor have any luck, having plundered and dissolved our monasteries, which were the centres of learning and spirituality as well as renowned places of hospitality? Damn him down to the lowest pits of Hell!

'It's history. Let it be!' I appealed, but I could see he wasn't listening.

'He wiped out our mediaeval culture and opened the door to an appalling Protestant regime that hounded our Catholic ancestors for centuries! May he roast on the spits of hell!' he cursed again.

'Enough!' I begged, realising it was a mistake to have accompanied him on this tour. He was still under the influence of the dissident history books of his school days. Susceptible as ever to the political satires of the Gaelic poets, he loved to quote. Still a sucker for slanted, dissident ballads he sang with gusto.

The message of the Belfast Agreement had not yet kicked in for him – and may never, ordaining him to remain a die-hard dissident, forever warring with England.

As we moved towards the Council Chamber, I was surprised to see him retrace his steps, his expression chased with menace.

'Where are you going?' I called after him.

'To his royal highness's bedroom.'

'But we've been there already!'

His excuse that he had forgotten to take a photo of it struck me as being rather odd, despite his feelings for Anne Boleyn. Sophisticated Anne, with her superior French manners and education, proved more alluring for Henry than her sister Mary, who had previously been his mistress. At least, unlike her sister, she was spared her head.

Something prompted me to follow Cormac. I didn't seem to remember him having a camera. I really regretted not having mine. The bed, with its rare canopy, its exquisite bedpane and its pristinely preserved frame, would have made for a truly memorable photo. Though few beds were as historical, I couldn't, for some reason, imagine Cormac, who loathed everything it stood for, wanting to photograph it.

'What the hell are you doing?' I exclaimed. Seeing him with one leg astride the rope that cordoned off visitors from the bed, while fumbling in his pocket for something, I sensed he was up to no good.

'What should have been done a long time ago.' His voice rang with fierce intent.

Aghast, I watched him whip his Ronson lighter from his

pocket, flip the lid, then flick it on to maximum flame.

For a moment, I froze, as I pictured the mayhem he was about to unleash.

'O no! Stop! You mustn't!' I choked back a scream that would otherwise have alerted the security.

'Why not? If it's the last thing I must do, it will be to torch that monster's bed.'

Whereupon, he tossed the lighter onto it and bolted.

I had flashes of the Counter-Reformation and of heretics being burned at the stake. Reprehensible though the Tudor had been, I still couldn't abide seeing so rare a piece of heritage being torched. Springing instinctively into action, I managed to seize the lighter before the bedpane caught fire. By then, Cormac had fled the castle, leaving me to pick up the pieces.

In frantic haste, I disposed of the Ronson through an open window and, with relief, watched it disappear into the moat. When I spotted Cormac's tam covering the CCTV camera in the room, I was hopeful that we both might have escaped the attention of the security guards long enough to make good our escape. Thankfully, there had been no other witnesses to his dastardly deed in the chamber at the time.

When I heard the rush of security men's feet approaching, I bolted in the opposite direction and managed to elude them. I could have throttled Cormac, had he not stayed out of reach until I chilled out.

We were on our flight home before I could bring myself to speak to him.

'What the hell got into you?' I finally brought myself to ask him, as I steadied my nerves with a stiff drink.

'History.' he declared defiantly. 'It has to be brought to book.'

I looked at him with disbelief.

'Do you realise you could have had us both locked up, you dick-head?'

A cynical smile flitted across his sardonic features.

'I'd swing for to see that bed burn.'

It wouldn't have mattered to him if the entire castle were reduced to ashes.

'Swinging would be too good for you,' I snapped and tossed back my whiskey.

If he were taken aback by my outburst, he didn't show it. Instead, he appealed to my modest nationalist sentiments.

'Chill out cousin! Where's your patriotism? Revisionist lackeys like you would still have us under the heel of John Bull.'

He justified what he considered would have been a high profile blow for the Cause, were it not for my reactionary intervention.

If he were expecting bouquets for his sinister heroism, he was in the wrong company.

Pulling a wry face, I told him that what he had done was utterly mindless and barbaric, and had no bearing whatever on patriotism. Quite frankly, I wanted nothing further to do with him.

He chuckled defiantly. 'You can see now why Henry the Eighth installed his own door locks whenever he stayed at the castle for one of his hunting parties.'

I refused to give him any hearing and proceeded instead to berate him.

'What a way to thank Emily! You should be ashamed of yourself.'

Signalling to the hostess for another Jameson, he declared that someone had to carry the torch of freedom for those who laid down their lives for it.

I shook my head emphatically, and firmly condemned the violent version of history he espoused.

'Try and get it into your fanatical excuse for a head, that that bed is a rare piece of heritage, which helps focus our minds on history,' I rebuked him.

Having finished his whiskey, he was surprisingly penitent: 'I really shouldn't have let it get to me,' he apologised.

I told him it was about time he grew up, time he accepted the democratic will of the people as expressed in the Belfast Agreement, and left it at that.

I was about to nod off in mid-flight when his mobile rang. It was Emily.

'So how did your visit to Hever Castle go?' I heard her inquire.

'Brilliant.' He joked he wouldn't mind spending his bridal night in King Henry's bed.

'It might end in bedlam,' she quipped. She was glad we enjoyed the tour.

Little did she realise it was about as enjoyable as a commando raid in broad daylight.

When I heard the chancer confess to her that it was such a pleasure to have met her and that he really enjoyed her company, I wondered what on earth he could be up to now. Trying to cover his tracks? Or playing politically correct to get off with her?

'The pleasure was all mine,' she assured him.

'We've got to get together before long,' I heard him insist, with a fervour that had me wondering if he were listening to his heart rather than his dissident head for a change.

'We really must. So why not pop over to Ashgrove whenever you feel free,' she invited.

I just can't wait to meet you again," he confessed, and suggested she might consider looking him up, assuring her he would only be too glad to show her around and renew her acquaintance with her ancestral roots.

From what I could gather, she'd only be too delighted, and expressed a wish to relive again her happy, childhood holidays in Ireland.

'Stay in touch Emily,' he begged.

'You too, dear. Cheers!'

'Cheers, honey!'

Back in Dublin airport, he had me guessing again, as I watched him making a bee-line for the check-in desk.

'Would you mind telling me where on earth you're off to this time?' I called after him, concerned, but relieved to be rid of him and to be reunited with Siobhán and the children. I was tired of being his keeper.

'London.'

'London!'

'Some unfinished business,' he chuckled.

Only love, I figured, could have turned him around.

MEMORIES OF A RAMBLING HOUSE

It must have been the dawn chorus this morning that sent me tripping down memory lane to the late Seán Lynott's popular rambling house I regularly frequented in my distant youth. That it survived for as long as it did, was as much to his credit as to the entertainment it provided for a community that hadn't much else going for it. Genial, cheerful and tolerant, Seán was the perfect host. On the rare occasions he had to call the younger men to order, when they got up to mischief, he did so with tact. Hence the appeal of his open house, which was the life and soul of our rural community – which has come to prefer, in recent times, the ear-shattering discos and binge drinking that are a feature of the Celtic Tiger to an abstemious house of song and dance; of stories and controversies; where romances that ended up the aisle frequently began, and where the dead were remembered with humour and affection. For those living on their own, it provided refuge from the desolateness of the rural winter.

For Seán too, I'm sure there were benefits, helping, as we must have, to shorten for him the long, bleak nights when the gales shrieked in the gable ends and his ancestral ghosts cast their shadowy presence about the hearth they once shared with him – their sole successor, now alone and, I suspect, uneasy, when the ramblers dispersed and the silence was as eerie as it was deafening.

To this, I attributed the origins of his rambling house, as much as his love of company. Year after year it continued, with new faces replacing old ones, lured by the *craic* and the camaraderie that were its drawing card – and, with the exception of one, regrettable incident still fresh in my memory, a tribute to Seán.

Far from laying the blame on him, I prefer to point a recriminatory finger at the Glen gang, who thought up the whole ghastly thing. Wild fellows with a fondness for pranks, they were only adjusting at the time to the conventions of the rambling house.

That ill-starred, November night, when the annual card raffle for the Christmas hamper had to be shelved due to the absence of some flu-stricken regulars, provided the new-comers with an opportunity to introduce us to bird-torching, a novel venture for most of us. We had shot grouse and pheasant in season, hunted hares for the coursing and the wren for St Stephen's Day, but we had never torched birds. With a long night on our hands, any pastime was considered preferable to none.

It wasn't until I saw the Glen gang arming us with sticks, as well as torches, that I suspected what was in store for our feathered friends. Curious but perturbed, I watched the ramblers creep with insidious intent into the grove that had long been a roosting site, where birds rested their tired wings at eventide, and reared their young uninterrupted.

Into this place of wonderment for generations of children – who climbed its trees for acorns and beech nuts, and scaled their topmost branches to view birds' nests – I, too, crept with bated breath, but without torch or stick, a witness to the unspeakable scene that was to follow.

'Now, let them have it!' I heard Murtagh whisper his heartless injunction.

Whereupon a score of men laid into the flocks of sleeping birds, dazzling them with their torches. Lurking behind a tree, I listened in disbelief to the flailing of ash and the thrashing of blackthorn sticks, as their wielders clinically despatched their unwitting victims with a savagery reminiscent of faction fighting.

I watched with apprehension a group shinning up trees with primate stealth, to wreak havoc on the upper branches, while others worked the lower ones as if they were felling apples. Even the redbreasts, considered unlucky to kill, were not spared. Surprised in their sleep, the wretched, dazed creatures mostly gave themselves up. The petrified shrieks of the few that managed to escape were drowned out by the blood-curdling cheers of men at their butchery.

Stunned, I listened to the succession of broken bodies tumbling through the latticework of shorn branches, followed by plumes of blood-boltered feathers plummeting like withered leaves in a late autumn gale.

Shocked that men, hitherto civilized and gentle, could suddenly become so barbaric, I had to cling for support to an ash tree. It was unlike anything I'd ever witnessed. Trust me, it had to be seen to be believed, for it was the behaviour of Neanderthals, rather than the caring men who'd normally decry cruelty in any shape or form towards bird or beast. In effect, I was witnessing the rape of the grove, a favourite of courting couples who valued it for its privacy and for its seasonal scents and colours that contributed to its popularity as a trysting place.

What amazed me most was the extent to which these men, in their frenzy, enjoyed their havoc, the grove resonating with their triumphal cries as they downed the last of their quarry. An appalling audit, I remember, the dead and injured birds that littered the ground, the full of a large, jute sack.

The aftermath, I vividly recall, made for feverish activity in the crowded kitchen, as birds were plucked and dressed, then cooked in a large pot on the big Stanley range, which was fired with logs and peat. Overcome by an ominous feeling, I refrained from the banter and merriment that were part of the ritual. Nor could I suppress my sense of outrage at seeing Murtagh pluck a blackbird while still alive, and then release it into the sub-zero, frosty night.

'How could you?' I protested, and left before the repast, the very thought of which made me wretch, as I hurried past the grove that had been effectively fauna-cleansed.

The torching must have given rise to collective misgivings, for it was never repeated nor spoken of again. Sometime later, a rattled Seán told us how his sleep had been shattered one night by a commotion in the kitchen. Convinced it was a burglar, he reached for his fowling piece, which he kept by his bedside for protection and crept into the kitchen, only to find it was something much more eerie than a burglar.

With the aid of the oil lamp, he eventually traced the racket to the range. Pulling open the door of the fuel-box, he recognised to his horror, the plucked blackbird, which Murtagh had released into the inclement night, being burnt to cinders. The wretched bird, he realised, had fallen down the flue while roosting on the chimney pot for heat.

That Christmas, the Grove failed to yield a single wren for the traditional Stephen's Day festival, giving Seán further pause for thought.

It gradually dawned on us that it had grown silent. As winter days lengthened into spring ones, Seán admitted to missing the dawn chorus that had long been his alarm clock. The spectacle of empty nests on bereft trees that April convinced him that the grove was blighted. There were nights, I gathered, when every gust of wind that strummed its deserted branches accused him of wrong-doing. On days when the grove should have been in full-throated song, it's hush had an air of unreality that unnerved him.

'It's cursed,' Kinsella declared, as we inspected it one night.

I disagreed. Now that I was doing science at secondary, I had less time for local superstitions and turned to Kearney for more credible answers.

'It wouldn't be the first time that a grove was forsaken,' he remarked.

'Really!' I was suddenly intrigued. Knowing him to be well-versed in folklore, I pressed him to continue.

'In pagan times, it seems to have been a place of worship, where the druids performed their sacrifices of beasts and birds to their deities. So revolting was the odour of rotting entrails, that the birds were believed to have abandoned it for long afterwards.'

'Would you blame them?' I heard Kinsella remark, then inquire if there had been any human sacrifices linked to the grove.

'None that I'm aware of. But other groves were not so lucky,' the folklorist informed us.

An outraged Kinsella declared that, if he had his way, he'd have those mindless yahoos from the Glen strung up from the highest branches, until the scald crows picked their bones clean for what they'd done.

I nodded, though I felt there were better ways of dealing with them.

Such men, I shuddered, were capable of anything. At least, the simple-minded pagans had a spiritual motive, however misguided.

Suffice that, for whatever reason, the grove remained silent. And a silent grove didn't make sense at the outset of the mating season. Soon Seán was on everybody's lips, as the grove became the subject of a protracted post-mortem, with logic and superstition competing for answers. And it was worrying him and keeping him awake at night.

Whenever the westerlies shook their branches, it seemed to him the trees were performing a dirge for the deceased birds that once sang on days when there was little to sing about. The previously vibrant grove looked set to become one of nature's appalling casualties.

Worse was to come. In the absence of the birds, the slugs, I noted, were wreaking havoc on Seán's vegetable plots, which had hitherto flourished in a sheltered clearance in the grove. His cabbages, riddled as if by a hail of gun fire, presented a sorry sight, while his lettuces scarcely survived beyond infancy.

'I still say it's cursed.' Kinsella was adamant as we surveyed the damage subsequently.

I merely shrugged, knowing it was pointless arguing with him.

From what I could see, Sean's fruit trees fared no better than his vegetables. The slugs were having a field day. Fat, slimy creatures, that clung to his every step whenever he inspected the grove. Squelch! Squash! In desperation, he watched them pilfering him of a valuable source of income from his customers in Abbeylaune, unless he could do something quickly to redress the situation. And in those pre-pesticide days, there wasn't much he could do, now that the balance of nature had been upset.

'The jinx hasn't passed.' I watched Kinsella strain a superstitious ear for the chirp of a bird, as spring gave way to summer.

'And it wont until someone can lift it,' Kearney predicted.

I could see it was getting to Seán, and heard how he was rocked to his fingertips when he went to check his new-born lambs one morning, only to find them dead, with their eyes plucked from their sockets by the scald-crows. It was not without precedent, but in Seán's frame of mind, it denoted something more sinister, which drove him, in a fit of remorse, into the grove, where he prayed that it be put right.

I remember the pall of gloom that hung over the rambling house, as our normally, irrepressible host grew more despondent by the day. The story telling and the jokes seemed out of place, and there was little appetite for music and dancing. Nothing could lift Seán's spirits, until I answered his door one evening when I'd dropped by, to a carefree gypsy with a jaunty bearing and a caged bird he claimed had the answer to Sean's problems. And going for a song.

'So you've heard?' Seán seemed surprised.

'People who travel the roads of Ireland like me hear lots of things that folk of fixed abode don't,' the footloose one said.

'What did you hear?' I watched Seán's expression tighten and his hands shake.

'That a terrible deed, which was not of yours, but of others' making, was done here,' he replied, nodding towards the grove. 'But rest assured that those directly responsible will pay dearly for it.'

'Bad cess to them,' I heard Seán direct his anger at them.

The gypsy nodded.

'If it's any consolation to you, the crows, at this very minute, are devouring their corn. And by the time the harvest comes around, they'll be threshing straw,' he predicted.

'And what can this bird of yours do to undo what they've done?' Seán inquired, cautious, I could tell, of the other's claims.

The gypsy smiled, revealing a mouthful of tawny teeth.

'You won't believe your eyes when you see it. Trust me, the blackbird of Derrycairn wouldn't hold candle-light to him. Sure 'tis sad I am to be parting with him,' he confessed with a convincing air.

I could see Seán gearing up for a purchase.

'You've come a long way to sell me a bird, stranger. And what might you be asking for him?'

The gypsy reached out a weather-beaten hand.

'A half-a-crown and he's all yours. Not a penny more nor less, for 'tis a crown of happiness you'll be wearing shortly, as befits a man with an open door and an open heart.'

Whereupon Seán reached into his pocket and fished out the required coin, which I watched him place in the other's palm.

'Now follow me!' the man of the road said.

When we reached the middle of the forsaken grove, I watched the gypsy ease open the cage door, then heard him whistle before releasing his captive. Freed from custody, it circled the choirs of trees ecstatically, weaving fluent patterns of flight among their branches before perching on the upper bough of a resplendent oak, where it broke into song. Soon, a second, and then a third joined it, and before we knew it, an assembly of warblers was turning the grove into an opera house, with the gypsy's tenor leading the choir.

'Didn't I promise you he'd solve your problems,' I heard the gypsy declare with satisfaction.

'May God reward you and roads rise to you,' Seán prayed and invited him indoors for a bite and a sup.

With the mating season in full swing again in the Grove, a recovered Seán would fall in love with Maeve, a winsome lass who turned many a head, and eventually Sean's, bringing to an end his lonely nights.

If their wedding had all our good wishes, we could somehow sense the end of a local era gradually unfolding. The demands of their rapidly increasing family would eventually bring the curtain down on the rambling house to which we'd be forever indebted for its fund of cherished memories that have helped to see us through a changing world that meant less and less to us as we grew older.

Why, I often ask, do we have to throw the baby out with the bathwater?

Why?

SPRING'S PRIMAL ANTHEM

It must have been the ecstatic piping of the blackbird in Barney's garden nearby that drew me out of doors this afternoon.

'Lovely day,' Edel greets. Lovely to look at. Single parent recently, wheeling out her new-born, first-born, spring-born son.

'Glorious,' I reply, every pore in my system responding to it.

No better woman. Kept it, though Molloy, her partner, fled the coop, when she refused to have it aborted. How could he? Even the vocalist in Barney's tree serenaded her. And the sun shone for her. And the eyes of young and old men were riveted by her alluring figure; the old feeling young again and the young losing the run of themselves in her presence.

'I haven't seen you recently,' Barney hails me and inquires if I'd come out to spot the talent?

I tell him I've been keeping house, in Louise's absence.

'When is she due back?'

'Tonight.' And not a minute too soon. How I miss her!

'That bird has run the winter out of me. Pavarotti has nothing on him.' Barney gestures towards the Sycamore, while reclining on his spade. His emblem. Works in the Botanic Gardens. *Rus in urbs.*

I nod, marvelling at the bird's response to the mating season. Whereupon, Barney confesses he was of two minds, recently, whether or not to chop down his stage. He would, too. His open-necked polo shirt revealing a man of heft, rather than refinement. Of width, rather than height. Of brawn, rather than brain. A man's man. What love-songs did he sing?

I try to talk him out of it. 'Spring wouldn't be the same without his solos and the tree.'

Barney frowns.

'I'm more concerned for my windows when it falls. And fall it will, given another gale like the recent one.' He glances at it suspiciously. Wind-bent, gnarled, but still greening to a creditable canopy. Mating tryst and nesting place. An eco-system in its own right.

'Fingers crossed there won't be any,' I appeal for a stay of execution.

Otherwise, it will be adieu to its rustle of spring, its autumnal riot of colours, its dawn chorus, resonant of my native Abbeylaune.

He smiles.

'I'll have to think about it.' I watch him jab his spade into the soil, withdraw it, then jab again, turning a sod for his minstrel. Les escargots. French delicacy. Not for me. Birds' delight.

'Fair play to you.' Edel, a victim of foul play. Putting distance between us with dainty steps! Tap, tap, tappety tap. Serenaded by Pavarotti. Tweet-tweet, tweet-tweet, tweet-tweet. Spring's primal anthem.

Hurry back to me, Louise! Spring is getting to me.

It must have been getting to Michael too. Suddenly bright-eyed and bushy-tailed. Wants a word. No man is an island. Only two doors down, yet I haven't seen him in ages. A recluse since Edel parted with him.

Suddenly outdoors. Cuckoo! Cuckoo! Spring is here. Loud sing. Love can be hell. Forgive Edel.

'Talk to you later, Barney. Michael wants a word.'

Barney looks surprised.

'I can't get wan out of him since Edel dropped him.'

Surprise! Surprise! Lovelorn Michael, taking again, I'm glad, an interest in his place and in his appearance. His neatly trimmed beard and his trendy haircut sign-posting a new self.

For whom? Edel? After all he'd been through for her! Would take her back, I'd wager, on the spur of the moment. The one, real love of his life, he insists.

'I seen her pushing her pram. Looks remarkably well,' he remarks.

Well, fell, hell. Belle, Belle, My Liberty Belle.

'You're not looking too bad yourself.' If only he'd straighten up and shake off his gloom. Still hurting, yet still smitten by her. The same and not the same woman, with the auburn tresses and the sun-kissed smile, to whom he still feels drawn. Now a mother. Could he love her again? Could she love him?

'There's a spring in her step,' he observes.

'Naturally. She has something to live for now,' I venture. Her little dote. Can Michael compete with that love? Can any man?

'I wish I had,' he sighs. More lead than levity in his. Lucky he's able to walk at all after the huge overdose he took.

After she walked out on him, he just fell apart. He let himself go, and the garden go, and his posture go. He drooped. Tilting more each day, his encounters with *terra firma* when in his cups, making for shock therapy.

'In time you will.'

Time cures. The heart outgrows its heart-aches. Finds a new ache. So the love songs tell us.

Molloy, Edel's ache. He used and abused her, then left her for high and dry. One of many short-taken by him.

Knowing Michael's abiding longings for her, I suggest he should kiss and make up.

He shakes his head. Strokes his beard. Droops.

'It's not that easy.'

I nod sympathetically. Been down that unrequited road more than once myself.

Admittedly, he was partly to blame. Kept her waiting. Then lost out to speedy Gonzales. The dashing Lothario in the Alfa Romeo, his fast-draw, ATM card out-gunning Michael's unemployment benefits. Missed out on the Celtic Tiger construction boom to look after his aging mother, when he would otherwise have been making a fortune as a painter and decorator.

Old Julie was the rub. Pernickety and possessive, she disapproved, he told me, of Edel. Oblivious to her virtues, she focused on her shortcomings. Too liberated, too assertive, too outspoken, too fond of style and of socializing, and clearly not religious enough by her standards.

Definitely not her cup of tea. She could never picture herself sharing her floor space with Edel, who considered at one point moving in with Michael, but having met with his mother's objections, upped and left him to her for Molloy, a troubadour with a master key to women's boudoirs.

'Women! Nothing but trouble,' Michael moaned.

Imagine, what it would be like without them! Adam without his Eve – unthinkable.

Two years on, his mother, now suffering from Alzheimer's, was in an old folks', leaving him the run of the house. If only Edel had waited. Or his mother moved in with her sister. Alternatives he pondered over and over again.

'What could she have seen in that scumbag?'

What does any woman see when she loses her head? Molloy seized the day.

'What she no longer sees, now that she has come to her senses.'

'You really think so?'

'I'm certain.' Now approaching the bend, she strides on shapely legs through the sun-soaked afternoon. A wiser woman.

Michael stoops, inserts another bulb into the soil, then straightens up. Tulips from Amsterdam. Red light. Her favourite flowers. Molloy planted her, then legged it. Scumbag!

Now a point of vanishing cerise. A shade that really suits her. Michael had the blues after she walked out on him. Used to hear him playing them on his DVD. The music of the broken.

I watch him grimace.

'If I ever get my hands on that low-life Molloy, as sure as hell, I'll throttle him.' Michael clenches and unclenches his fist.

Sir Galahad. Revenge not ours. Love your enemy. Christian way. Easier said than done.

'I believe he has skipped it across the pond. Rumoured to have ran up a massive debt on his ATM card.' Artful dodger. Evading, too, his child-support payments. A shaggin' cuckoo.

Still defensive of her, Michael wishes a plague upon his house.

'Better, I suppose, to have loved than not,' I mutter, urging him to be grateful to her for the experience.

He scowls, then squashes down the soil around the tulip.

'That blackbird must be hard up for a mate,' Barney chuckles as he joins us. Minus his spade.

Michael nods.

'I see Edel is free again. With looks like hers, it won't be for long,' Barney predicts for his benefit.

I agree. Different in the past. Puritanical Ireland is dead and buried. No more Magdalene laundries either. Men, I'd wager, will soon be knocking on her door with flowers for her and toys for her baby.

'The ball is back in your court.' He urges Michael to bat. Early thirties if he's a day. Gave up the chase after he'd got the bullet. No other woman so far capable of stepping into Edel's elegant shoes. Wine-red, high-heeled, leg-enhancing stilettos.

Michael shakes his head. Still not sure of himself, nor of Edel, I suspect.

'Once bitten . . . you know what they say.'

'No earthly reason to be twice shy.' Barney doesn't believe in any of that clap-trap.

A man of action. With no time for sentiment. Stoic in adversity. Just pick yourself up, dust yourself down and get on with it. Thirty wedding anniversaries to his credit this autumn. Would do it all over again with Martha. Would she with him, given that he was believed to be a bit of a Taliban behind closed doors?

Michael stalls. Pleads for time.

'You mustn't let another season of romance pass you by or you'll regret it,' Barney tries to reason with him.

I could hear its rustle in the leaves and grasses. Sense its joy in the laughter of children at play in the nearby park. Its delirium in the birds and insects, and its turbulence in men's hearts. The very air resonated with it. And my beloved Louise was on her way back to me from a sunnier clime.

But hark! Here comes Edel. Sprightly, shapely, chic. Homeward-bound.

'Now's your chance!' Barney exclaims.

Michael droops, then turns the other way.

'Perhaps another time.' Cannot switch on and off the emotions like a tap. Barney ought to know better.

'Do you want me to do gooseberry for you?' Barney offers.

'No thanks.' Proper order.

'What the hell's wrong with you?' I hear Barney ask, determined to reconcile the former lovers. Fixer. Can Humpty Dumpty be fixed?

Michael pauses before replying.

'Molloy is scarcely out of her hair. She needs time to recover.'

I could see Barney frowning.

'Why not catch her on the rebound?' Catch a fallen star. Molloy caught her on the hop.

'I don't want to rush my fences.' Didn't jump when he should have. Jump-shy.

'I'm telling you she's yours for the asking,' Barney persists. No beating about the bush. Refused, I gather, to take no for an answer from Martha when she pleaded for time to consider his proposal, shortly after meeting her. The first woman, I gathered, for whom he ever fell. Which is not to say that any of his previous women ever fell for him. And knowing him, better for both parties that he be the one who fell, for having fallen, he could only blame himself if he fell for the wrong woman.

'I'll leave it for now.' Michael's courage fails him.

'The story of your life.' I could see Barney losing his patience with him.

Michael gapes at him with dismay.

'There's the question of the child.' *In loco parentis*. Surrogate for Molloy.

'What about it?' Barney seems bemused.

'It's not mine.'

'So what? You still love her, don't you? And in time you'll come to love it.' Stunningly, she approaches. Tap, tap, tappetty, tap.

Michael wrestles with his feelings as more joyous sounds emanate from the perambulator. Her bundle of love.

'I'm still not sure if I should pick up the pieces for Molloy.'

'Don't hold it against the child. And surely you wouldn't wish she'd disposed of it?' Barney remonstrates.

'Good God, no!' Barbaric. Unchristian.

'Then what's your problem?' Barney still doesn't get it, that recovering from a broken romance is not like recuperating from a head-cold.

'I'm not sure if I'm ready to be a father.' I could see his point. The baby's the rub. Feed me. Change me. Sing to me. Think twice.

Barney shakes his head. Fathered a big family without a bother, then left the rearing to Martha. Wouldn't get away with it nowadays.

'You'll learn, like we all did.'

Not quite as instinctive as motherhood. A slower, learning curve.

As she drew alongside, Edel remarks it was well for us having nothing better to do but stand around chin-wagging.

'Some of us aren't fit for much else,' Barney accounts for our inertia, then inquires how her little man is doing.

'Not a bother on him,' she says, then asks if we could recommend someone who'd paint and decorate his room.

Back with her parents since moving out of Molloy's love nest. An attractive pied-a-terre, I gather, on the South side.

'Michael Angelo here.' Barney jerks his thumb at her unrequited lover.

Michael strokes his beard, then nods. Incapable of refusing our local Cleopatra.

'Great! That'll spare me ringing around.' She looks relieved. His Sistine contract.

'And no better or more capable man for the job,' Barney references him.

'You don't have to tell me.' I watch her post Michael an inviting smile. Come back to me. I miss you. 'So when can you start?'

'Whenever suits you.' Ready and rearing to go I can tell.

'Tomorrow?'

'Okay.' His posture now erect, and his voice resonating with purpose.

'And if it's convenient, you might drop by tonight to discuss the colour scheme?' I hear her suggest, in a voice both soft and appealing.

'A good idea.'

Something bright and warm to reflect both your moods.

'Any particular time?'

Throw in 'my love' while you're at it. You may as well, for it's written all over you.

'By nine o'clock this little fellow should be down for the night.'

Until he starts teething. Forty winks between ear-shattering, sleep-wrecking howls. Trouble with the choppers coming and going.

'Fine.' A twinkle in his eye and a smile replacing the scowl he wore for ages. All presumably forgiven.

'And don't forget the wine and the flowers,' Barney reminds him.

There's a lilt in Edel's laughter and promise in her ruby lips not lost on Michael. I can hear Pavarotti belting out a fresh refrain. The sky doesn't have a single cloud. And Louise will be back in my arms shortly.

There are days, you'll agree, when life is magical, and others when it's a bitch.

REQUIEM FOR THE WALL

When the forbidding wall that separated our two opposed communities was demolished, Leonard went into denial. The wall, as far as he was concerned, was still there. I tried telling him things had changed, but I might as well have been talking to the wall. The man was in the grip of a mindset some attributed to a wall complex. Others, to wall syndrome. For as long as I've known him he's had a wall of one kind or another between himself and our system.

'I was born on the wrong side of the Wall,' I heard him crib, prior to its demolition.

Tea-breaks in the factory canteen were his peak cribbing times.

'Many on the other side have had reason to regret they were ever born,' Hans, a towering, thoughtful type from the other side, disagreed. Since his arrival, he'd become Leonard's sparring partner. The terrier versus the St Bernard, with a lot of barking but no biting so far.

'You're still seriously deluded,' I heard Leonard, for whom the grass was always greener on the other side, accuse him.

'At least on this side, delusions are not rammed down your neck,' Hans retorted. And he should know, having seen it from both sides.

We lived on the western side of the Wall, which had been

erected a long time ago to protect the others' way of life from ours.

I want to make it clear, the wall was of their making, not ours. And it didn't help not being able to see for ourselves how the other side lived, and having to settle for Leonard's version of it, which according to Hans, had very little to do with the grim one he fled.

I wouldn't mind seeing the real thing for myself, but I knew that any attempt to access it would be foiled by its guardians – trigger-happy bullies, who behaved as if they were protecting the Holy Grail. Hans's escape from it, I understand, was nothing short of miraculous, given the bullet wounds he received while scaling the Wall in his efforts to join Deirdre, his pen pal and partner to be.

Deirdre had opened his eyes to our side and, in turn, to the other side long before he arrived. If it kicked Leonard in the head, I'm certain he wouldn't recognise the latter for what it was.

'What's the big deal about this side?' He was curious, though more on his guard since Hans began to rattle his cage.

After a studied pause, I heard Hans rejoin in his broad, other side accent, 'I can speak my mind here. Over the Wall, I mightn't as well have a mind.'

'You can speak for all you're worth here for all the hearing you'll get,' Leonard said.

Which wasn't surprising in his case, seeing how few bothered to listen to him.

'And I can worship without fear in public,' Hans added.

Leonard, a self-professed agnostic, shook his head.

'It must come as a bit of a surprise to you to find how empty the churches here are these days,' he said and left us to ourselves.

Seeing his failure to grasp that the system on the other side had had its day, and in fact, only ever had a false dawn, Hans dismissed him as walleyed.

Those who followed in his intrepid footsteps and who lived to tell the tale, Leonard regarded as dissidents and malcontents. It never occurred to him how dissident he could be. He had to have an axe to grind.

Admittedly, as our shop steward, he had served us well, though we could have done with less of his sermonizing about the other side.

Careful not to get on the wrong side of him, I could see Hans struggling to keep his cool during his early days on our side. Initially, he held back from confronting Leonard who, in any case, was locking horns on our behalf with the boss, McMurragh, about whom he had nothing good to say. I'm sure McMurragh felt similarly about Leonard, and must have found him a pain in the proverbials down the years with his pickets, his hard-line stances on pay, on working conditions and his sniping at the profit principle the boss epitomised, unlike – if you were to believe him – his counterpart on the other side.

After a selective, tour-guided holiday there, Leonard went into over-drive. They really must have got to him for he was convinced more than ever that our firm should be run on similar lines to theirs.

'Nonsense! It would be rowing back to a failed system,' Hans no longer held back, having seen for himself how outmoded such firms were.

He needn't have worried. We were happy enough with the way ours was run and didn't need any advice from Leonard.

'Unlike here, people there are more valued than machines,' he tried to persuade the defector.

'Which wouldn't be hard, seeing how valueless the machines are,' Hans replied and addressed his sandwich.

A frustrated Leonard banged his mug on the canteen table.

'Can't you see that profit rules the roost here?' he snapped.

Hans refused to be taken in by the other's cant.

'What you've failed to see is that loss is more the order of the day there. Why do you think I came over the wall?'

'You saw our glass half full when, in fact, it was far from it,' the shop steward ventured.

Hans disagreed with a contemptuous wave of his hand.

'From where I came, there were lots of times when you didn't even have a glass.'

I'd take his word for it any day before Leonard's.

'But nobody else had either,' Leonard disagreed. I knew Hans wouldn't fall for that.

'Like hell! There were those who always had, but you weren't supposed to see. So I'd seriously suggest you change your distorted specs for a pair like mine.' Hans jestingly offered him his.

Leonard pushed them away from him.

'No thanks. I might end up as cock-eyed as you.'

An amused Hans suggested that he acquire a periscope big enough to peep over the Wall, confident that it would open his eyes to the other side. 'And just be careful your eyeballs don't pop from their sockets,' he warned, and he bolted from the canteen in response to the siren's shrill summons to work.

That was all before the Wall fell, though it didn't take the Wall to fall for most of us to see that the other side was nothing like what Leonard would have us to believe.

If there's one thing life has taught me, it's that things never remain the same.

You think you're sitting pretty and the next thing, your chair is kicked from under you. It was likewise with the Wall we all thought was permanent. Now a heap of rubble and a withering indictment of its author. Unless you're a Luddite, you move on.

Which is what Leonard still can't bring himself to do.

'Time'll tell who's right.' He jutted a warning finger at Hans subsequently.

'Time has already told it. In fact it has been telling it for a long time.'

I could see Hans was beginning to tire of his adversary's ongoing self-deception.

'Maybe he is wired differently to the rest of us,' I ventured.

I'd be the first to admit that not everyone can change. Which is tough. Like Leonard, they're happier with the way things were than the way they've become. Even if that means settling for less. And for a system that has run aground.

Sooner or later, I guess he'll have to face the facts, as Hans did, unless he wants to go on living in fantasy-land.

'His pride won't allow him.' Hans claimed to have finally figured him.

As the months went by, I was convinced that Leonard had become snared by his own propaganda.

Now that the Wall had crumbled, we were amazed that, despite being privately shaken for awhile, he was suddenly as upbeat as ever. We were convinced he'd lost the plot. It took Hans to twig that he had re-invented the Wall and that he was essentially the same old dyed-in-the-wool Leonard. In fairness, not without a certain integrity, if your preference be for someone who sticks through thick and thin to his guns, even if they are misfiring, than for one who bends with every breeze.

'It'll rise again,' I heard him predict one day in the canteen. 'History repeats itself.'

Hans shook his head derisively.

'No way. Never,' he was adamant.

An intractable Leonard was confident it would survive in

the minds and hearts of the people who, having come to see its worth, would rebuild it some day.

Hans sighed audibly.

'It's history,' he snapped.

'It had a lot going for it.' I listened to Leonard lament its passing with a lump in his throat.

'And a hell of a lot not. Try and get it, it's a dream that went sour.'

Hans, I gathered, had long foreseen its collapse and with it, Leonard's fall from grace soon after his arrival.

'The man's a wallnut,' the escapee declared as we returned to work.

Beleaguered though Leonard be, I knew he'd go down fighting, though Hans disagreed.

'His back is against a wall that's no longer there.' He glowed with satisfaction. But not for long, as things suddenly began to move faster than any of us could ever have imagined.

With the Wall down, the other side began arriving on our doorstep in droves in search of work. If they brought home to Leonard some unsettling truths about their side, they provided him oddly with a fresh cause.

'We're going to be snowed under,' I heard him explode as he browsed over the latest statistics provided by his favourite tabloid.

'I'm not surprised,' Hans rejoined.

It was soon clear to us that the migrants regarded our side as their Promised Land – their El Dorado with a booming tiger economy, which was the envy of their backward one.

Much to Leonard's chagrin, an opportunistic McMurragh welcomed them into his expanding work-force, knowing they'd readily offer their labour for well below the standard wage, which would be many times what they earned on the other side.

A serious issue for us, given that the more he employed, the more our livelihoods were at risk. To give Leonard his due, he didn't take it lying down.

'There's only one way to deal with them,' he declared to Hans and myself in the canteen during the tea-break.

'I'm not so sure there's even one. But tell us in any case,' Hans encouraged.

I could sense another squabble brewing. Another clash of irreconcilable perspectives.

'Rebuild the wall.' I wasn't sure if I'd heard him rightly above the din of the canteen, by now a Babel of migrant accents.

'You can't be serious!' Hans thundered.

The shop steward looked him straight in the eye.

'Can you not see we're being over-run. It's an invasion. As if we've hadn't enough of them down through history.'

We were rocked by Leonard's outburst. Had he finally woken up to the grim realities of the other side and the consequences for our side?

'And that's only the first wave. With a thriving economy like this you can expect many more,' I heard Hans forecast worse to come.

I could see a worried look flit across the other's features.

'Something has to be done about it before it's too late.' Leonard's tone had an ominous ring to it, like when the firm was laying off staff or putting us on short time.

Hans, on the other hand, was unperturbed.

'Why worry?' he appealed. 'The economy is on a roll. And consider the benefits to your gene pool from intermarriage with our beautiful, blonde, fair-skinned women and our tall, well-built, young macho men.'

As if to prove his point to his pint-sized protagonist, he raised himself to his full six foot plus height and flexed his enviable muscles.

'And that's nothing to what we're going to be, now that we can afford to feed ourselves properly,' he predicted.

'The good times simply can't last.' Leonard was less optimistic. I often wondered if he weren't happier with less good ones.

'They'd have to be pretty bad not to be better than the ones from where the migrants are coming from. Try walking a mile of the road in their shoes and you'll see what I mean,' Hans suggested.

I watched Leonard shaking his head glumly.

'Our way will corrupt them,' he worried.

'It hasn't done me any harm so far. Which is why I intend to stay,' Hans vowed as he ripped into his succulent burger.

'Will the others?' I heard Leonard ask with a worried expression.

'I doubt it. Some, possibly. Most will return as soon as their own economy picks up.'

When we thought we'd heard the last of the Wall, Leonard ruefully remarked one day, during the tea break, that it came down too soon.

'It didn't come down half soon enough,' Hans bellowed.

Leonard heaved a sigh.

'They needed more time to catch up with us.'

'Nonsense! The longer it stood, the more catching up they'd have to do.'

Whereupon, I noted Leonard trying a new tack. 'What's fair about paying the migrants less than the standard rate?'

'It's unfair. But putting back the wall would be a lot less fair. A little will go a long way with them when they return,' Hans reasoned and helped himself to another burger.

'But it's not fair the way they're being used against us,' Leonard countered.

'I agree. But that's how it is and will continue to be, unless . . .' Hans paused, as he often did, while formulating his ideas in his adopted lingo, which he continued to study at evening classes. Though stuck for the occasional word, he was already quite fluent, and with a lot to say about the other side that was of interest to everyone bar Leonard.

'Unless what?' his protagonist pressed.

'They're paid the same wages as everybody else,' Hans, who worked for less than we did, suggested.

I could see Leonard shaking his head.

Whereupon, Hans continued with his line of reasoning.

'Equal pay will mean equal employment opportunities. With the economy booming, you need them as much as they need you.'

It made good sense to me, but had yet to register with Leonard.

'I can foresee trouble ahead when the boom ends,' he predicted gloomily.

I listened to him lament again for the good old days, before the Wall came down, when there was very little outside competition for jobs.

'Not any more. Things have changed. Pay them a pittance and you, too, will end up working for less,' Hans warned.

A militant Leonard began gearing up for action.

'If we don't make a stand, we'll soon be queuing at the labour exchange. It's the old story: profit before people. The only winner in all this will be McMurragh.'

I could see his point.

An unruffled Hans finished his burger. Like his fellow migrants, he was making up for years of measly meals.

Amazed, I watched our rejuvenated shop steward embracing a new cause that would help to re-invent him, now that his dreams were in tatters. Without one he was rudderless. In a matter of weeks, he would be leading us in one of the city's biggest ever, protest marches against the abuse of cheap, migrant labour. Once again, the spokesperson for his imperilled colleagues. And it was bringing out the best in him.

'They say you can't teach an old dog new tricks, but you can still rely on him to guard your house,' Hans remarked to me, amazed by the new-born Leonard.

The protest, like most of its kind, had a limited success. Regulations put in place affirming equality, for employment purposes, would continue to be flouted. And never more so than when the economy subsequently crashed.

'Don't say I didn't warn you?' I listened to Leonard crow over Hans in the canteen.

How he could be in such high spirits, with the Recession biting and unemployment hitting record levels, amazed me.

Admittedly, the migrants were returning home as fast as they came, which must have been some relief to him. But hardly sufficient grounds for elation, with construction business collapsed, the banks broke, and workers queuing in their thousands at the labour exchanges as their firms folded up. A grim scenario, and yet Leonard was on song and sporting an uncanny smile rather than his habitual scowl.

'How can you be so happy?' I heard Hans, who was worried sick about losing his job, take issue with him one day.

'Admit it, I was right all along.'

'Right about what?' I watched Hans glaring at him.

'That the system on the other side was the better one.' I couldn't believe my ears.

'Get a life, man!' Hans barked.

'By the looks of things, you're not going to have much of one on this side for the foreseeable future,' I heard Leonard predict, convinced that history was set to vindicate him.

Hans was unmoved.

'Believe me, I've been through worse times,' he assured his protagonist.

Leonard shook his head.

'The worst is yet to come. Right now, pal, we're in a sinking ship that's going down faster than the Titanic. There has to be a better alternative to the greed-driven system that has left us in the mess we'll be in for years to come.'

Hans paused before giving him his carefully considered answer.

'Yes. A properly regulated one.'

Perhaps, one of these days, the truth will dawn on Leonard as it eventually dawned on Hans and on the migrants, who have no desire to turn the clock back.

I'm glad Hans has no regrets about his decision, having come he insists, to our side more out love for Deirdre than for the good life.

A man after my own heart now throbbing for Helga, one of those tall, blonde beauties from the other side who turned my head in oblique angles soon after her arrival.

Trust me, there is simply no wall that can keep out love.

THE WAITRESS

Seeing him walk through the revolving door of the restaurant, a jubilant June exclaimed: 'Don't tell me Adrian's back!'

The fatigue she felt earlier, from catering for an engagement party, suddenly evaporated. She was inexplicably on fire, if a little unsure how to take him after his spell in Paris.

'I knew he'd return,' Maeve chuckled, her eyes twinkling with mischief.

'Really! You should have been a clairvoyant,' June rejoined, and asked her colleague if she wouldn't mind taking his order this once.

Maeve declined, insisting that it was June Adrian preferred.

'I'd love to know what attraction this place has for him.' June hesitated as she struggled to regain her composure.

'The food, the ambience and especially you,' her junior volunteered, a little envious of the head waitress's stunning looks, which turned men's heads wherever she went.

'I'm afraid he's out of my league,' June disagreed, while stealing another glimpse of Adrian. A slimmer, trendier version of his previous self and wearing his hair longer.

Maeve didn't think so. Why was he forever chatting her up? And that glint in his eye during their exchanges. She didn't miss a trick.

'You mean, sussing me out. Peeling me, layer by layer, until he finds whatever it is he's looking for.'

June could feel her heart-beat increasing. Privately, she hoped things would continue as heretofore between them. In his absence, he was no less present in her thoughts. No man in her past life had ever measured up to him and none had come between them in the meantime.

'Your hidden talents. We keep telling you you're a born actress,' Maeve piped.

'A born waitress will do fine.' She shrugged off the tribute, which she had earned for her hilarious impersonations at staff parties.

'Trust me, he can't wait for you to take his order. So, take a deep breath, June, and give him that winning smile that endears you to everyone,' Maeve suggested and left her to attend one of the boss's more esteemed clients.

June braced herself, picked up the menu and waited upon her favourite customer, whose warm embrace reassured her that nothing had changed between them.

'Nice to see you again, June.' His gaze enveloped her affectionately.

'And you, too. And by the way, thanks for your card. So tell me, how did Paris go?'

'It's a stunning city, but it's Dublin for me.'

'And the Parisian belles?' she inquired, a smile playing on her attractive features.

'Chic, attractive, but give me an Irish woman any day,' he assured her.

She liked his French jacket and was amused by those Gallic gestures he had picked up.

'Really! Still, what wouldn't I give to have been in your shoes. I'd hoped to get away to Lanzarote for a break, but had to cancel it at the last minute when one of the staff left. It would be my luck.' She shrugged resignedly.

When a concerned Adrian told her she was married to her job, she assured him she hadn't felt any need for a divorce so far. And less so, she might have added, now that he was back.

In his company, the restaurant took on a magical quality, turning her work into recreation. More importantly, despite their differences, he gave her food for thought.

'You must let go or you'll become part of the furniture,' he warned. She shook her head.

'You'll have the boss letting me go if he over-hears you,' she cautioned him lightly, and left him to browse over the menu.

Her employer's good opinion meant everything to her.

When she returned to take his order, he suggested mildly that she mustn't let the boss own her.

Seeing Maeve eavesdropping, while taking an order at a nearby table, she declared: 'I prefer to think we have a mutual claim on each other.'

'So I've noticed.'

At times she wondered if there were anything about her that he didn't notice. Not that she disapproved of his interest or wasn't grateful to him for putting things in perspective for her. It was just that he was a freer spirit, while she was a fixture. And content to remain one.

'Is he still single?' Adrian's tone implied her boss ought to be married.

She assured him, while lighting his table lamp, that he was one of the most sought-after bachelors in town.

A successful business man obviously, unlike him – a misfit in the world of commerce he had turned his back on for philosophy.

Having scanned the menu, Adrian inquired if she fancied him, while searching her exquisite features for confirmation.

'He's my employer for goodness sake!' she exclaimed.

Knowing that the boss disapproved of her dallying with her clients, she took Adrian's order and hoped to get back to him later. The tables were already filling up with patrons demanding prompt service. She took her job seriously.

'The usual!' he said, presuming, rightly, she would remember. They didn't get a chance to speak again until she was presenting him with the bill. And then only briefly.

'Try and give that self beneath the head waitress a look in,' he advised and slipped her a gift of expensive French perfume as he was leaving. She thanked him profusely.

'It's great to be back and to find you amiable as ever,' he confessed and bade her good night.

She felt special again. Adrian had put the bounce back in her step and a song in her heart. She felt so elated it took her some time to gather her wits.

'Paris hasn't changed him. I can see he still has the hots for you,' Maeve noted as the last patrons were departing and the pressures were off.

'It's business as usual, Maeve. Nothing more.' June kept her feelings to herself. Privately, she began to live for Adrian's visits.

'*In vino veritas*,' he declared one night, while doing justice to more of his favourite French wine than usual.

'You don't really believe that?' she said, having never seen much evidence for it .

He disagreed, believing there was nothing like a helping of the grape to free up those truths that can set one free.

'From what?' she asked, while topping up his glass.

'Let's say one's job.'

And with a suddenness that caught her off guard, inquired if she ever considered changing hers. He must be losing it!

Firmly, she replied: 'I like what I'm doing.'

He regarded her appraisingly, then suggested she was capable of better.

'I'm quite comfortable here,' she insisted.

He frowned, then stole a quick glimpse of her.

'Too comfortable, perhaps?'

She glanced suspiciously at him.

'Do you realise what you're asking of me? That I pack in my job!'

'Why not? I did it.'

She held the bottle suspended, wondering if she were hearing rightly.

'There are more creative careers.'

He twirled his glass thoughtfully.

'I'm sure there are, and a lot more stressful, too.' She shied away from his suggestion.

'But more suited to your ability. And more rewarding in the long run,' he persisted.

Assuming a commanding stance, she said: 'Surely, I ought to be the best judge of that,' and flicked back a strand of her wavy, auburn hair.

He disagreed, suggesting it would help if she were to see herself, occasionally, as he did.

Determined not to be swayed, she dug her heels in.

'The one I see, which seemingly you can't, will do me fine.'

He shook his head, the allowed a brief silence to hang between them.

Realising that he had her best interests at heart, she relented, and asked him how he saw her. She held her breath while awaiting his answer.

'A well programmed robot.'

She felt like screaming and giving him a piece of her mind. Instead, she told him to go and see an optician and turned on her heels. She would have passed him on to Maeve had he not detained her by the wrist and assured her that no offence was intended.

Emphatically, she responded: 'It's what the boss expects. And the guests pay for. And it's not for negotiation.'

She considered the idea of Adrian reinventing her a bit much. One of these days, she'd give him her frank assessment of himself and see how he'd take it.

'Just don't take the boss home with you,' he advised.

She smiled.

'So far. I've left him after me in the restaurant. Satisfied?'

She wondered if she were becoming the object of rivalry. Or if he were just playing games with her.

He nodded. He was ready for his main course. Poached salmon, which she served under the vigilant eye of the boss, who subsequently had Maeve take Adrian his dessert and his coffee, on the pretext that he needed June to wait on a celebrity from the theatrical world. Agreeable though she found him, she'd prefer to have been serving Adrian, treasuring, despite their differences, every moment of his company.

Her heart did a little jig when he next showed up, his greeting as warm as ever.

'You gave me the slip last week,' he reproved her lightly, adding that Maeve did his cholesterol no favour when she served him with someone's chocolate mousse.

A meticulous June apologised for her colleague's error, but he made light of it as she took his order.

When she returned with his soup, the chef's speciality, that never failed to live up to its billing, he inquired yet again what it was about the job that appealed to her.

Previously, they had agreed to differ about various matters and left it at that. On the question of her career, he was much more persistent.

Dropping her voice in case the boss overheard her, she confided: 'It's the reason I rise each morning with a sense of purpose and retire to bed at night with a sense of security. It's what and who I am.'

'It's what you are not.'

She looked reprovingly at him.

'You don't hear me complaining.'

'I sometimes wish I did.'

Having shut a nearby window on the chill, night air from the river, she gave him other reasons.

'I'm happy. I can cope. I make a decent living. What more can I ask for?'

'Much more. Trust me, you're wasting your talents here.'

He held her gaze with a fervour she found compelling and, in turn, disturbing.

'But suppose I don't have what it takes for the place you've in mind?'

He shook his head.

'*But* is your problem. Your mindset. Your ball and chain.'

'My safety net,' she corrected him, privately enjoying their contest of wits.

If he failed to convince her that the world was at her feet, she was chuffed nonetheless, if somewhat bemused, by his interest in her career, which she felt was the right one for her.

'You'll never know until you've tried your hand at something else,' he suggested.

She disagreed firmly.

'I really believe some invisible hand led me here, all the way from Abbeylaune, where my family have been waiters for generations.

Besides, I'd miss our little weekly *tête-à-tête* were I to leave,' she teased him, while keeping one eye on the boss, who was presently pre-occupied with the celebrity from the theatrical world, whom Maeve was elected to serve on this occasion, prompting concern on June's part that her junior wouldn't trigger a cardiac crisis for the restaurant with another misplaced chocolate mousse.

Adrian frowned. His refusal to accept her caused her, at times, to doubt if her feelings for him were reciprocal. Clearly, he had her best interests at heart. And, while she enjoyed their exchanges, she was hopeful he'd eventually let up.

Duty calling, she darted off to take a young couple's order, then to minister to Ms Levine, a finicky spinster whom no man could please. After that, it was a theatre-bound party who required her service. By the time she got back to Adrian, he had finished his coffee and was preparing to leave.

She apologised to him, explaining that it was one of the restaurant's busier nights.

He understood. As he slid into his overcoat, he advised her not to give too much credence to fate, reminding her that she was the one in the driving seat.

She nodded though she didn't quite agree with him.

'Take care, honey!'

He gave her arm an affectionate little squeeze.

'You, too.'

She gave him a sweet smile, suddenly sensing a chemistry she felt was mutual. Increasingly, she took him home with her in her thoughts, fantasised about him in bed, and in her chilled out moments, sifted their exchanges for any romantic hints on his part.

None of her previous dates had been so attentive or had her think about herself the way he did. He made her feel alive and precious. She couldn't wait for his next visit, and began to like the idea of having him manage her life. Well . . . up to a point.

Whenever Adrian failed to show up, her heart sank and she went about her work mechanically, a prey to doubts and sensitive to an emotional void that only he could fill.

When he'd reappear, she would move into over-drive. Skip between the tables like a ballerina. Carry laden trays with the grace and agility of a juggler, while dancing attendance like a ministering angel on appreciative customers. Only Adrian was unimpressed.

'Watching your performance was as near to method-acting as you can get.'

He accused her of role playing, as she served him his fruit cocktail on one of those spirited occasions.

Defensively, she responded: 'You won't see a soldier in the parade ground with his hands in his pocket.'

He shook his head. 'It's cartoon stuff! And it's not cool.'

'What is it you're looking for?' She was close to losing her cool.

'Someone who can think and step outside of the box. '

'Who day-dreams and serves you with the wrong desert? I just can't please you, can I?'

She left him to his fruit cocktail. Why couldn't he just accept her?

The boss must have sensed her frustration, for he took her aside afterwards.

'Keep it business-like with him,' he cautioned, implying that she was his, not Adrian's responsibility. She suspected Maeve of carrying stories about her to him.

Despite their disagreement, June was incapable of distancing herself from Adrian.

On those occasions when he let up and regaled her with colourful accounts of his time in Paris, he awoke in her a desire to travel. To brush up her French and sample those Left Bank cafés he raved about. Gradually, she realised she was settling into a rut and needed to have a life outside of her work.

His proposal, however, that she go back to college, made little sense to her initially.

'And who'll foot the bill for my new shoes when I've shaken the dust of this place from my old ones? Do you expect me to go barefoot?' she exclaimed.

He shook his head emphatically.

'I'd suggest, for starter,s that you sign up for evening classes. That way, you can hold on to the day job and your shoes for the time being.'

'And then I suppose you'll have me singing for my supper.'

'Trust me. You won't go hungry, anymore than I did in Paris. '

She frowned, then decided she had a question for him.

'What, as a matter of interest, did you do for your keep there? The rounds of the cafés, like Edith Piaff, singing, *'Je ne regrette rien.'* Those nuggets of wit gleaned from the restaurant's clientele stood her good stead in her exchanges with him.

He kept her guessing, reminding her, instead, that he walked out of a well-paid, if unsuitable job, to finish his doctorate, which would secure him a junior post in a philosophy department. He had no regrets for having followed his star.

'Good for you. But I think I've found mine.' She took her leave of him. It was one of those nights when the staff were on their toes.

'You must grow out of this place,' Adrian said, when she got back to him with the bill.

She grinned.

'I might not be able to handle the growing pains.'

'There's no growing without them,' he assured her.

He gave her an extra-generous tip and an encouraging pat as he was leaving.

June would do some soul-searching in the days ahead. At times, she wondered if Adrian over-estimated her and, at other times, if she under-rated herself. Come to think of it, her respectable Leaving Cert results would guarantee her a decent job any day.

Now that Adrian had dispelled her belief that waitressing was her destiny, she toyed increasingly with the idea of trying her hand at something else. With Celtic Tiger Dublin bristling with opportunities, there was no reason why she should be buried in her boots in the restaurant. She had seen her friends frequently change jobs and usually for the better.

Initially, it was largely to please Adrian that she signed up for an acting course and applied to have her shifts at the restaurant rescheduled so she could remain in touch with him.

The boss's response was predictably one of deep concern.

'It's Adrian, isn't it?' he asked.

She nodded, blushing.

Whereupon, he inquired if Adrian were a pebble on her beach.

'Good heavens, no!'

'Good.' He looked relieved.

'Why good, if I might ask?'

'I care for you, June. I wouldn't like you to be misled.' Her boss oozed concern.

Jane smiled.

'You don't have to worry on that score, sir.'

She responded to his suggestion that they dine together some night and take in a show afterwards with a tactful 'perhaps another time,' preferring to keep their relationship on a business footing.

Pressed for her real reason, she would have to admit that the chemistry between herself and Adrian was absent with the boss, who took her refusal graciously.

'And now I'd better take Ms Levine's order, or I shall hear

about it.' She excused herself. It was nice to know that the boss, too, had her best interests at heart.

When Adrian eagerly inquired how she was getting on at her evening course, she replied: 'Brilliant! I'm really enjoying it.'

'But why acting?' He seemed bemused.

She chuckled.

'I suppose it comes naturally to me.'

'So I've noticed.'

He was glad she had finally taken his advice.

Before Christmas, he announced that he had been given two complimentary tickets for the theatre and invited her to accompany him on her night off.

She was thrilled with his offer and asked him the name of the play.

'It's called "Lucky Breaks". Have you heard of it?'

'It rings bells.' It was as much as she'd divulge. In fact, it triggered a raft of memories for her.

Things would take a lucky turn for June that week-end as one of the leading actresses suddenly took ill. In a panic, the producer turned to the School of Acting for a stand-in. Happily for him, June had performed the part in her school production. Gifted with an exceptional memory, she could still recall her lines. Her natural acting ability, honed by some rigorous, last minute rehearsing, just about readied her for the part.

She planned it as a little surprise for Adrian and texted him to say she wouldn't be joining him in the parterre, but would meet up with him after the show, having been assigned some backstage duties by the School of Acting.

Thunder-struck would have been more like his reaction when she walked onto the stage and carried off the role with professional panache. What a talent! It was as if she were tailored for the part. He made no secret of it that he was swept off his feet.

'What a debut! You were brilliant,' he exclaimed, applauding her performance in the theatre bar afterwards.

'I'm so glad you were impressed.' She was thrilled by his response.

'So much so I'm convinced you've got to turn professional,' he said, promising if ever she did, he would be prepared to help out.

She thanked him, but felt she shouldn't burn her boats at the restaurant just yet. Besides, she didn't want to be dependent on Adrian. If she were going to make it as an actress, it would be under her own steam.

As they taxied home, she was on cloud nine. In her wildest dreams, she could never have seen herself sharing a stage with celebrated actors, being fêted on her début by appreciative fans and presented with a bouquet of flowers by the grateful producer whom she had waited upon at the restaurant. Adrian's good opinion was the icing on the cake.

'I told you all along you had what it takes. You just didn't believe in yourself,' he said, still reeling from her performance.

She rewarded him with an appreciative kiss as he dropped her off. She would have liked to have him in for a night-cap, but felt it was a bit soon for familiarity of that kind.

Maeve didn't think so.

'He's absolutely stage-struck. Trust me, he's yours for the asking.'

'Well , until he asks, I'll not to be too trusting.' June refused to lose the run of herself.

True, there were nights when she fantasised about him ripping open her bodice, then taking her in a frenzy of desire. Fantasies, strictly. In reality, it would be a different story. She would resist his advances, postpone the pleasure, and then, when the time was right, she'd give herself to him. That's if it ever came to that.

Then, remembering the boss's warning, she'd return to her senses. She would have to wait and see whether he was anything more than just her mentor. Mentally stimulating though she found him, something she'd read about philosophers not being the marrying type, put a further brake on her ardour.

In the meantime, things continued to gather momentum. Outings to the theatre were followed by nightcaps at his or her place, where she'd re-enact for him snippets from her latest role. At other times, they'd improvise imaginary scenes that often ended with them in each others' arms. While he loved the theatre, it was clear to her that his talents were elsewhere.

'I'd better hold on to the day job,' he'd chuckle, putting her on a superior footing to him in that respect.

Gradually it dawned on her that there were more exciting and more creative options than the restaurant. The fetters that had bound her for so long were already loosening. She began to gear up for an exciting, new career on the stage.

When Adrian proposed to her one night after a sparkling performance, she lost her nerve for a moment. She asked for time to consider it and advised against rushing their fences at this point. When he persisted, her response was as measured as his was precipitate.

'I'm still not sure if we're right for each other.'

Doubts! The leap in the dark. That surrender of her selfhood and the risk to her new career caused her to freeze and, in turn, to ponder if it weren't the compromise required for marriage.

'But of course we are!'

He, at any rate, was convinced. She still needed time to think. Flirting with him was one thing. Entering an enduring relationship was a more serious matter. Not that she wanted to end her days like Ms Levine, anymore than ending them in an unhappy union.

'I'm even less sure if you're ready to give up your freedom just yet.'

She tried to put things on hold until he was sure about his decision.

He shook his head.

'I've had my fill of it. Why do you think I returned from Paris? And dine week-in, week-out at the Gilded Cage? Can't you see I need you?'

Her mentor was suddenly very human and vulnerable in a way that moved her. Yet, she held back.

'I read somewhere that philosophy and marriage don't mix.' There were times when she saw him as an inveterate bachelor.

He nodded to the contrary.

'If the exception proves the rule, then let me be that exception,' he declared with his hand on his heart.

She worried it might mean having to give up the theatre, now that she'd fallen in love with it again.

He shook his head. 'The restaurant possibly. But that will be for you to decide.'

Still shaken, she excused herself while she sought the refuge of the restroom before coming to a decision, the significance of which hit her with the force of a tsunami that had caught her off-guard.

'I love you, June,' he called after her.

After a nail-biting wait for Adrian, she returned with her response: a very positive 'yes'.

'Let me hear it again!' He was on his feet and enfolding her in his embrace.

'Yes! Yes! Yes!'

He kissed her repeatedly, then signalled to the waiter for the obligatory champagne.

Life, she had come to realise, was a stage where she could play many roles.

THE ZEALOTS STRIKE BACK

Few, least of all yours truly, would have thought that the Zealots, who had long been on the back foot, would ever again try to regain their former stranglehold over the academies. Hence, it was with a sense of shock and disbelief that I read about their new campaign of Submersion. Those dark clouds approaching from the West all day were never more ominous. I rang Culainn. *Hiberno defensor*. His voicemail said: 'Not in. Try later.' It might have added – try Maeve's, for they were inseparable of late.

Idiot!

Frankly speaking, *Erse – the Zealots' lingo* – has been teetering on the brink of extinction even in its own strongholds for generations. Yet, whenever the last rites are about to be administered, it's somehow given the kiss of life by its dwindling faithful. Canny survivors, I'll hand it to them. Most believed they were permanently out for the count after the *coup de grâce* administered by the redoubtable Culainn and the Lingo Choice campaign.

And what a showdown that was! I sensed it simmering since Culainn and myself were in shorts. Even then, he was gearing up for the fray. By the time he was wearing the long ones, his critical flair was matched by his verbal firepower, which few could match. As his desk-mate I ought to know, having been on the receiving end more than once. Like most of my classmates at the junior academy in Abbeylaune, I kept my head down and left it to Culainn to put his neck out.

'It's a waste of time. We never speak it outside of the academy,' I heard him repeatedly chafe during our final year. I usually did his Erse homework for him. He had no problems with his Hiberno one.

'We don't have any choice but to learn it.' I was resigned to it, having, in any case, a reasonable flair for it, though nothing like a native speaker.

'We should have,' Culainn continued to claim, like most in Abbeylaune then, that it was effectively a dead language, its demise fast-tracked by the cheerless way it was taught.

I knew that, without it, certain doors would remain closed to me. The old story of vested interests, the Zealots knew how to exploit. In any case, I wanted to follow in my uncle's footsteps and become an instructor in the capital. Which, in retrospect, was a bit calculating on my part. A trick Culainn didn't miss.

What the hell's come over you, Culainn? You must be taking leave of your senses dating Maeve, the Zealot, tv pin up. Can't you see she's the Wooden Horse of their propaganda machine. Stunning, talented and charismatic I'll grant you, but surely not your type. You walk different roads. For feck sake, get a grip! You're having the wool pulled over your eyes.

'There's frig-all for us who can't learn it. Just a job on some building site across the pond.' He was speaking up more and more for his fellow-plodders.

I remember him remarking, on another occasion, how they were having serious problems with the mother tongue because of the emphasis on Erse. Being punished for it didn't exactly do it any favour. Smack! Smack! Four of the best of the Zealot's (his nickname in Abbeylaune) cane if you hadn't your home-work done, and shivering in your shoes even if you had, of his flak for grammatical errors red-pencilled like scars all over your pages.

As I saw it – a scared academy, with the Zealot scared of the Zealot inspector, who was scared of the Zealot minister who, in turn, was scared of the Zealot Taoiseach. The lingo itself scared of dying though, between you and me, on a life-support machine, while still masquerading as our first official lingo. A claim that riled Culainn.

'Erse is not my first lingo,' he snapped in the school yard one day when he'd taken stick for messing up his grammar. 'And it doesn't look as if it will ever be my second lingo either.'

'Nor ours.' The plodders rallied to his support, albeit, out of earshot of the Zealot.

Don't tell me Culainn, you've turned your back on them. The hard-done victims of that system. Are you going to stand by while they're being put back on the educational rack?

I could see, even in the junior academy, from where he was coming. Granted, Hiberno, by now our mother tongue, was once imposed by the Invader on our ancestors. So what! He saw no reason why we should have to suffer for it. After all, it was no fault of ours. Or no reason why Hiberno should be treated as the enemy of Erse that expired by and large with our forefathers.

But try telling the Zealots, who still haven't got it, that after generations of conversing in it, we've made Hiberno our own. That it's our medium. That we live in it, make love in it, eat, sleep and drink in it. From my experience, nothing would give them greater pleasure than to bin it and its literary treasures. Any wonder that Culainn was already trumpeting our grievances with it while still in the junior academy.

'What's the point in wasting so much time on it when we should be doing a continental language?' I frequently heard him echoing the views still expressed today by many in a multicultural Abbeylaune.

Maeve must have you wrapped around her little finger. How else could you have forgotten those classmates who left the junior academy, illiterate in both lingoes and with nothing to show for their time but bitter memories. Catch on man!

I played my cards with the Zealot and achieved a certain competence in Erse, despite the drudgery of its grammar and its irrelevance as a spoken medium outside of the Zealot colony – a shrinking catchment on the Western seaboard that continued to wield a disproportionately big stick over the entire, academic system we'd come to detest.

Far from being the happiest days of our lives, Culainn labelled those at the junior academy as among the saddest ones.

Can you not see that Submersion would be a nightmare for those with learning disabilities? Not to mention the foreign nationals now flocking to our shores and schools availing of the Celtic Tiger. Why make learning hell for them?

For Culainn, I knew, his school days were agony. I can still see him gazing absently out the window or reading comics under the seat, estranged from Erse and its text books. Much to the Zealot's annoyance, Culainn had a real talent for Hiberno, our down-graded mother tongue. Due to his forbidden reading, his essays were brilliant. Even Fiachra, the Zealot's son, a really bright spark if it weren't for his father's interference, was no match for him.

Culainn, whose father was less interfering, made a lot more sense to us than Fiachra whenever Fiachra tried to make sense of the nonsense we couldn't see much sense in, like having to learn everything through Erse. I can still hear them arguing.

'It's our mother tongue.' Fiachra would spring to its defence. A chip off the old block. And every bit as narrow-minded and as fanatical, his frail physique kitted out from head to toe in Zealotwear.

'You mean our great, great, grandmother's tongue,' a taller, more robust Culainn would rejoin to the amusement of the plodders.

'I mean our mother tongue,' Fiachra would insist.

'And if I don't learn it?'

Fiachra would sneer.

'You'll be a West Brit.'

His father was said to frown upon fellow-Zealots who weren't native speakers. Their bilingualism was an anathema to him; their prudent use of Hiberno tantamount to a profanity.

'Even if I can't? And feel like the donkey of the class anytime I try to?'

'Of course you can.' For Zealots, any language was preferable to Hiberno.

'Can you not get it? I can't,' a frustrated Culainn would explode to a chorus of braying from the plodders. 'He-haw, he-haw.'

'Nonsense! You can. But you don't want to.' Fiachra, who was on patriotic fire, would persist, further enflaming Culainn.

'Are you thick? Can't you see I don't want to because I can't. I want to talk like everyone else talks and say what I want to, which I can't in your lingo. So does that make me any less patriotic than you?'

'Definitely. Either you speak Erse or you're a West Brit.' Fiachra would remain resolute.

'No way!' we chorused, rallying to Culainn's support and shouting down Fiachra who had no idea what it was like to be the class donkey.

Whereupon Culainn would inquire if anyone wanted to be a patriotic donkey?

No hand would be raised. There were lots of hands that would have gladly plucked out Fiachra's tongue for trying to pluck out ours, as Culainn reminded him.

I could tell Culainn wasn't liked by the Zealot, who must have sensed in him a rebel he'd never subdue.

Try ringing him again. Beep! Beep! No joy. Wake up Culainn! Or 'tis destroyed you'll be surely by your infatuation. And get it into your besotted head this programme for Submersion is the thin edge of the wedge. Personally, I can't imagine Maeve losing much sleep over its dire consequence for disadvantaged, inner city plodders.

As his years at the senior academy drew to a close, it was clear to me that Culainn was gearing up for a showdown. Consumed with the spirit of rebellion, I frequently watched him vent his frustration on the statue erected in the town's square to a noted Erse scholar for his contribution to its grammar – our bugbear.

His final examination results would provide the match to light his fuse. If he came out on top in Hiberno, he came out at the bottom in Erse; failed his exam because of it. Failed, fair is fair, unfairly. The fate of many like him.

I could tell he was livid by the way he shook his clenched fist at the Academy. It must have been some consolation to him that his parting shot at the Zealot system was applauded wildly by the plodders, who raised him aloft on their shoulders, sensing, I suspect, that they had found the intrepid spokesperson who, in time, would settle their scores and put to right the wrongs done to them by Zealots.

I wonder if he still has the bottle for battle. Or if Maeve hasn't put out his fire.

I'd go on to become a junior academy instructor in the capital's inner city while he, like so many of his classmates, went to work on the buildings in the 'land of the invader' before drifting into journalism, where he found his feet and was soon hitting the headlines, his talent for Hiberno opening doors to him that the Zealots closed for so many of his generation.

Imagine my delight as I read your brief missive. 'Returning to the old sod. Just landed a job with the Irish Voice. I'll hook up with you shortly in the capital. Will be gunning for the Zealots.'

Try texting him! Since taking up with Maeve, the Zealots have been gathering momentum behind his besotted back. Took his eye off them after the Lingo Choice Movement had folded up its tent, forgetting that they never give up.

So different to the crusader who returned from the 'land of the invader' all fired up for the cause. An instinctive reporter, he sensed the public mood was ripe for action and promptly joined the Lingo Choice Movement – a rallying point for the educationally aggrieved. Well-honed for the campaign ahead by his maturing spell abroad, he would soon become its most eloquent mouthpiece. Like so many other disgruntled academics, I rallied to his support.

Culainn was truly magnetic. With his striking looks and imposing stature, he had the charisma that makes for leadership. Crowds flocked to protest meetings to hear him speak and to air their grievances as well as demand an end to the Zealot regime. *Vox populi* had begun to assert itself.

A manifesto, which Culainn read and circulated at meetings, became our Magna Carta and our roadmap for an exciting new educational era, which had the support of those generations whose learning had been stymied by the Zealot system.

Zealot reaction, I recall, was predictably swift and harsh. An elite minority, they realised they had much to lose. I could tell they weren't going to give up without a fight.

I watched them try to shout down Culainn at meetings, then harass him afterwards. They accused him of being a traitor, a *shóneen*, and a West Brit. I remember how, on one occasion, he was forced to run for his life and take refuge in a confectioner's until the police came to his rescue. Whenever the Zealots referred to him afterwards as the fruitcake, an unflappable Culainn reminded them they had had their loaf and eaten it. Had they got their hands on him, I knew they'd have made a meal of him.

Still no reply. Try the Irish Voice. Regularly works from home. One of the advantages of the lap-top. Far cry from the nib pen and the inkwell of our junior academy days.

Culainn, I could tell, was not one to back off. Years of festering anger had steeled him for battle. With the Zealot citadel shaken to its very foundations, and the Opposition now in government and committed to his manifesto, victory was his. The Zealot stranglehold on the academies was broken and few would lament its passing.

A triumphal Culainn was confident that school-days would once again be the happiest days.

The new government would soon introduce a popular new curriculum that could now be taught in Hiberno. Gone were the depressing days of the Zealot system. The humiliation and frustration experienced by the plodders. The heart-break of exam failure arising from failing Erse. The many doors closed to those without it. Culainn was rightly hailed as a hero.

Still no response. Maeve's bondsman. Wonder do they do bondage? And if he woos her in Erse?

The discredited Zealots would never forgive him. They'd had it. Unless, of course, the politicians played into their hands, which wouldn't surprise me, if votes were at stake and principles stood in the way of the perks of office.

For a while, the Zealots were seemingly content to nibble away at Culainn's gains, while continuing to wring academic concessions for their lingo. As I said, they never give up. Take my word for it, they were careful never again to accuse any one who didn't speak their vernacular of being a *shóneen* or a West Brit.

Could it have been a Pyrrhic victory?

Despite being on the ropes, it never ceased to amaze me that Erse was still essential for access to certain jobs and, crucially, for entry to the Instructors' Academy, retaining a discriminatory control over that key stronghold.

A satisfied Culainn refrained from a final solution. He had fought the good fight and was at peace with himself and, eventually, with the Zealots.

Was Maeve the olive branch? Beware the Zealots bearing gifts Culainn!

With the Lingo Choice Movement in abeyance, I could see them gradually regrouping and gearing up for a comeback. Already, they were setting up their own academies and were recovering lost ground. The returned Patriotic Party, mindful of their voting power at election time, continued to give into them.

An unwitting ploy that never made sense to me. But there was little I could do. With Culainn no longer interested and recently dating a high profile Zealot, I felt helpless. If every man has his price then Maeve was his.

When he confided in me that he'd found the woman of his dreams – the *Spéirbhean* who imbued him with a vision of Erse culture so seductive that he fell for it head-over-heels, I shuddered. Spellbound, he rhapsodised how she had opened his eyes to the beauty of its poetry. The magic of its music, its dance and its songs had him more in thrall than her alluring figure. Its myths and legends, I gathered, were as bewitching as her raven-dark hair. Maeve was his pathfinder and his conduit to his ancestral, cultural roots. Not that I had any crib with that, as long as he didn't lose sight of his mission.

So besotted, was he by his *Spéirbhean,* he began to sport the Zealot insignia on his lapel, as well as their emblematic gansey. He was even trying his hand at their ancient way of singing, though he hadn't a note in his head, and was taking lessons in Erse-dancing, despite having, as the saying goes, two left feet.

To rid him of his former image, Maeve had him replace his shoulder-length locks with a tight hair-cut.

'You're dropping your guard,' I warned him, uncomfortable with his new self, and with the proliferation of their academies.

He waved aside my concern.

'At least they're optional,' he replied casually.

'And do you not think it's unfair to the plodders that doing subjects through Erse in the state examinations should carry extra bonus points?'

He merely shrugged.

Should I try ringing Maeve's gaff? Better wait until I catch him on his own.

And what a kick in the pants was in store for him when I caught up with him that evening and informed him of the Zealot's programme for Submersion and of the political support it was receiving from unlikely quarters.

'Jesus!' he exclaimed, realising he'd been hoodwinked. 'It's turning the clock back to the awful system that educationally stymied our generation.'

'Indeed. Regrettably you turned a blind eye to it.' I didn't pull my punches.

'How can you say that?' He sounded bewildered.

'How else could you've been so oblivious to the activities behind the scenes of someone very close to you?' I berated him.

'Tell me for chrissake.' His adrenalin, I sensed, was by now beginning to shoot through the roof.

Reluctantly, I named her.

'No way! She couldn't! Who told you?' His voice resonated with disbelief.

'I keep an eye on the Irish periodicals.'

I could hear him cursing himself at the other end of the line.

'Worse, the Opposition are remaining neutral in the hope of attracting the Erse speakers' vote in the forthcoming election. So much for politicians.' I continued to up the ante.

'Oh no! The Zealots never give up. How could I have taken my eyes off them?' He reproached himself.

'Love blind-folded you.' I could picture him kicking himself.

Whereupon, he inquired how my colleagues felt.

'What do you expect? They're up in arms. Submersion, with its planned, piece-meal take-over of the curriculum, is simply not on for inner city pupils. We have enough problems as it is trying to teach them Hiberno.'

'It's the cuckoo back in the pipit's nest,' he exploded, as he remembered, with bitterness, having had to write letters in Hiberno for illiterate, fellow emigrants to their families at home while living in the 'land of the invader'.

'Picture what it will be like for the plodders having to return to that system?' I put it to him.

'It doesn't bear thinking,' he whined.

'But what about Maeve? Your cultural beacon.'

'Never mind her.' He promptly requested the gist of their programme in Hiberno, confessing that his love affair with Erse was over.

I gave it to him straight.

From the moment of conception, the Zealot embryo is a complete person. And any attempt to terminate it will be deemed a criminal offence.

Being pro-life he had no problem with that.

To induce Zealots to out-produce Hibernos, they will be entitled to double the normal children's allowance.

'They'll breed like rabbits,' he quickly changed his tune.

Children of Zealot-Hiberno marriages must be raised as Zealots.

'Utterly divisive,' he barked.

Though I expected him to slam down the phone any minute, I proceeded resolutely to put him on red alert.

All Hiberno-speaking children are to be fostered out for a period of each year to Zealot parents after the age of five.

'They won't stop till they clone themselves,' he wailed and bade me continue.

All communication in Zealot playschools, pre-schools, kindergartens and, in time, in their Hiberno counterparts, must be conducted exclusively through the medium of Erse that will shield our native culture from foreign influence. And where words fail, there must be silence or gestures rather than resort to Hiberno.

'They'll turn us into Trappists. Before we know it, they'll have us breaking wind in Erse,' he howled.

'Can you take any more?' I inquired concerned for his blood pressure.

'Continue!'

Double marks will be awarded in exams for Erse. All other subjects done through its medium will carry double bonus points.

'It's the lunatics taking over the asylum.' I could hear him pounding his desk with his fist.

'Have you had enough?'

'A crawful, but carry on.'

Huge tracts of the Golden Vale, and the Boyne Valley are to be set aside by a reconstituted Land Commission for the purposes of creating new Erse colonies who, in turn, will propagate their lingo

382   *Echoes of the Celtic Tiger*

in the way the Invader once propagated his.

'It will be to hell or to Connacht for Hibernos,' he groaned, denouncing the manifesto as a blueprint for the dictatorship of the Zealots.

Determined to drive home to him the critical import for the academies of this misguided policy, I pressed ahead, however painful it would be for him.

'And how about this for audacity?'

'All religious services are to be conducted through Erse.'

'They'll empty the churches.' He decided he'd heard enough, convinced that Submersion would result in cultural cleansing.

I agreed. Whatever affections he had for Erse were by now clearly dented.

When he chilled out, he thanked me for the tip-off.

'So what do you propose to do?' I pressed, refusing to let him off the hook.

I could hear him sigh. Then snarl.

'Let us go to war.' There was a ring of resolution to his voice that I found reassuring.

I could see a shaft of sunlight shooting through the rain clouds. Then I realised there was something that needed clearing up.

'But your *Spéirbhean* . . . how is she going to react?' I inquired again.

His response was harshly forthright.

'I'm through with her.'

I wasn't sure if I were hearing rightly.

'You can't just up and leave her, simply because she's promoting her lingo,' I protested.

'It's over. We walk different roads,' he insisted.

'You know what they say about opposites?' Oddly, I didn't want to see Maeve hurt. From what I gathered, she had a nice side to her.

After a prolonged pause he confessed: 'To step into Zealot shoes, I'd have to step out of mine. My Hiberno lingo is me.'

He made no secret of it that parting with her, however painful, was essential to his sanity. He had to stop lying to himself.

I might have guessed. Their relationship, I gathered, had become fraught with conflict. Attempts at bilingualism didn't work. She was a fundamentalist. To bridge the divide was too big an ask. Try as he did, he could never become fluent in Erse or feel at home in it. And seeing the problems migrant workers from Europe were having with a second language confirmed it. I could have predicted it from day one.

Culainn has learned, to his cost, that there can be no permanent truce with the Zealots. They simply will not accept that Hiberno is now our mother tongue. Blame history, but don't try to undo it. It's been tried and failed. Hiberno, the people's lingo that has given us poets and writers of world renown, is here to stay as our first, official language. Only the foolhardy would disagree.

Not that I have any problem with Erse having its place as a subject in the curriculum, nor with a snatch of bilingualism on the street. My love of its music, its games and dances, and especially its folklore, remains undiminished. When it comes to Submersion I draw the line, remembering all too vividly the cock-up it made of our schooling and the misery it caused the plodders whom it deprived of indispensable survival skills.

To the barricades, Hibernos!